LONG AGO, IN THE FARAWAY WORLD OF SKULLBANIA, THE WICKED WIZARD VENOMOUS DROOL TRIED TO CONQUER AND RULE ITS PEOPLE.

HE WAS DEFEATED BY BRAVE BARBARIANS WHO CUT HIM INTO PIECES. SINCE THEN, DROOL'S FOLLOWERS HAVE BEGUN COLLECTING THE PIECES IN THE HOPES THAT THEY CAN REBUILD DROOL AND RESTORE HIM TO POWER. BUT THEY ARE MISSING ONE PIECE—HIS BIG TOE!

AND SO OUR HERO, A YOUNG BARBARIAN NAMED FANGBONE, HAS COME TO OUR WORLD TO GUARD AND HIDE THE BIG TOE OF DROOL. FANGBONE JOINS EASTWOOD ELEMENTARY'S CLASS 3G AND, WITH THE HELP OF HIS FRIEND BILL, BEGINS TO LEARN THE STRANGE AND CURIOUS WAYS OF A THIRD-GRADER.

BUT BE WARNED, READER: WHEN THE TOE WIGGLES . . .

EVIL WILL STRIKE!

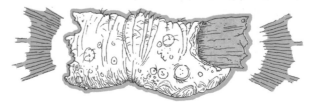

FANGBONE!

THIRD-GRADE BARBARIAN

THE BIRTHDAY PARTY OF DREAD

MICHAEL REX

G. P. PUTNAM'S SONS
AN IMPRINT OF PENGUIN GROUP (USA) INC.

G. P. PUTNAM'S SONS
A DIVISION OF PENGUIN YOUNG READERS GROUP.
PUBLISHED BY THE PENGUIN GROUP.
PENGUIN GROUP (USA) INC., 375 HUDSON STREET, NEW YORK, NY 10014, U.S.A.
PENGUIN GROUP (CANADA), 90 EGLINTON AVENUE EAST, SUITE 700, TORONTO, ONTARIO
M4P 2Y3, CANADA (A DIVISION OF PEARSON PENGUIN CANADA INC.).
PENGUIN BOOKS LTD, 80 STRAND, LONDON WC2R ORL, ENGLAND.
PENGUIN IRELAND, 25 ST. STEPHEN'S GREEN, DUBLIN 2, IRELAND
(A DIVISION OF PENGUIN BOOKS LTD).
PENGUIN GROUP (AUSTRALIA), 250 CAMBERWELL ROAD, CAMBERWELL, VICTORIA 3124, AUSTRALIA (A
DIVISION OF PEARSON AUSTRALIA GROUP PTY LTD).
PENGUIN BOOKS INDIA PVT LTD, 11 COMMUNITY CENTRE,
PANCHSHEEL PARK, NEW DELHI - 110 017, INDIA.
PENGUIN GROUP (NZ), 67 APOLLO DRIVE, ROSEDALE, AUCKLAND 0632, NEW ZEALAND
(A DIVISION OF PEARSON NEW ZEALAND LTD).
PENGUIN BOOKS (SOUTH AFRICA) (PTY) LTD, 24 STURDEE AVENUE,
ROSEBANK, JOHANNESBURG 2196, SOUTH AFRICA.
PENGUIN BOOKS LTD, REGISTERED OFFICES: 80 STRAND, LONDON WC2R ORL, ENGLAND.

PUBLISHED SIMULTANEOUSLY IN CANADA.
PRINTED IN THE UNITED STATES OF AMERICA.
DESIGN BY RYAN THOMANN. TEXT SET IN CC WILD WORDS.
THE ART WAS CREATED IN INK AND COLORED DIGITALLY.

LIBRARY OF CONGRESS CATALOGING-IN-PUBLICATION DATA IS AVAILABLE UPON REQUEST.
ISBN 978-0-399-25523-6
3 5 7 9 10 8 6 4 2

TO DECLAN AND GAVIN,
WHO WERE THE FIRST TWO
WARRIORS IN FANGBONE'S ARMY!

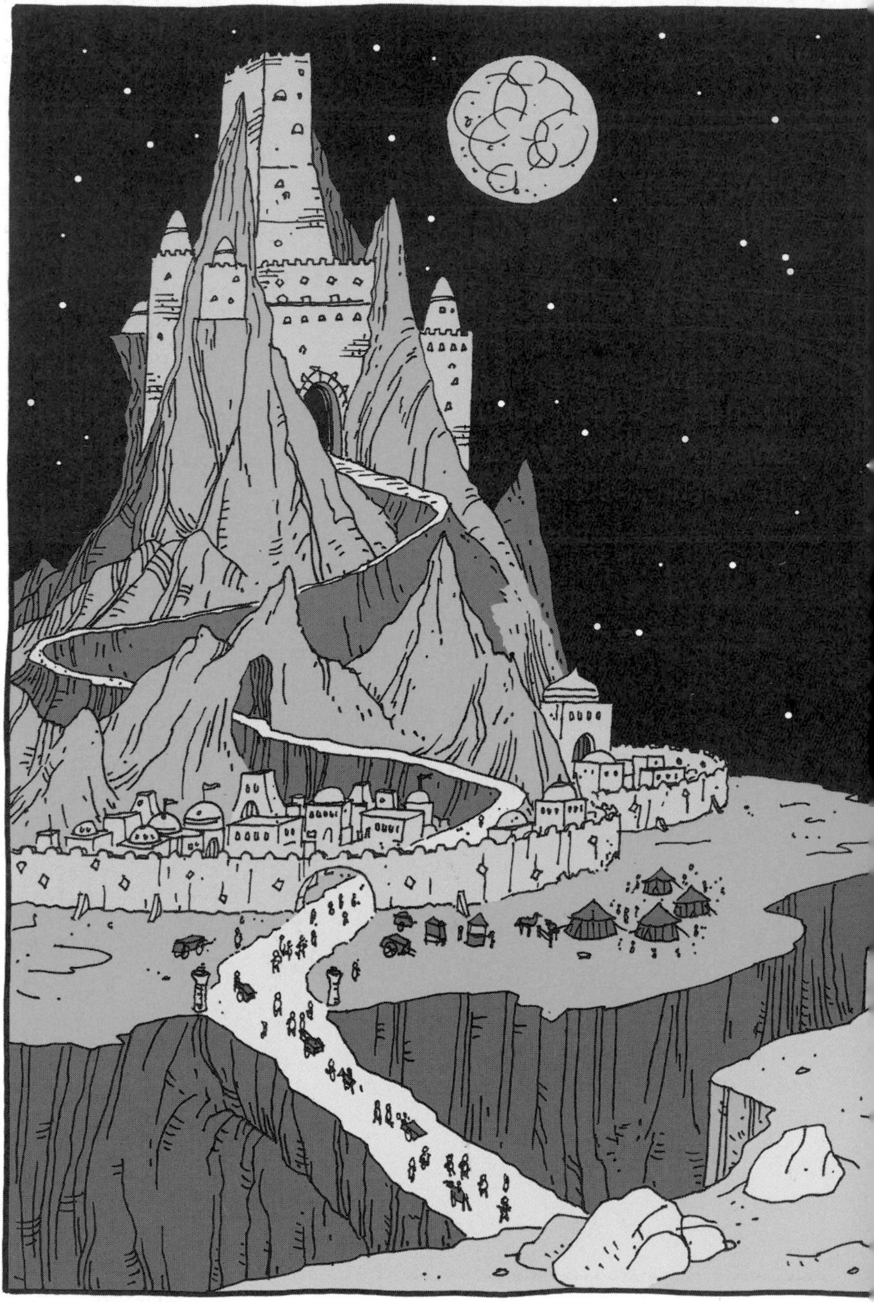

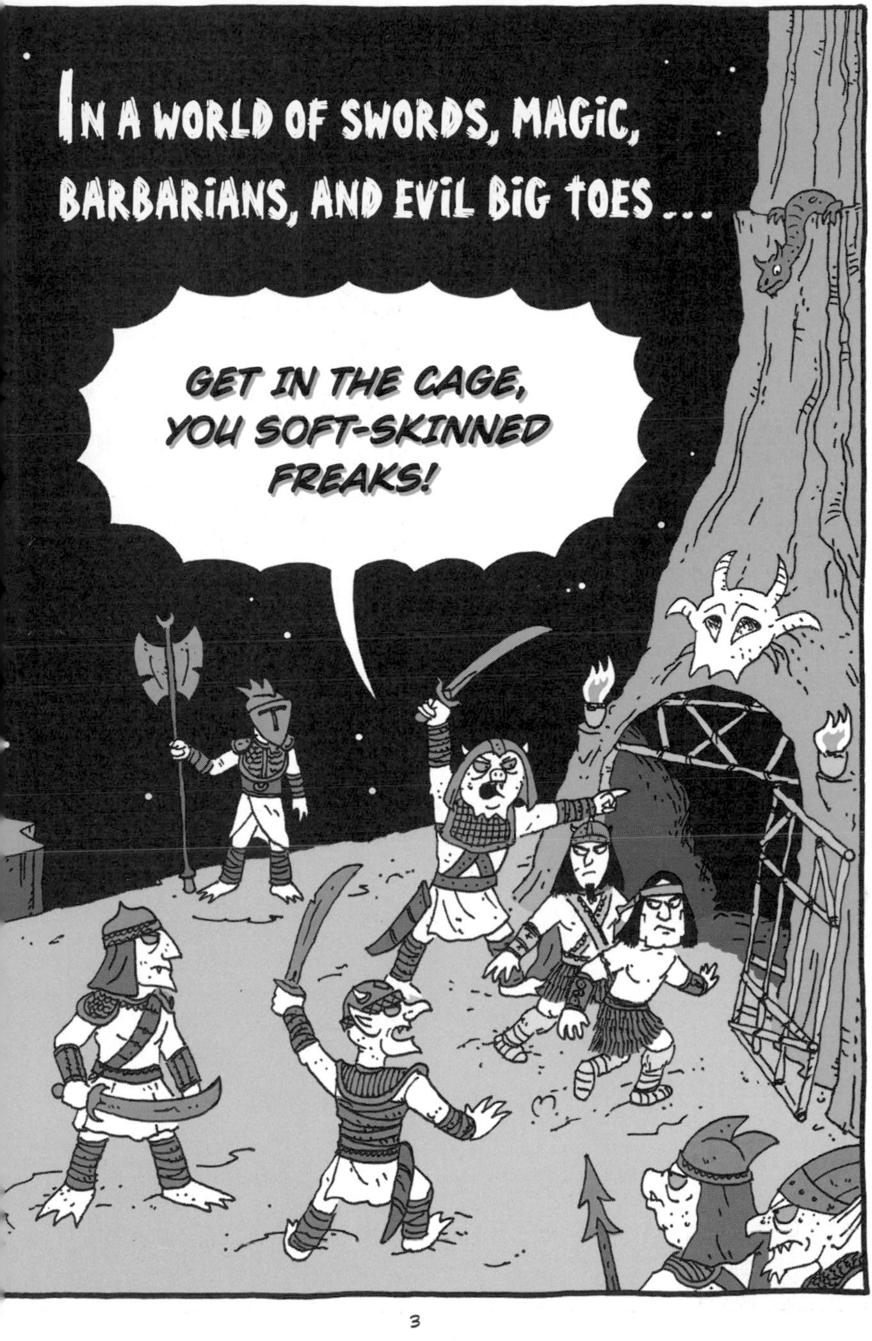
IN A WORLD OF SWORDS, MAGIC, BARBARIANS, AND EVIL BIG TOES . . .
GET IN THE CAGE, YOU SOFT-SKINNED FREAKS!

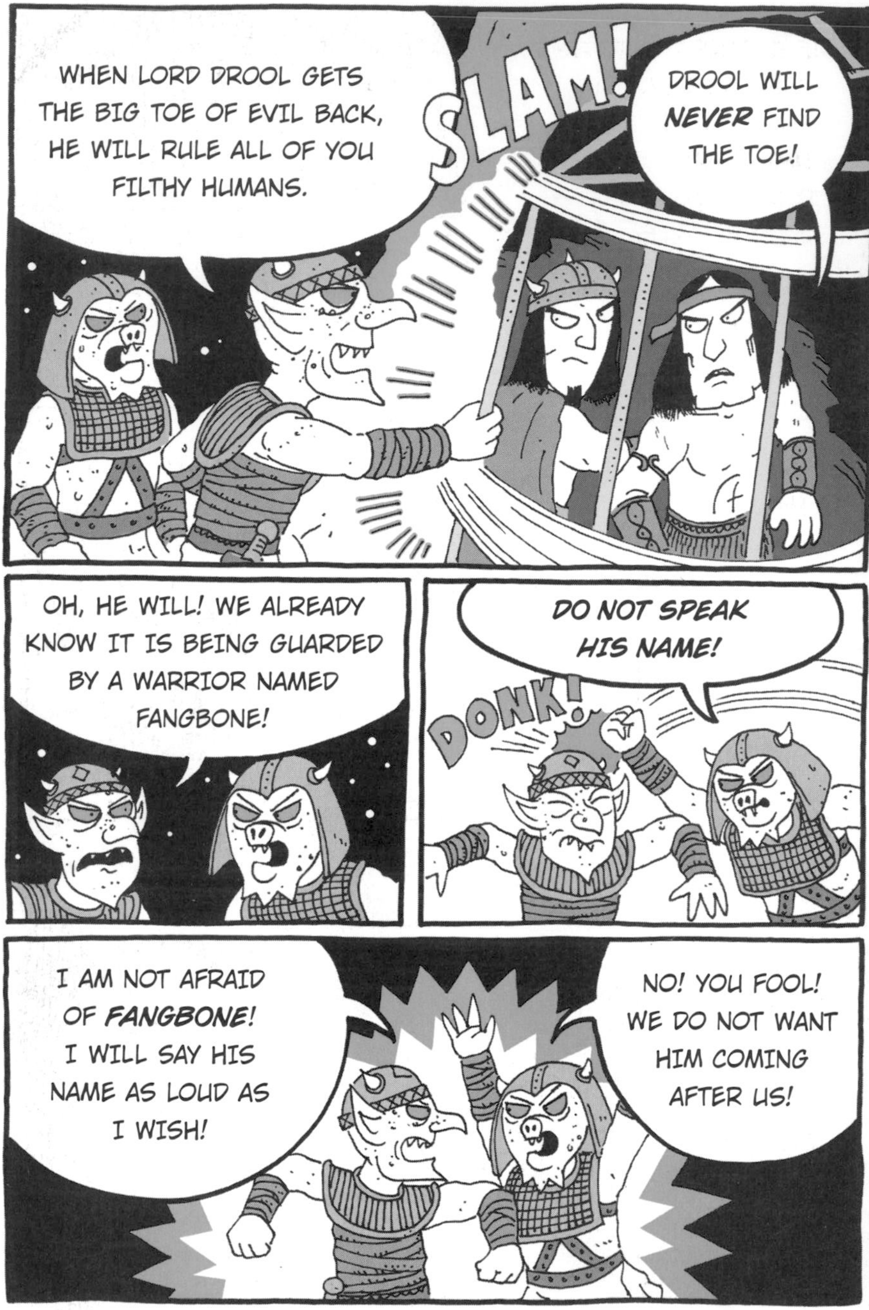
WHEN LORD DROOL GETS THE BIG TOE OF EVIL BACK, HE WILL RULE ALL OF YOU FILTHY HUMANS.
SLAM!
DROOL WILL *NEVER* FIND THE TOE!
OH, HE WILL! WE ALREADY KNOW IT IS BEING GUARDED BY A WARRIOR NAMED FANGBONE!
DO NOT SPEAK HIS NAME!
DONK!
I AM NOT AFRAID OF *FANGBONE*! I WILL SAY HIS NAME AS LOUD AS I WISH!
NO! YOU FOOL! WE DO NOT WANT HIM COMING AFTER US!

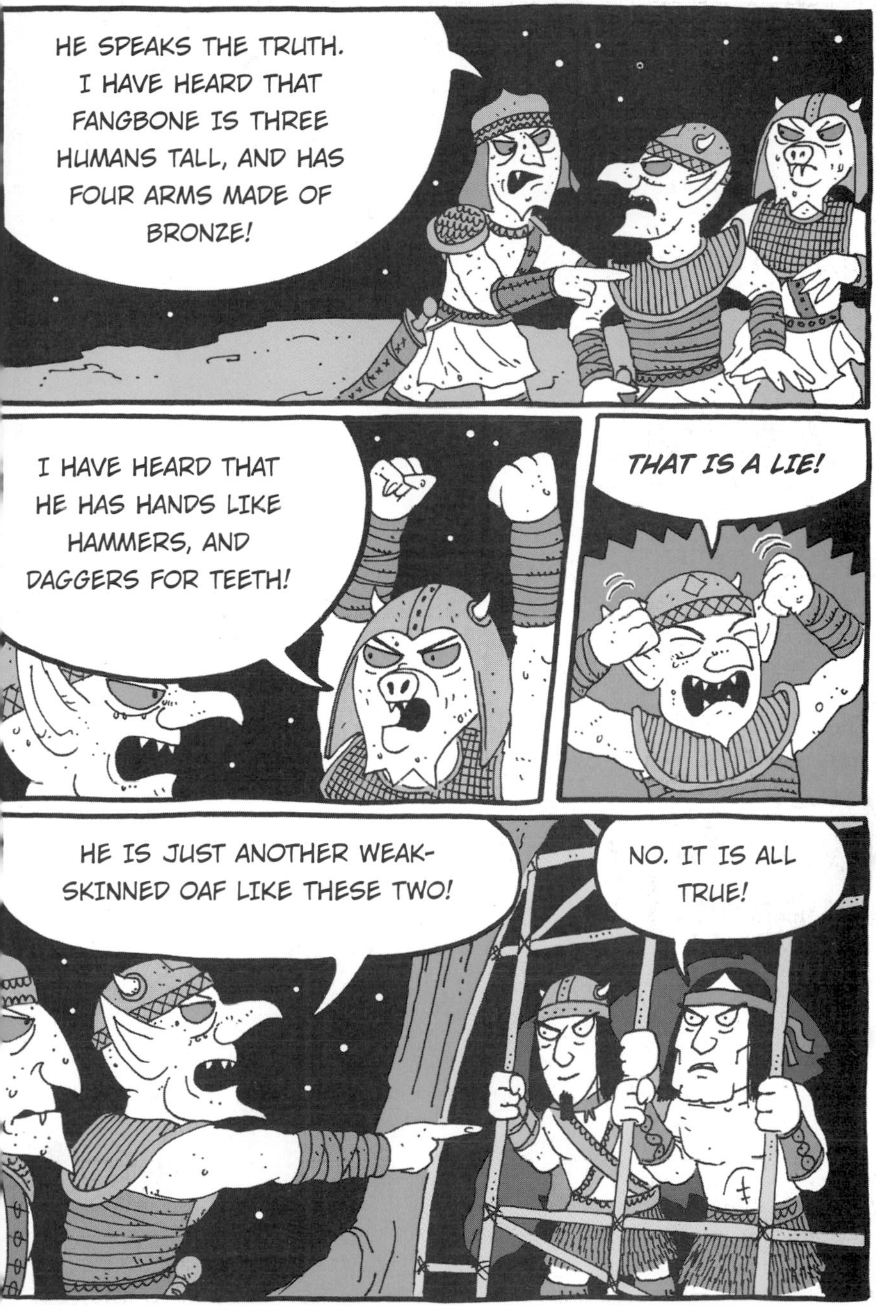
HE SPEAKS THE TRUTH. I HAVE HEARD THAT FANGBONE IS THREE HUMANS TALL, AND HAS FOUR ARMS MADE OF BRONZE!
I HAVE HEARD THAT HE HAS HANDS LIKE HAMMERS, AND DAGGERS FOR TEETH!
THAT IS A LIE!
HE IS JUST ANOTHER WEAK-SKINNED OAF LIKE THESE TWO!
NO. IT IS ALL TRUE!

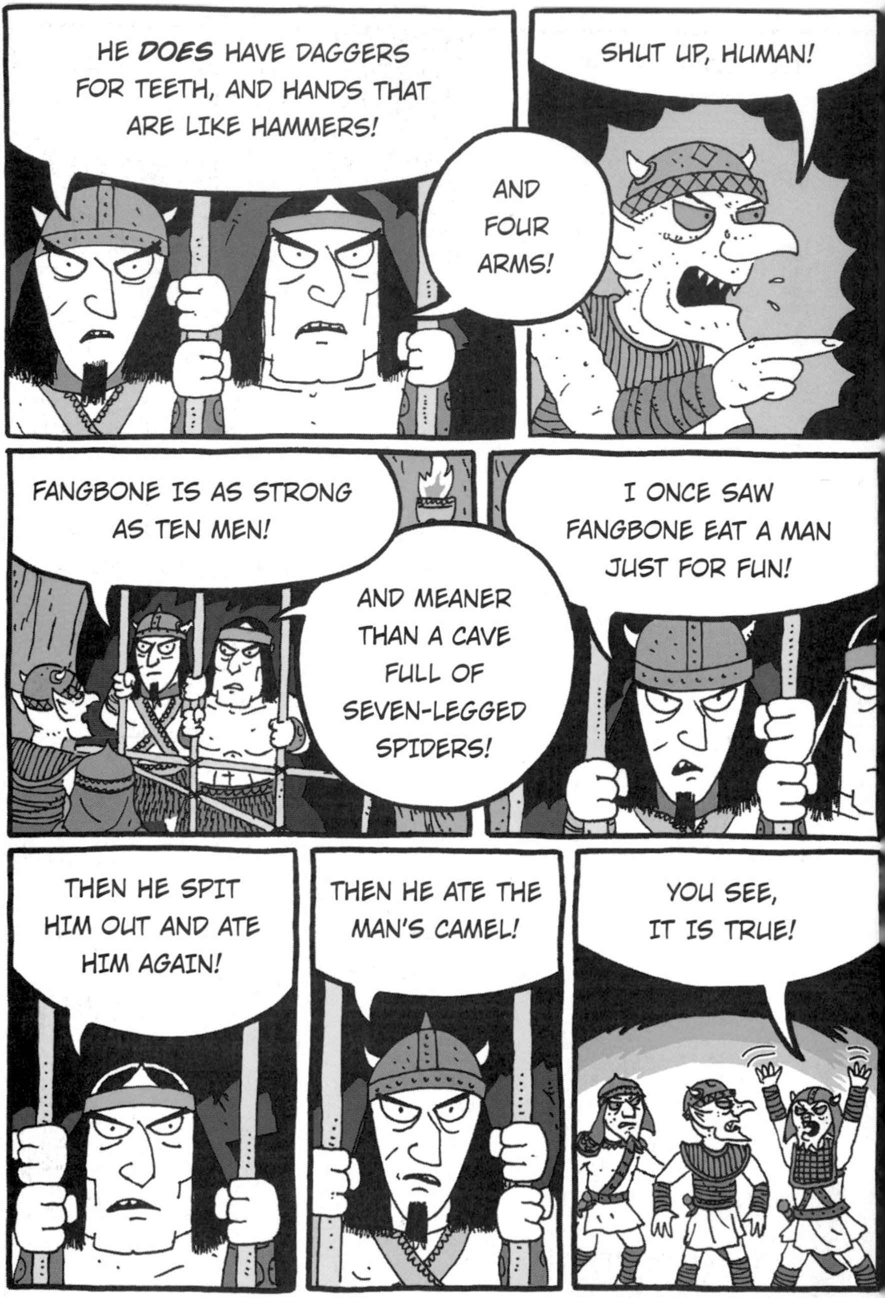
HE DOES HAVE DAGGERS FOR TEETH, AND HANDS THAT ARE LIKE HAMMERS!
AND FOUR ARMS!
SHUT UP, HUMAN!
FANGBONE IS AS STRONG AS TEN MEN!
AND MEANER THAN A CAVE FULL OF SEVEN-LEGGED SPIDERS!
I ONCE SAW FANGBONE EAT A MAN JUST FOR FUN!
THEN HE SPIT HIM OUT AND ATE HIM AGAIN!
THEN HE ATE THE MAN'S CAMEL!
YOU SEE, IT IS TRUE!

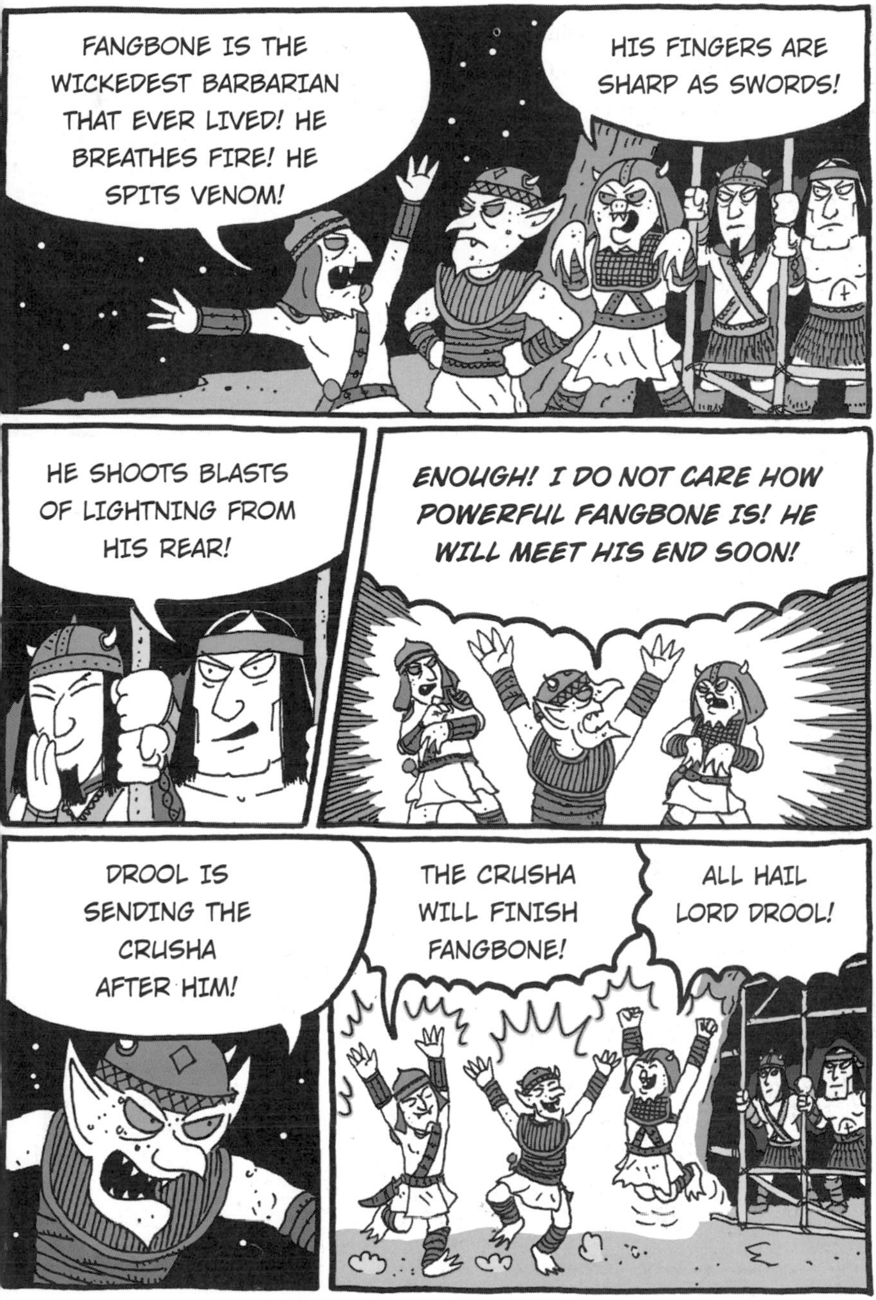
FANGBONE IS THE WICKEDEST BARBARIAN THAT EVER LIVED! HE BREATHES FIRE! HE SPITS VENOM!
HIS FINGERS ARE SHARP AS SWORDS!
HE SHOOTS BLASTS OF LIGHTNING FROM HIS REAR!
ENOUGH! I DO NOT CARE HOW POWERFUL FANGBONE IS! HE WILL MEET HIS END SOON!
DROOL IS SENDING THE CRUSHA AFTER HIM!
THE CRUSHA WILL FINISH FANGBONE!
ALL HAIL LORD DROOL!

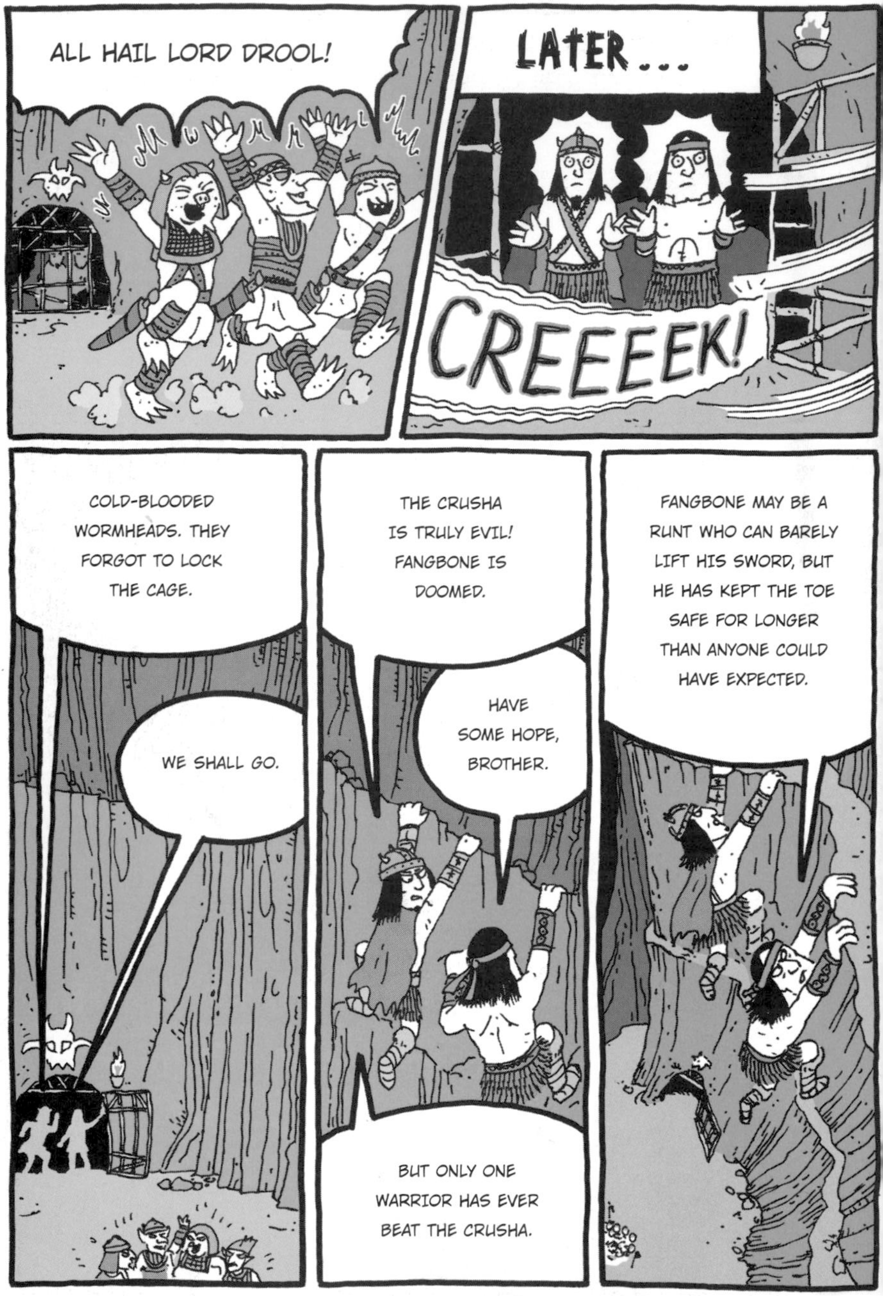
ALL HAIL LORD DROOL!
LATER . . .
CREEEEEK!
COLD-BLOODED WORMHEADS. THEY FORGOT TO LOCK THE CAGE.
WE SHALL GO.
THE CRUSHA IS TRULY EVIL! FANGBONE IS DOOMED.
HAVE SOME HOPE, BROTHER.
BUT ONLY ONE WARRIOR HAS EVER BEAT THE CRUSHA.
FANGBONE MAY BE A RUNT WHO CAN BARELY LIFT HIS SWORD, BUT HE HAS KEPT THE TOE SAFE FOR LONGER THAN ANYONE COULD HAVE EXPECTED.

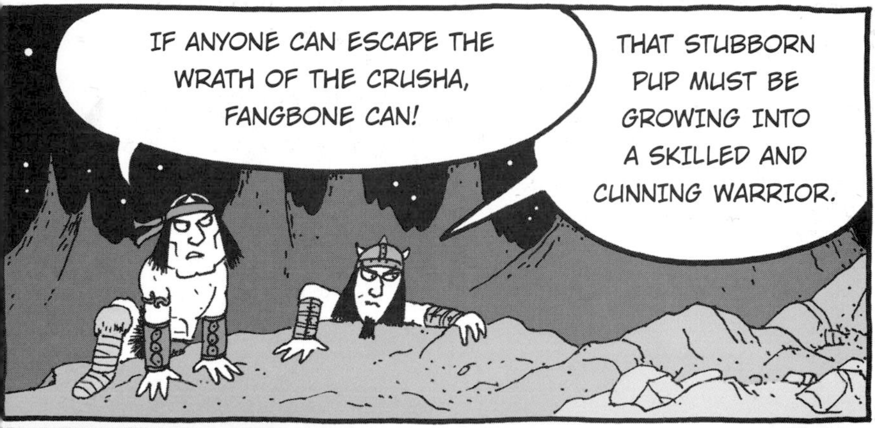
IF ANYONE CAN ESCAPE THE WRATH OF THE CRUSHA, FANGBONE CAN!
THAT STUBBORN PUP MUST BE GROWING INTO A SKILLED AND CUNNING WARRIOR.

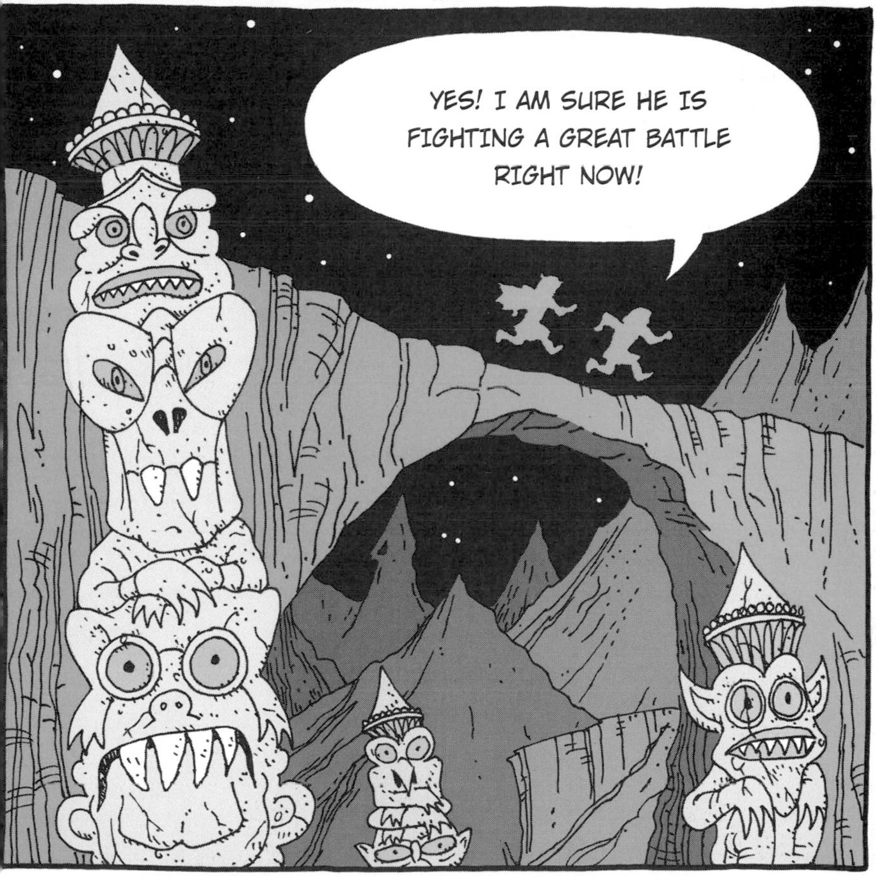
YES! I AM SURE HE IS FIGHTING A GREAT BATTLE RIGHT NOW!

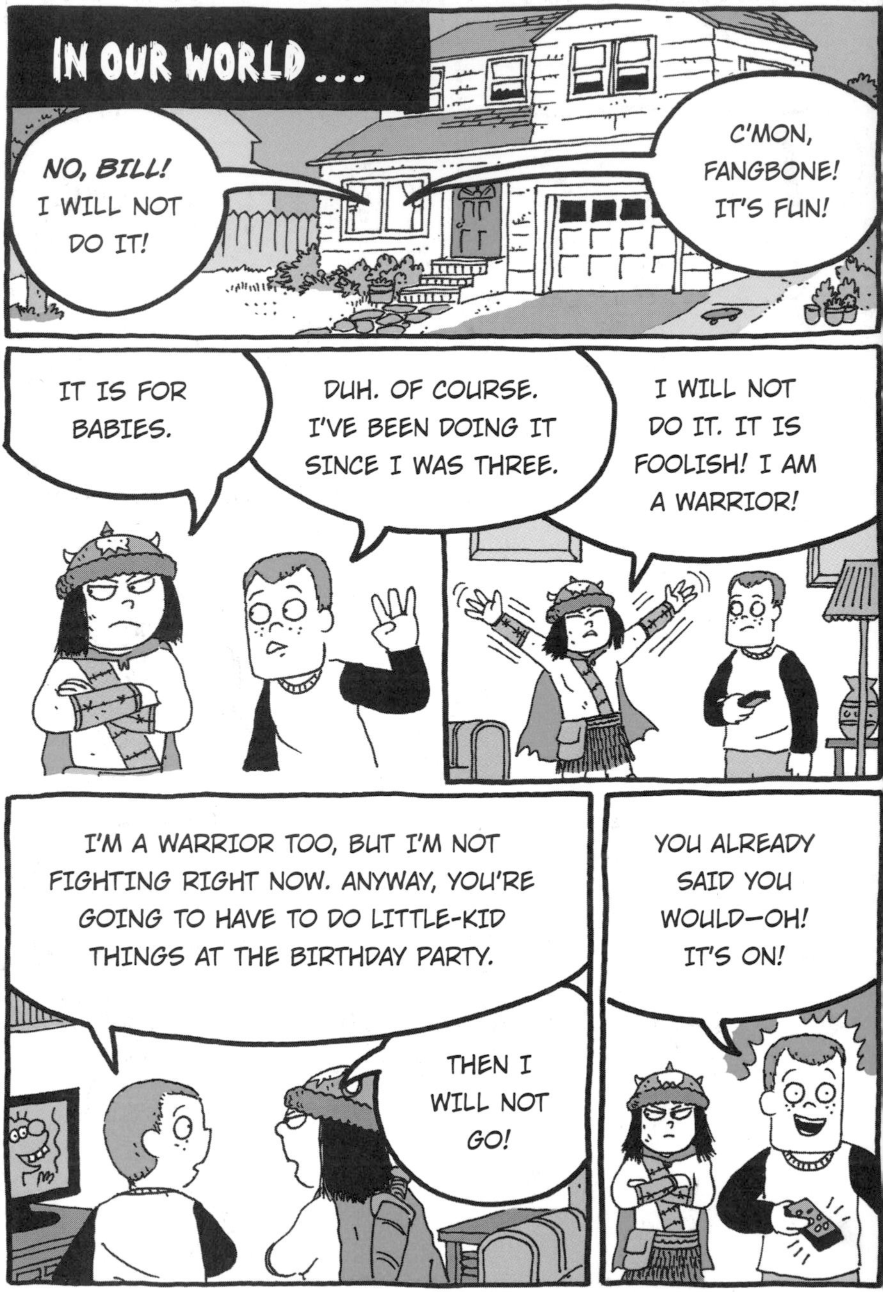
IN OUR WORLD . . .
NO, BILL! I WILL NOT DO IT!
C'MON, FANGBONE! IT'S FUN!
IT IS FOR BABIES.
DUH. OF COURSE. I'VE BEEN DOING IT SINCE I WAS THREE.
I WILL NOT DO IT. IT IS FOOLISH! I AM A WARRIOR!
I'M A WARRIOR TOO, BUT I'M NOT FIGHTING RIGHT NOW. ANYWAY, YOU'RE GOING TO HAVE TO DO LITTLE-KID THINGS AT THE BIRTHDAY PARTY.
THEN I WILL NOT GO!
YOU ALREADY SAID YOU WOULD—OH! IT'S ON!

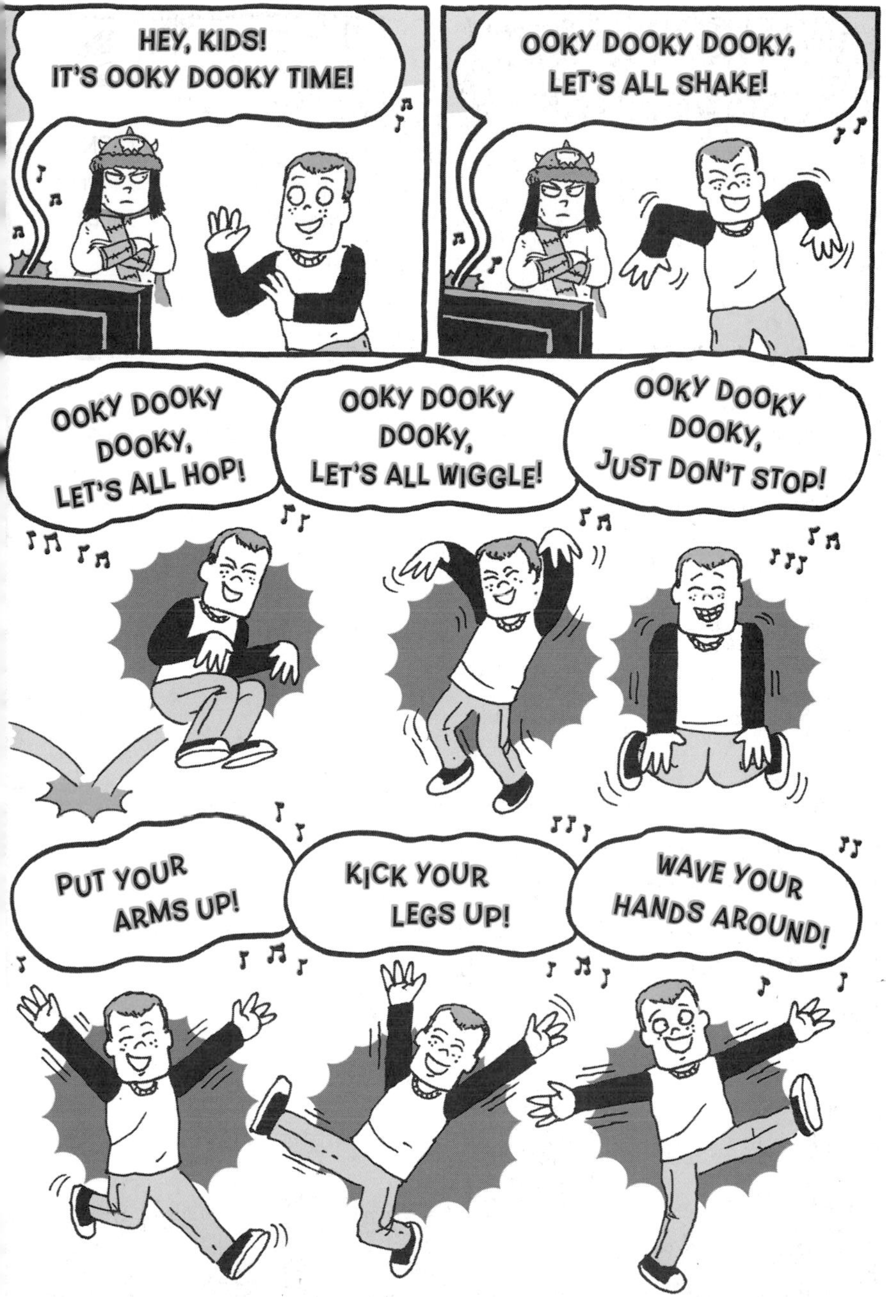
HEY, KIDS! IT'S OOKY DOOKY TIME!
OOKY DOOKY DOOKY, LET'S ALL SHAKE!
OOKY DOOKY DOOKY, LET'S ALL HOP!
OOKY DOOKY DOOKY, LET'S ALL WIGGLE!
OOKY DOOKY DOOKY, JUST DON'T STOP!
PUT YOUR ARMS UP!
KICK YOUR LEGS UP!
WAVE YOUR HANDS AROUND!

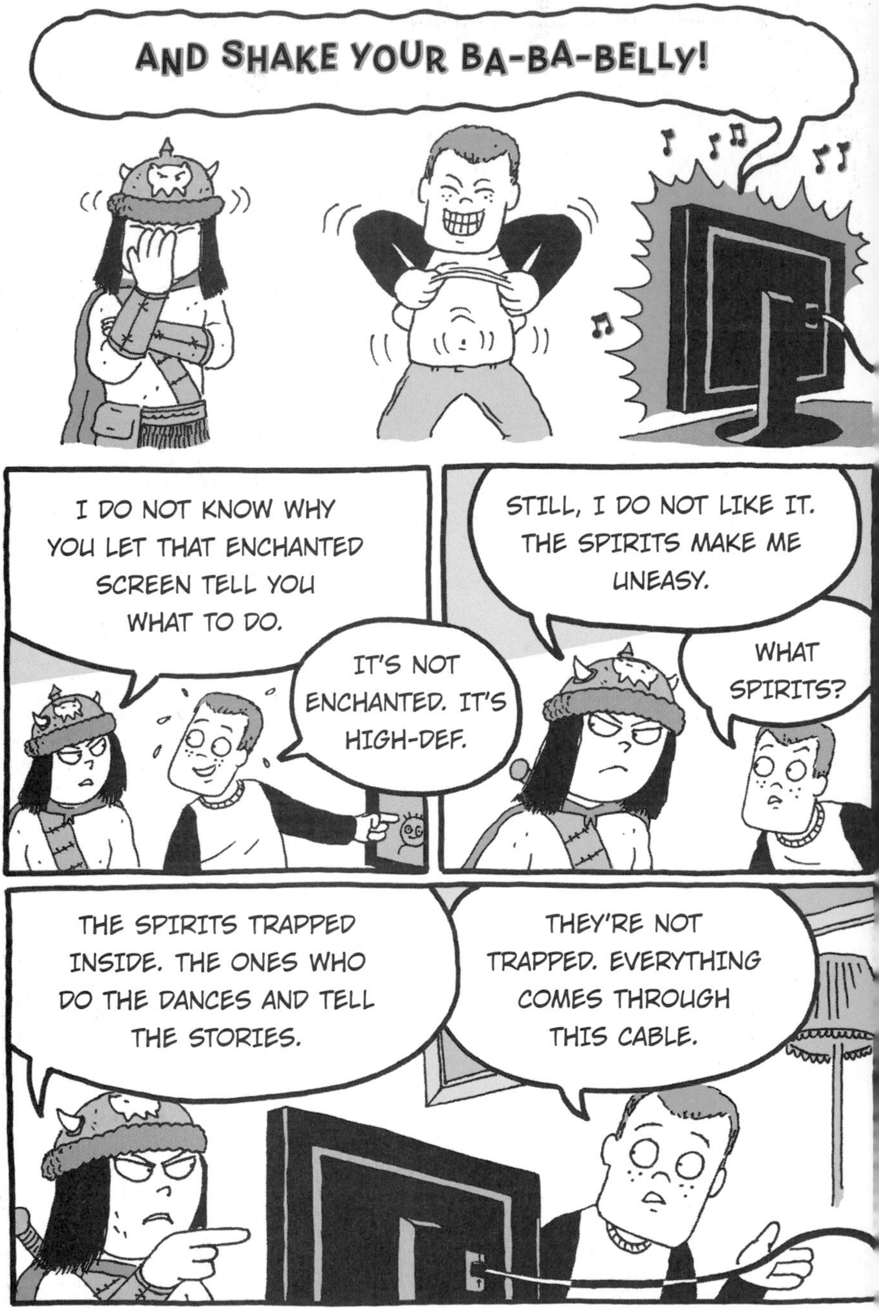
AND SHAKE YOUR BA-BA-BELLY!
I DO NOT KNOW WHY YOU LET THAT ENCHANTED SCREEN TELL YOU WHAT TO DO.
IT'S NOT ENCHANTED. IT'S HIGH-DEF.
STILL, I DO NOT LIKE IT. THE SPIRITS MAKE ME UNEASY.
WHAT SPIRITS?
THE SPIRITS TRAPPED INSIDE. THE ONES WHO DO THE DANCES AND TELL THE STORIES.
THEY'RE NOT TRAPPED. EVERYTHING COMES THROUGH THIS CABLE.

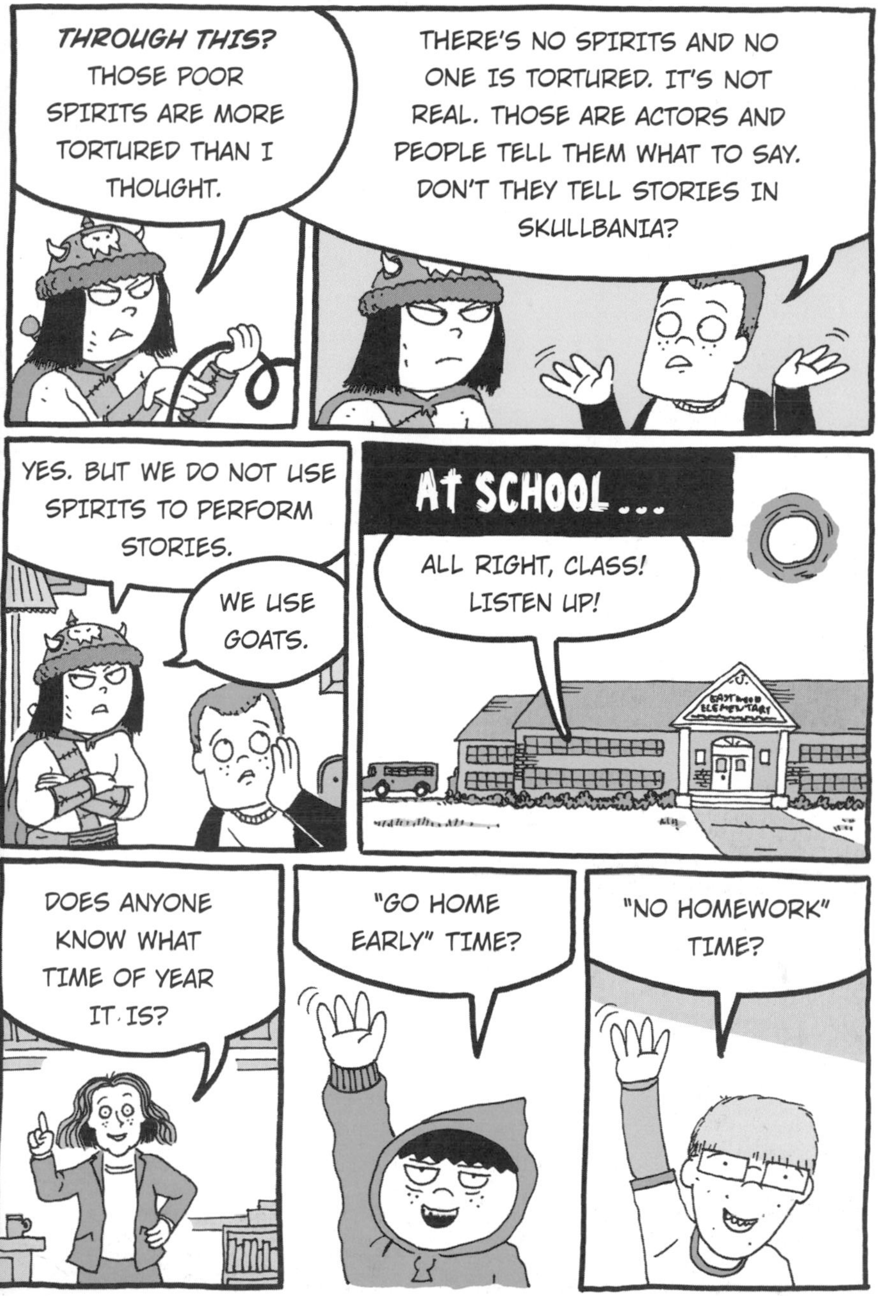
THROUGH THIS? THOSE POOR SPIRITS ARE MORE TORTURED THAN I THOUGHT.
THERE'S NO SPIRITS AND NO ONE IS TORTURED. IT'S NOT REAL. THOSE ARE ACTORS AND PEOPLE TELL THEM WHAT TO SAY. DON'T THEY TELL STORIES IN SKULLBANIA?
YES. BUT WE DO NOT USE SPIRITS TO PERFORM STORIES.
WE USE GOATS.
At SCHOOL . . .
ALL RIGHT, CLASS! LISTEN UP!
DOES ANYONE KNOW WHAT TIME OF YEAR IT IS?
"GO HOME EARLY" TIME?
"NO HOMEWORK" TIME?

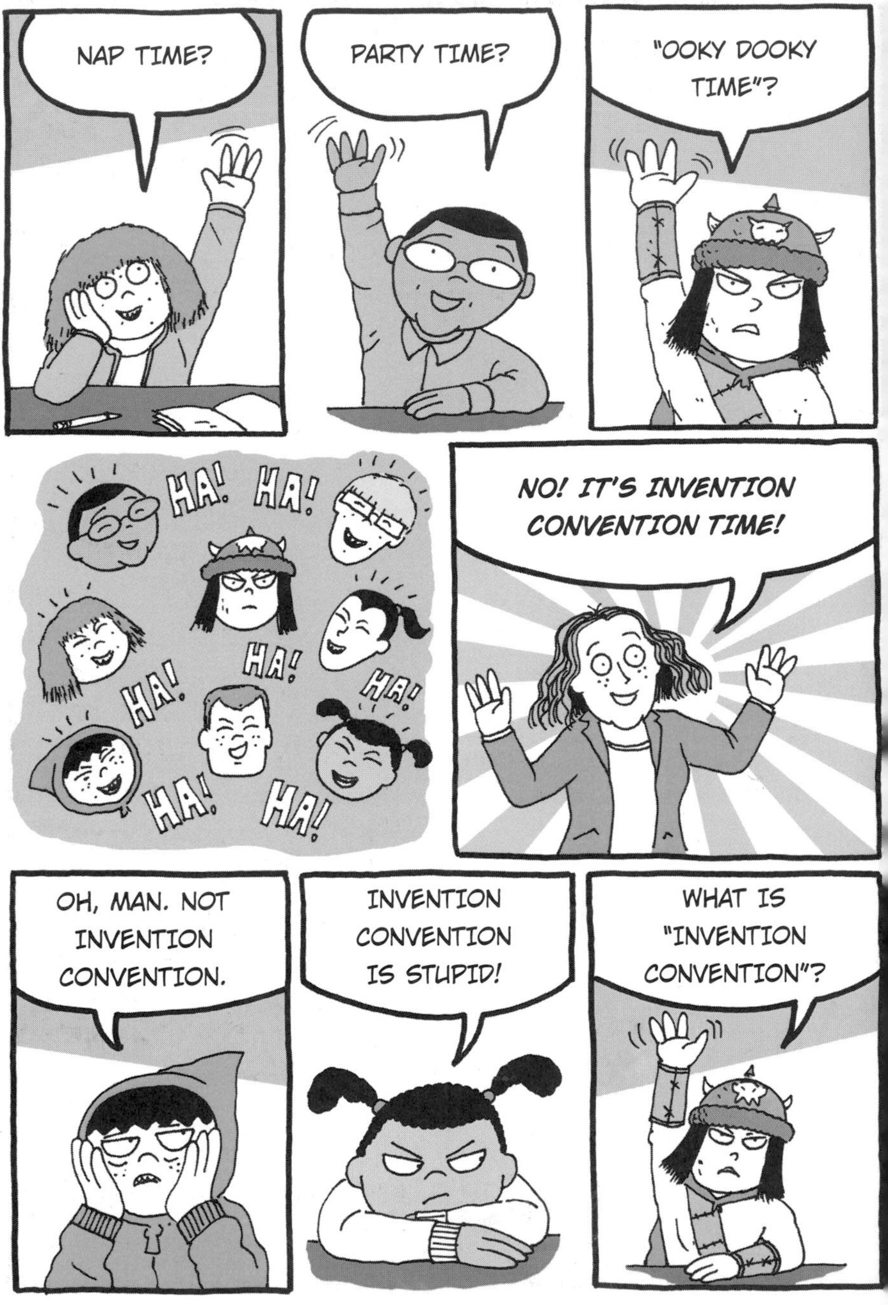
NAP TIME?
PARTY TIME?
"OOKY DOOKY TIME"?
HA! HA! HA! HA! HA! HA! HA!
NO! IT'S INVENTION CONVENTION TIME!
OH, MAN. NOT INVENTION CONVENTION.
INVENTION CONVENTION IS STUPID!
WHAT IS "INVENTION CONVENTION"?

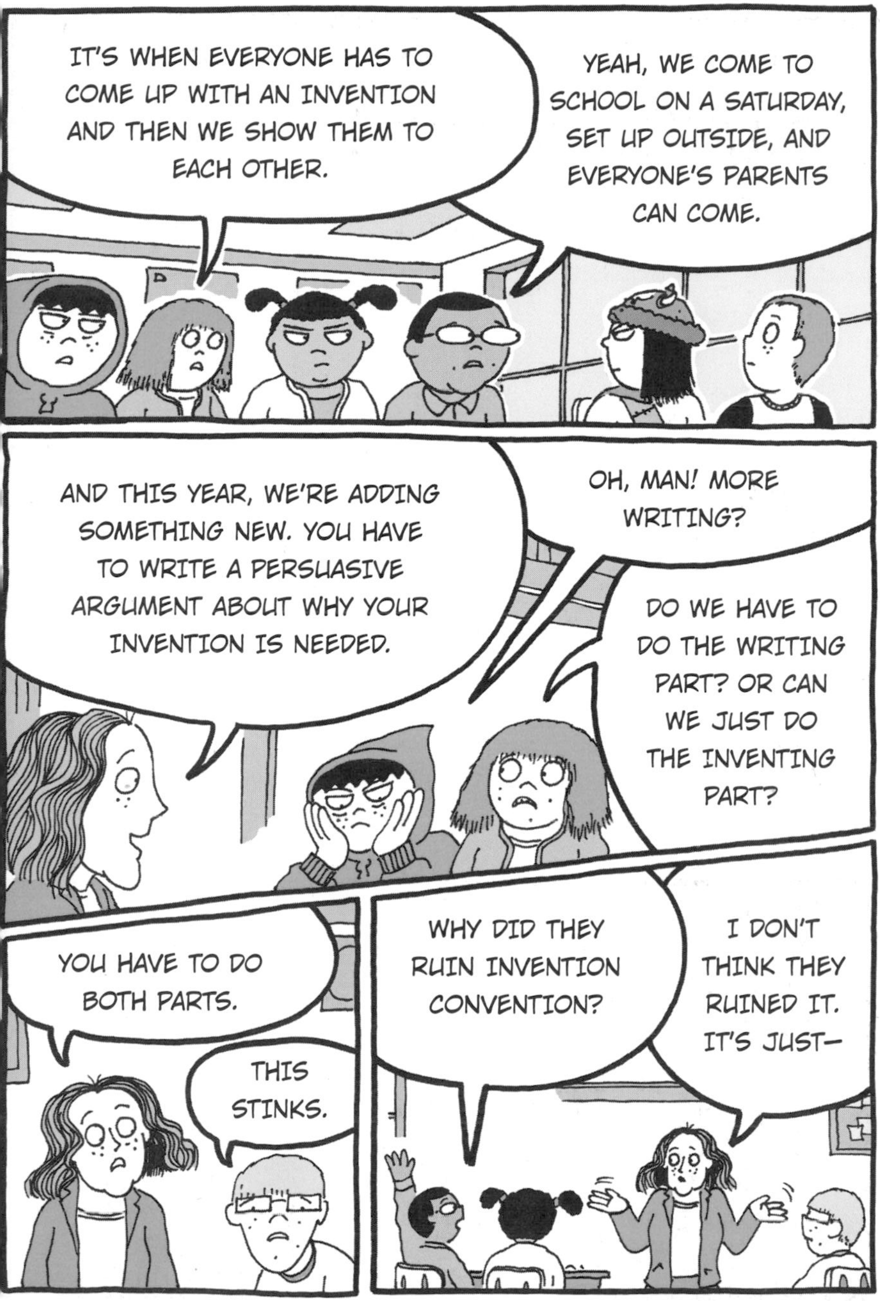
IT'S WHEN EVERYONE HAS TO COME UP WITH AN INVENTION AND THEN WE SHOW THEM TO EACH OTHER.
YEAH, WE COME TO SCHOOL ON A SATURDAY, SET UP OUTSIDE, AND EVERYONE'S PARENTS CAN COME.
AND THIS YEAR, WE'RE ADDING SOMETHING NEW. YOU HAVE TO WRITE A PERSUASIVE ARGUMENT ABOUT WHY YOUR INVENTION IS NEEDED.
OH, MAN! MORE WRITING?
DO WE HAVE TO DO THE WRITING PART? OR CAN WE JUST DO THE INVENTING PART?
YOU HAVE TO DO BOTH PARTS.
THIS STINKS.
WHY DID THEY RUIN INVENTION CONVENTION?
I DON'T THINK THEY RUINED IT. IT'S JUST—

 HARDER.

 LAMER.

 STUPIDER.

 MISS GILLIAN? WHAT IS "PERSUASIVE ARGUMENT"?

IT'S WHEN YOU TRY TO GET PEOPLE TO CHANGE THEIR MINDS.

 YOU GIVE THEM GOOD REASONS TO THINK THE WAY YOU DO.

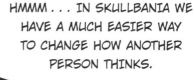 HMMM . . . IN SKULLBANIA WE HAVE A MUCH EASIER WAY TO CHANGE HOW ANOTHER PERSON THINKS.

 REALLY, HOW?

 WE HIT THEM ON THE HEAD WITH A SWORD!

LATER...

BILL? CAN I TALK WITH YOU?

SURE.

BILL, YOUR GRADES HAVEN'T BEEN VERY GOOD THE LAST FEW WEEKS, AND—

ARE YOU GONNA CALL MY MOM?

WELL . . . I SHOULD LET HER KNOW—

PLEASE DON'T! I'LL GET IN TROUBLE!

I CAN MAKE MY GRADES BETTER! I'LL WORK REALLY HARD! I'LL DO MY HOMEWORK TWICE!

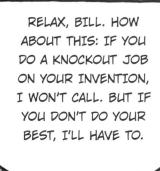

RELAX, BILL. HOW ABOUT THIS: IF YOU DO A KNOCKOUT JOB ON YOUR INVENTION, I WON'T CALL. BUT IF YOU DON'T DO YOUR BEST, I'LL HAVE TO.

DO YOU UNDERSTAND ME, BILL?

YES.

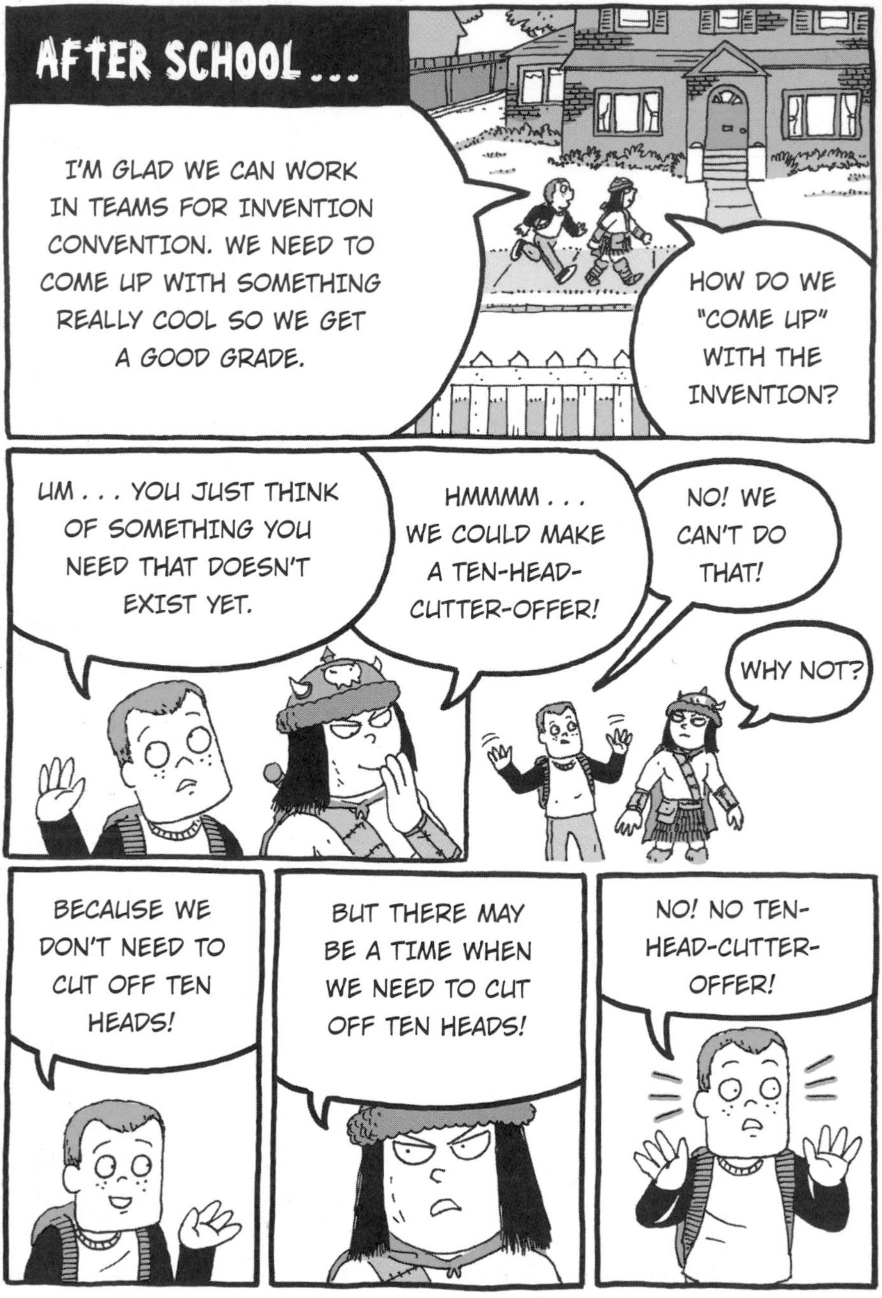
AFTER SCHOOL . . .
I'M GLAD WE CAN WORK IN TEAMS FOR INVENTION CONVENTION. WE NEED TO COME UP WITH SOMETHING REALLY COOL SO WE GET A GOOD GRADE.
HOW DO WE "COME UP" WITH THE INVENTION?
UM . . . YOU JUST THINK OF SOMETHING YOU NEED THAT DOESN'T EXIST YET.
HMMMM . . . WE COULD MAKE A TEN-HEAD-CUTTER-OFFER!
NO! WE CAN'T DO THAT!
WHY NOT?
BECAUSE WE DON'T NEED TO CUT OFF TEN HEADS!
BUT THERE MAY BE A TIME WHEN WE NEED TO CUT OFF TEN HEADS!
NO! NO TEN-HEAD-CUTTER-OFFER!

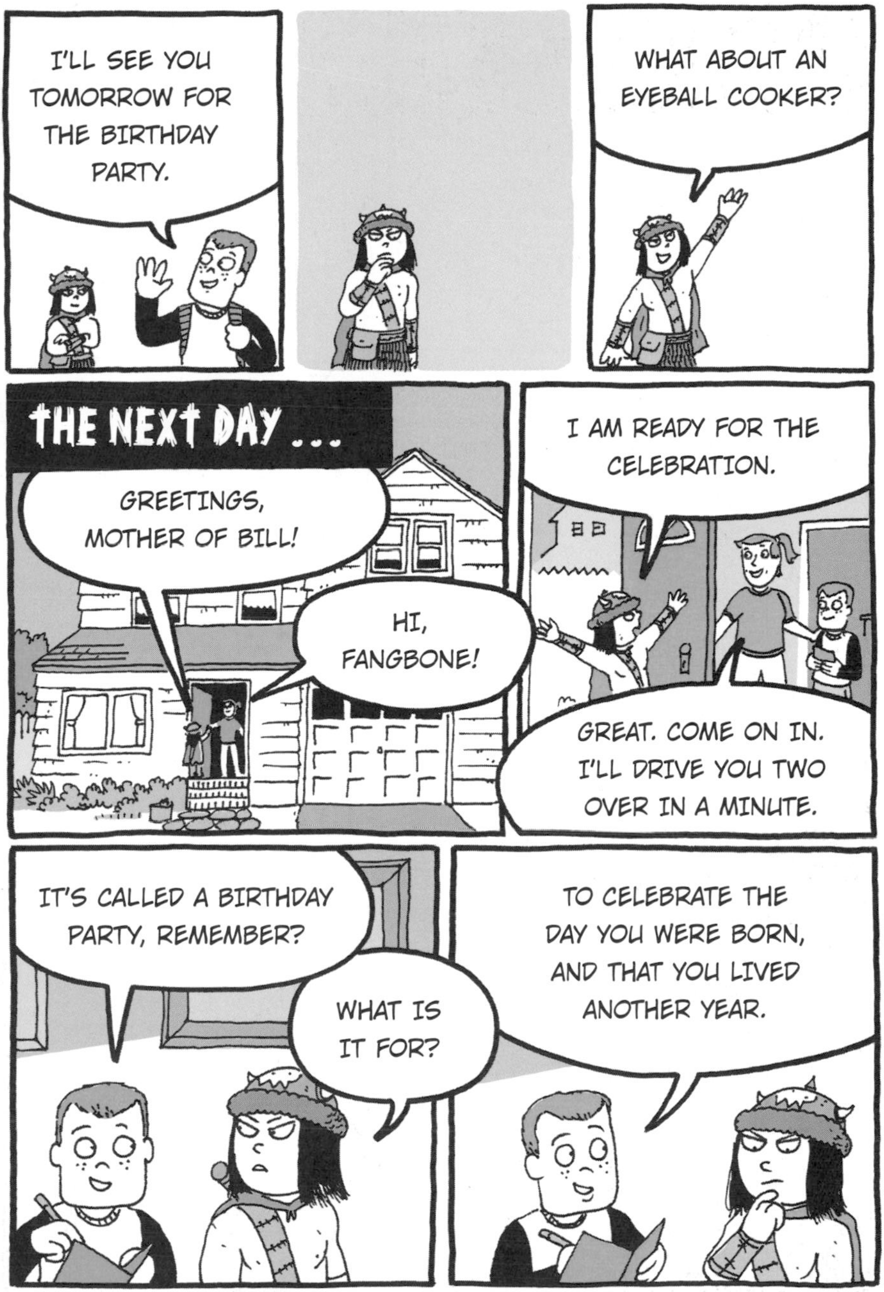
I'LL SEE YOU TOMORROW FOR THE BIRTHDAY PARTY.
WHAT ABOUT AN EYEBALL COOKER?
THE NEXT DAY . . .
GREETINGS, MOTHER OF BILL!
HI, FANGBONE!
I AM READY FOR THE CELEBRATION.
GREAT. COME ON IN. I'LL DRIVE YOU TWO OVER IN A MINUTE.
IT'S CALLED A BIRTHDAY PARTY, REMEMBER?
WHAT IS IT FOR?
TO CELEBRATE THE DAY YOU WERE BORN, AND THAT YOU LIVED ANOTHER YEAR.

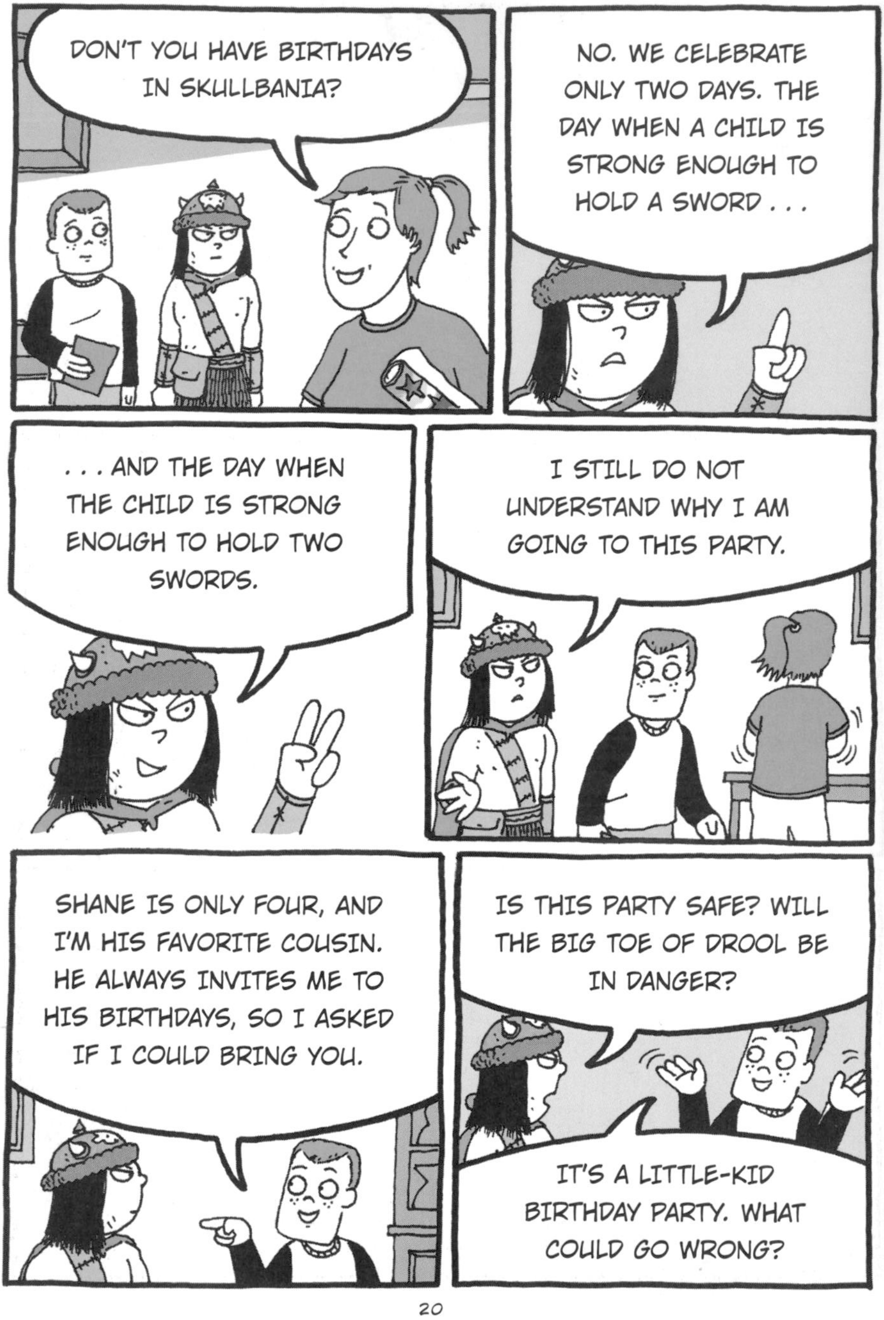
DON'T YOU HAVE BIRTHDAYS IN SKULLBANIA?
NO. WE CELEBRATE ONLY TWO DAYS. THE DAY WHEN A CHILD IS STRONG ENOUGH TO HOLD A SWORD . . .
. . . AND THE DAY WHEN THE CHILD IS STRONG ENOUGH TO HOLD TWO SWORDS.
I STILL DO NOT UNDERSTAND WHY I AM GOING TO THIS PARTY.
SHANE IS ONLY FOUR, AND I'M HIS FAVORITE COUSIN. HE ALWAYS INVITES ME TO HIS BIRTHDAYS, SO I ASKED IF I COULD BRING YOU.
IS THIS PARTY SAFE? WILL THE BIG TOE OF DROOL BE IN DANGER?
IT'S A LITTLE-KID BIRTHDAY PARTY. WHAT COULD GO WRONG?

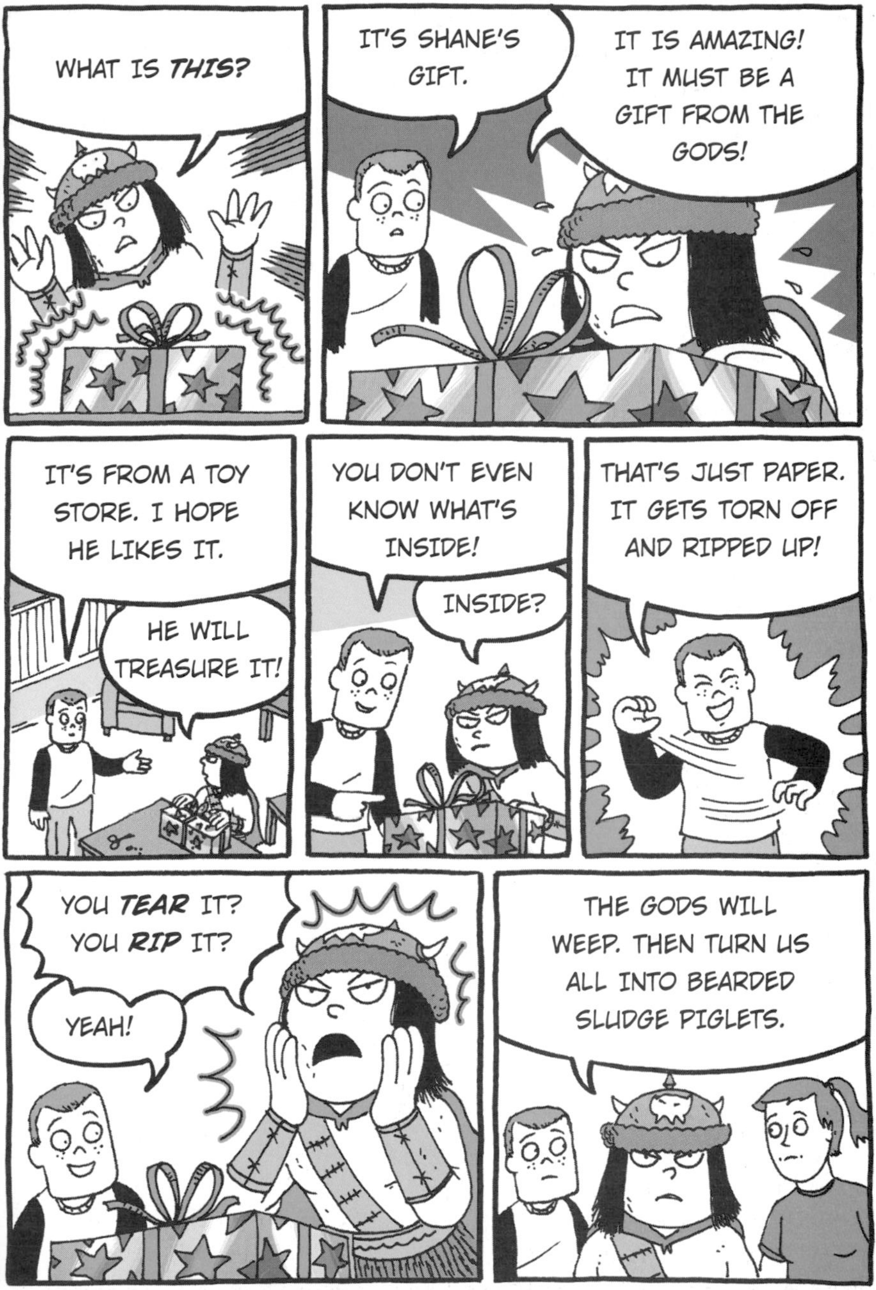
WHAT IS *THIS?*
IT'S SHANE'S GIFT.
IT IS AMAZING! IT MUST BE A GIFT FROM THE GODS!
IT'S FROM A TOY STORE. I HOPE HE LIKES IT.
HE WILL TREASURE IT!
YOU DON'T EVEN KNOW WHAT'S INSIDE!
INSIDE?
THAT'S JUST PAPER. IT GETS TORN OFF AND RIPPED UP!
YOU *TEAR* IT? YOU *RIP* IT?
YEAH!
THE GODS WILL WEEP. THEN TURN US ALL INTO BEARDED SLUDGE PIGLETS.

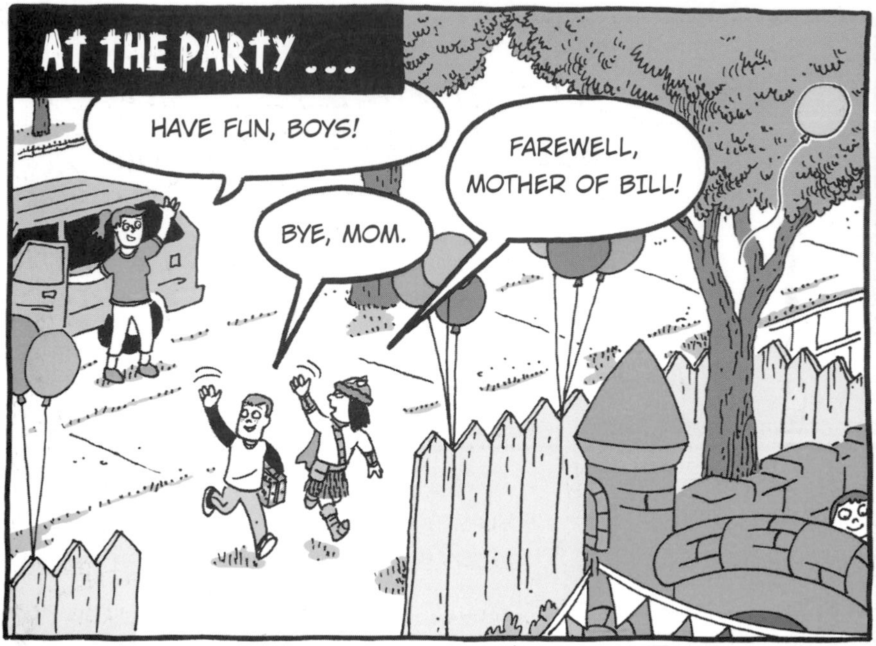
AT THE PARTY . . .
HAVE FUN, BOYS!
BYE, MOM.
FAREWELL, MOTHER OF BILL!

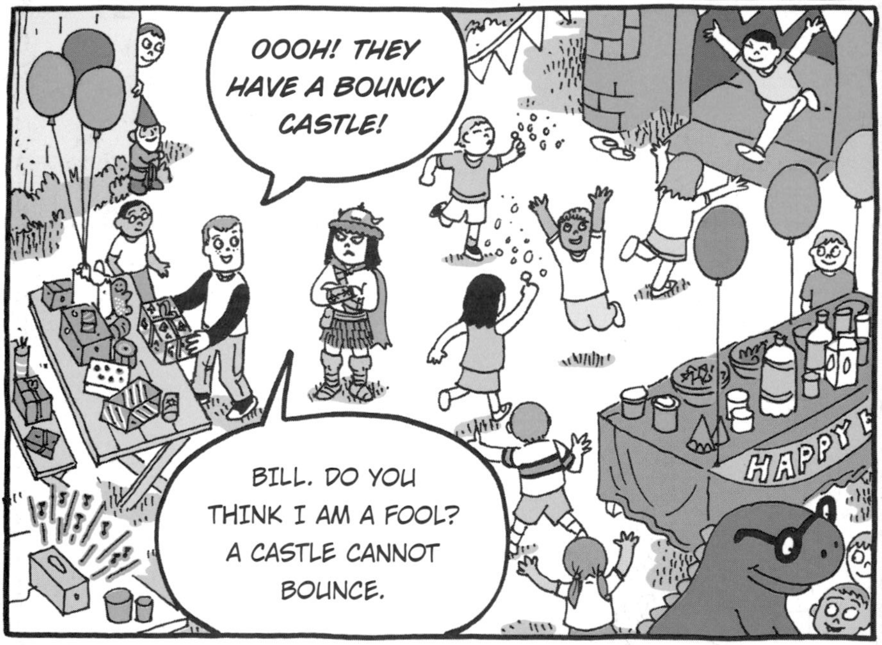
OOOH! THEY HAVE A BOUNCY CASTLE!
BILL. DO YOU THINK I AM A FOOL? A CASTLE CANNOT BOUNCE.
HAPPY

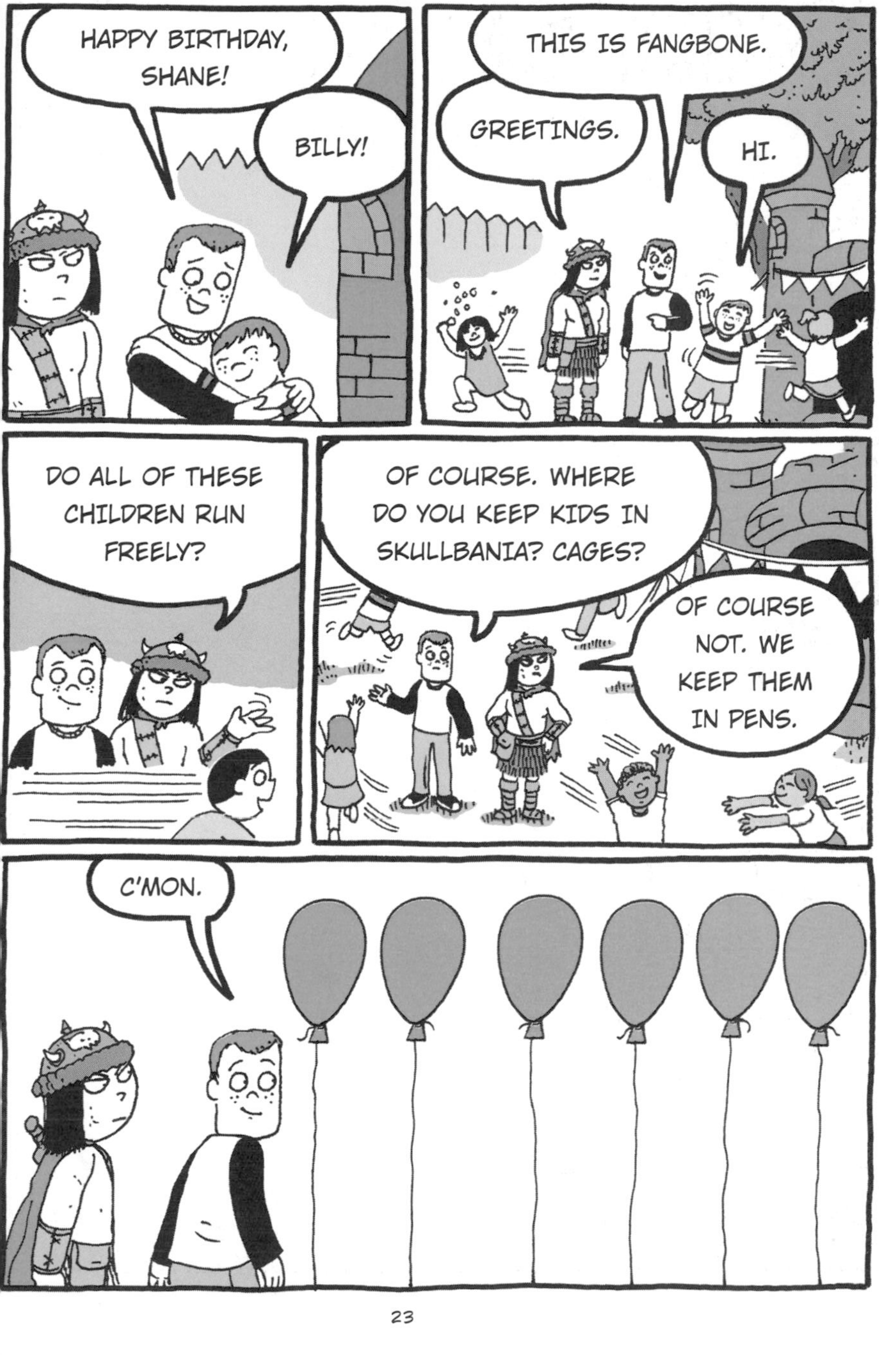
HAPPY BIRTHDAY, SHANE!
BILLY!
THIS IS FANGBONE.
GREETINGS.
HI.
DO ALL OF THESE CHILDREN RUN FREELY?
OF COURSE. WHERE DO YOU KEEP KIDS IN SKULLBANIA? CAGES?
OF COURSE NOT. WE KEEP THEM IN PENS.
C'MON.

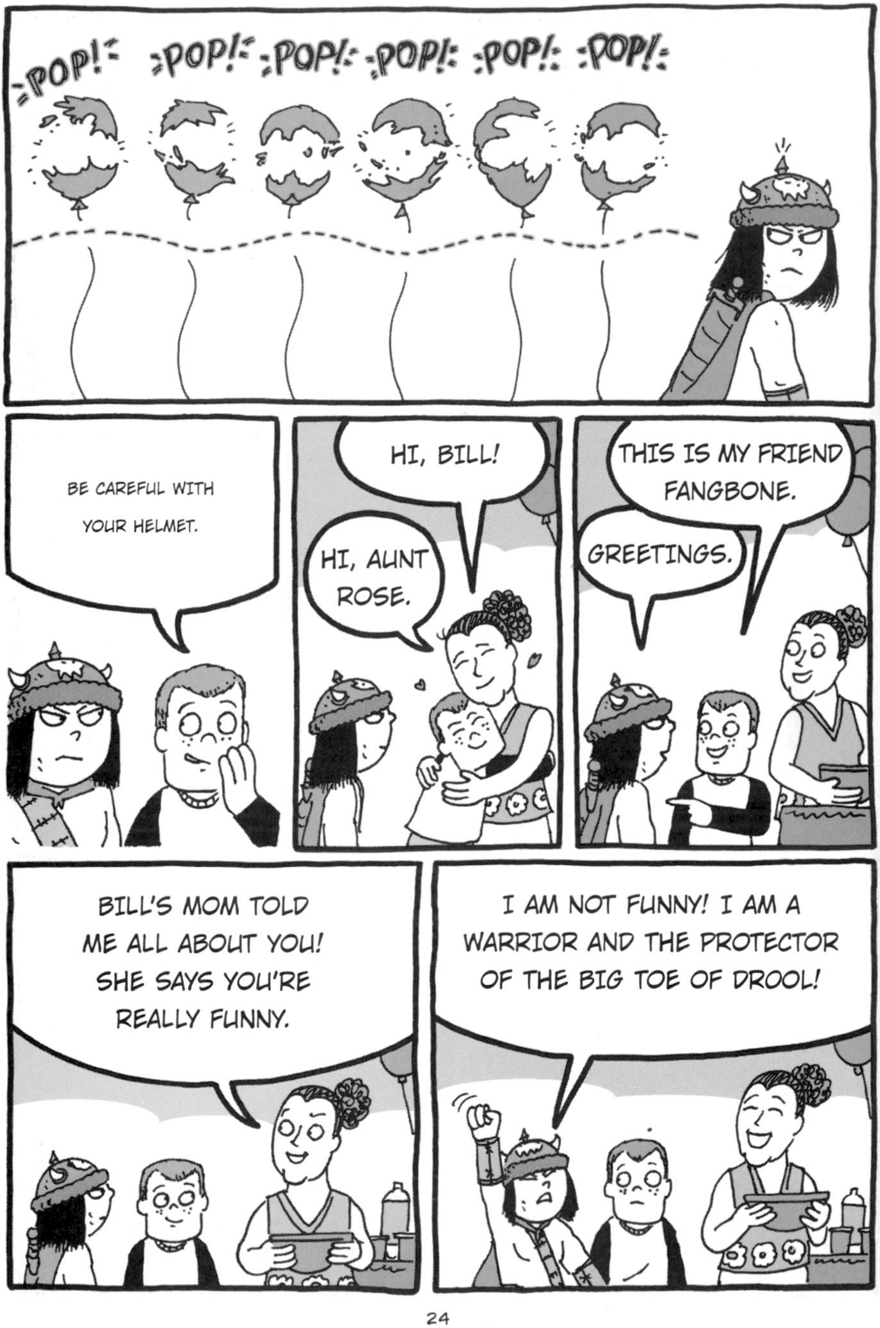
POP! POP! POP! POP! POP! POP!
BE CAREFUL WITH YOUR HELMET.
HI, BILL!
HI, AUNT ROSE.
THIS IS MY FRIEND FANGBONE.
GREETINGS.
BILL'S MOM TOLD ME ALL ABOUT YOU! SHE SAYS YOU'RE REALLY FUNNY.
I AM NOT FUNNY! I AM A WARRIOR AND THE PROTECTOR OF THE BIG TOE OF DROOL!

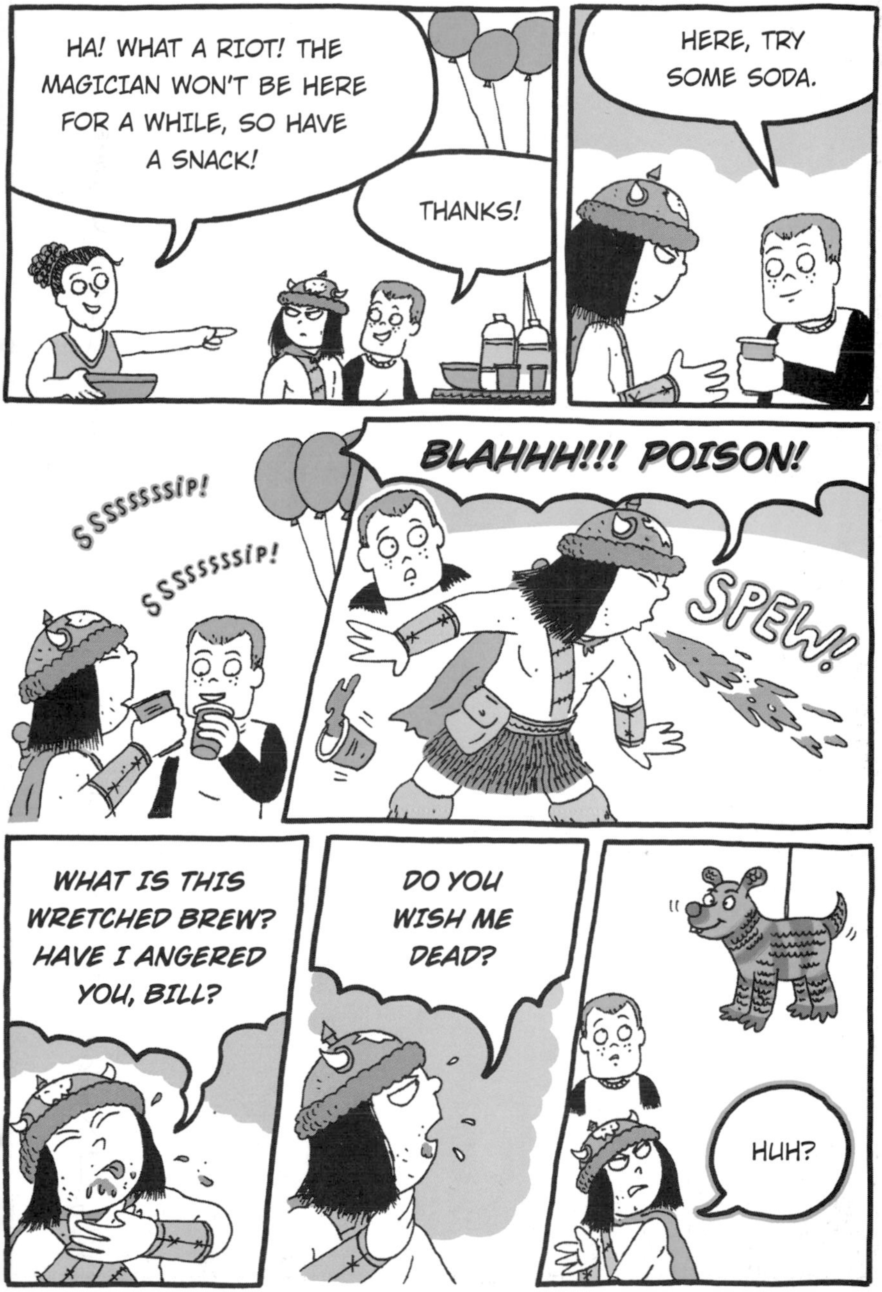
HA! WHAT A RIOT! THE MAGICIAN WON'T BE HERE FOR A WHILE, SO HAVE A SNACK!
THANKS!
HERE, TRY SOME SODA.
SSSSSSSSIP!
SSSSSSSSIP!
BLAHHH!!! POISON!
SPEW!
WHAT IS THIS WRETCHED BREW? HAVE I ANGERED YOU, BILL?
DO YOU WISH ME DEAD?
HUH?

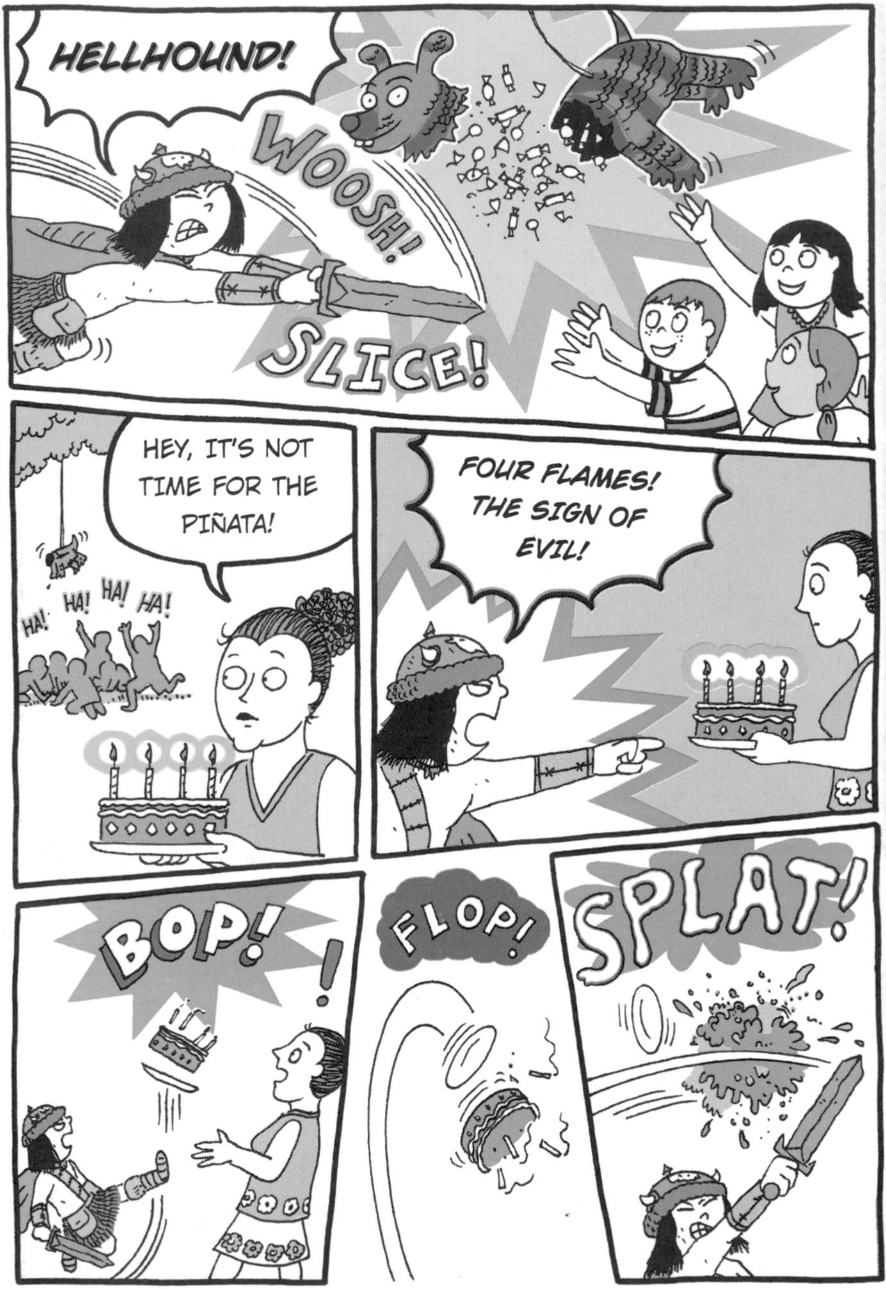
HELLHOUND!
WOOSH!
SLICE!
HEY, IT'S NOT TIME FOR THE PIÑATA!
HA! HA! HA! HA!
FOUR FLAMES! THE SIGN OF EVIL!
BOP!
!
FLOP!
SPLAT!

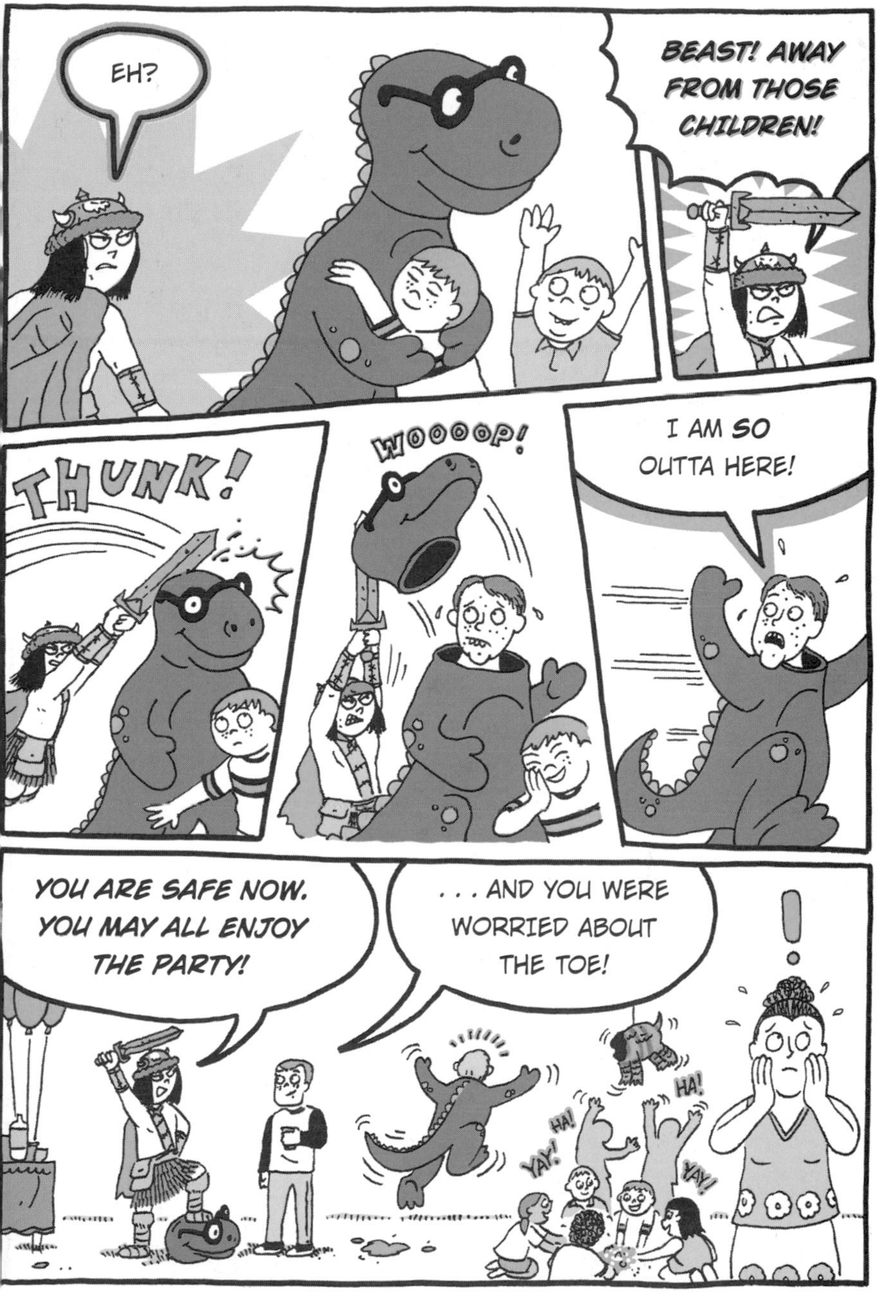
EH?
BEAST! AWAY FROM THOSE CHILDREN!
THUNK!
WOOOOP!
I AM SO OUTTA HERE!
YOU ARE SAFE NOW. YOU MAY ALL ENJOY THE PARTY!
. . . AND YOU WERE WORRIED ABOUT THE TOE!
!
HA!
YAY!
HA!
YAY!

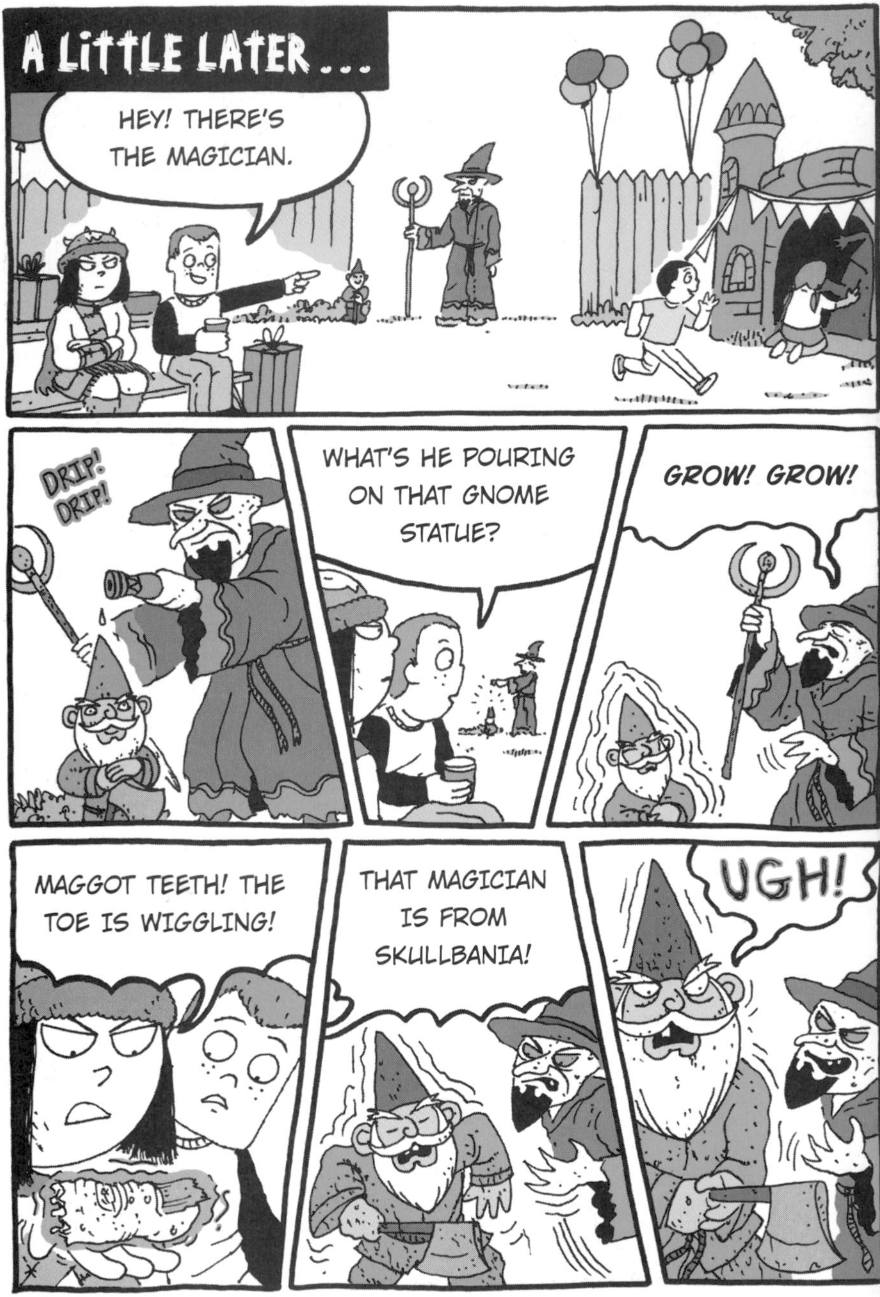
A LITTLE LATER . . .
HEY! THERE'S THE MAGICIAN.
DRIP! DRIP!
WHAT'S HE POURING ON THAT GNOME STATUE?
GROW! GROW!
MAGGOT TEETH! THE TOE IS WIGGLING!
THAT MAGICIAN IS FROM SKULLBANIA!
UGH!

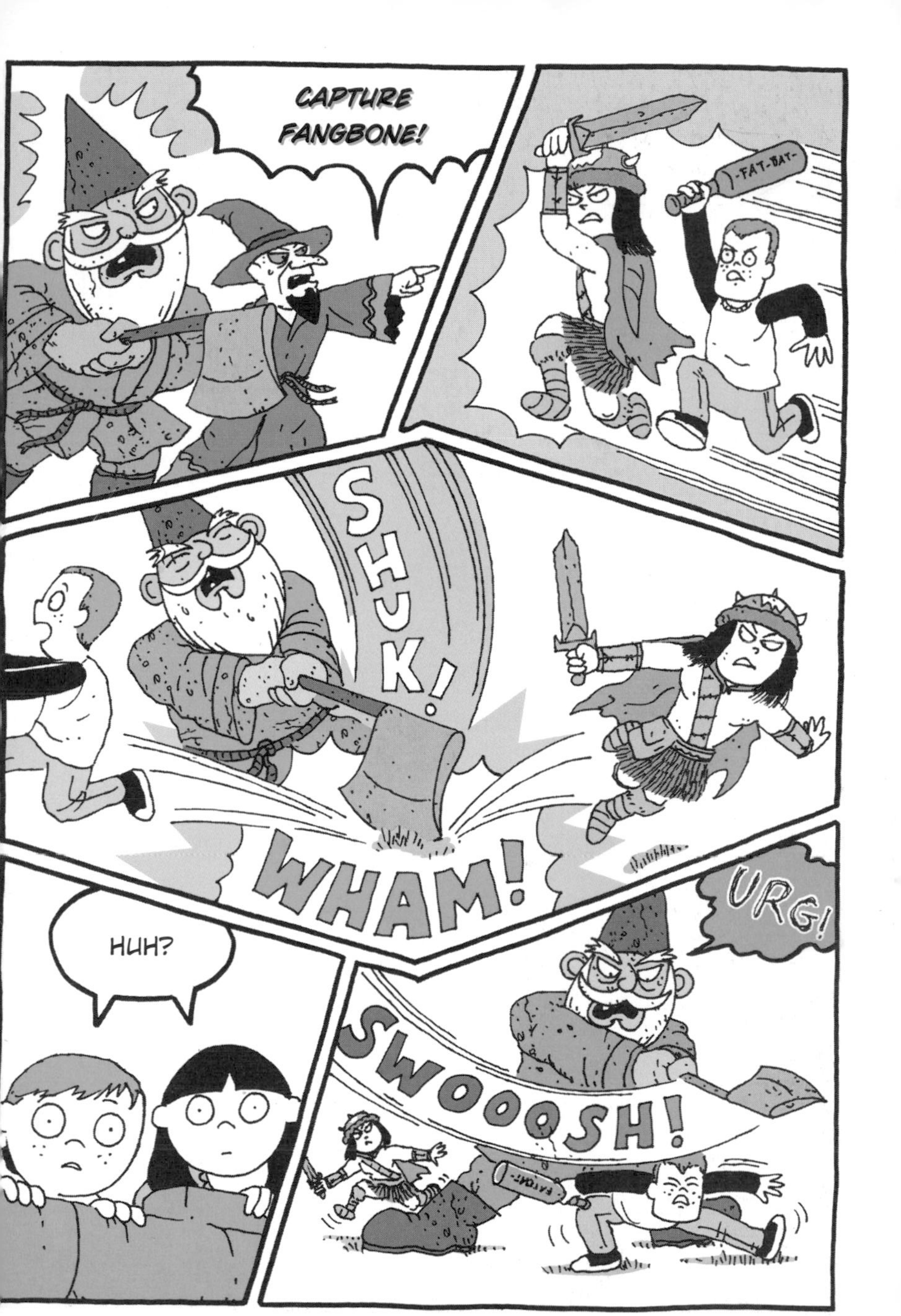

CAPTURE FANGBONE!
-FAT-BAT-
SHUK!
WHAM!
URG!
HUH?
SWOOOSH!

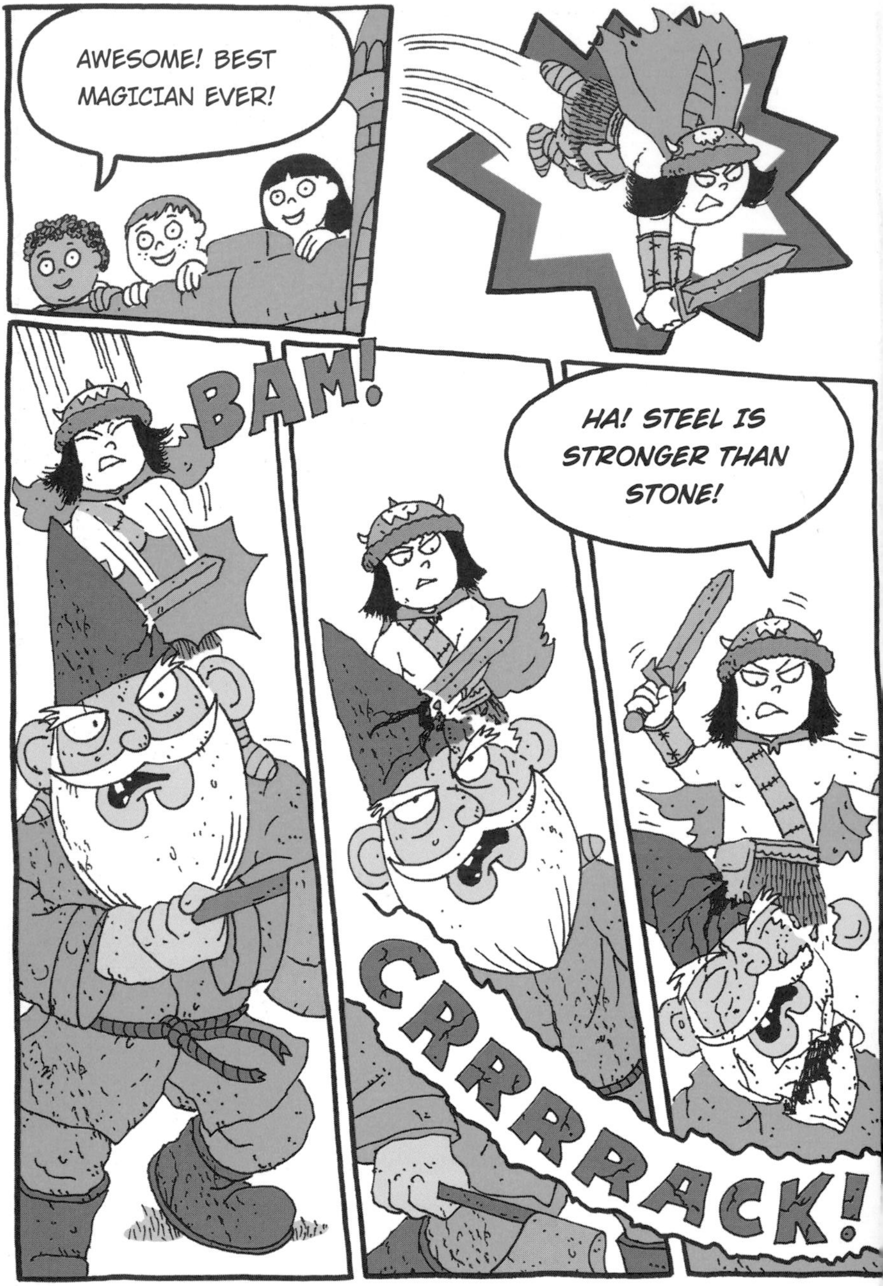
AWESOME! BEST MAGICIAN EVER!
BAM!
HA! STEEL IS STRONGER THAN STONE!
CRRRRACK!

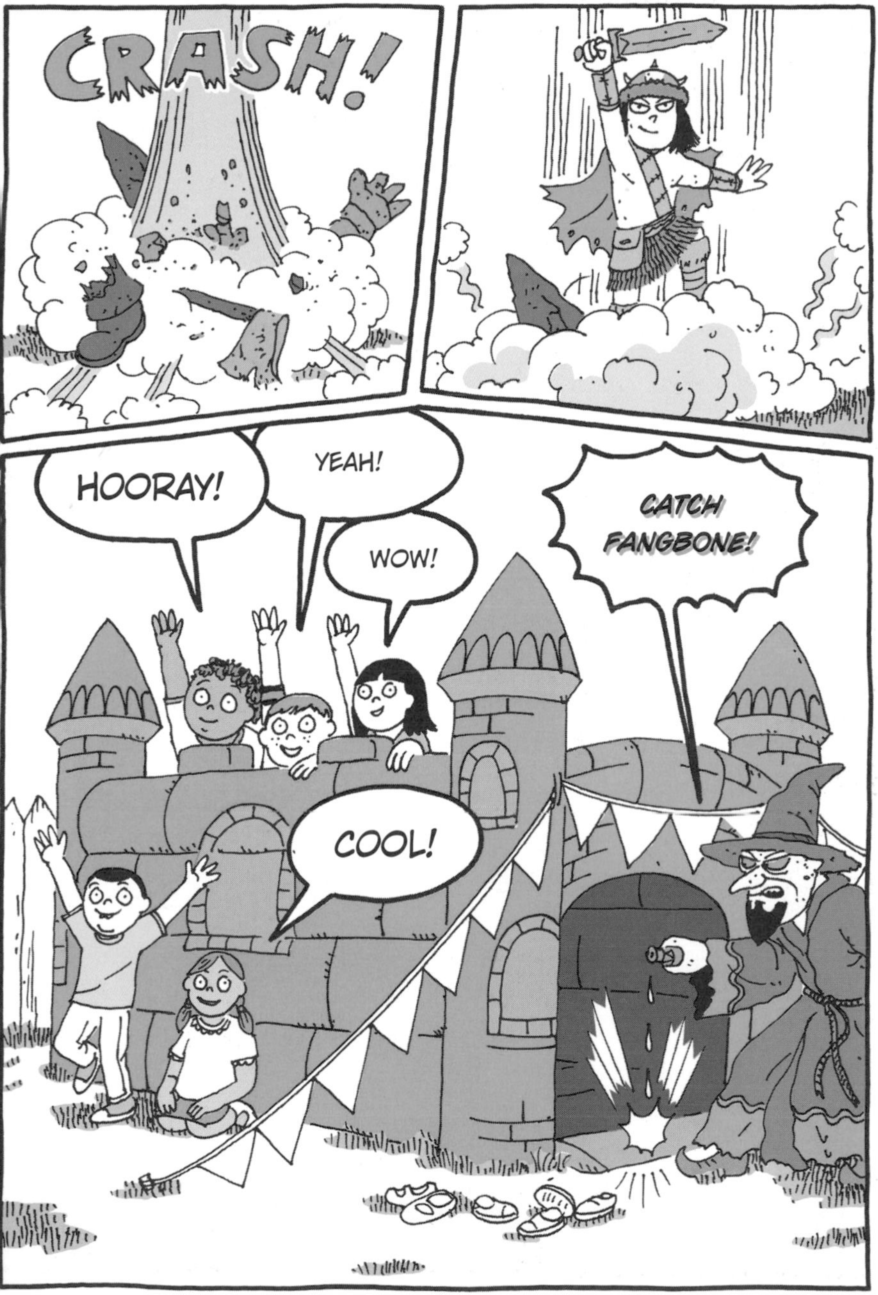
CRASH!
HOORAY!
YEAH!
WOW!
CATCH FANGBONE!
COOL!

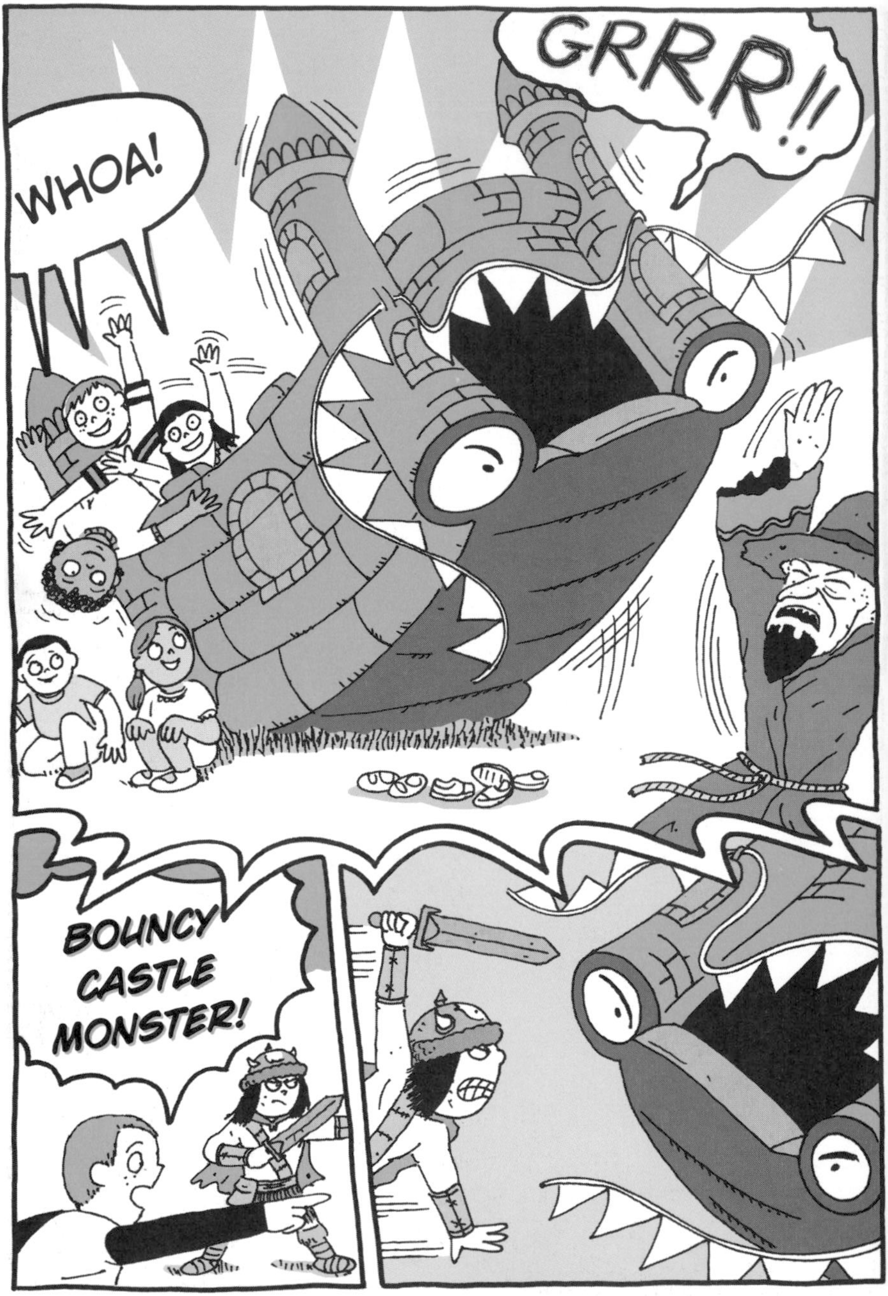
WHOA!
GRRR!!
BOUNCY CASTLE MONSTER!

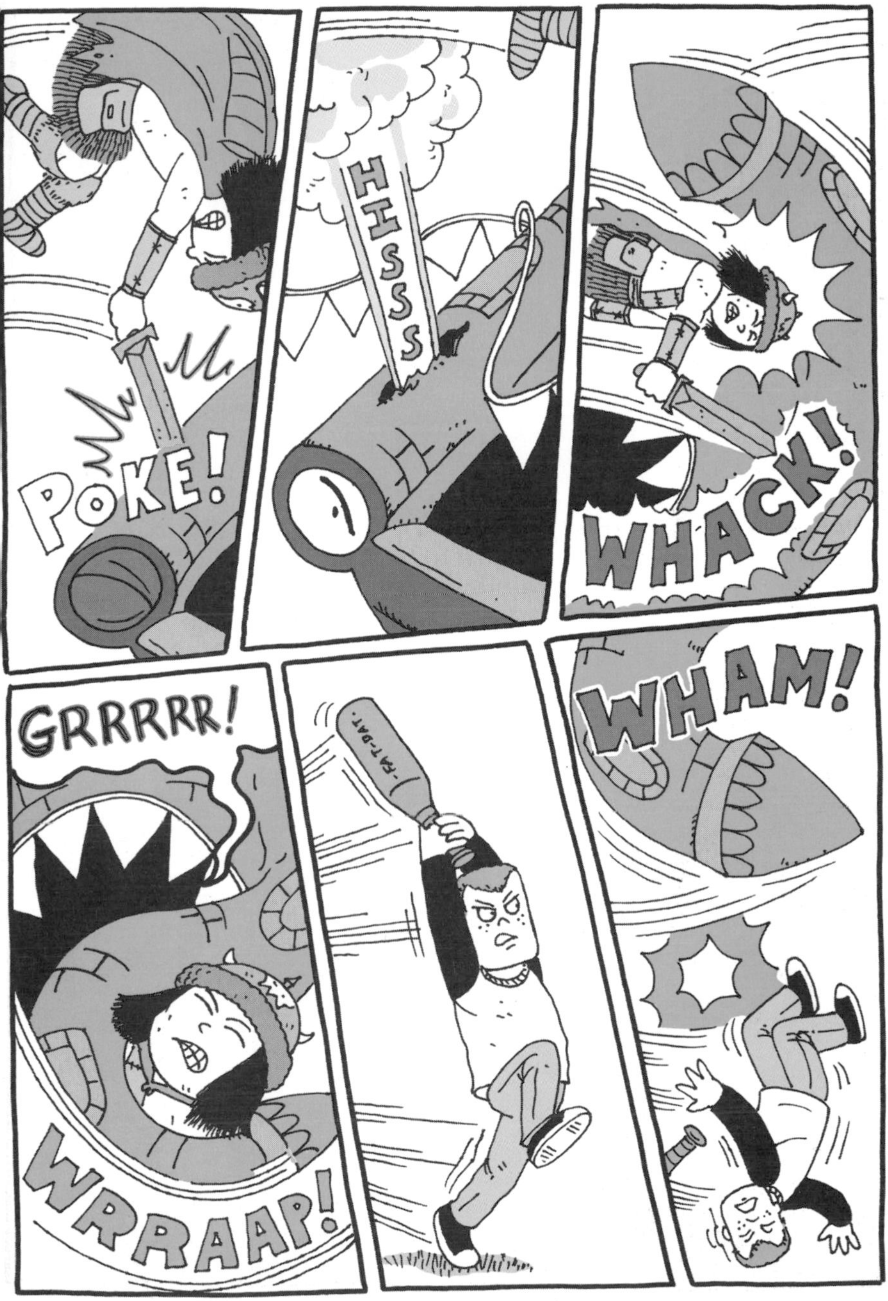
POKE!
HISSS
WHACK!
GRRRRR!
WRRAAP!
·RAT-BAT·
WHAM!

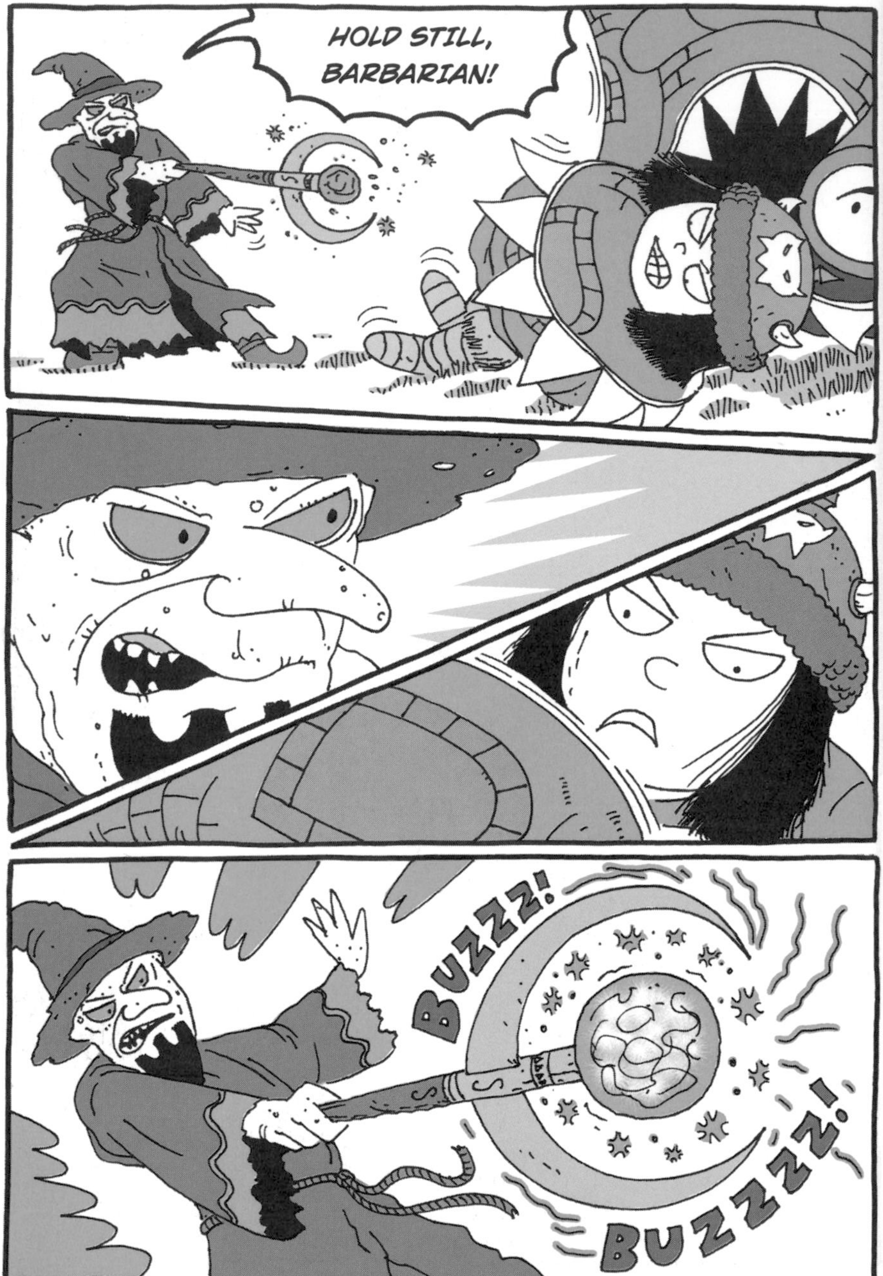
HOLD STILL, BARBARIAN!
BUZZZ!
BUZZZZ!

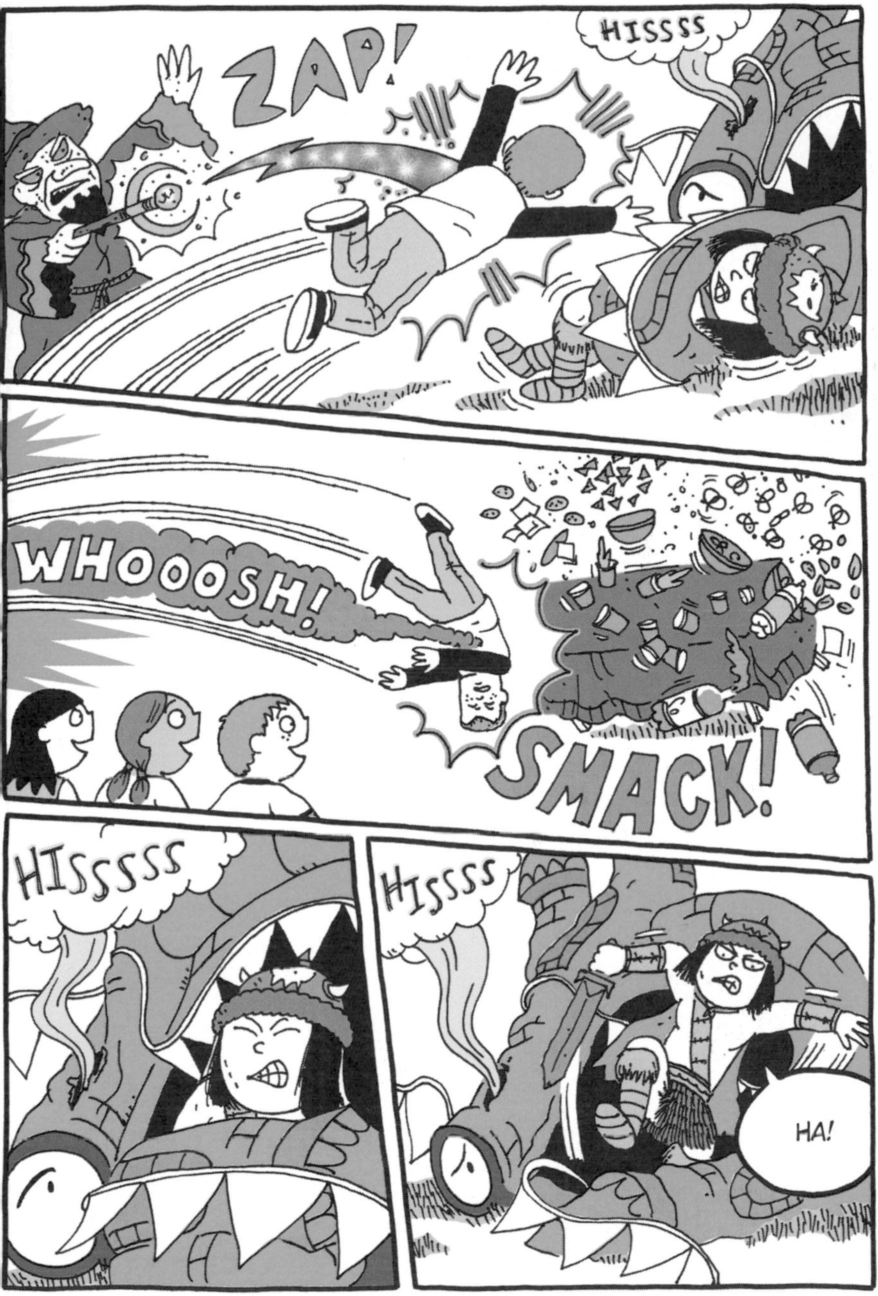
ZAP!
HISSSS
WHOOOSH!
SMACK!
HISSSSS
HISSSS
HA!

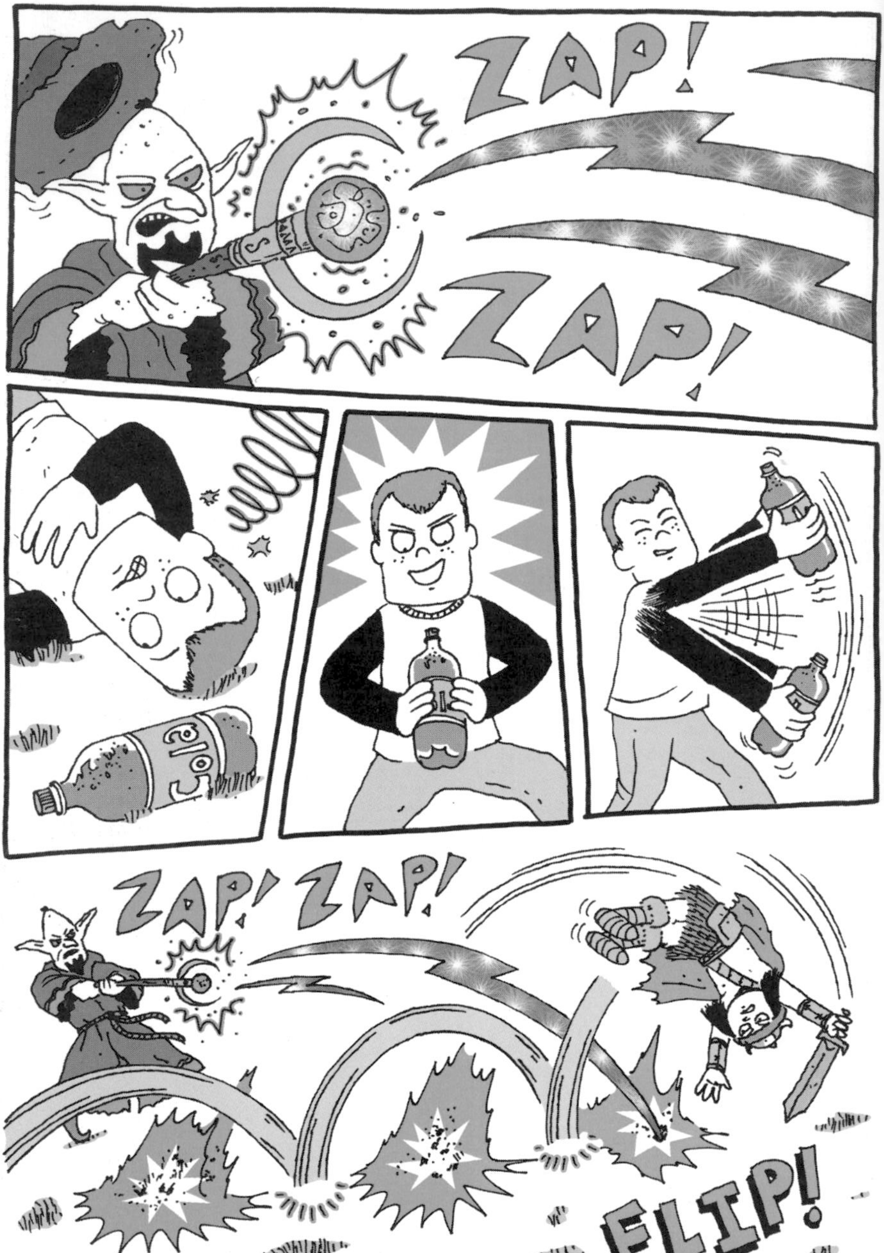
ZAP!
ZAP!
ZAP! ZAP!
FLIP!

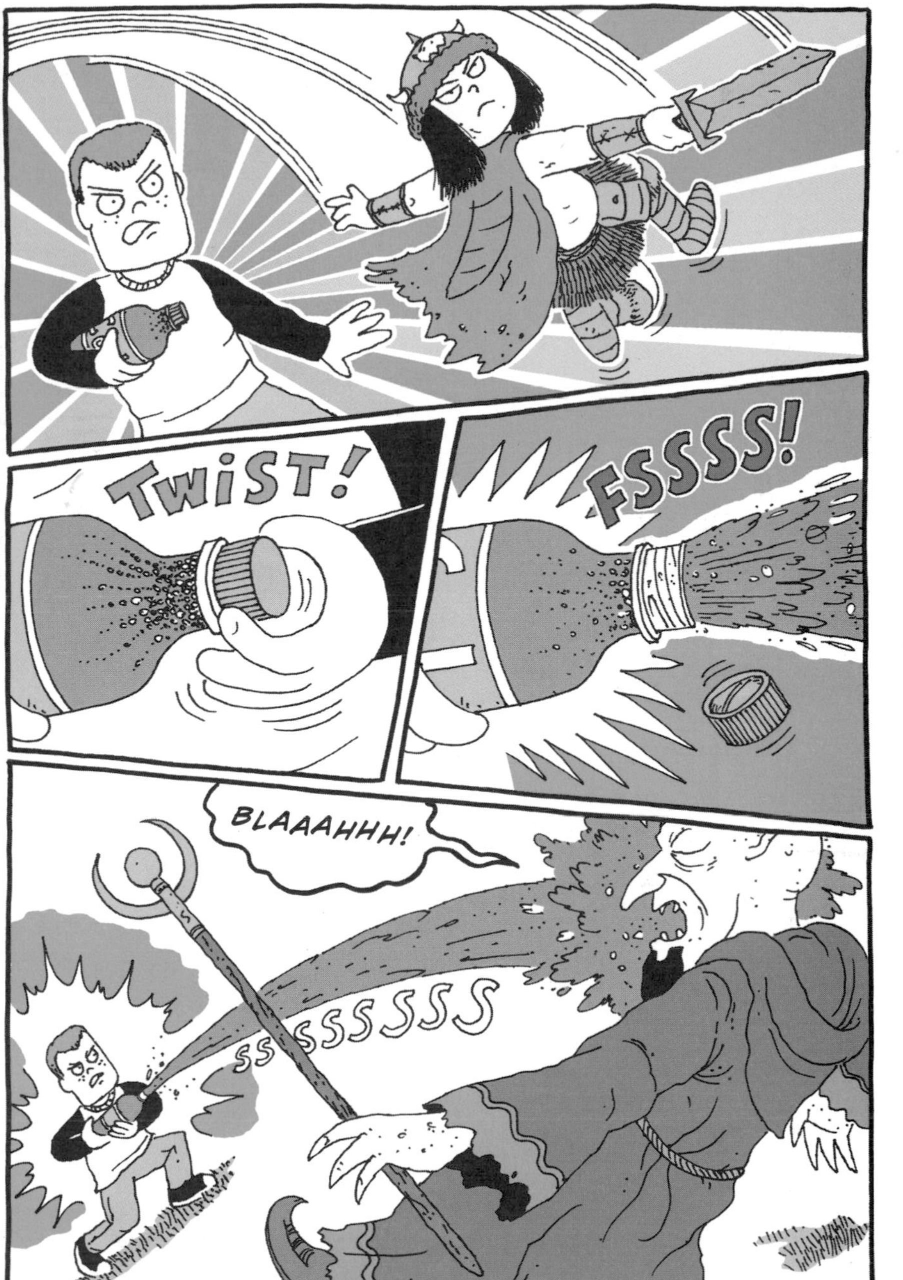
TWIST!
FSSSS!
BLAAAHHH!
SSSSSSSSS

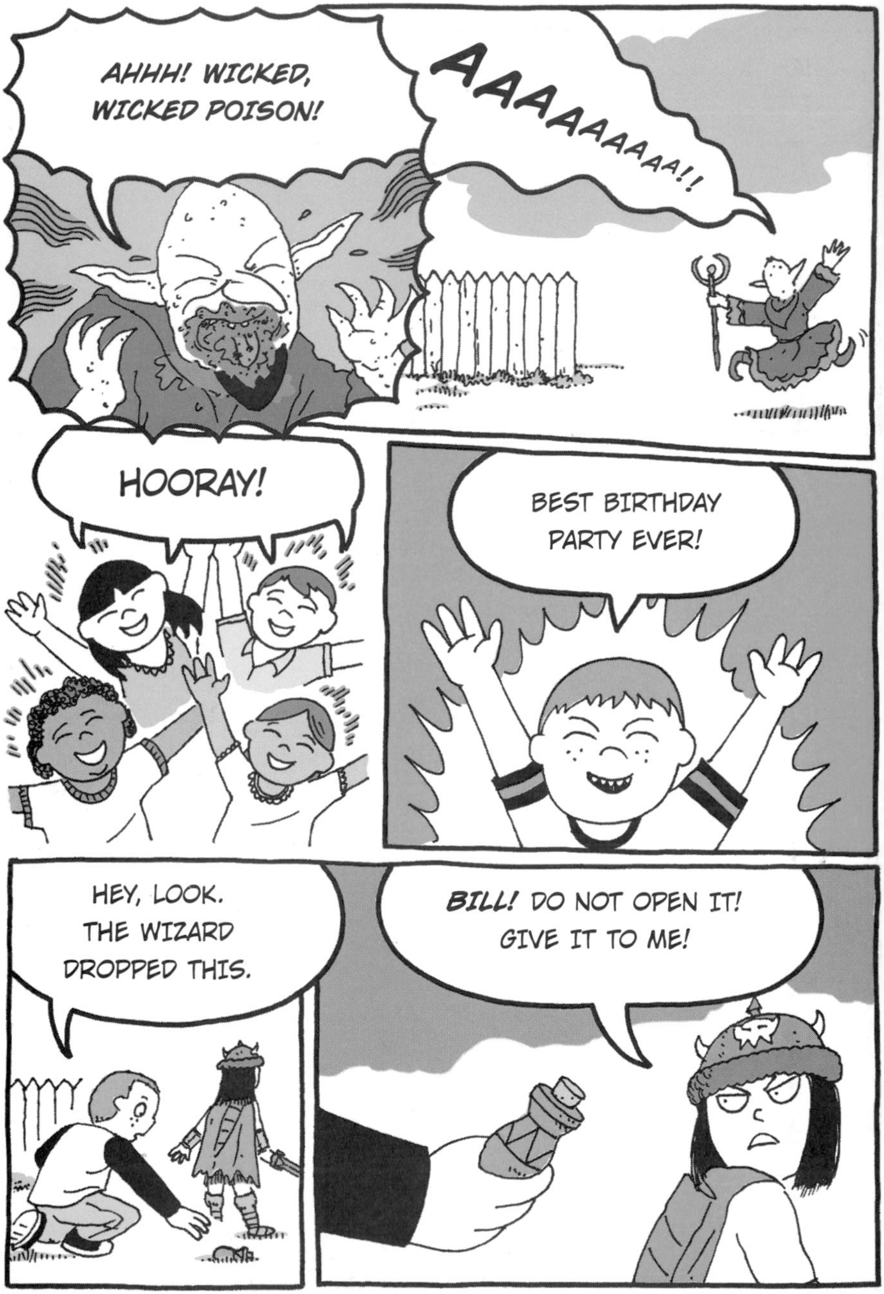
AHHH! WICKED, WICKED POISON!
AAAAAAAAAA!!
HOORAY!
BEST BIRTHDAY PARTY EVER!
HEY, LOOK. THE WIZARD DROPPED THIS.
BILL! DO NOT OPEN IT! GIVE IT TO ME!

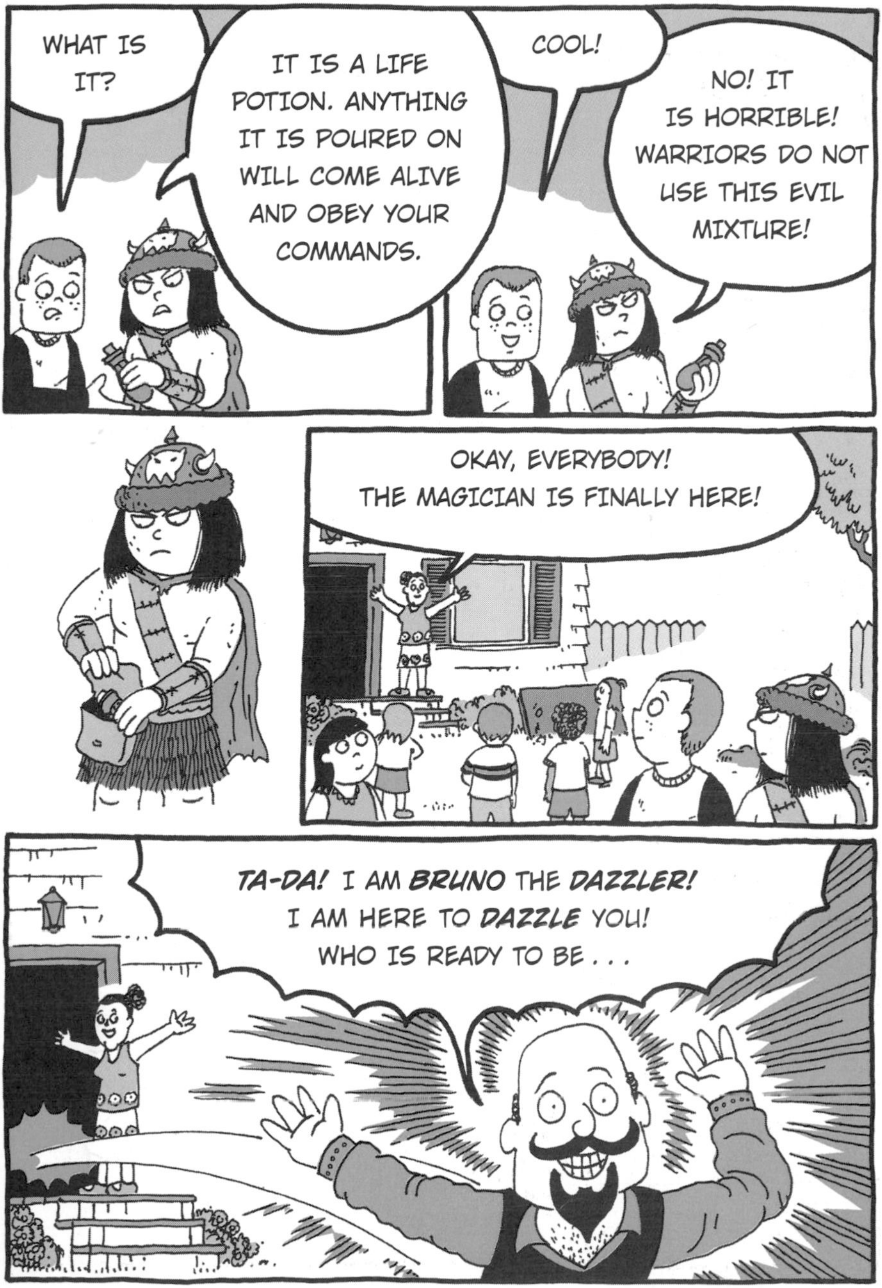
WHAT IS IT?
IT IS A LIFE POTION. ANYTHING IT IS POURED ON WILL COME ALIVE AND OBEY YOUR COMMANDS.
COOL!
NO! IT IS HORRIBLE! WARRIORS DO NOT USE THIS EVIL MIXTURE!
OKAY, EVERYBODY! THE MAGICIAN IS FINALLY HERE!
TA-DA! I AM BRUNO THE DAZZLER! I AM HERE TO DAZZLE YOU! WHO IS READY TO BE . . .

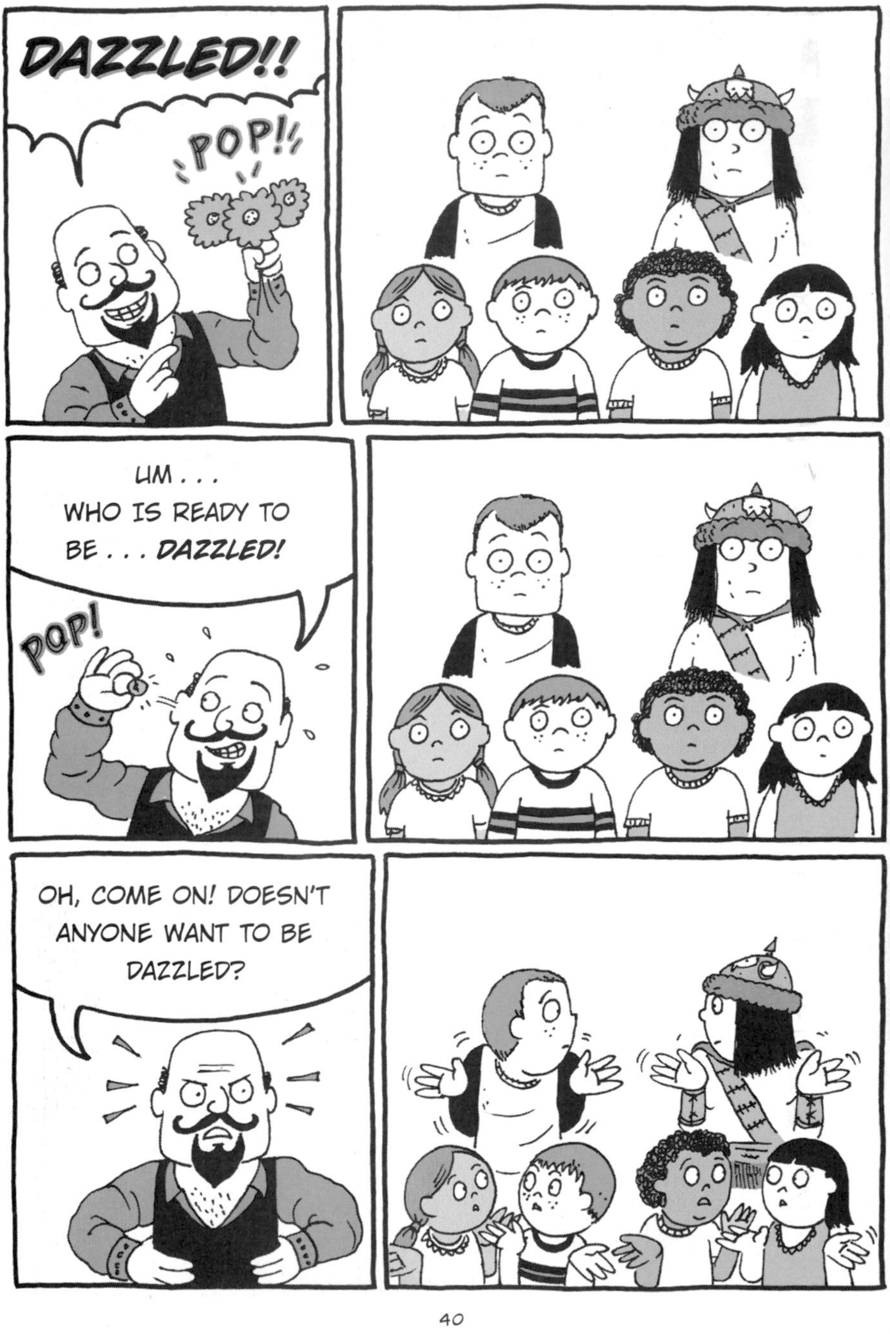
DAZZLED!!
POP!!
UM . . .
WHO IS READY TO
BE . . . DAZZLED!
POP!
OH, COME ON! DOESN'T
ANYONE WANT TO BE
DAZZLED?

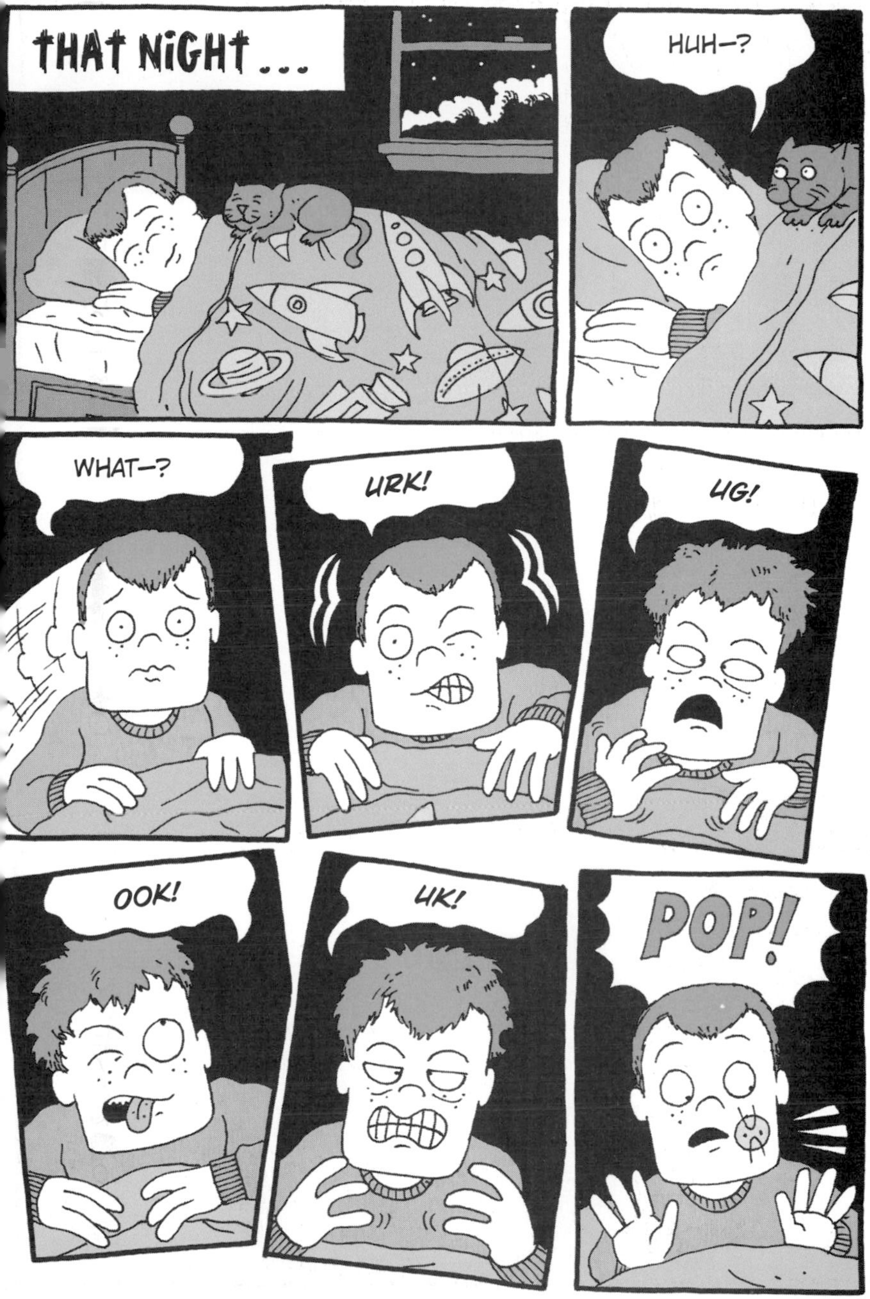
THAT NIGHT . . .
HUH-?
WHAT-?
URK!
UG!
OOK!
UK!
POP!

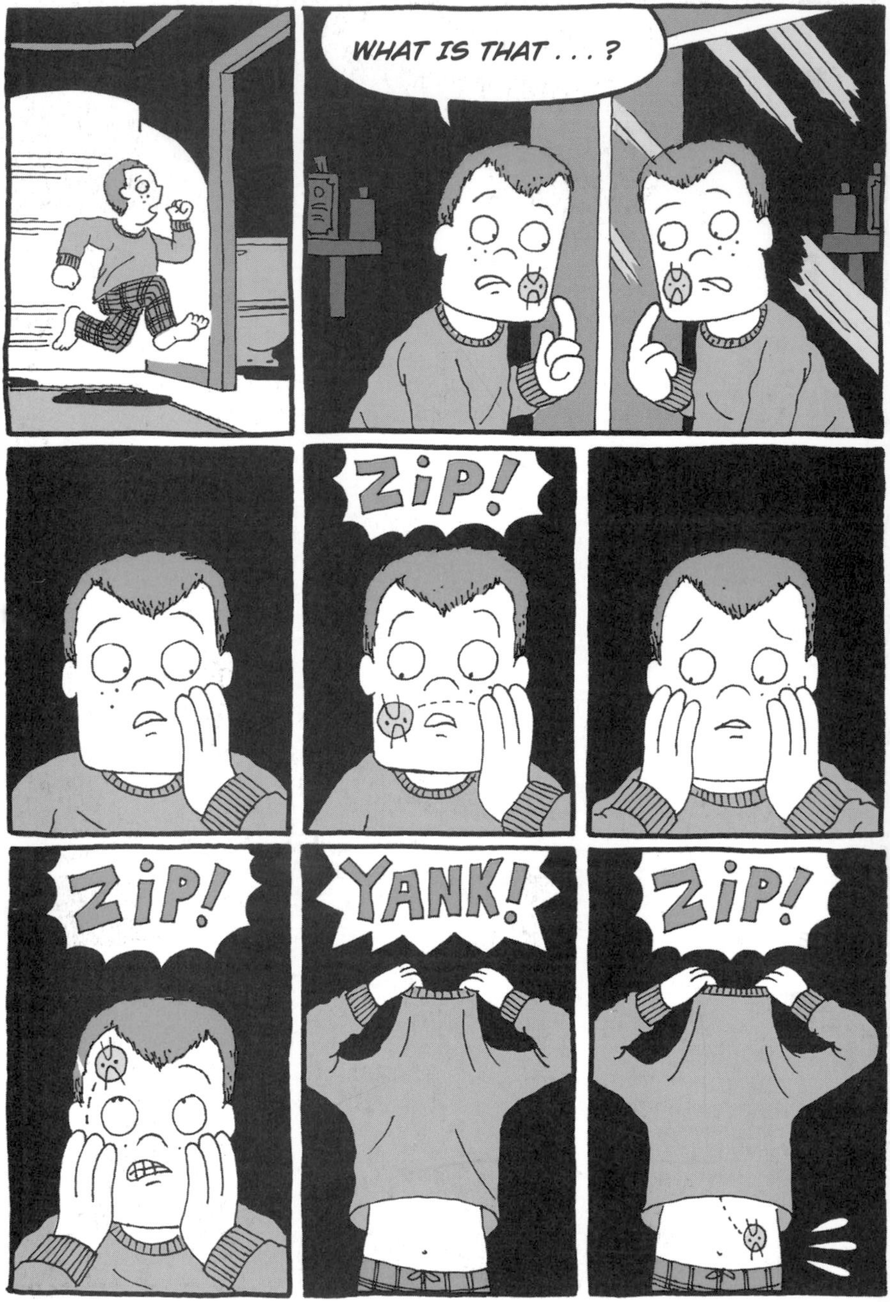
WHAT IS THAT . . . ?
ZiP!
ZiP!
YANK!
ZiP!

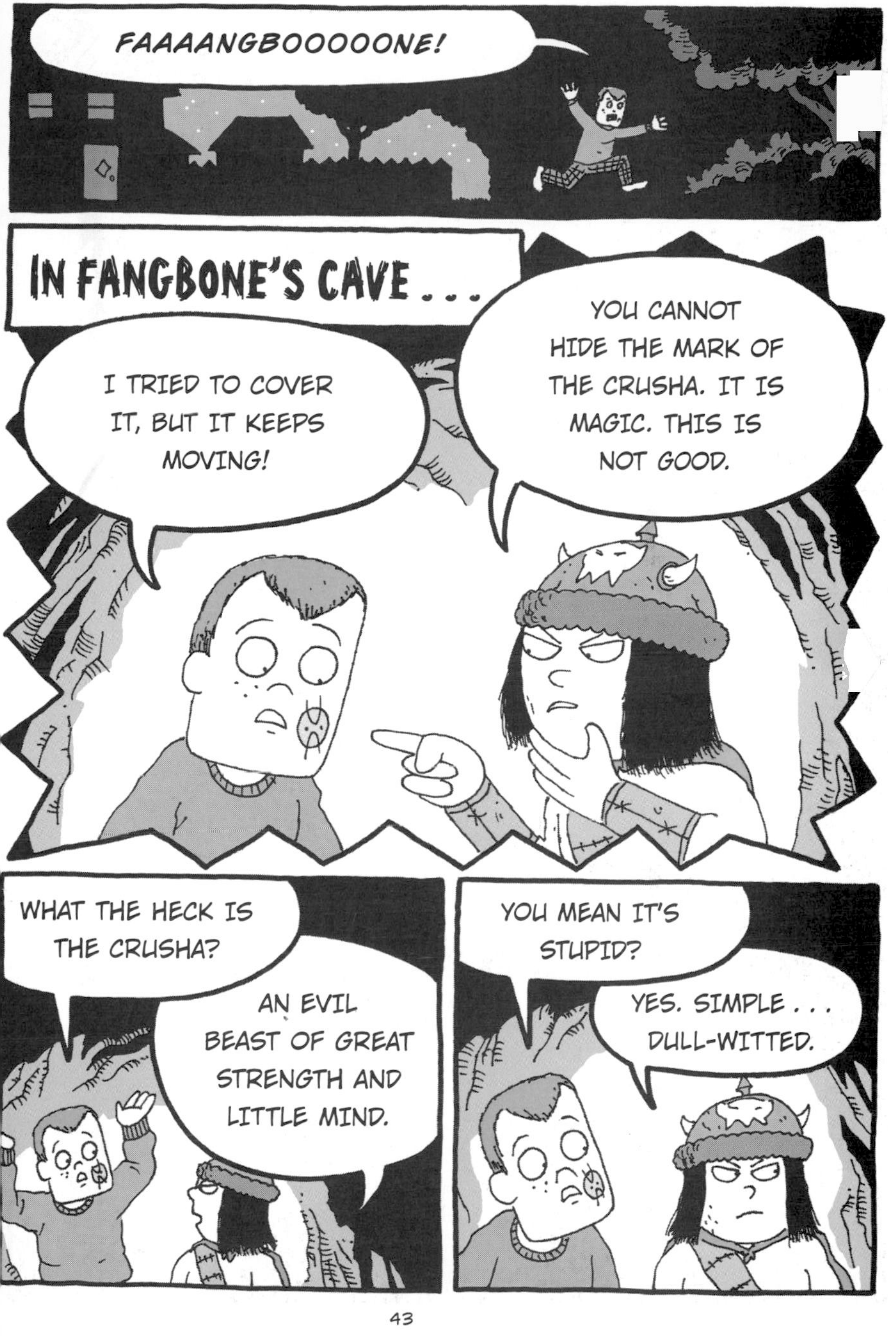
FAAAANGBOOOOONE!
IN FANGBONE'S CAVE . . .
I TRIED TO COVER IT, BUT IT KEEPS MOVING!
YOU CANNOT HIDE THE MARK OF THE CRUSHA. IT IS MAGIC. THIS IS NOT GOOD.
WHAT THE HECK IS THE CRUSHA?
AN EVIL BEAST OF GREAT STRENGTH AND LITTLE MIND.
YOU MEAN IT'S STUPID?
YES. SIMPLE . . . DULL-WITTED.

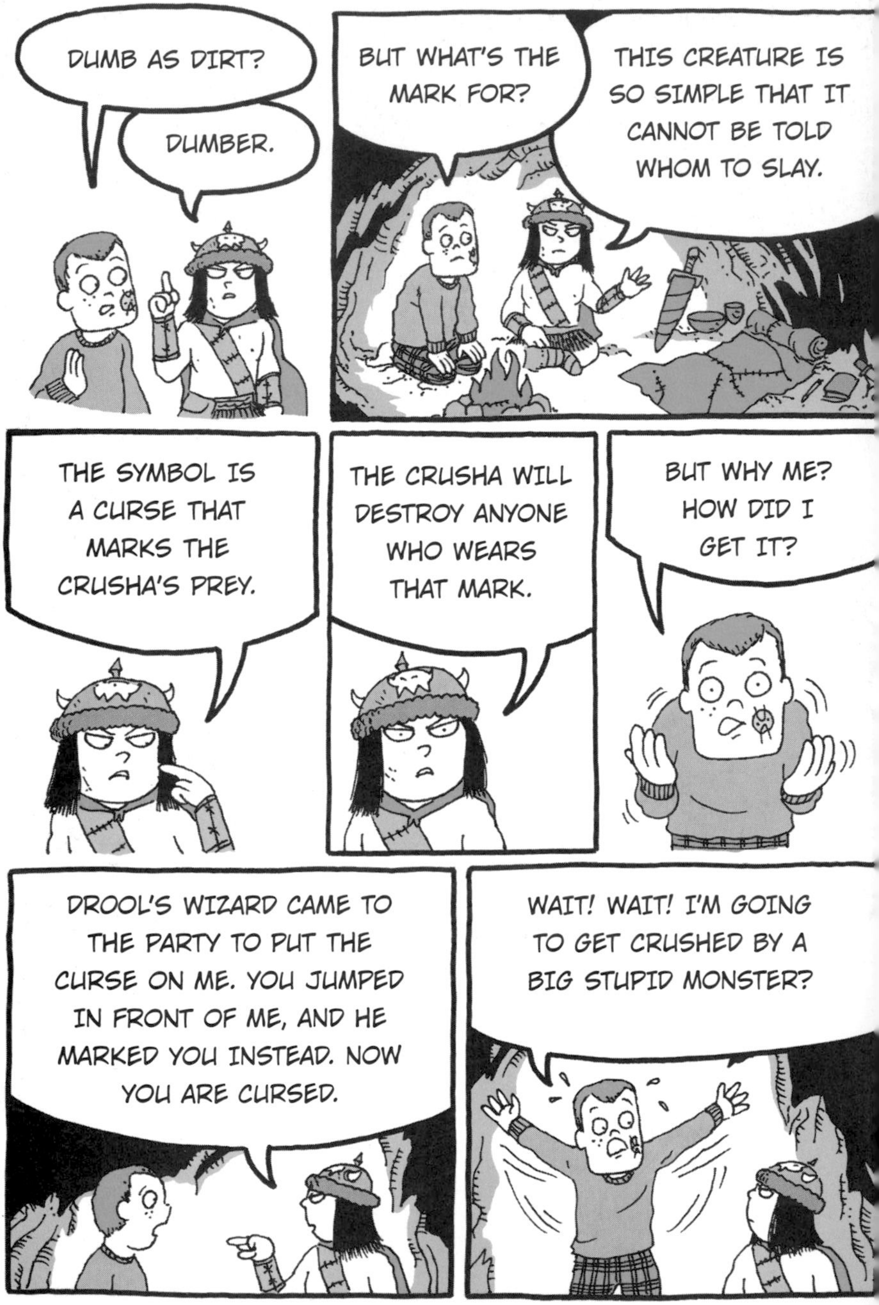

DUMB AS DIRT?
DUMBER.
BUT WHAT'S THE MARK FOR?
THIS CREATURE IS SO SIMPLE THAT IT CANNOT BE TOLD WHOM TO SLAY.
THE SYMBOL IS A CURSE THAT MARKS THE CRUSHA'S PREY.
THE CRUSHA WILL DESTROY ANYONE WHO WEARS THAT MARK.
BUT WHY ME? HOW DID I GET IT?
DROOL'S WIZARD CAME TO THE PARTY TO PUT THE CURSE ON ME. YOU JUMPED IN FRONT OF ME, AND HE MARKED YOU INSTEAD. NOW YOU ARE CURSED.
WAIT! WAIT! I'M GOING TO GET CRUSHED BY A BIG STUPID MONSTER?

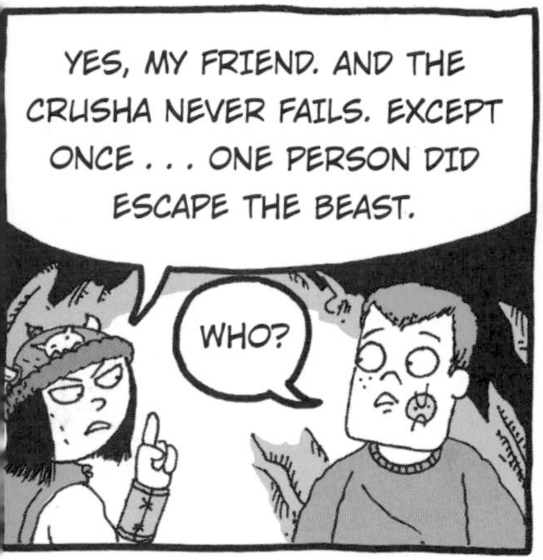
YES, MY FRIEND. AND THE CRUSHA NEVER FAILS. EXCEPT ONCE . . . ONE PERSON DID ESCAPE THE BEAST.
WHO?

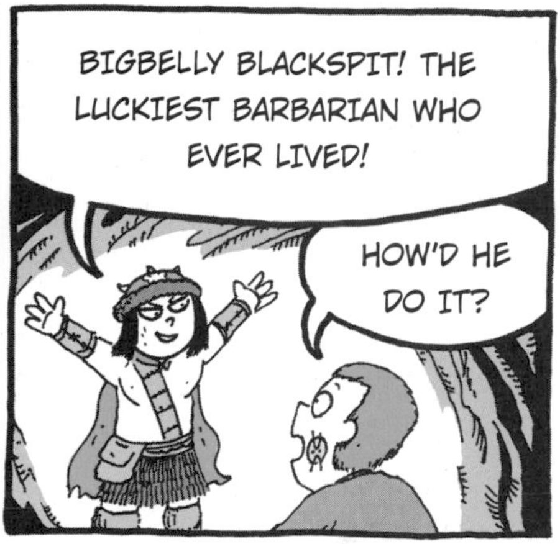
BIGBELLY BLACKSPIT! THE LUCKIEST BARBARIAN WHO EVER LIVED!
HOW'D HE DO IT?

THE CRUSHA CHASED BIGBELLY INTO THE DESERT. IT SMASHED THE GROUND TO BITS, BUT MISSED BIGBELLY. A GIANT CRACK OPENED UP, AND BIGBELLY SLIPPED BELOW THE SURFACE.

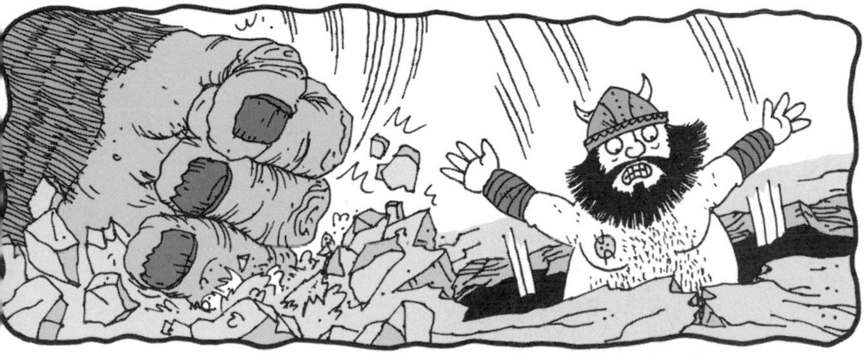

THE CRUSHA THOUGHT IT HAD DESTROYED BIGBELLY, SO IT WALKED AWAY.

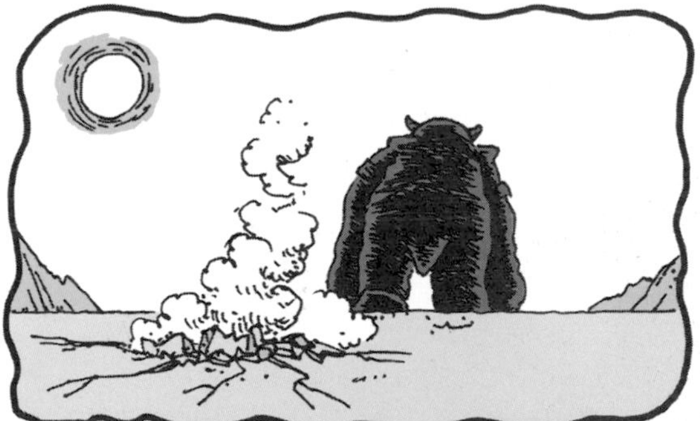

BIGBELLY CRAWLED LOWER UNDERGROUND AND FELL INTO THE TOMB OF THE ANCIENT WOLFWORMS, WHERE HE FOUND ROOMS FULL OF GOLD AND JEWELRY.

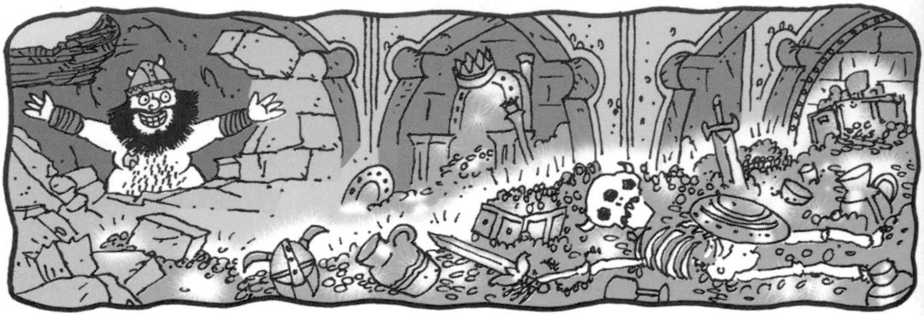

THEN, HE MADE HIS WAY OUT OF THE TOMB AND FOUND A GOLDEN BOAT WAITING IN AN UNDERGROUND RIVER.

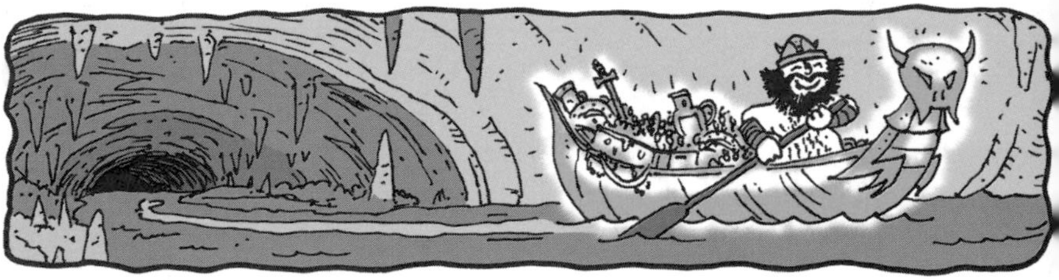

HE TRAVELED DOWN THE RIVER AND ENDED UP IN THE CAVERN OF LOVELY LADIES, WHERE HE MARRIED 13 WIVES!

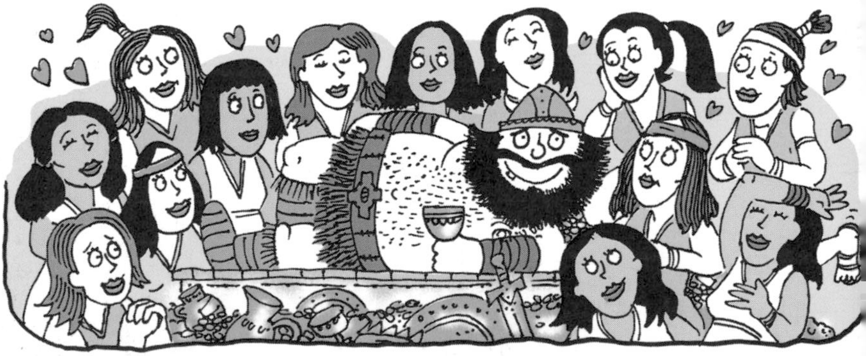

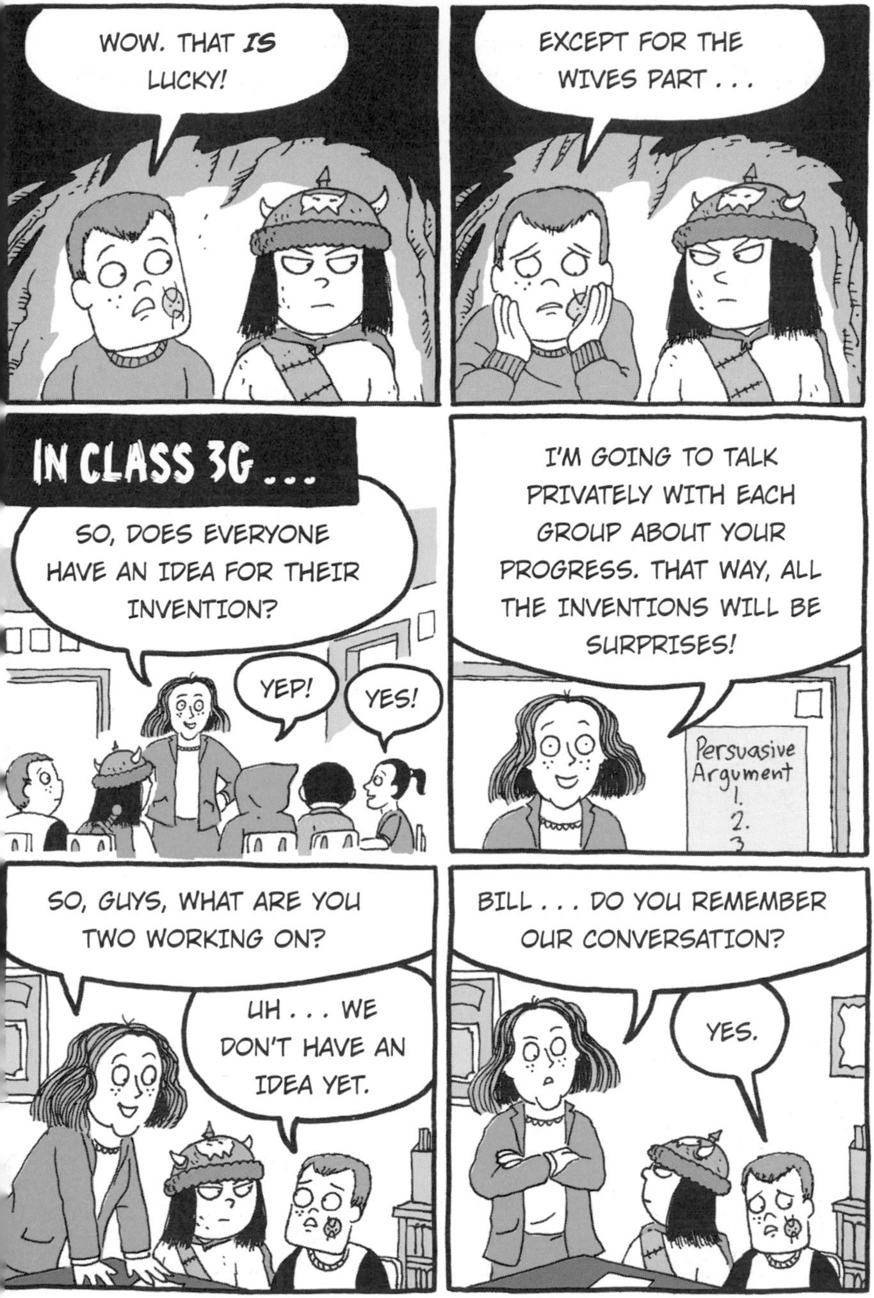
WOW. THAT IS LUCKY!
EXCEPT FOR THE WIVES PART . . .
IN CLASS 3G . . .
SO, DOES EVERYONE HAVE AN IDEA FOR THEIR INVENTION?
YEP!
YES!
I'M GOING TO TALK PRIVATELY WITH EACH GROUP ABOUT YOUR PROGRESS. THAT WAY, ALL THE INVENTIONS WILL BE SURPRISES!
Persuasive Argument
1.
2.
SO, GUYS, WHAT ARE YOU TWO WORKING ON?
UH . . . WE DON'T HAVE AN IDEA YET.
BILL . . . DO YOU REMEMBER OUR CONVERSATION?
YES.

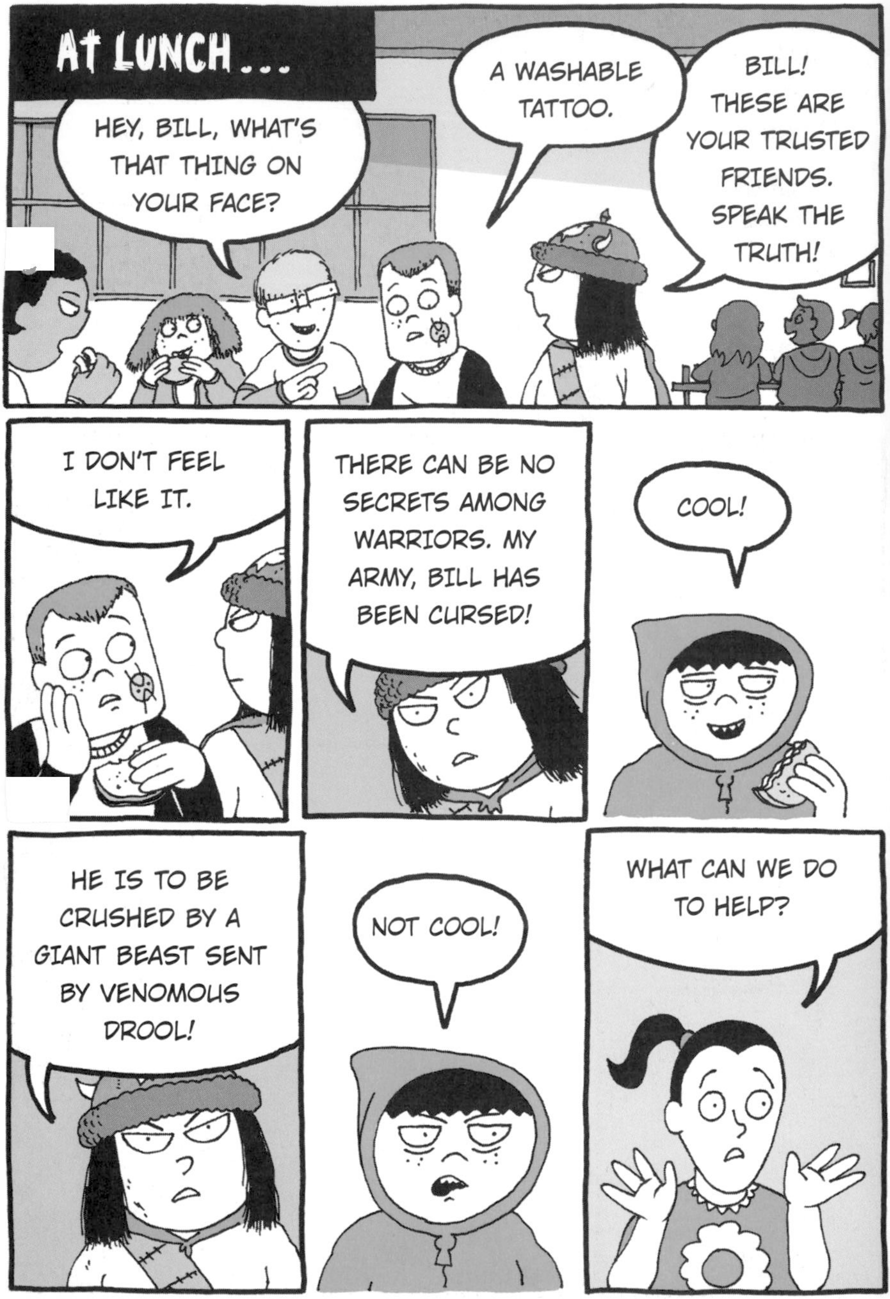

At LUNCH...
HEY, BILL, WHAT'S THAT THING ON YOUR FACE?
A WASHABLE TATTOO.
BILL! THESE ARE YOUR TRUSTED FRIENDS. SPEAK THE TRUTH!
I DON'T FEEL LIKE IT.
THERE CAN BE NO SECRETS AMONG WARRIORS. MY ARMY, BILL HAS BEEN CURSED!
COOL!
HE IS TO BE CRUSHED BY A GIANT BEAST SENT BY VENOMOUS DROOL!
NOT COOL!
WHAT CAN WE DO TO HELP?

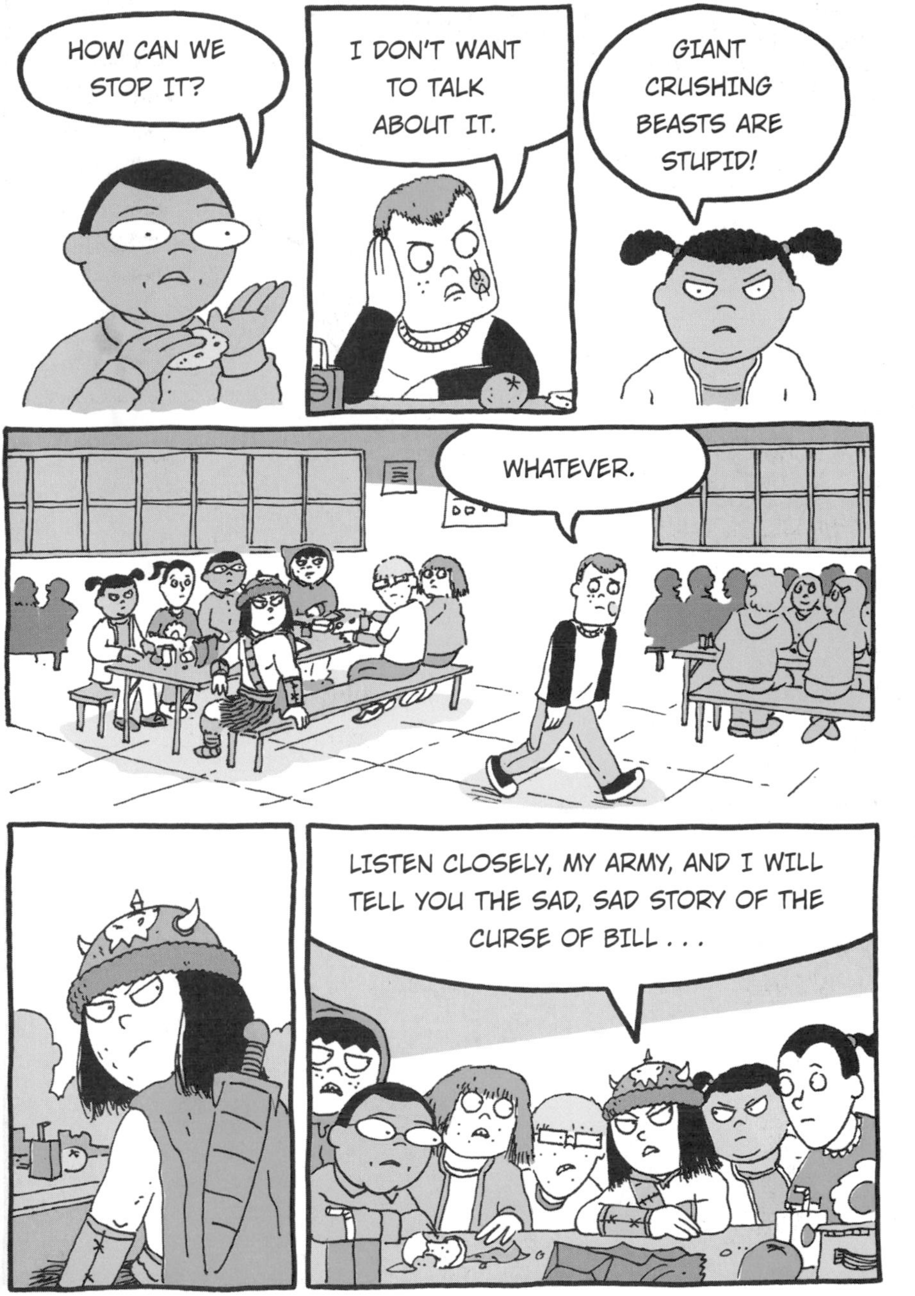
HOW CAN WE STOP IT?
I DON'T WANT TO TALK ABOUT IT.
GIANT CRUSHING BEASTS ARE STUPID!
WHATEVER.
LISTEN CLOSELY, MY ARMY, AND I WILL TELL YOU THE SAD, SAD STORY OF THE CURSE OF BILL . . .

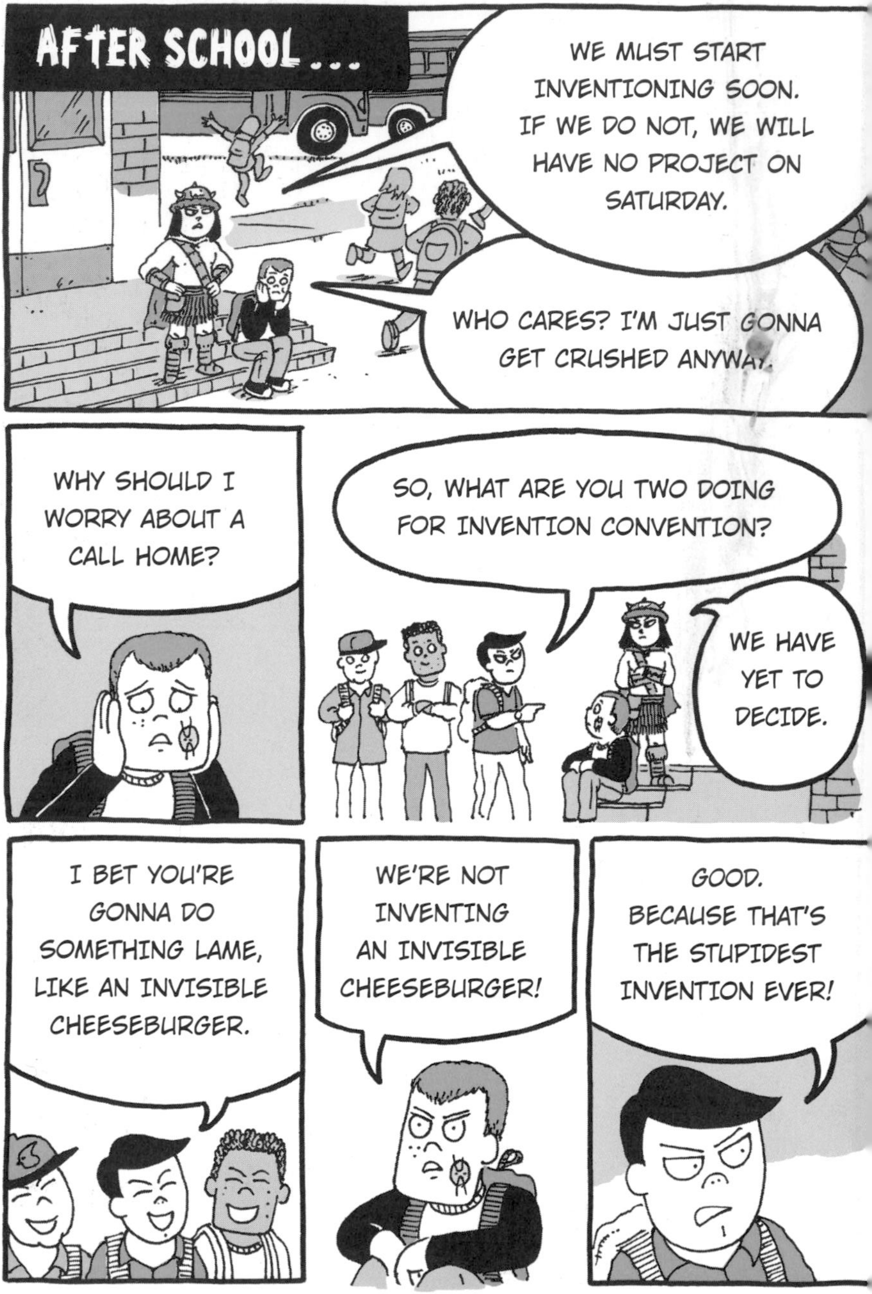
AFTER SCHOOL . . .
WE MUST START INVENTIONING SOON. IF WE DO NOT, WE WILL HAVE NO PROJECT ON SATURDAY.
WHO CARES? I'M JUST GONNA GET CRUSHED ANYWAY.
WHY SHOULD I WORRY ABOUT A CALL HOME?
SO, WHAT ARE YOU TWO DOING FOR INVENTION CONVENTION?
WE HAVE YET TO DECIDE.
I BET YOU'RE GONNA DO SOMETHING LAME, LIKE AN INVISIBLE CHEESEBURGER.
WE'RE NOT INVENTING AN INVISIBLE CHEESEBURGER!
GOOD. BECAUSE THAT'S THE STUPIDEST INVENTION EVER!

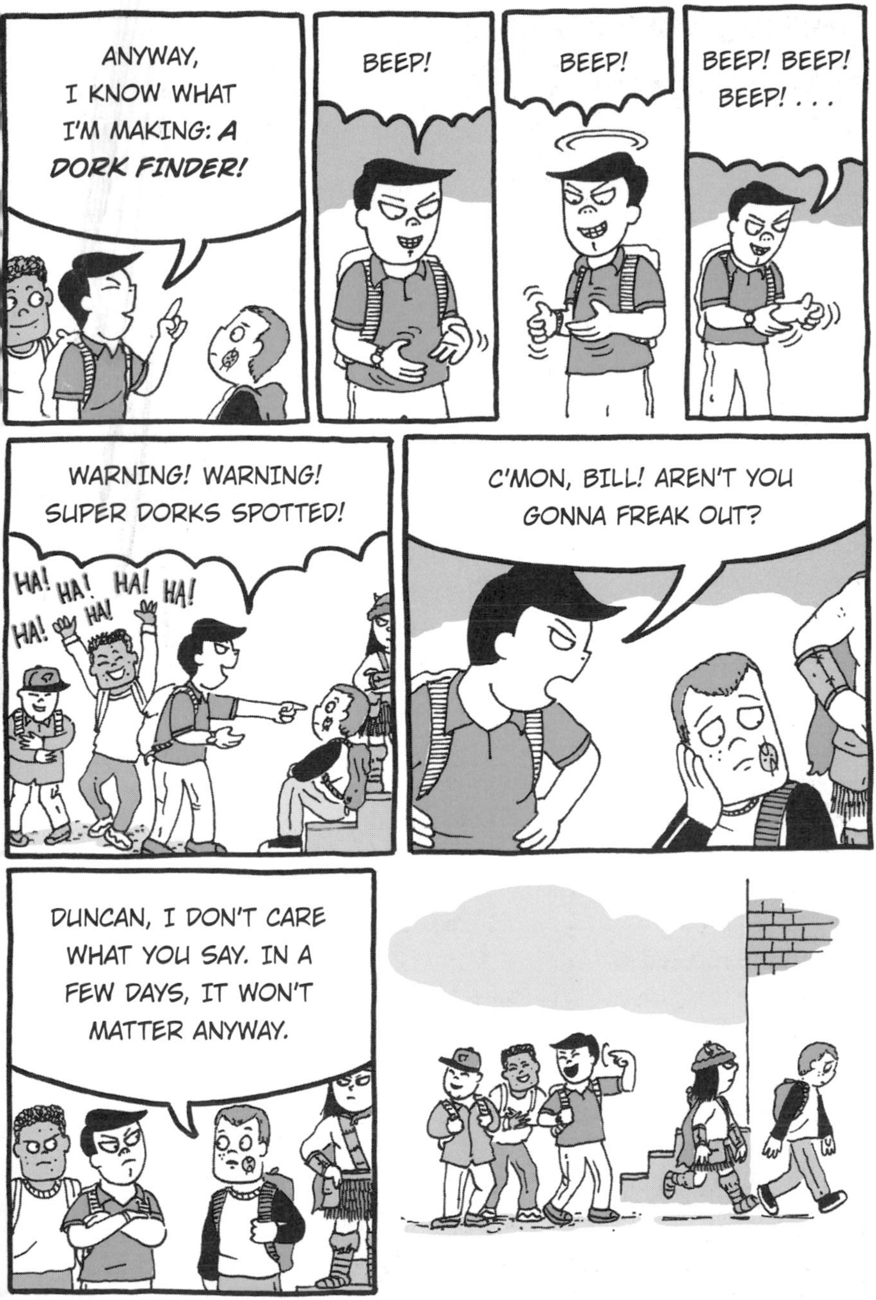
ANYWAY, I KNOW WHAT I'M MAKING: A *DORK FINDER!*
BEEP!
BEEP!
BEEP! BEEP! BEEP! . . .
WARNING! WARNING! SUPER DORKS SPOTTED!
HA! HA! HA! HA! HA! HA!
C'MON, BILL! AREN'T YOU GONNA FREAK OUT?
DUNCAN, I DON'T CARE WHAT YOU SAY. IN A FEW DAYS, IT WON'T MATTER ANYWAY.

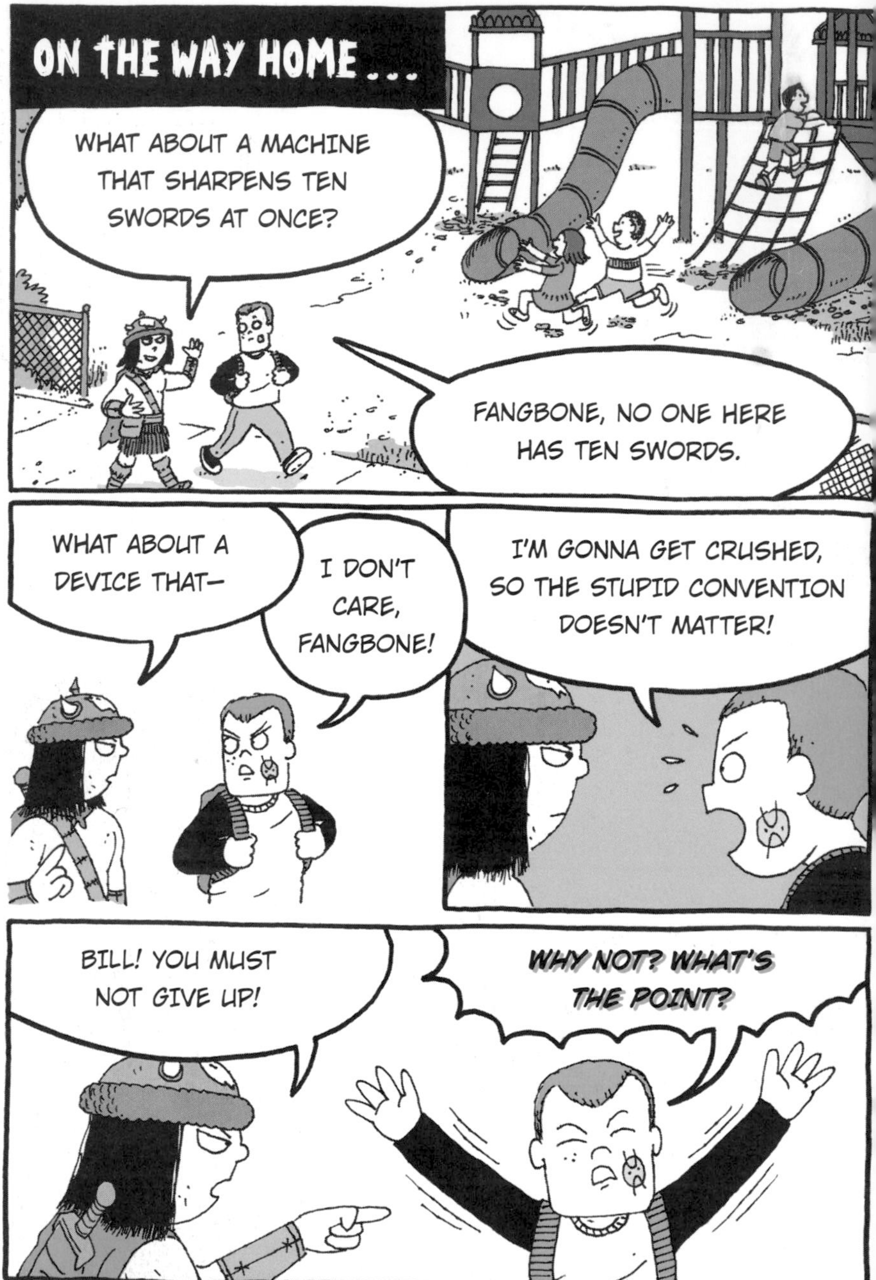
ON THE WAY HOME...
WHAT ABOUT A MACHINE THAT SHARPENS TEN SWORDS AT ONCE?
FANGBONE, NO ONE HERE HAS TEN SWORDS.
WHAT ABOUT A DEVICE THAT—
I DON'T CARE, FANGBONE!
I'M GONNA GET CRUSHED, SO THE STUPID CONVENTION DOESN'T MATTER!
BILL! YOU MUST NOT GIVE UP!
WHY NOT? WHAT'S THE POINT?

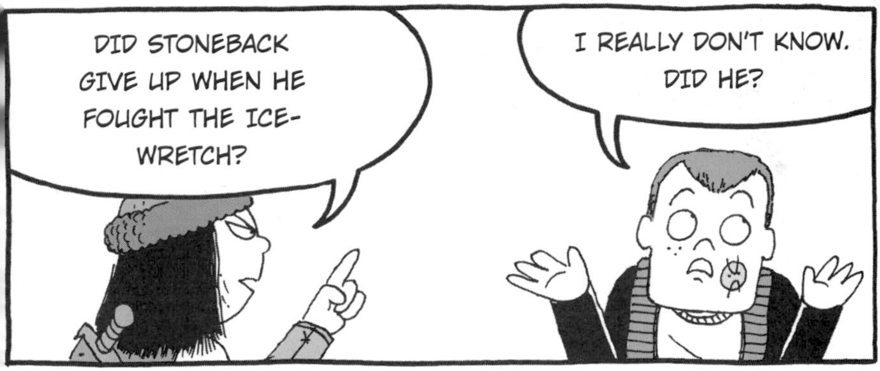
DID STONEBACK GIVE UP WHEN HE FOUGHT THE ICE-WRETCH?
I REALLY DON'T KNOW. DID HE?

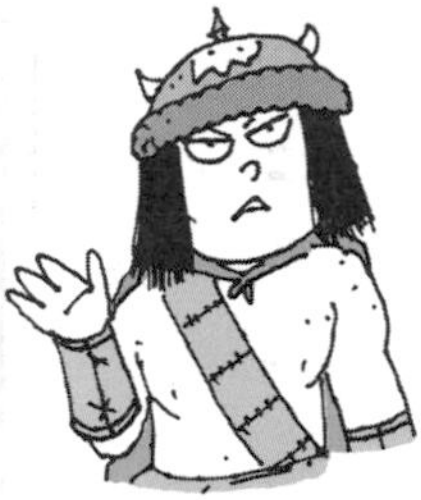

NO! OF COURSE NOT! AS STONEBACK WAS SEARCHING FOR HIS BRIDE, ZIZELLA, HE CROSSED THE FREEZING MOUNTAINS OF CRANIA. HE CAME TO A BRIDGE THAT CROSSED A GREAT CHASM. A BRUTAL CREATURE CALLED THE ICE-WRETCH WAS GUARDING THE BRIDGE!

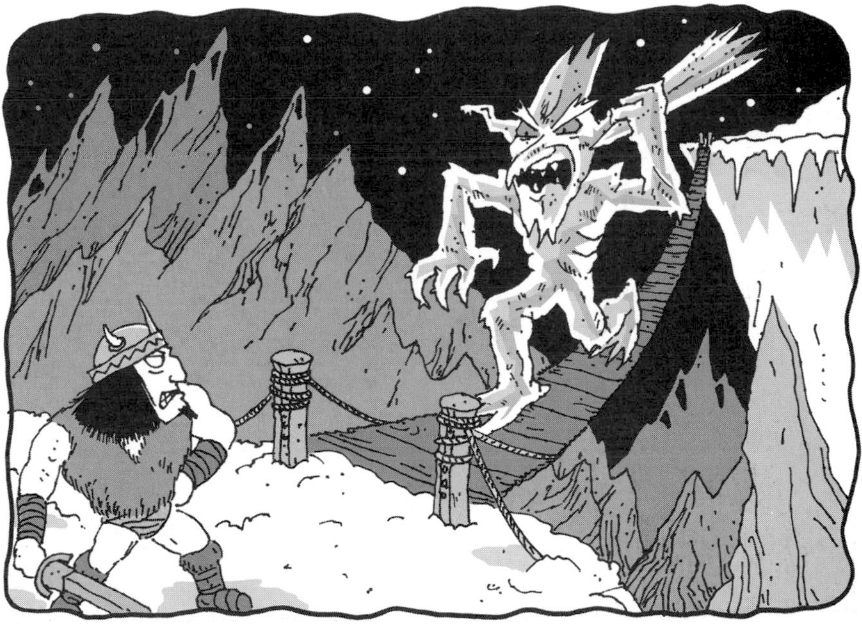

THE WRETCH WANTED GOLD AND SILVER FROM STONEBACK TO CROSS, BUT STONEBACK HAD NONE, SO HE CHALLENGED THE WRETCH TO A BATTLE. IF HE WON, HE COULD CROSS; IF HE LOST, HE WOULD TURN BACK.

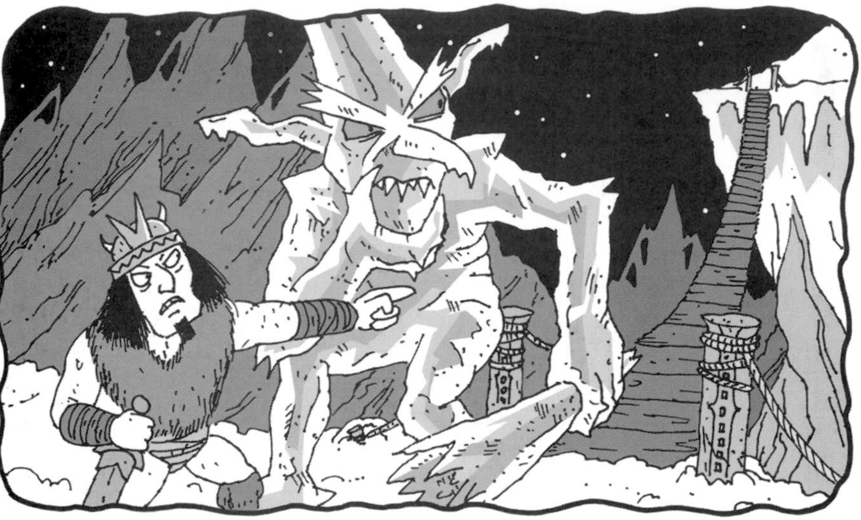

AS THEY FOUGHT, STONEBACK SLASHED AT THE WRETCH, CHIPPING CLOUDS OF ICE FROM ITS BODY. THE ICE DRIFTED DOWN THE MOUNTAIN AND BECAME THE WORLD'S FIRST SNOWFALL.

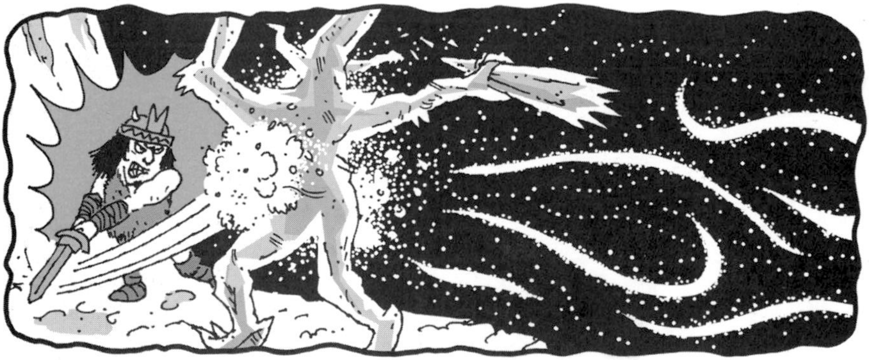

THE ICE-WRETCH KNOCKED STONEBACK ALL OVER WITH ITS CLUB. STONEBACK TURNED HIS BACK ON THE BRIDGE AND THE WRETCH HIT HIM SO HARD THAT HE FLEW ACROSS THE GREAT CHASM, LANDING ON THE OTHER SIDE.

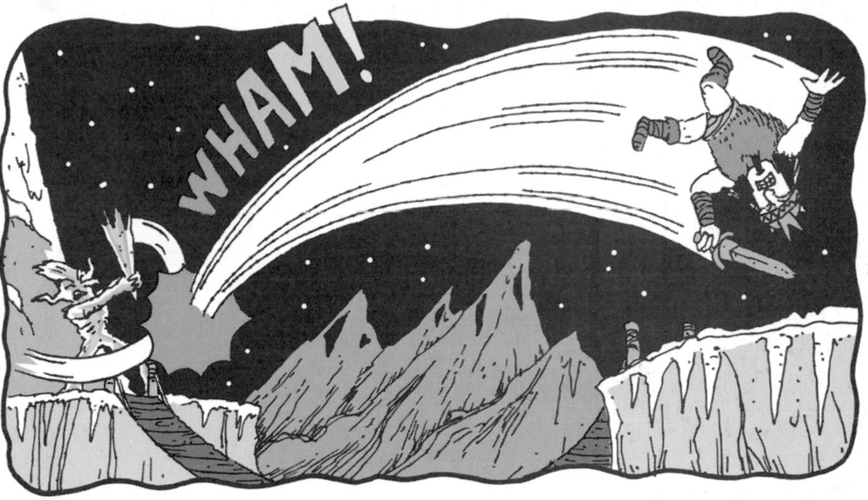
WHAM!

STONEBACK HAD CROSSED WITHOUT PAYING OR WINNING THE BATTLE! THE ICE-WRETCH WAS FURIOUS AND STONEBACK CONTINUED ON HIS QUEST FOR ZIZELLA.

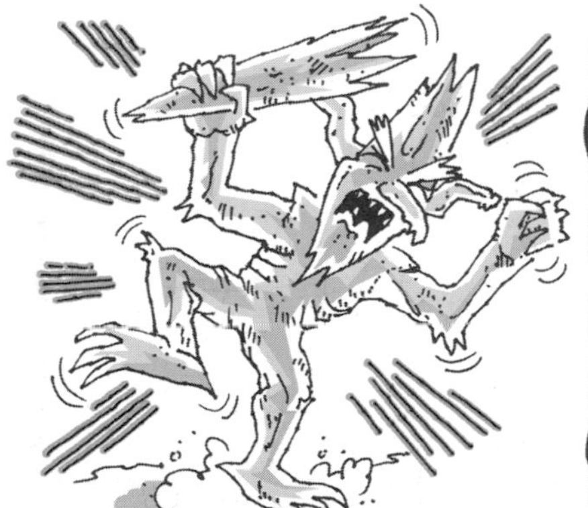

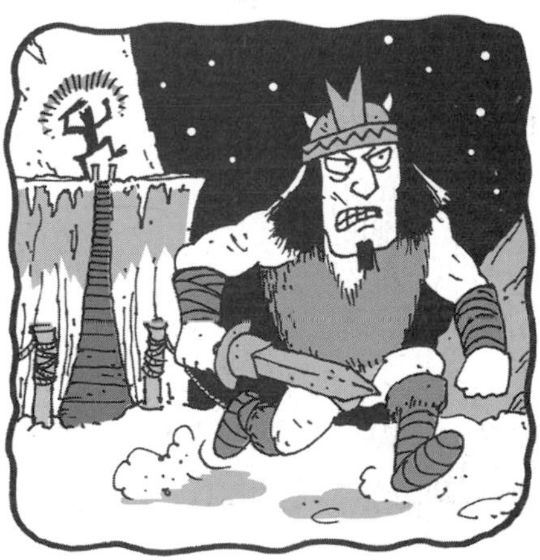

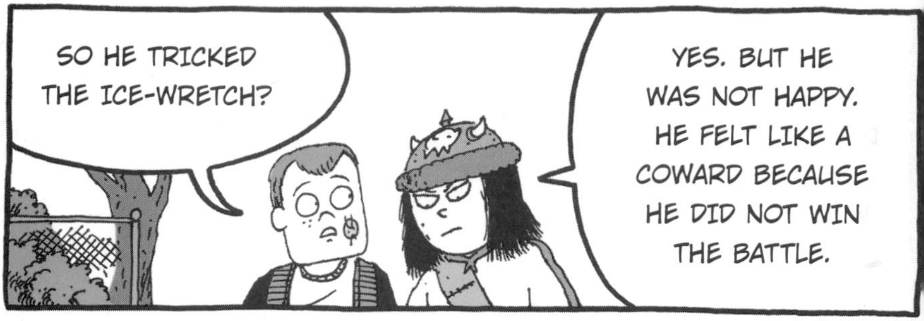
SO HE TRICKED THE ICE-WRETCH?
YES. BUT HE WAS NOT HAPPY. HE FELT LIKE A COWARD BECAUSE HE DID NOT WIN THE BATTLE.

A YEAR LATER, HE RETURNED TO CHALLENGE THE ICE-WRETCH AGAIN. BUT THEY WERE BOTH FIERCE FIGHTERS, AND NEITHER WARRIOR WON.

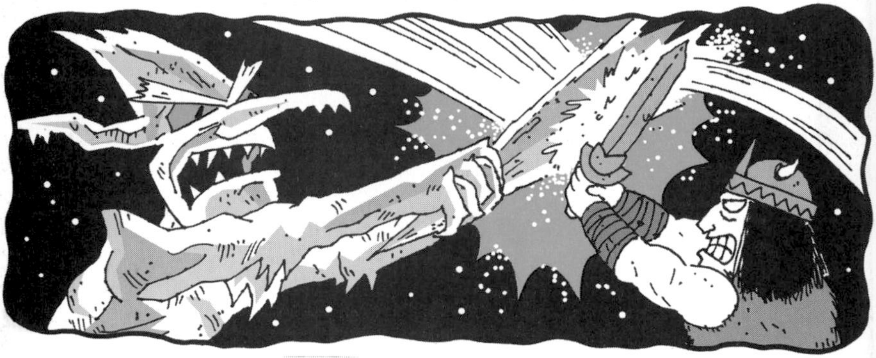

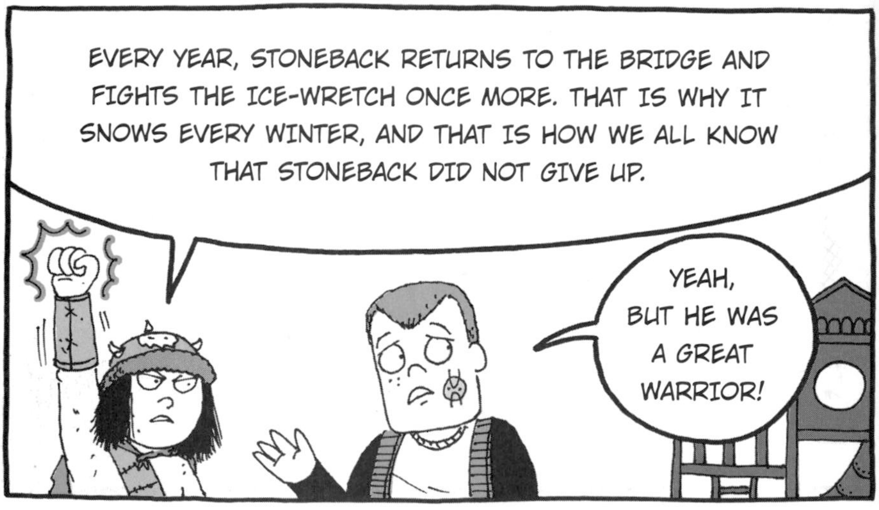
EVERY YEAR, STONEBACK RETURNS TO THE BRIDGE AND FIGHTS THE ICE-WRETCH ONCE MORE. THAT IS WHY IT SNOWS EVERY WINTER, AND THAT IS HOW WE ALL KNOW THAT STONEBACK DID NOT GIVE UP.
YEAH, BUT HE WAS A GREAT WARRIOR!

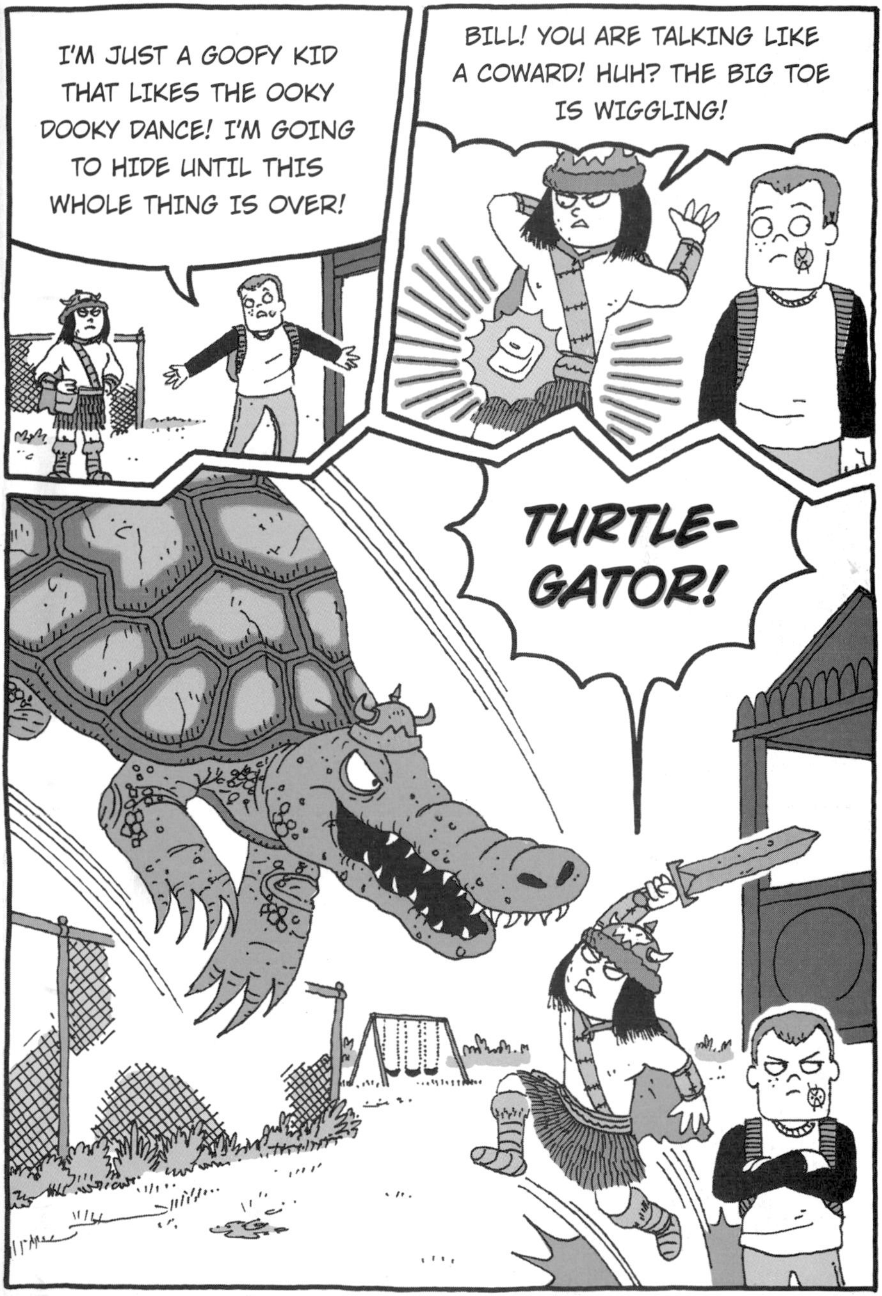
I'M JUST A GOOFY KID THAT LIKES THE OOKY DOOKY DANCE! I'M GOING TO HIDE UNTIL THIS WHOLE THING IS OVER!
BILL! YOU ARE TALKING LIKE A COWARD! HUH? THE BIG TOE IS WIGGLING!
TURTLE-GATOR!

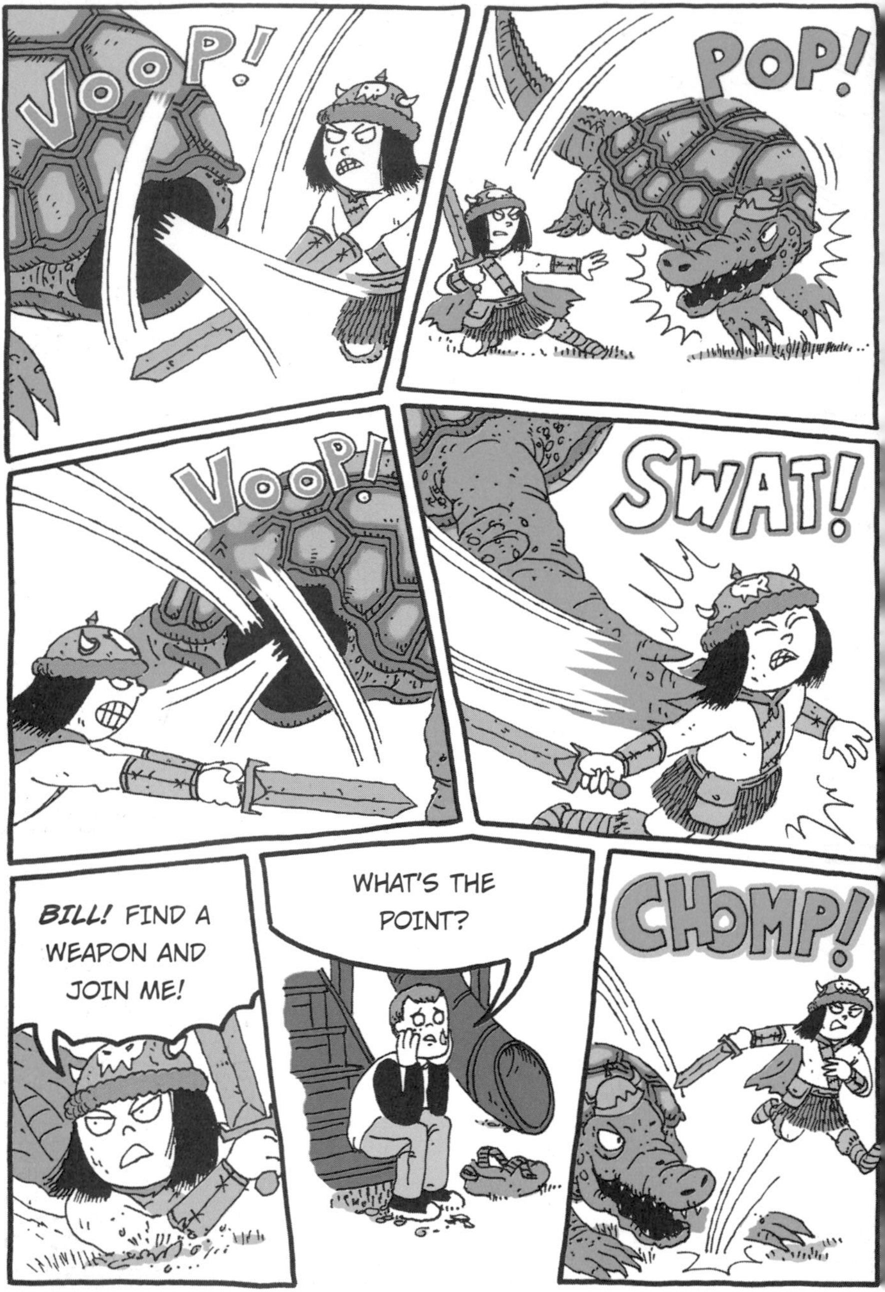
VOOP!
POP!
VOOP!
SWAT!
BILL! FIND A WEAPON AND JOIN ME!
WHAT'S THE POINT?
CHOMP!

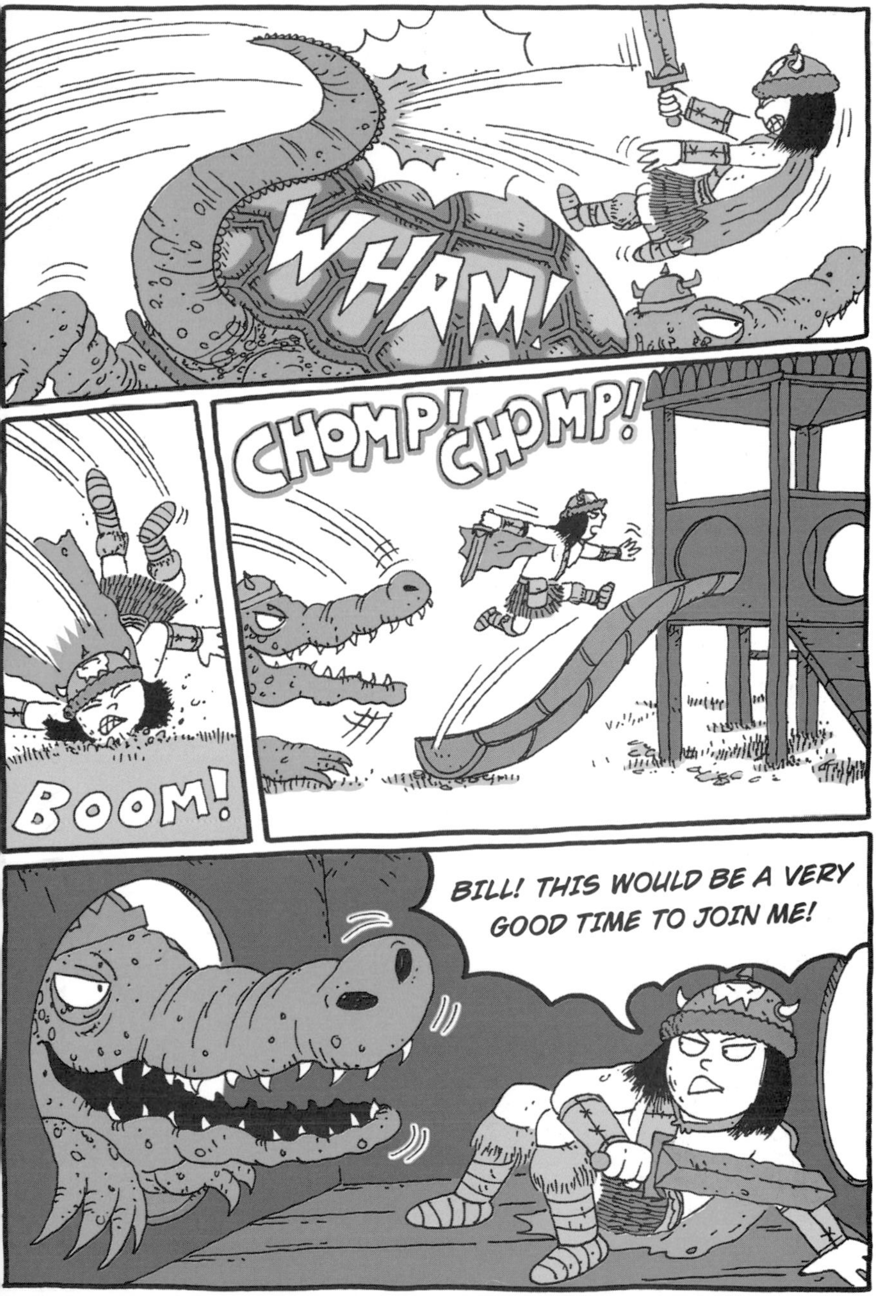
WHAM!
BOOM!
CHOMP! CHOMP!
BILL! THIS WOULD BE A VERY GOOD TIME TO JOIN ME!

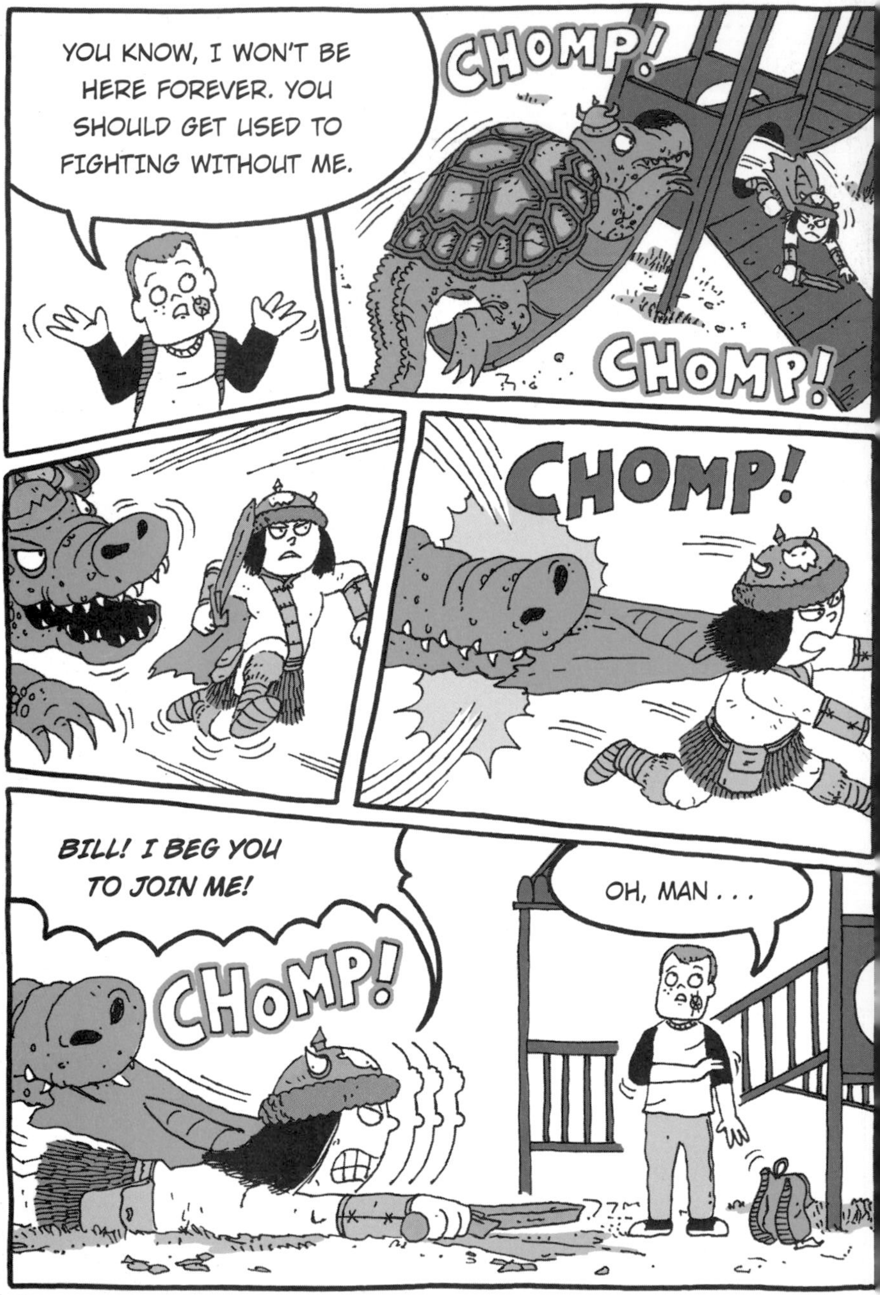
YOU KNOW, I WON'T BE HERE FOREVER. YOU SHOULD GET USED TO FIGHTING WITHOUT ME.
CHOMP!
CHOMP!
CHOMP!
BILL! I BEG YOU TO JOIN ME!
CHOMP!
OH, MAN . . .

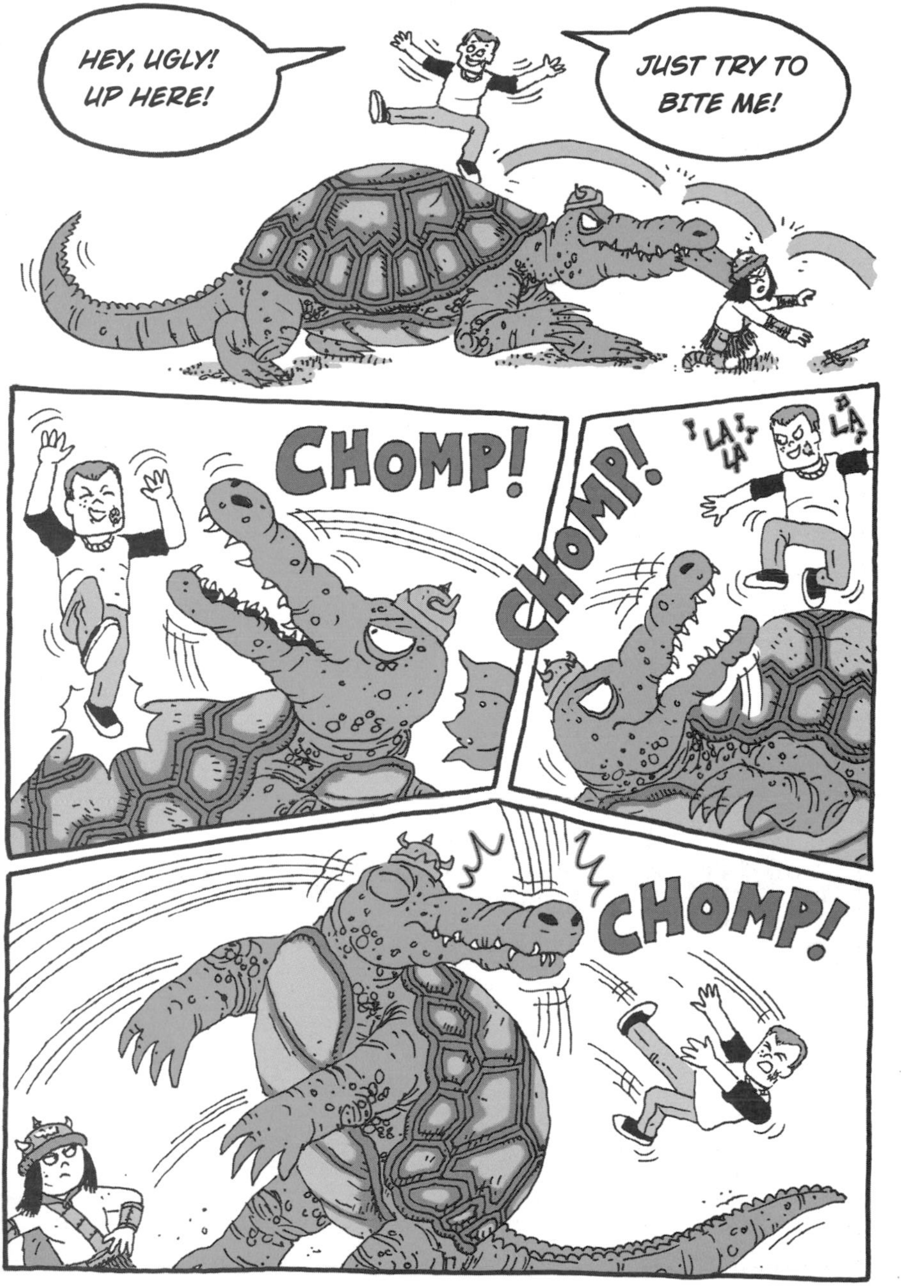
HEY, UGLY! UP HERE!
JUST TRY TO BITE ME!
CHOMP!
CHOMP!
LA LA
LA
CHOMP!

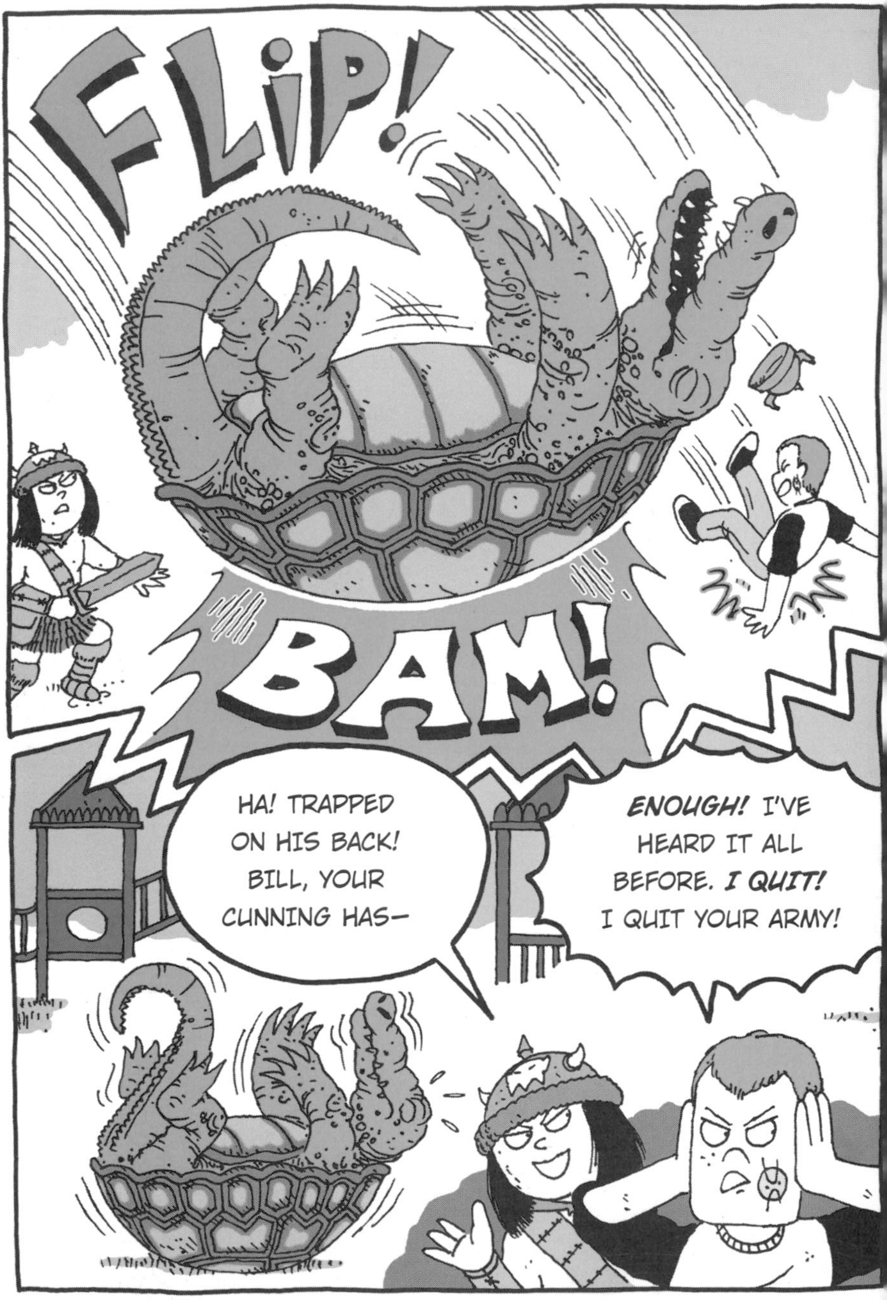
FLIP!
BAM!
HA! TRAPPED ON HIS BACK! BILL, YOUR CUNNING HAS—
ENOUGH! I'VE HEARD IT ALL BEFORE. I QUIT! I QUIT YOUR ARMY!

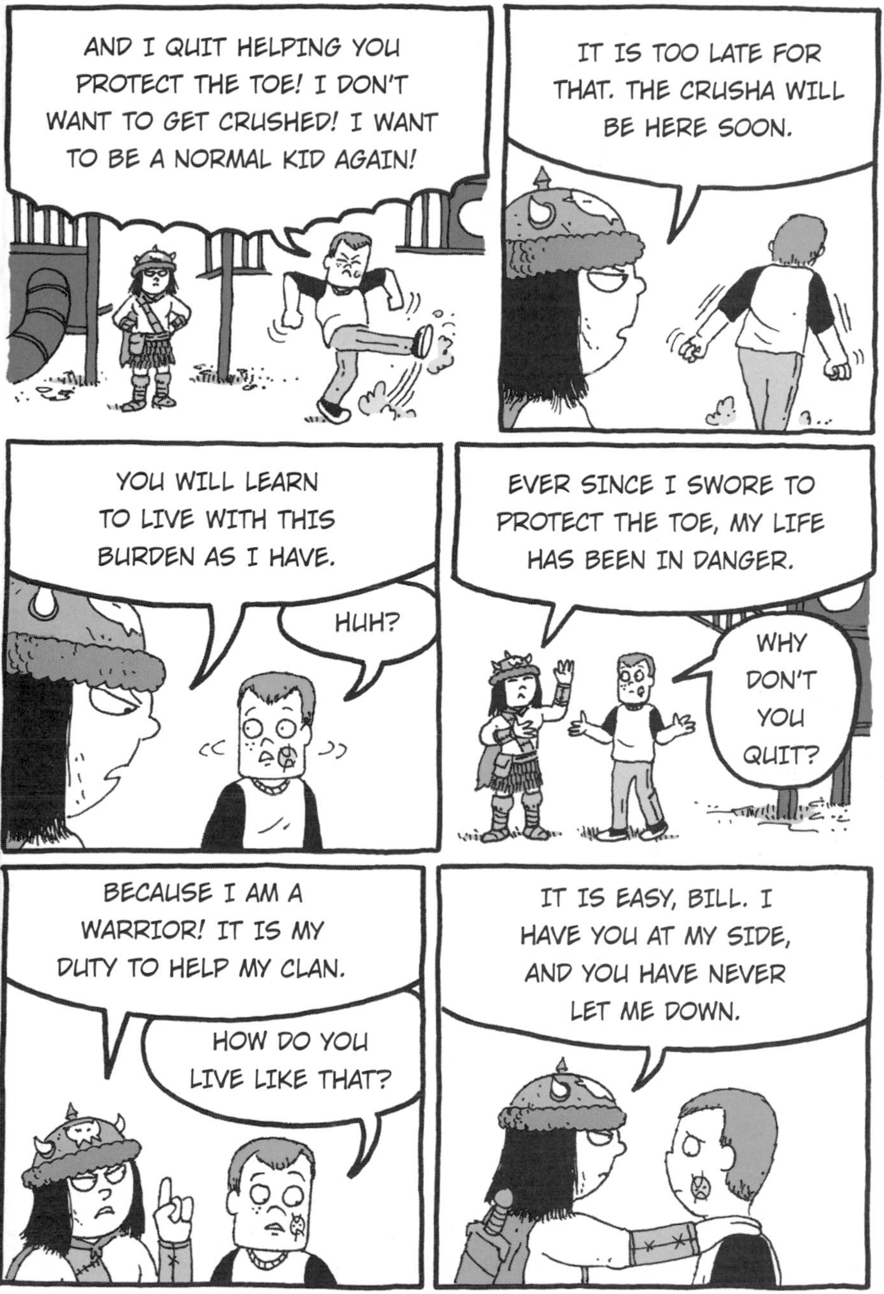
AND I QUIT HELPING YOU PROTECT THE TOE! I DON'T WANT TO GET CRUSHED! I WANT TO BE A NORMAL KID AGAIN!
IT IS TOO LATE FOR THAT. THE CRUSHA WILL BE HERE SOON.
YOU WILL LEARN TO LIVE WITH THIS BURDEN AS I HAVE.
HUH?
EVER SINCE I SWORE TO PROTECT THE TOE, MY LIFE HAS BEEN IN DANGER.
WHY DON'T YOU QUIT?
BECAUSE I AM A WARRIOR! IT IS MY DUTY TO HELP MY CLAN.
HOW DO YOU LIVE LIKE THAT?
IT IS EASY, BILL. I HAVE YOU AT MY SIDE, AND YOU HAVE NEVER LET ME DOWN.

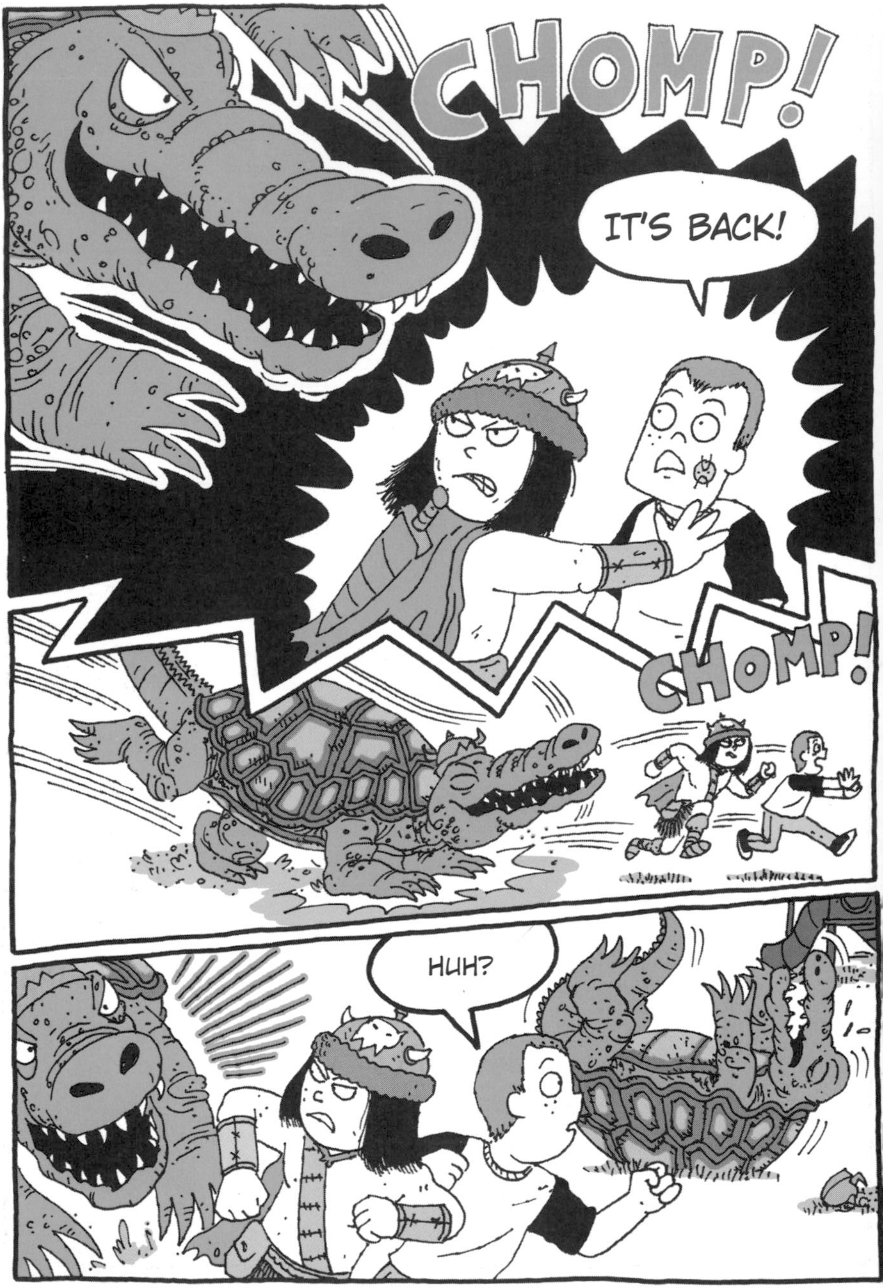
CHOMP!
IT'S BACK!
CHOMP!
HUH?

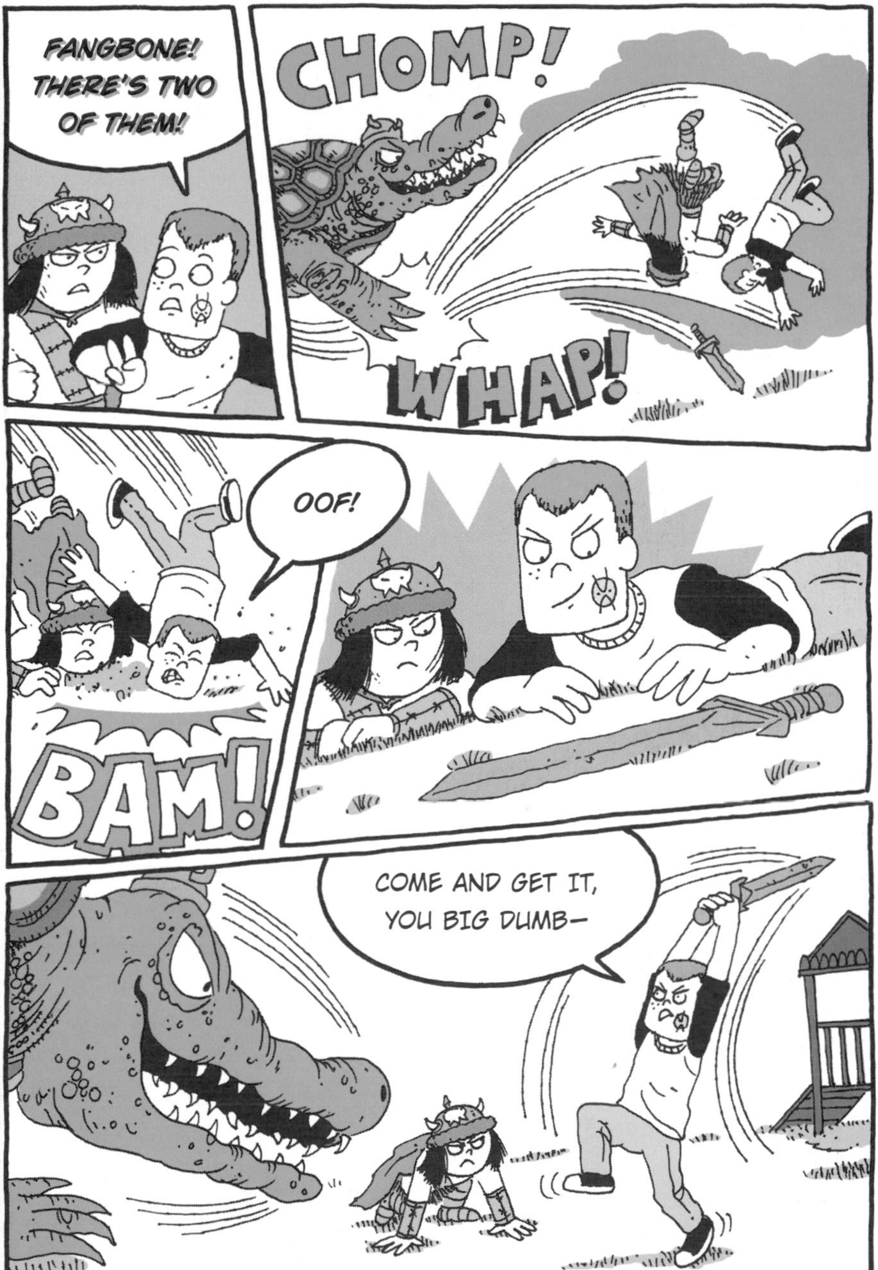
FANGBONE! THERE'S TWO OF THEM!
CHOMP!
WHAP!
OOF!
BAM!
COME AND GET IT, YOU BIG DUMB—

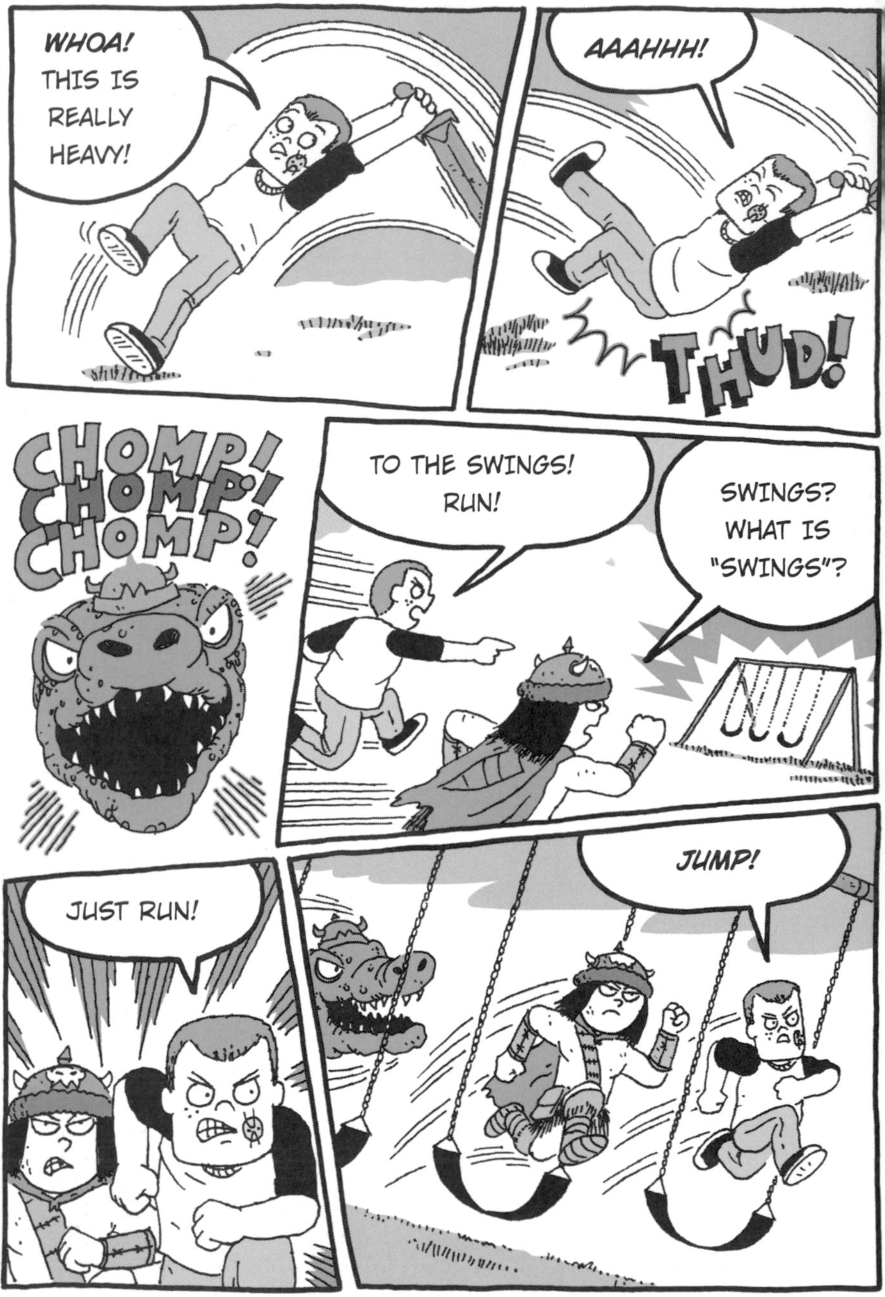
WHOA! THIS IS REALLY HEAVY!
AAAHHH!
THUD!
CHOMP! CHOMP! CHOMP!
TO THE SWINGS! RUN!
SWINGS? WHAT IS "SWINGS"?
JUST RUN!
JUMP!

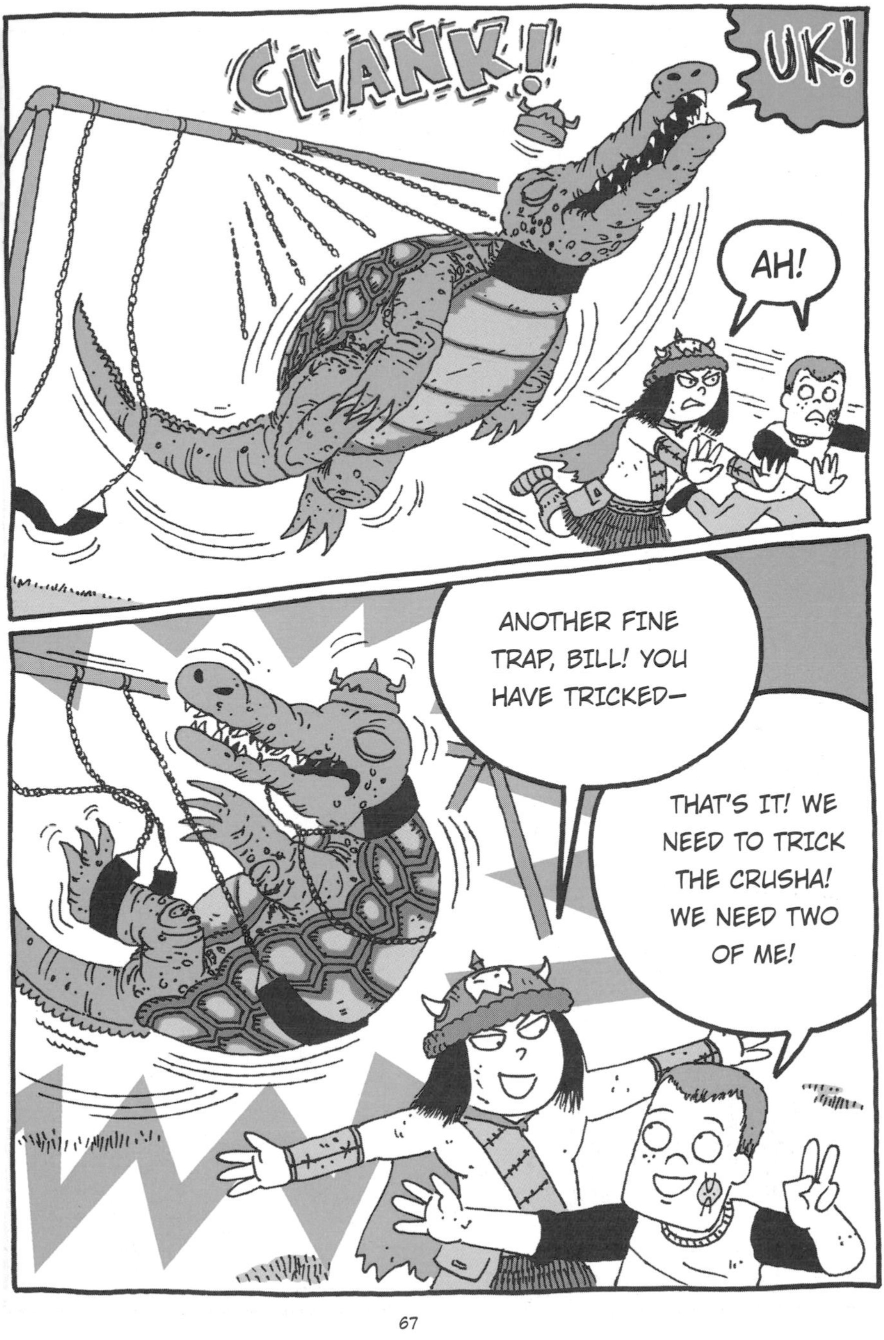
CLANK!
UK!
AH!
ANOTHER FINE TRAP, BILL! YOU HAVE TRICKED—
THAT'S IT! WE NEED TO TRICK THE CRUSHA! WE NEED TWO OF ME!

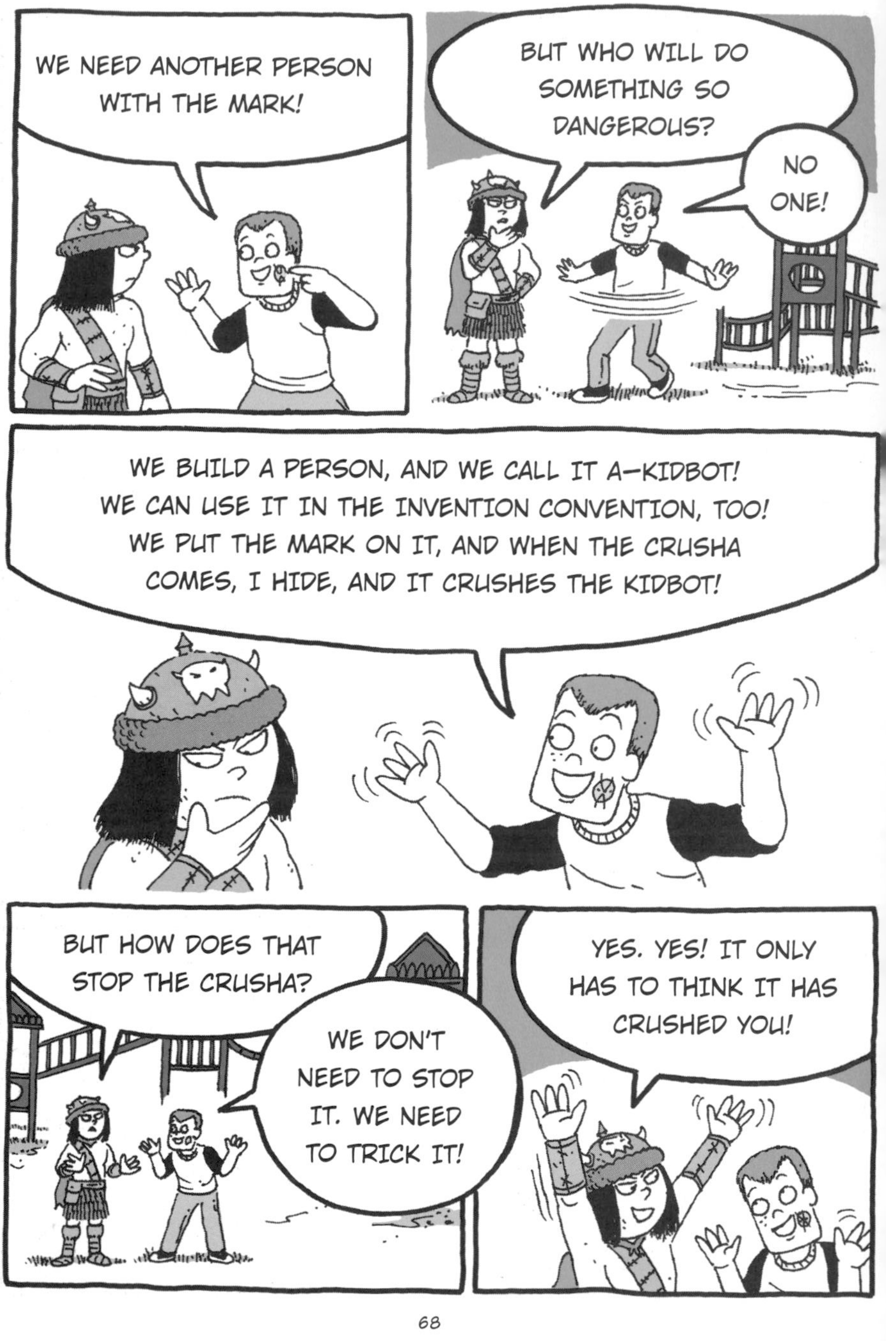
WE NEED ANOTHER PERSON WITH THE MARK!
BUT WHO WILL DO SOMETHING SO DANGEROUS?
NO ONE!
WE BUILD A PERSON, AND WE CALL IT A—KIDBOT! WE CAN USE IT IN THE INVENTION CONVENTION, TOO! WE PUT THE MARK ON IT, AND WHEN THE CRUSHA COMES, I HIDE, AND IT CRUSHES THE KIDBOT!
BUT HOW DOES THAT STOP THE CRUSHA?
WE DON'T NEED TO STOP IT. WE NEED TO TRICK IT!
YES. YES! IT ONLY HAS TO THINK IT HAS CRUSHED YOU!

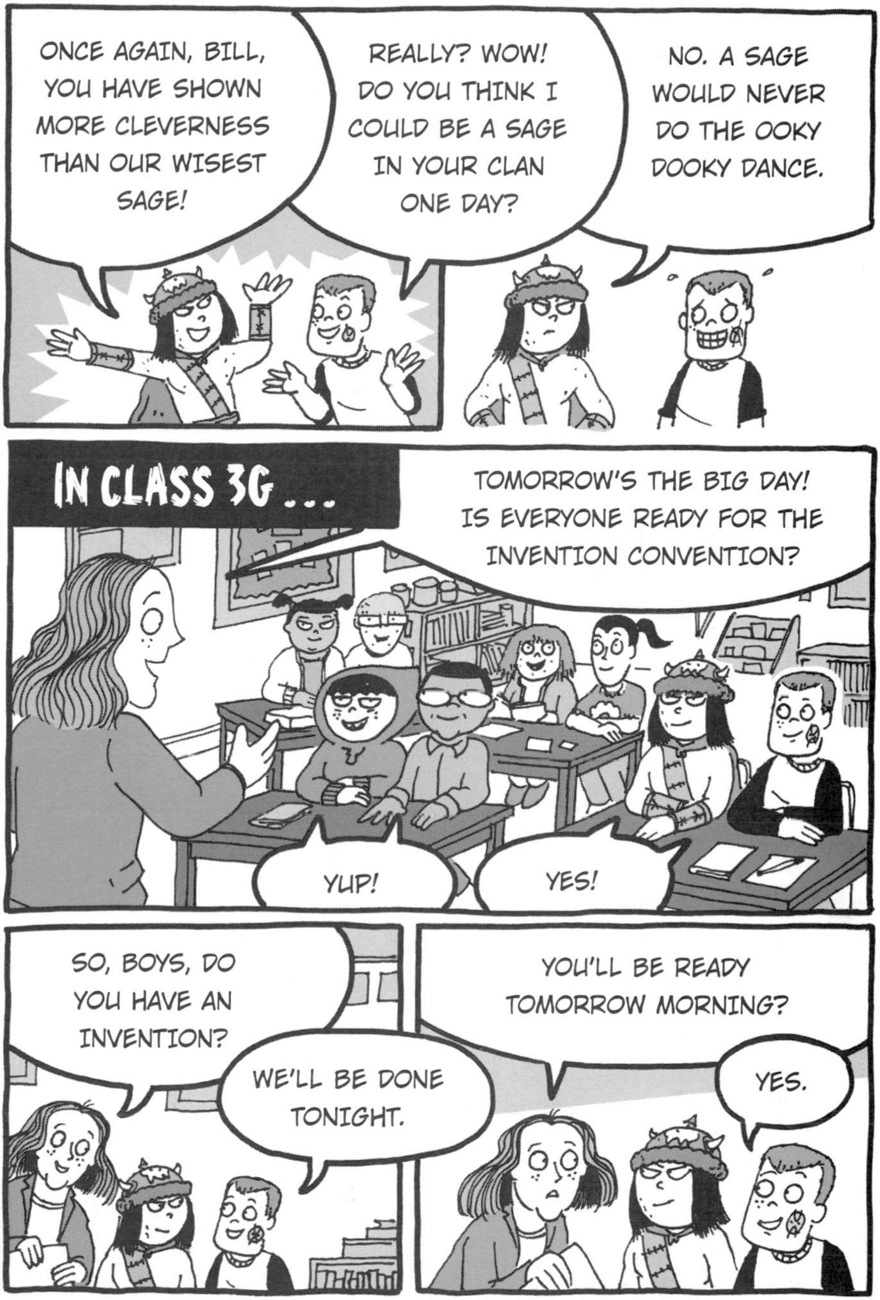
ONCE AGAIN, BILL, YOU HAVE SHOWN MORE CLEVERNESS THAN OUR WISEST SAGE!
REALLY? WOW! DO YOU THINK I COULD BE A SAGE IN YOUR CLAN ONE DAY?
NO. A SAGE WOULD NEVER DO THE OOKY DOOKY DANCE.
IN CLASS 3G . . .
TOMORROW'S THE BIG DAY! IS EVERYONE READY FOR THE INVENTION CONVENTION?
YUP!
YES!
SO, BOYS, DO YOU HAVE AN INVENTION?
WE'LL BE DONE TONIGHT.
YOU'LL BE READY TOMORROW MORNING?
YES.

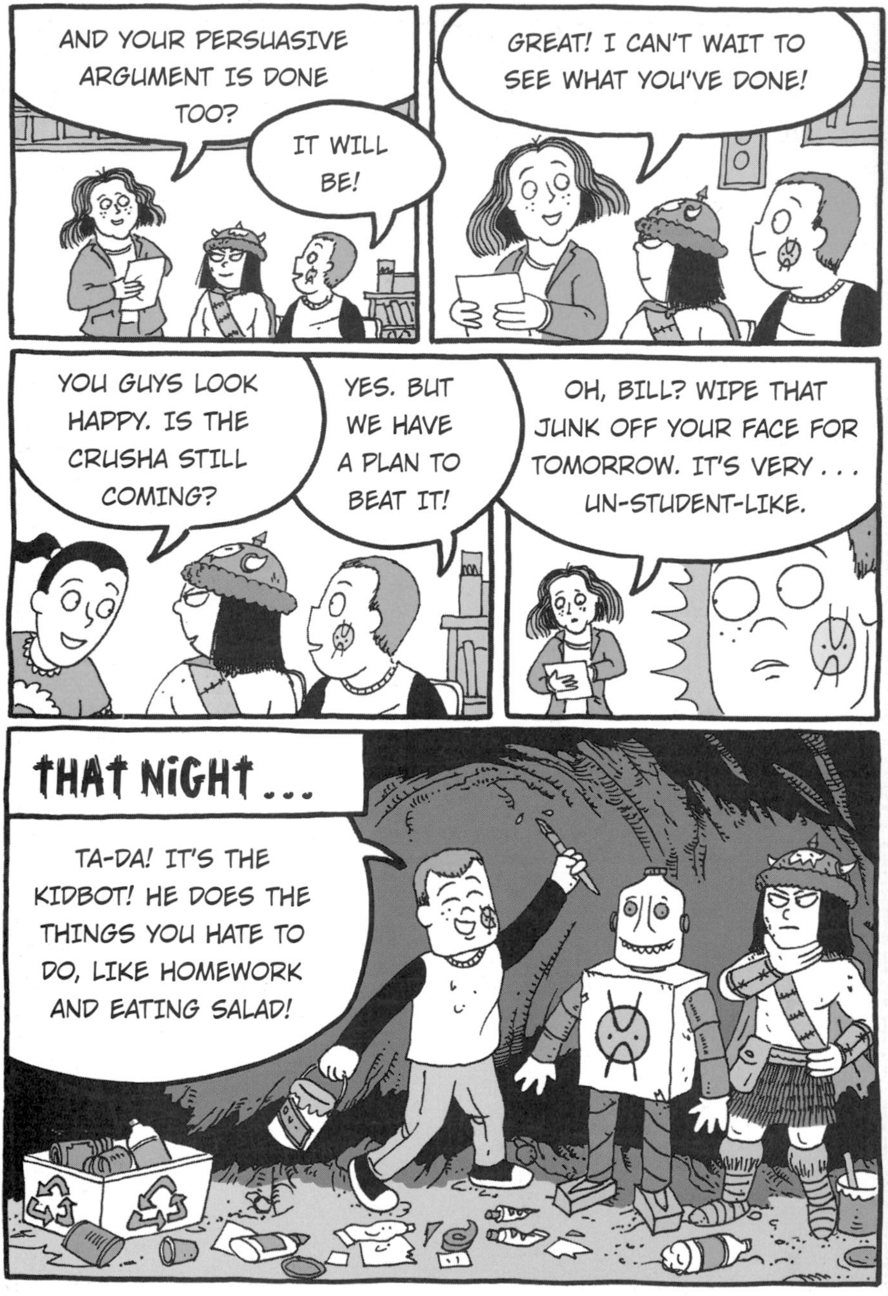
AND YOUR PERSUASIVE ARGUMENT IS DONE TOO?
IT WILL BE!
GREAT! I CAN'T WAIT TO SEE WHAT YOU'VE DONE!
YOU GUYS LOOK HAPPY. IS THE CRUSHA STILL COMING?
YES. BUT WE HAVE A PLAN TO BEAT IT!
OH, BILL? WIPE THAT JUNK OFF YOUR FACE FOR TOMORROW. IT'S VERY . . . UN-STUDENT-LIKE.
THAT NIGHT . . .
TA-DA! IT'S THE KIDBOT! HE DOES THE THINGS YOU HATE TO DO, LIKE HOMEWORK AND EATING SALAD!

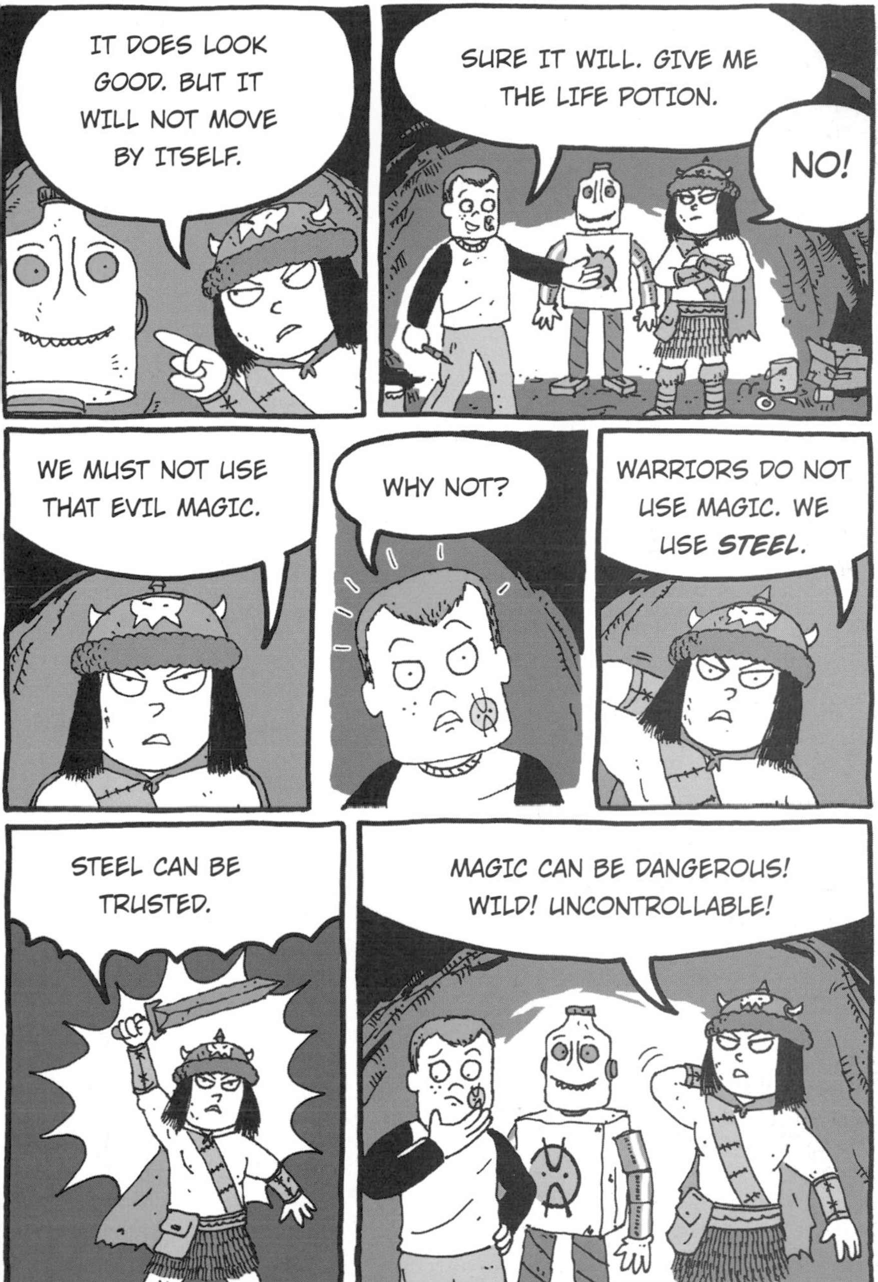
IT DOES LOOK GOOD. BUT IT WILL NOT MOVE BY ITSELF.
SURE IT WILL. GIVE ME THE LIFE POTION.
NO!
WE MUST NOT USE THAT EVIL MAGIC.
WHY NOT?
WARRIORS DO NOT USE MAGIC. WE USE STEEL.
STEEL CAN BE TRUSTED.
MAGIC CAN BE DANGEROUS! WILD! UNCONTROLLABLE!

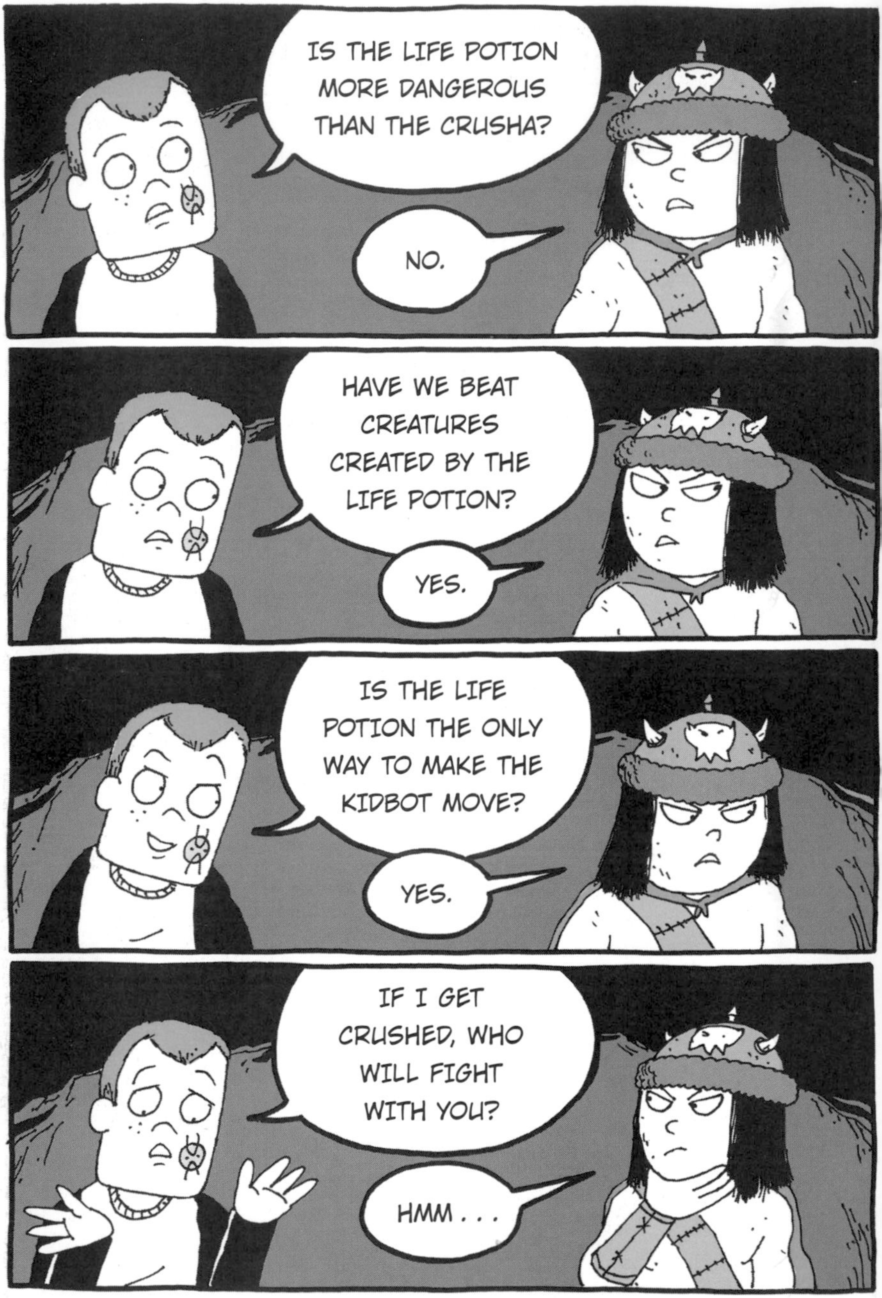
IS THE LIFE POTION MORE DANGEROUS THAN THE CRUSHA?
NO.
HAVE WE BEAT CREATURES CREATED BY THE LIFE POTION?
YES.
IS THE LIFE POTION THE ONLY WAY TO MAKE THE KIDBOT MOVE?
YES.
IF I GET CRUSHED, WHO WILL FIGHT WITH YOU?
HMM . . .

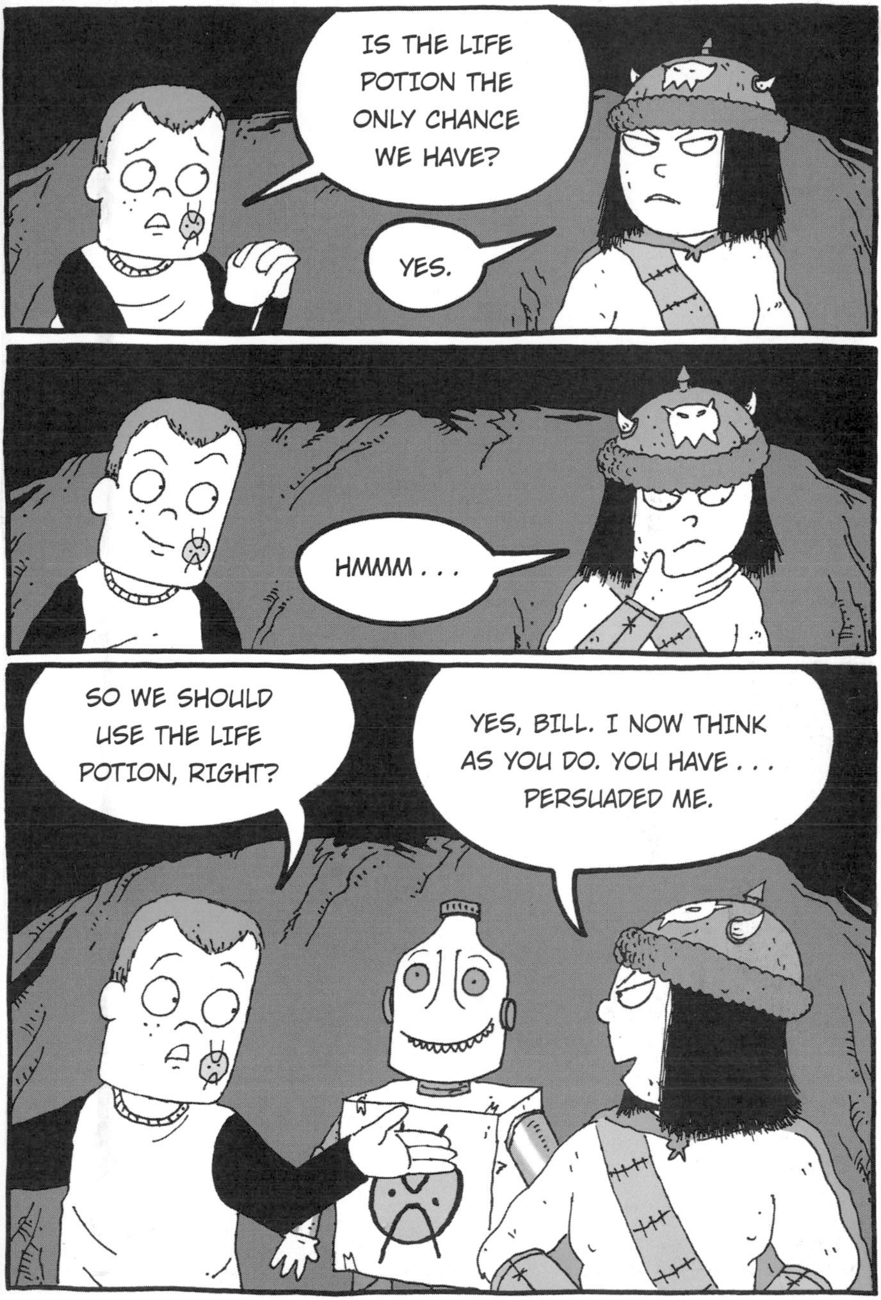
IS THE LIFE POTION THE ONLY CHANCE WE HAVE?
YES.
HMMM . . .
SO WE SHOULD USE THE LIFE POTION, RIGHT?
YES, BILL. I NOW THINK AS YOU DO. YOU HAVE . . . PERSUADED ME.

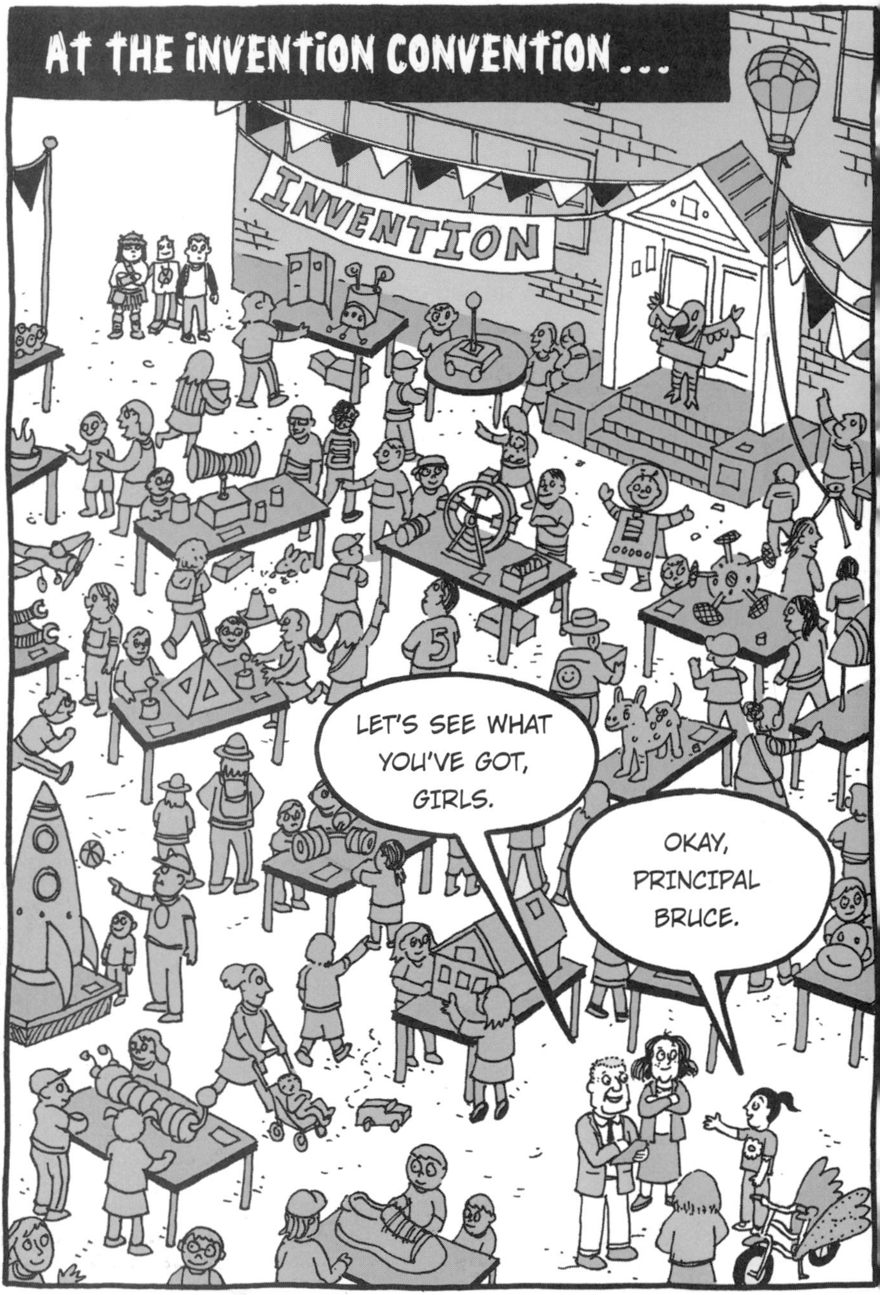
AT THE INVENTION CONVENTION . . .
INVENTION
LET'S SEE WHAT YOU'VE GOT, GIRLS.
OKAY, PRINCIPAL BRUCE.

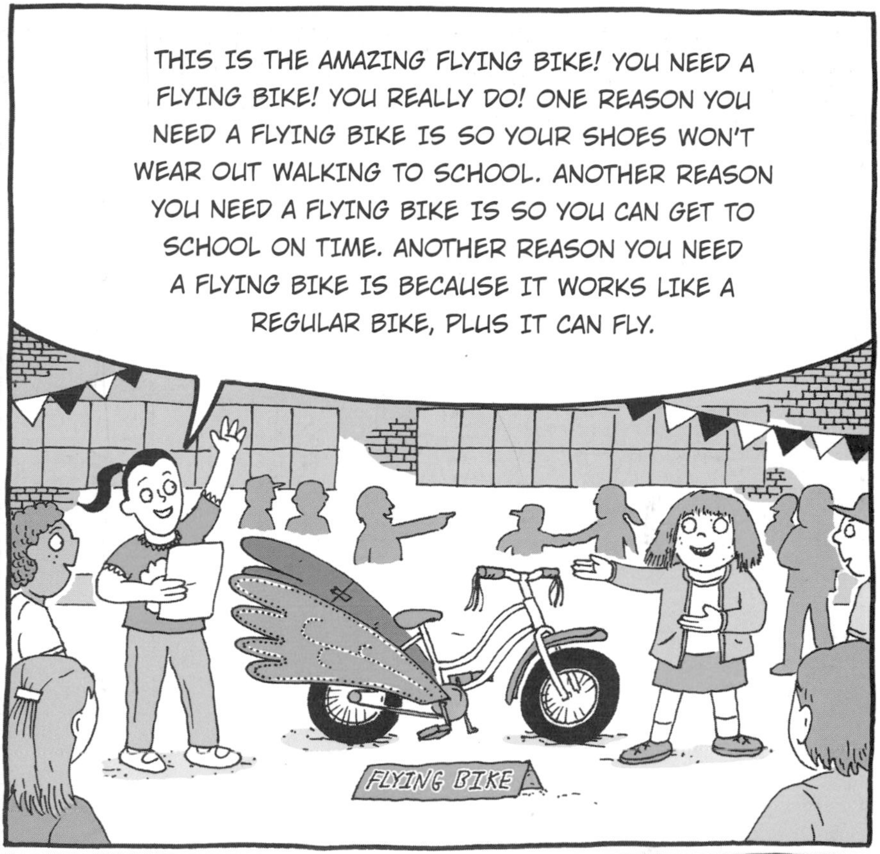
THIS IS THE AMAZING FLYING BIKE! YOU NEED A FLYING BIKE! YOU REALLY DO! ONE REASON YOU NEED A FLYING BIKE IS SO YOUR SHOES WON'T WEAR OUT WALKING TO SCHOOL. ANOTHER REASON YOU NEED A FLYING BIKE IS SO YOU CAN GET TO SCHOOL ON TIME. ANOTHER REASON YOU NEED A FLYING BIKE IS BECAUSE IT WORKS LIKE A REGULAR BIKE, PLUS IT CAN FLY.
FLYING BIKE

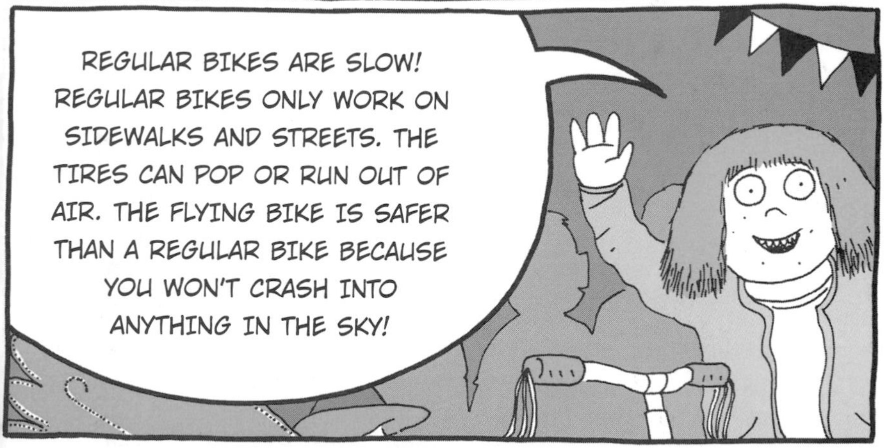
REGULAR BIKES ARE SLOW! REGULAR BIKES ONLY WORK ON SIDEWALKS AND STREETS. THE TIRES CAN POP OR RUN OUT OF AIR. THE FLYING BIKE IS SAFER THAN A REGULAR BIKE BECAUSE YOU WON'T CRASH INTO ANYTHING IN THE SKY!

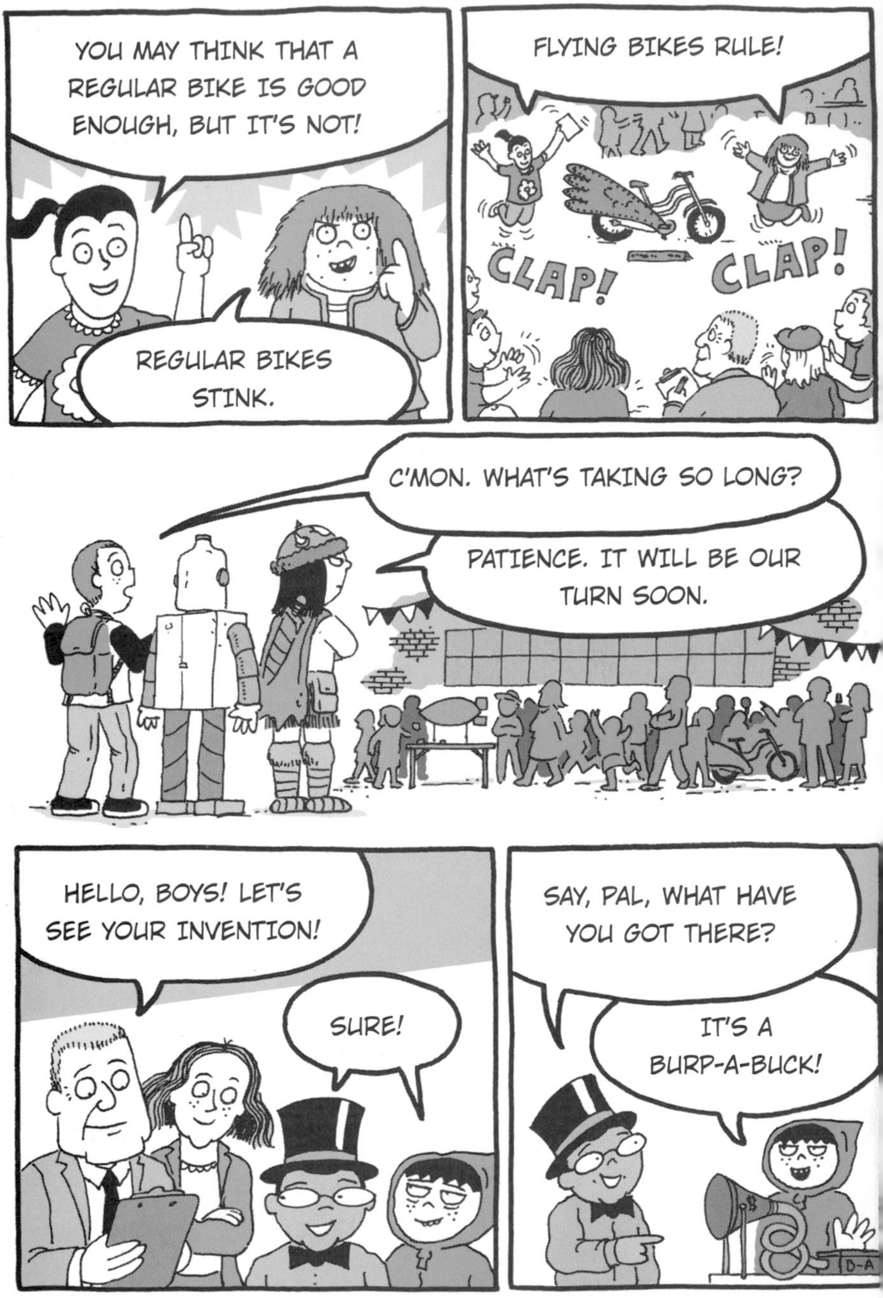
YOU MAY THINK THAT A REGULAR BIKE IS GOOD ENOUGH, BUT IT'S NOT!
REGULAR BIKES STINK.
FLYING BIKES RULE!
CLAP!
CLAP!
C'MON. WHAT'S TAKING SO LONG?
PATIENCE. IT WILL BE OUR TURN SOON.
HELLO, BOYS! LET'S SEE YOUR INVENTION!
SURE!
SAY, PAL, WHAT HAVE YOU GOT THERE?
IT'S A BURP-A-BUCK!
B-A

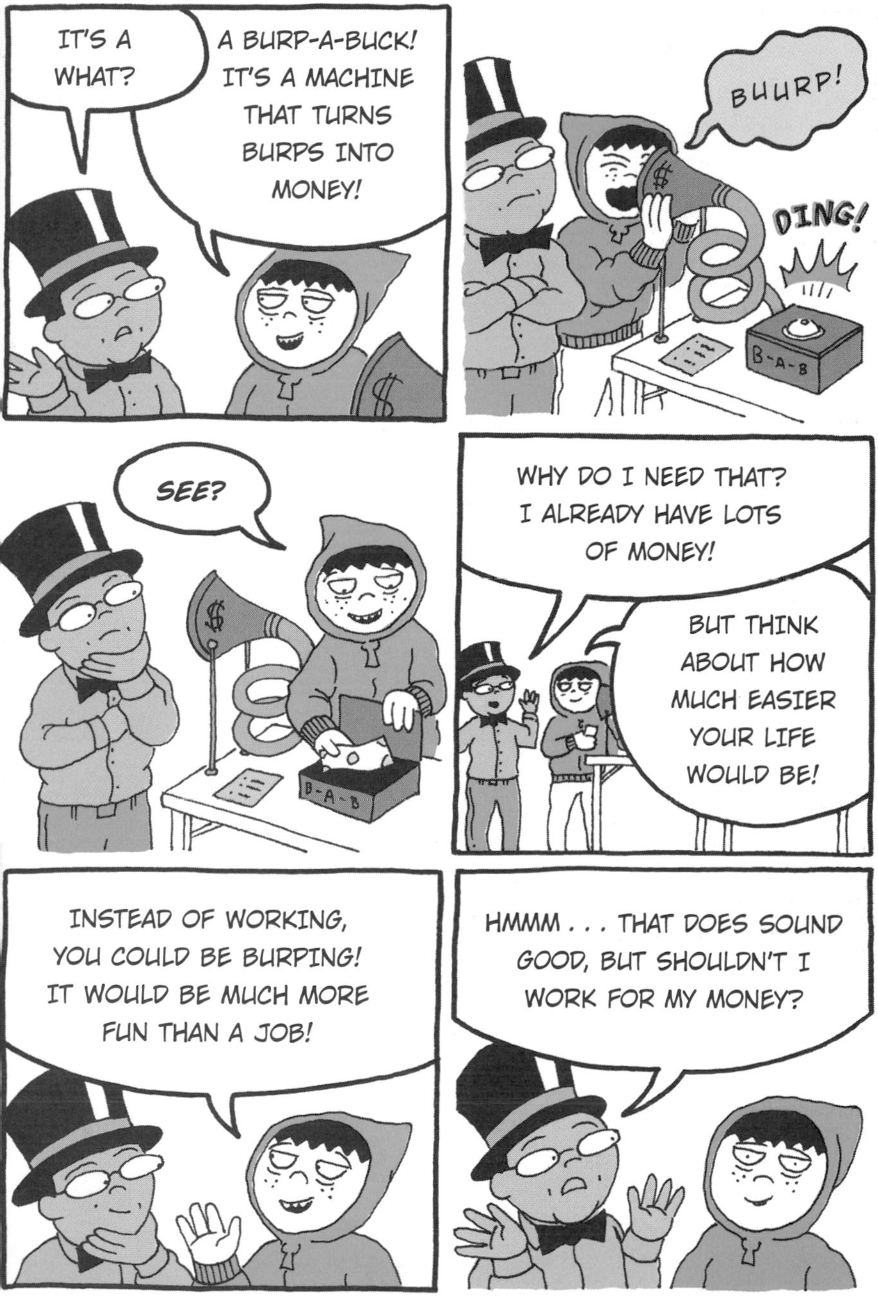
IT'S A WHAT?
A BURP-A-BUCK! IT'S A MACHINE THAT TURNS BURPS INTO MONEY!
BUURP!
DING!
B-A-B
SEE?
B-A-B
WHY DO I NEED THAT? I ALREADY HAVE LOTS OF MONEY!
BUT THINK ABOUT HOW MUCH EASIER YOUR LIFE WOULD BE!
INSTEAD OF WORKING, YOU COULD BE BURPING! IT WOULD BE MUCH MORE FUN THAN A JOB!
HMMM . . . THAT DOES SOUND GOOD, BUT SHOULDN'T I WORK FOR MY MONEY?

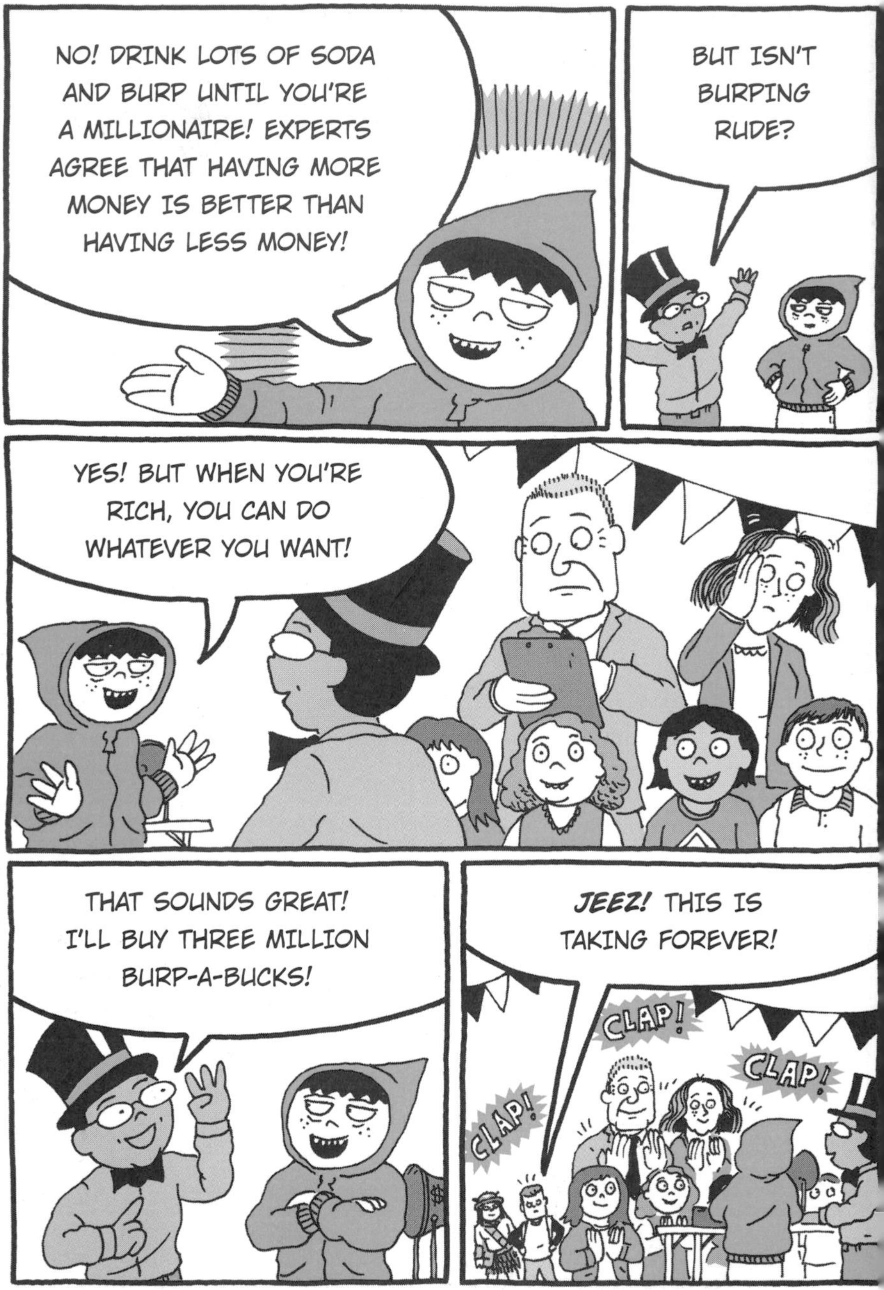
NO! DRINK LOTS OF SODA AND BURP UNTIL YOU'RE A MILLIONAIRE! EXPERTS AGREE THAT HAVING MORE MONEY IS BETTER THAN HAVING LESS MONEY!
BUT ISN'T BURPING RUDE?
YES! BUT WHEN YOU'RE RICH, YOU CAN DO WHATEVER YOU WANT!
THAT SOUNDS GREAT! I'LL BUY THREE MILLION BURP-A-BUCKS!
JEEZ! THIS IS TAKING FOREVER!
CLAP!
CLAP!
CLAP!

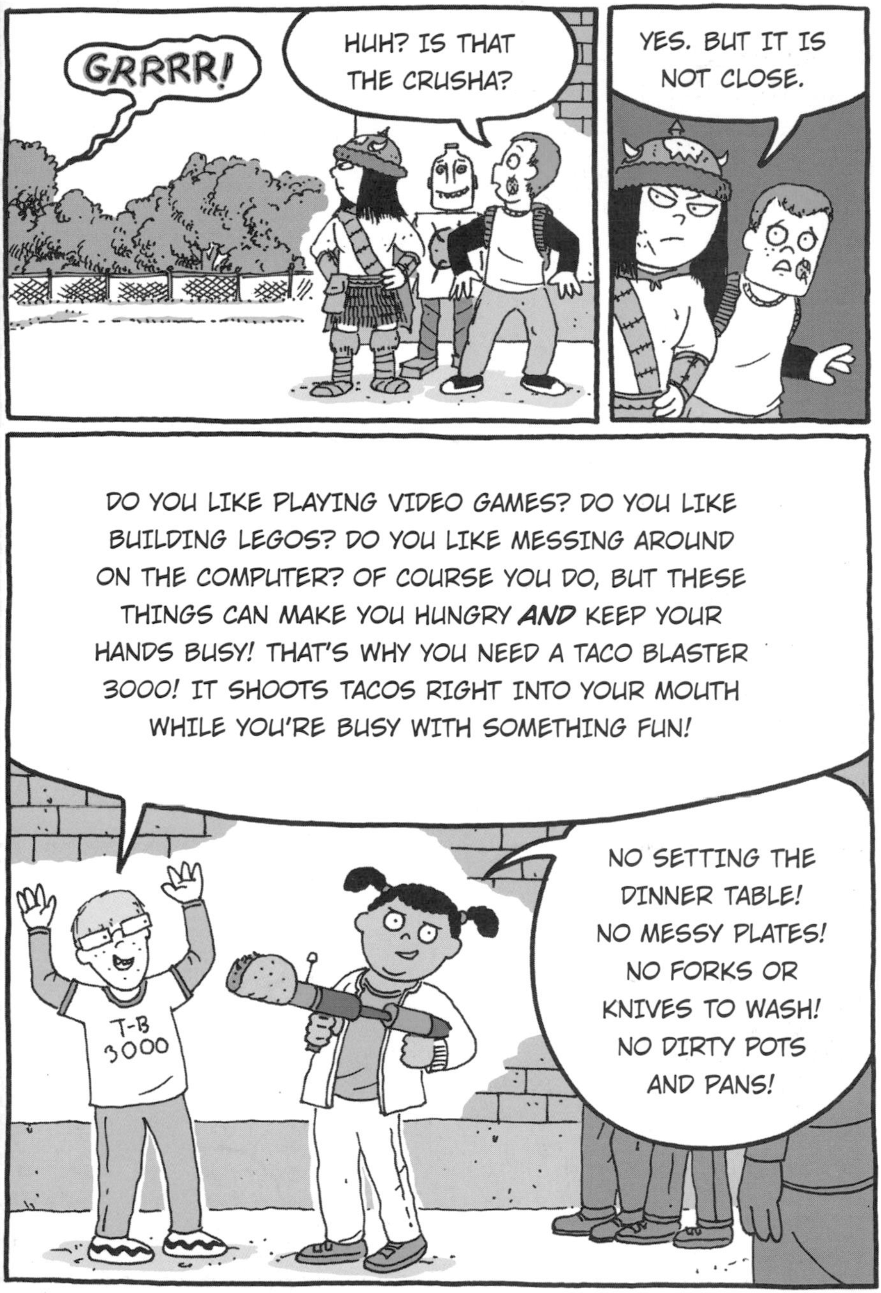
GRRRR!
HUH? IS THAT THE CRUSHA?
YES. BUT IT IS NOT CLOSE.
DO YOU LIKE PLAYING VIDEO GAMES? DO YOU LIKE BUILDING LEGOS? DO YOU LIKE MESSING AROUND ON THE COMPUTER? OF COURSE YOU DO, BUT THESE THINGS CAN MAKE YOU HUNGRY AND KEEP YOUR HANDS BUSY! THAT'S WHY YOU NEED A TACO BLASTER 3000! IT SHOOTS TACOS RIGHT INTO YOUR MOUTH WHILE YOU'RE BUSY WITH SOMETHING FUN!
T-B 3000
NO SETTING THE DINNER TABLE! NO MESSY PLATES! NO FORKS OR KNIVES TO WASH! NO DIRTY POTS AND PANS!

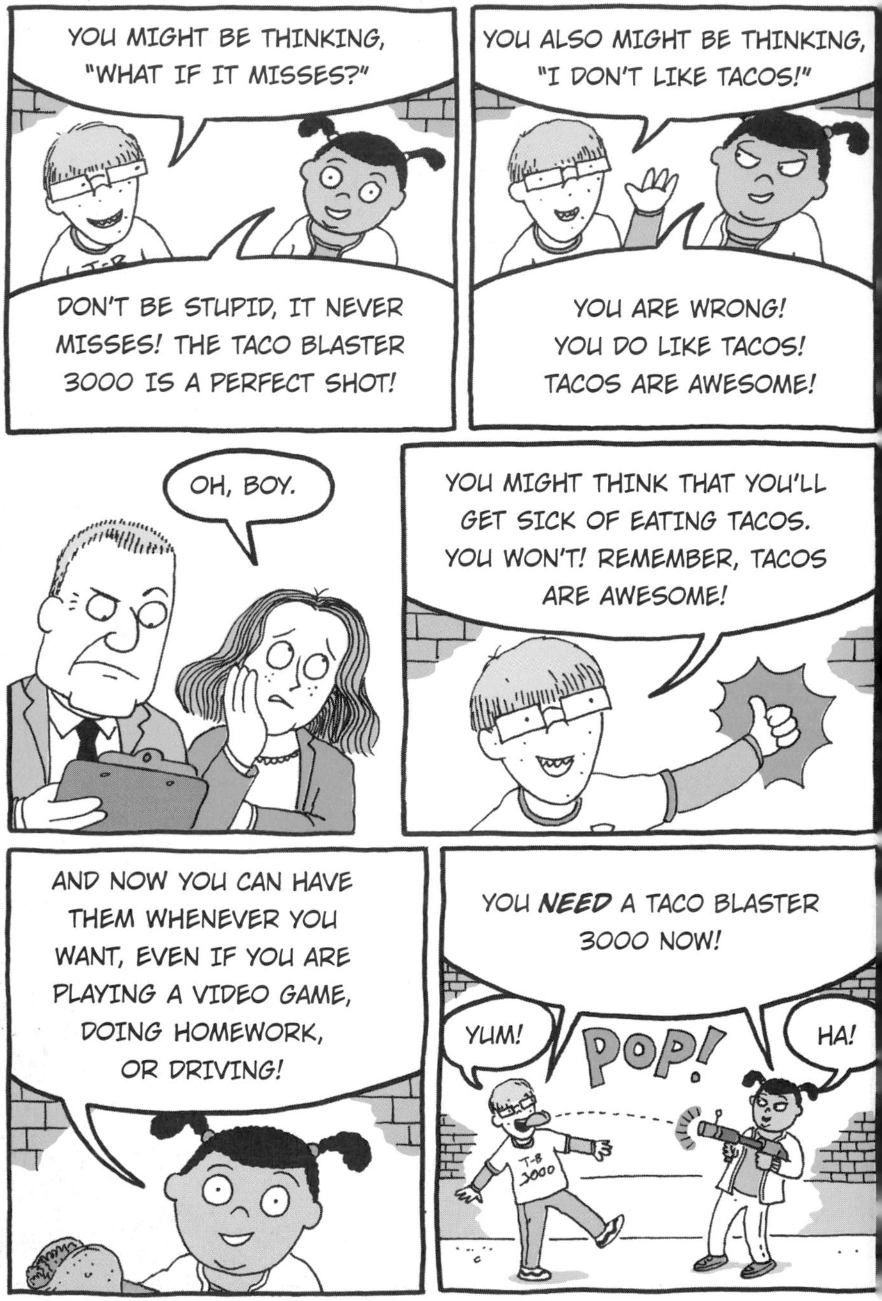
YOU MIGHT BE THINKING, "WHAT IF IT MISSES?"
DON'T BE STUPID, IT NEVER MISSES! THE TACO BLASTER 3000 IS A PERFECT SHOT!
YOU ALSO MIGHT BE THINKING, "I DON'T LIKE TACOS!"
YOU ARE WRONG! YOU DO LIKE TACOS! TACOS ARE AWESOME!
OH, BOY.
YOU MIGHT THINK THAT YOU'LL GET SICK OF EATING TACOS. YOU WON'T! REMEMBER, TACOS ARE AWESOME!
AND NOW YOU CAN HAVE THEM WHENEVER YOU WANT, EVEN IF YOU ARE PLAYING A VIDEO GAME, DOING HOMEWORK, OR DRIVING!
YOU **NEED** A TACO BLASTER 3000 NOW!
YUM!
POP!
HA!
T-B 3000

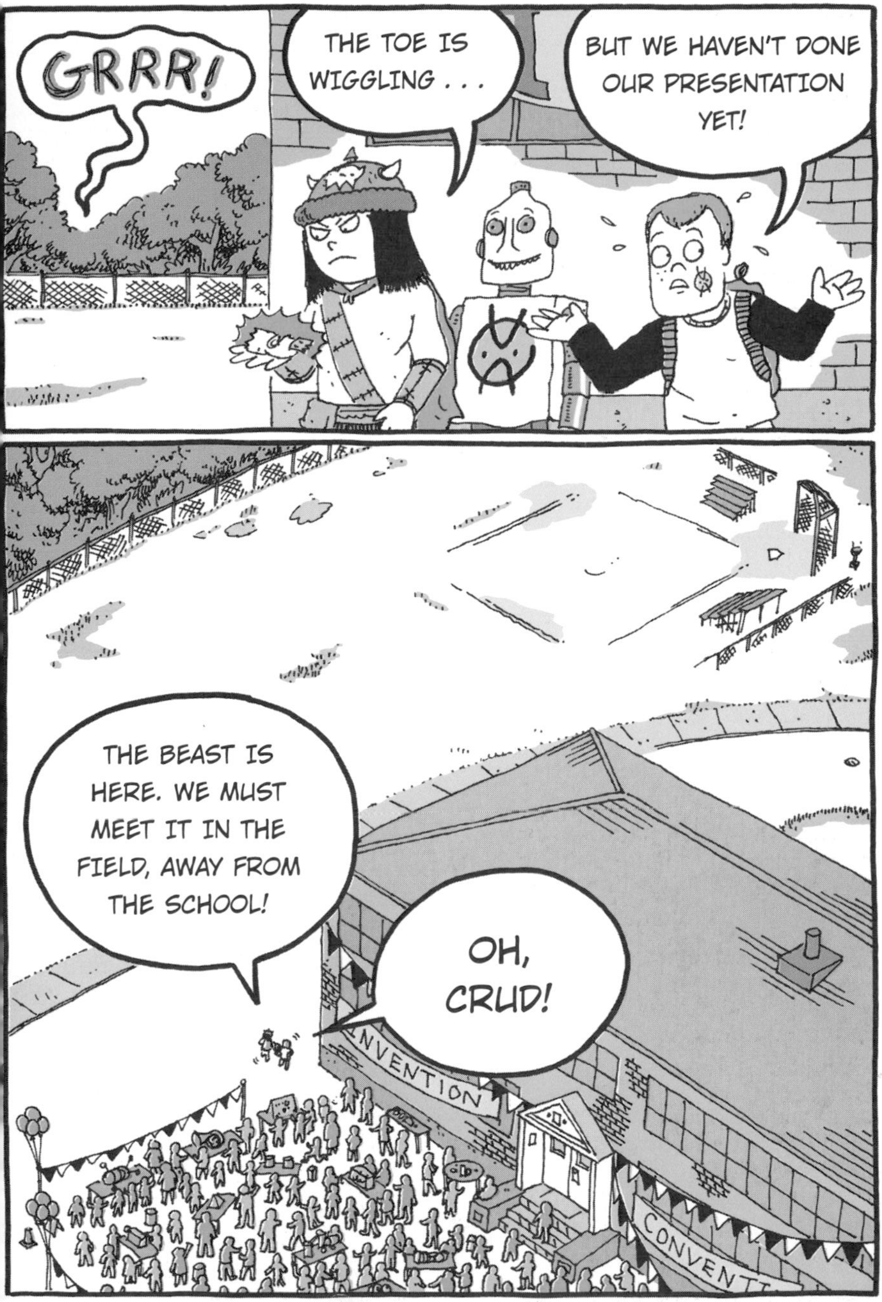
GRRR!
THE TOE IS WIGGLING . . .
BUT WE HAVEN'T DONE OUR PRESENTATION YET!
THE BEAST IS HERE. WE MUST MEET IT IN THE FIELD, AWAY FROM THE SCHOOL!
OH, CRUD!
NVENTION
CONVENTI

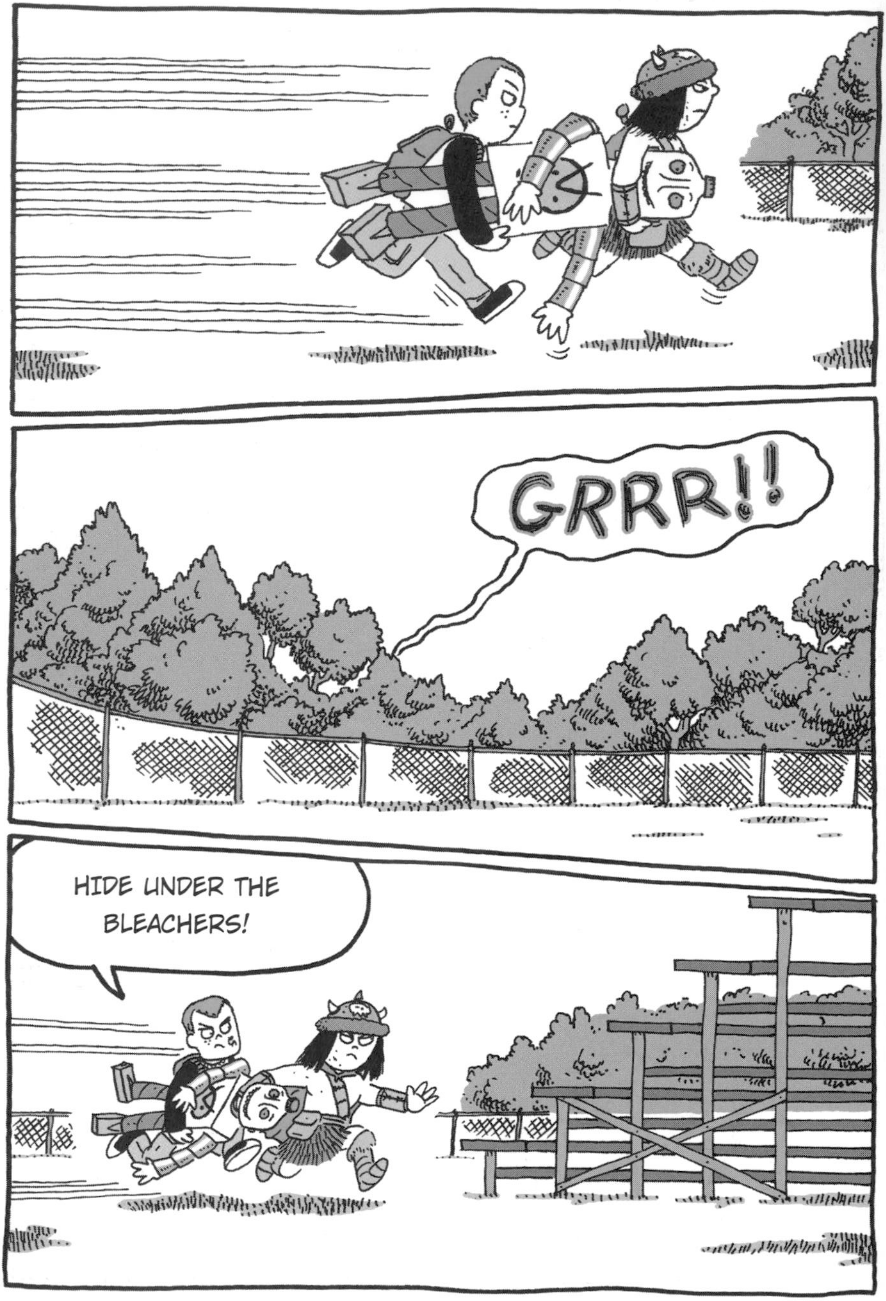
GRRR!!
HIDE UNDER THE BLEACHERS!

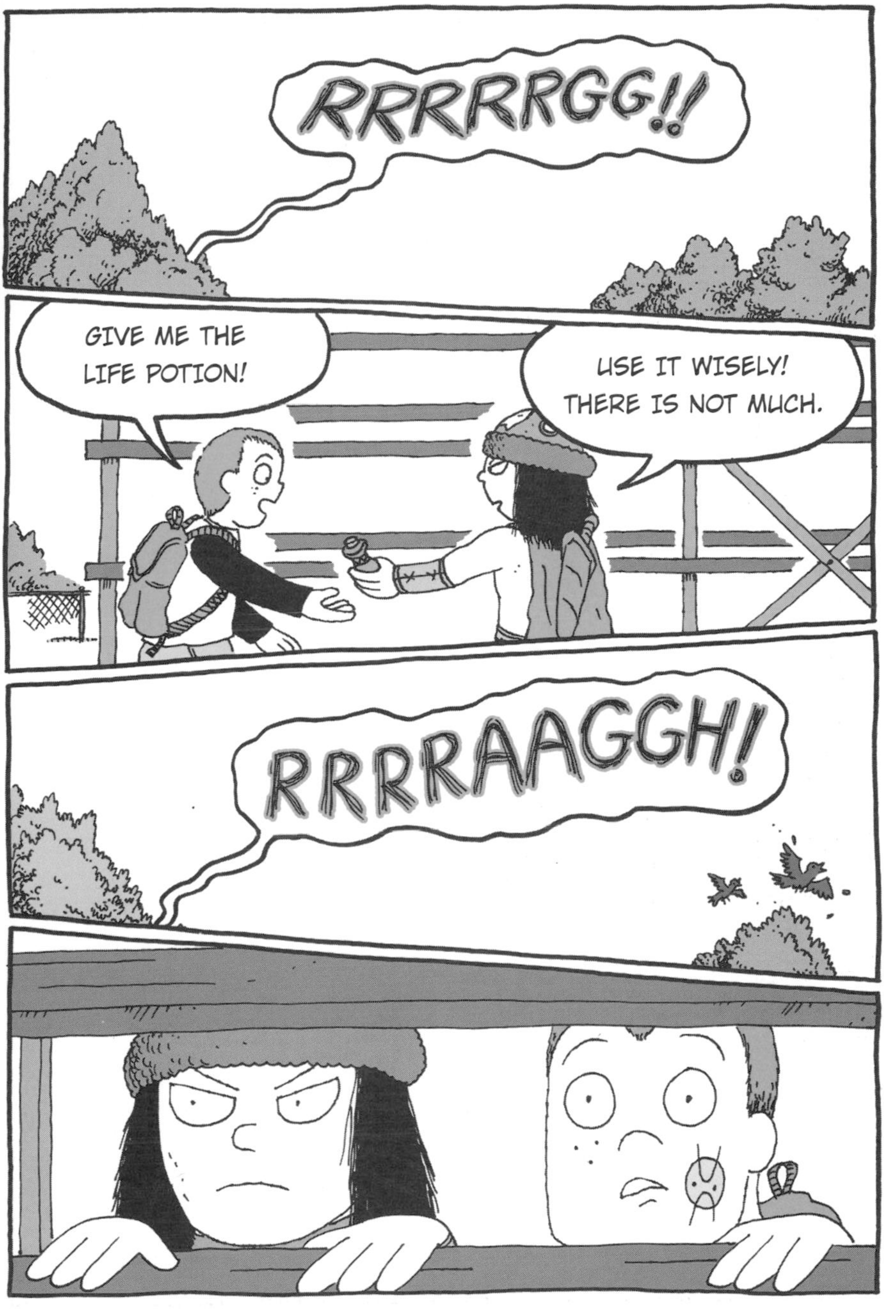
RRRRRGG!!
GIVE ME THE LIFE POTION!
USE IT WISELY! THERE IS NOT MUCH.
RRRRAAGGH!

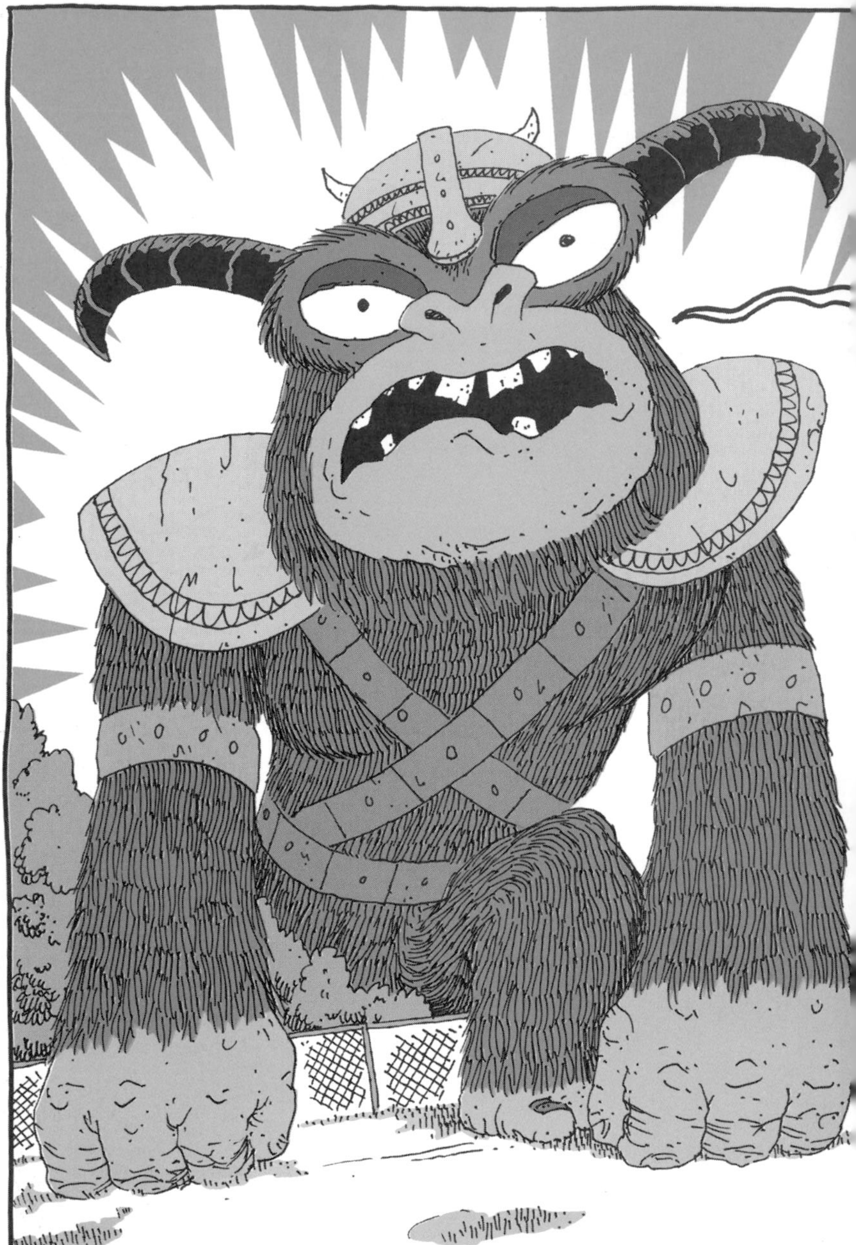

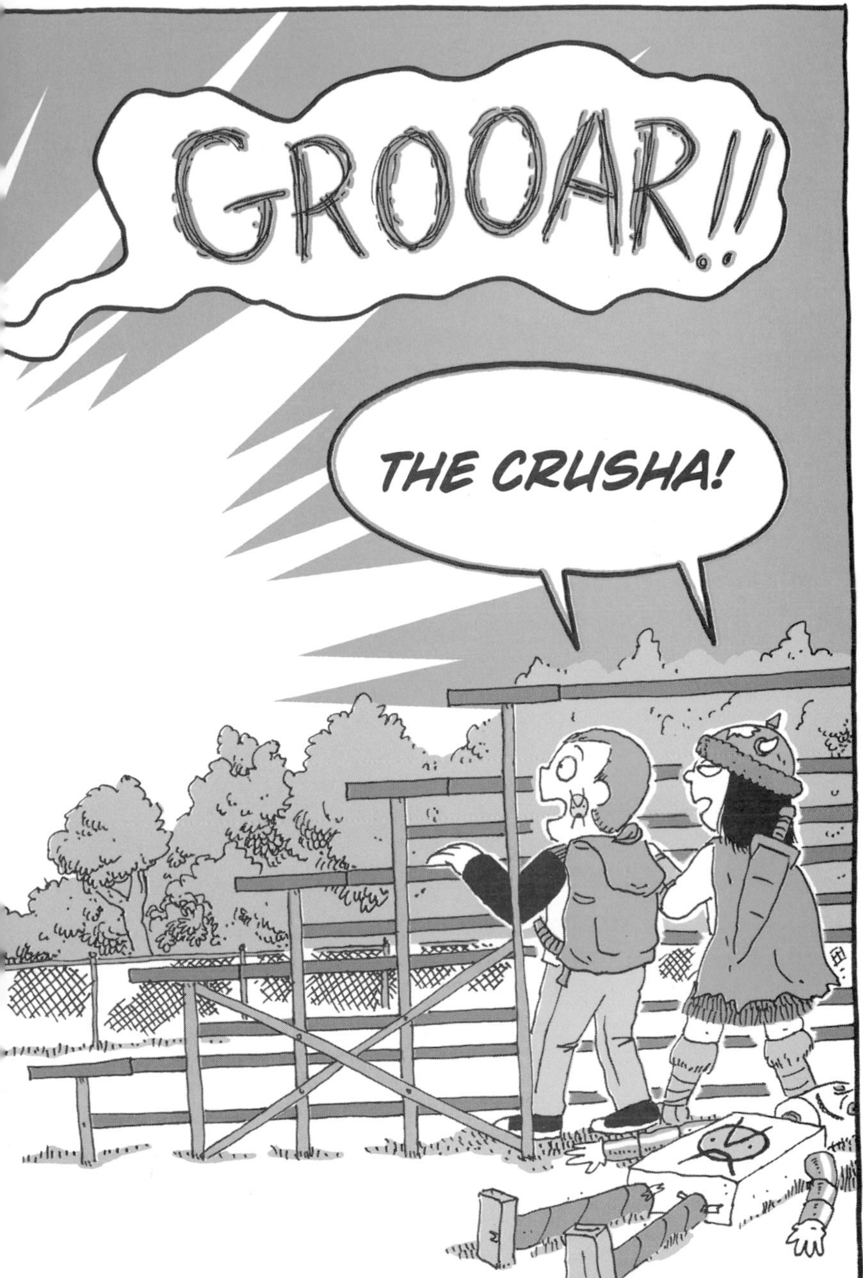
GROOAR!!
THE CRUSHA!

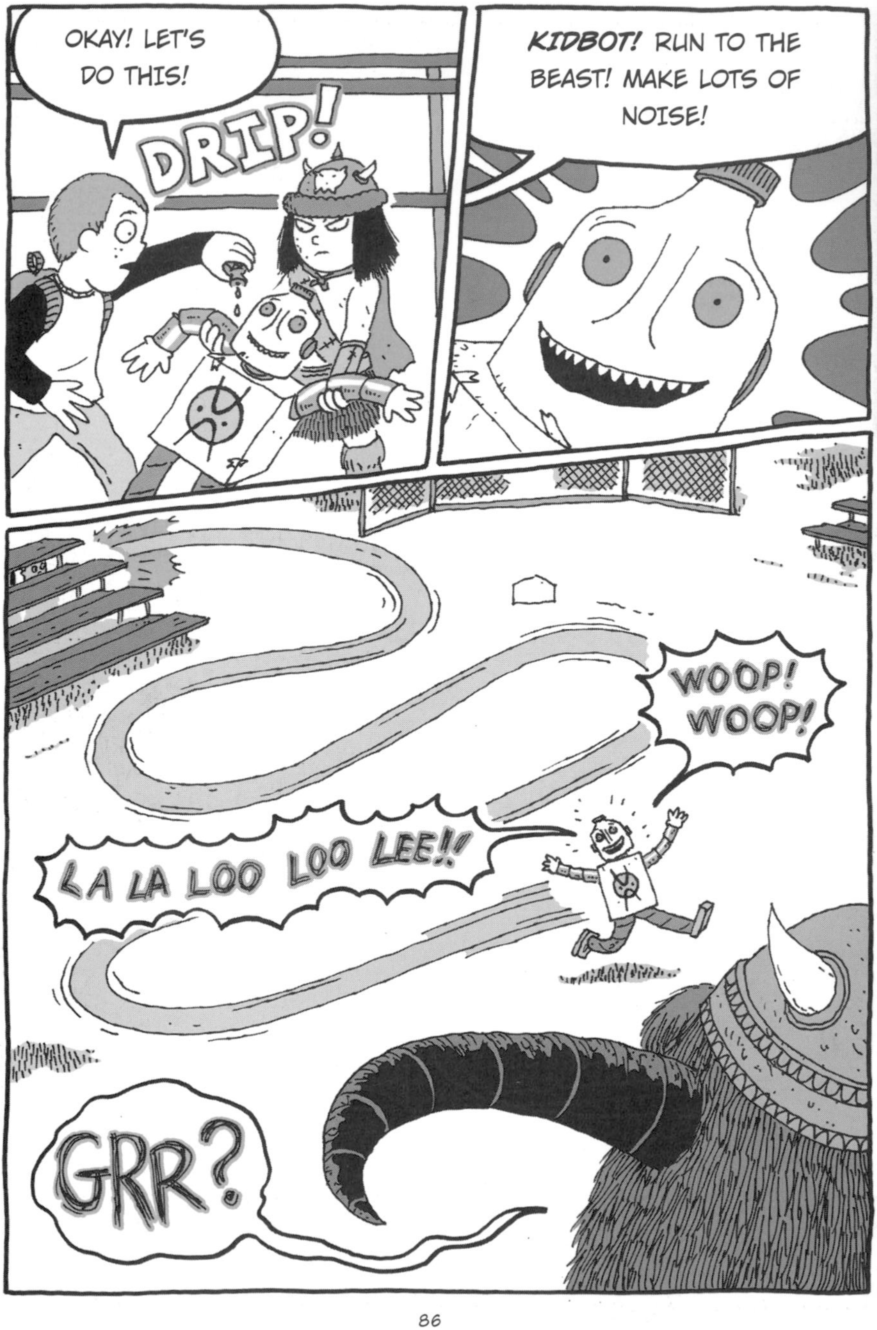
OKAY! LET'S DO THIS!
DRIP!
KIDBOT! RUN TO THE BEAST! MAKE LOTS OF NOISE!
WOOP! WOOP!
LA LA LOO LOO LEE!!
GRR?

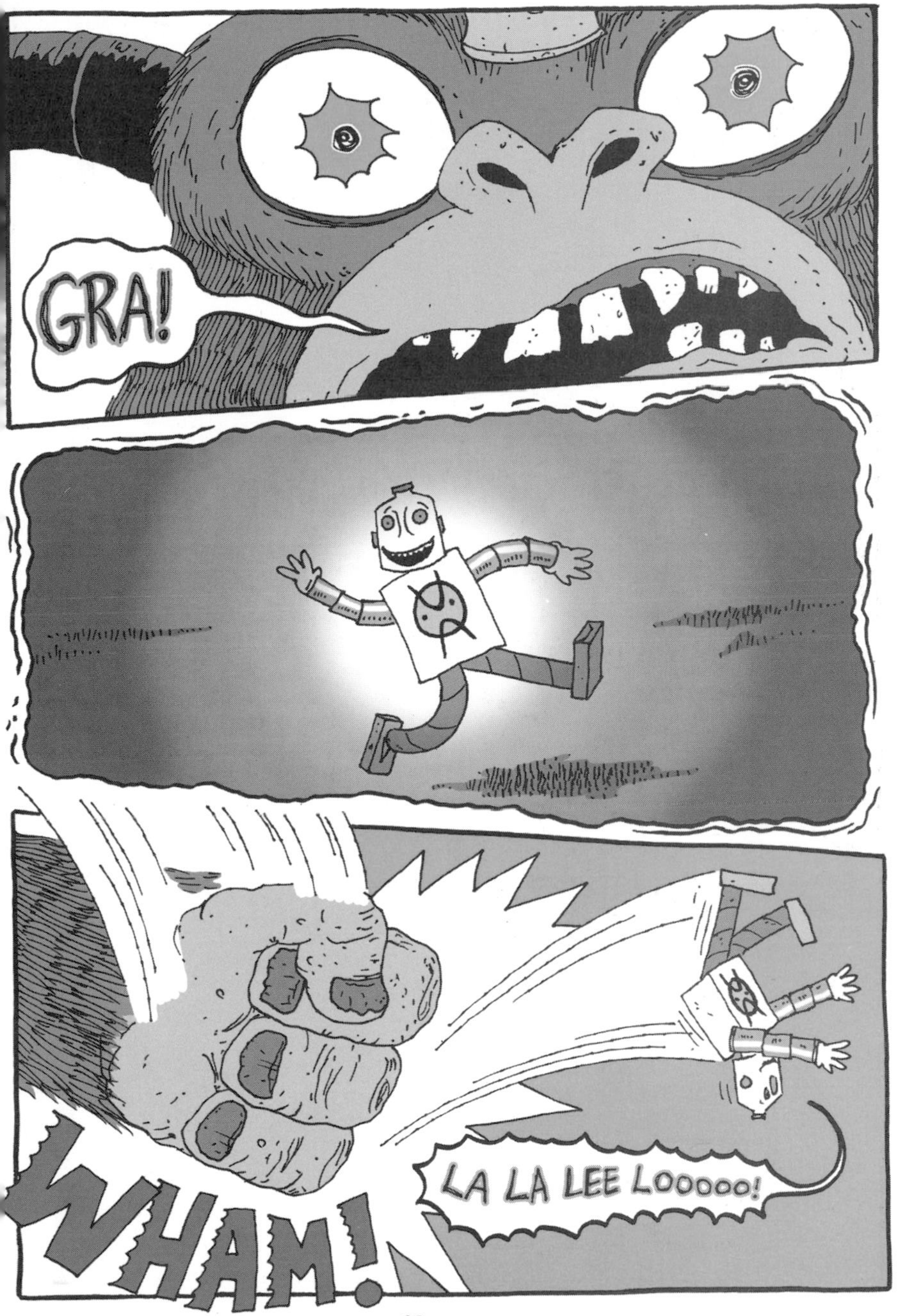
GRA!
WHAM!
LA LA LEE LOOOOO!

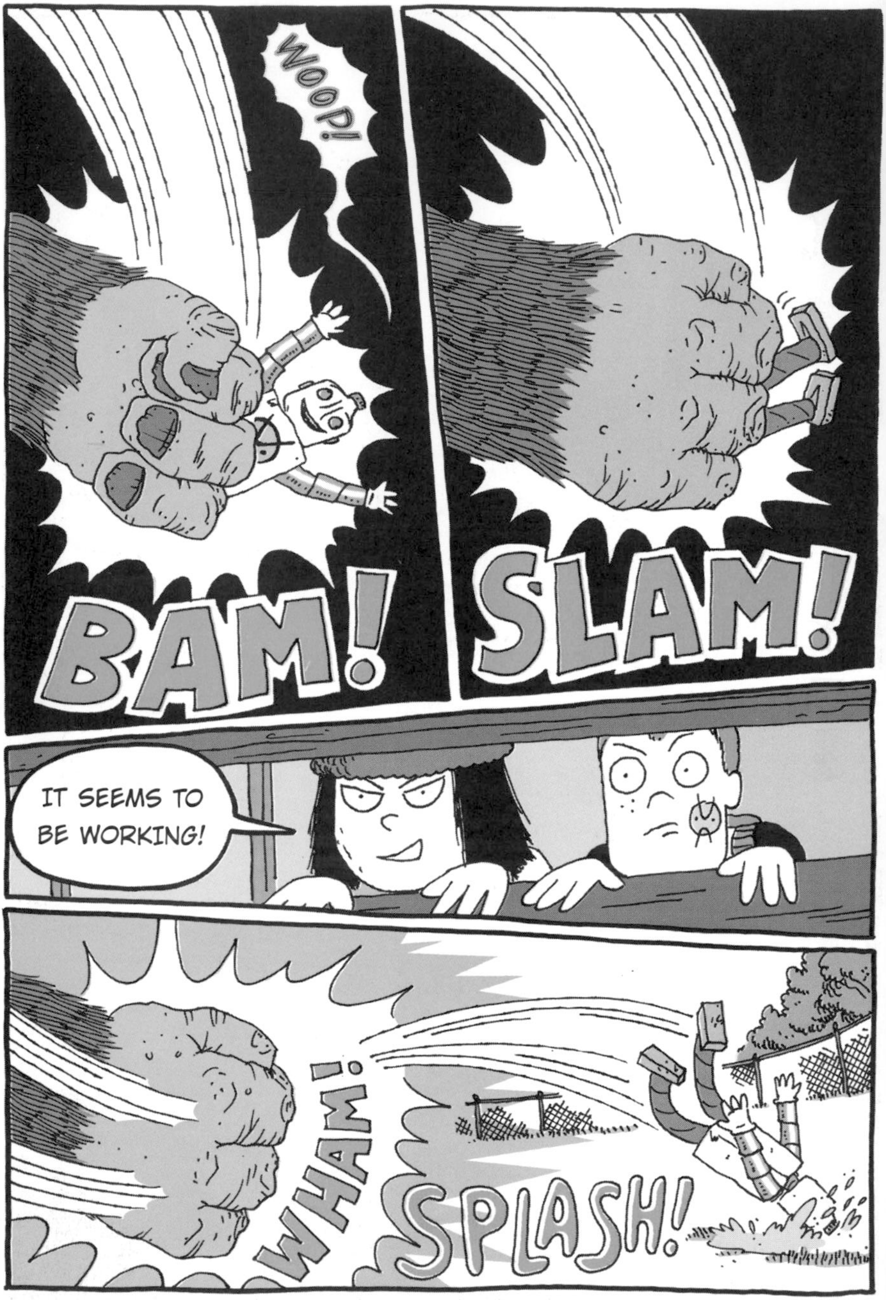
WOOP!
BAM!
SLAM!
IT SEEMS TO BE WORKING!
WHAM!
SPLASH!

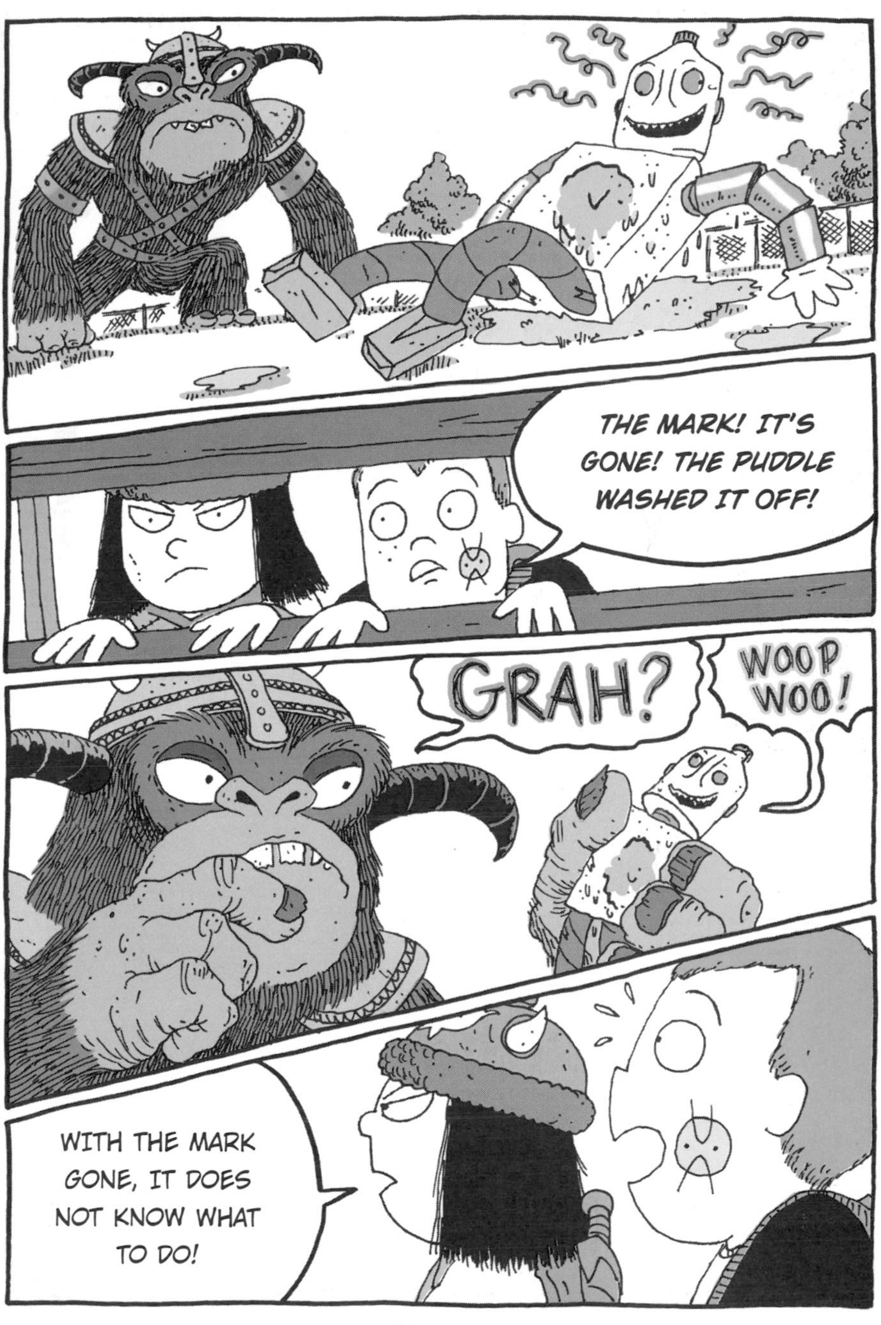
THE MARK! IT'S GONE! THE PUDDLE WASHED IT OFF!
GRAH?
WOOP WOO!
WITH THE MARK GONE, IT DOES NOT KNOW WHAT TO DO!

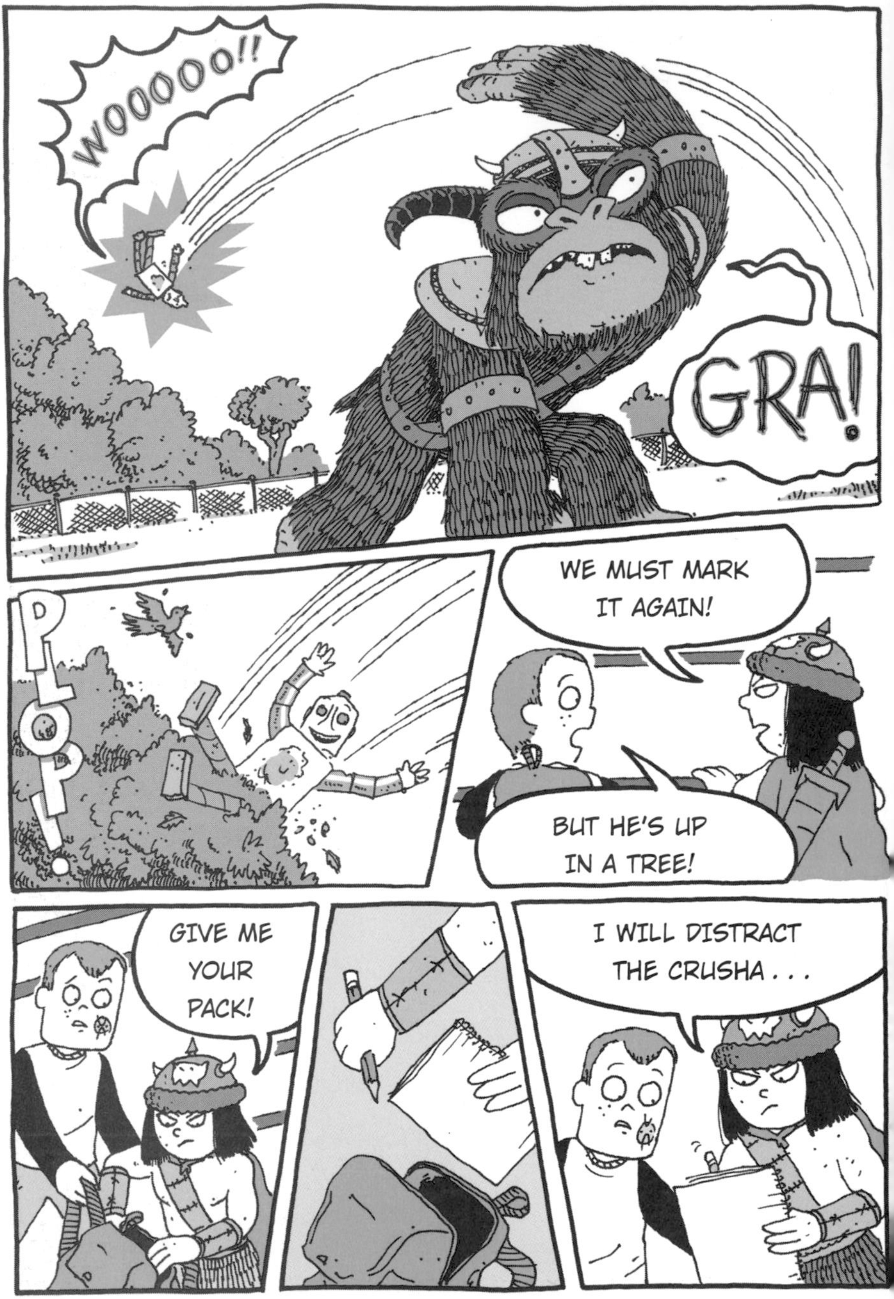
WOOOOOO!!
GRA!
PLOP!
WE MUST MARK IT AGAIN!
BUT HE'S UP IN A TREE!
GIVE ME YOUR PACK!
I WILL DISTRACT THE CRUSHA . . .

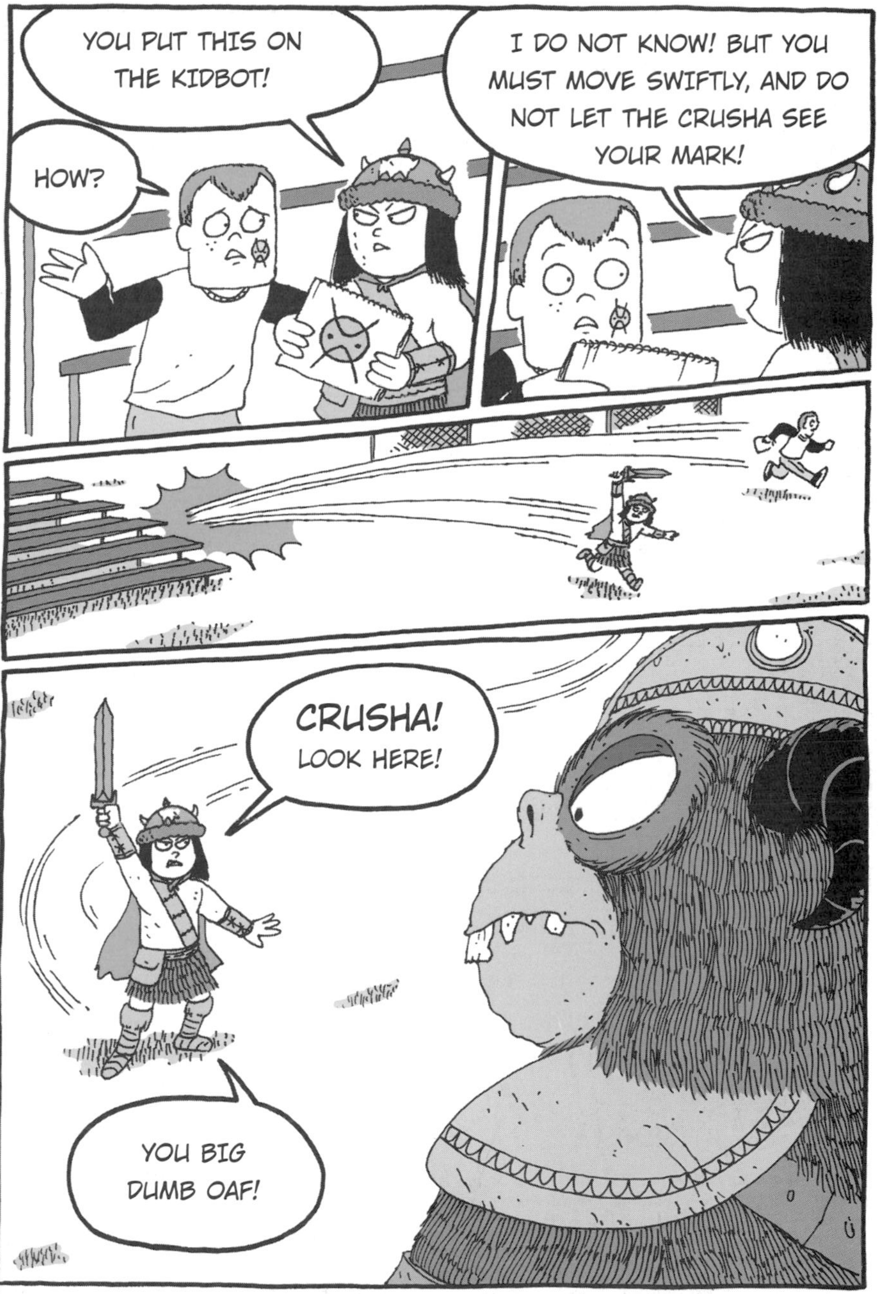
YOU PUT THIS ON THE KIDBOT!
HOW?
I DO NOT KNOW! BUT YOU MUST MOVE SWIFTLY, AND DO NOT LET THE CRUSHA SEE YOUR MARK!
CRUSHA! LOOK HERE!
YOU BIG DUMB OAF!

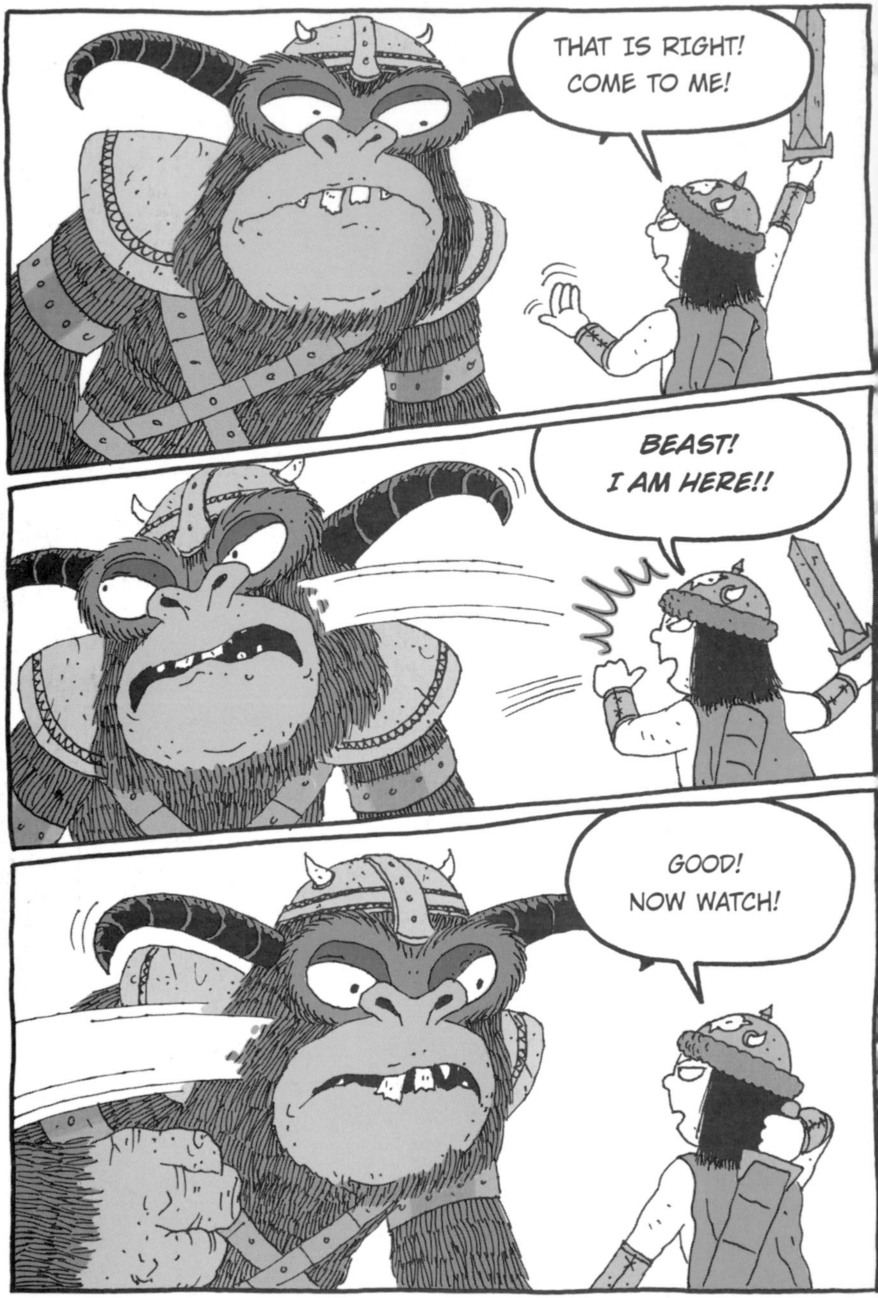
THAT IS RIGHT! COME TO ME!
BEAST! I AM HERE!!
GOOD! NOW WATCH!

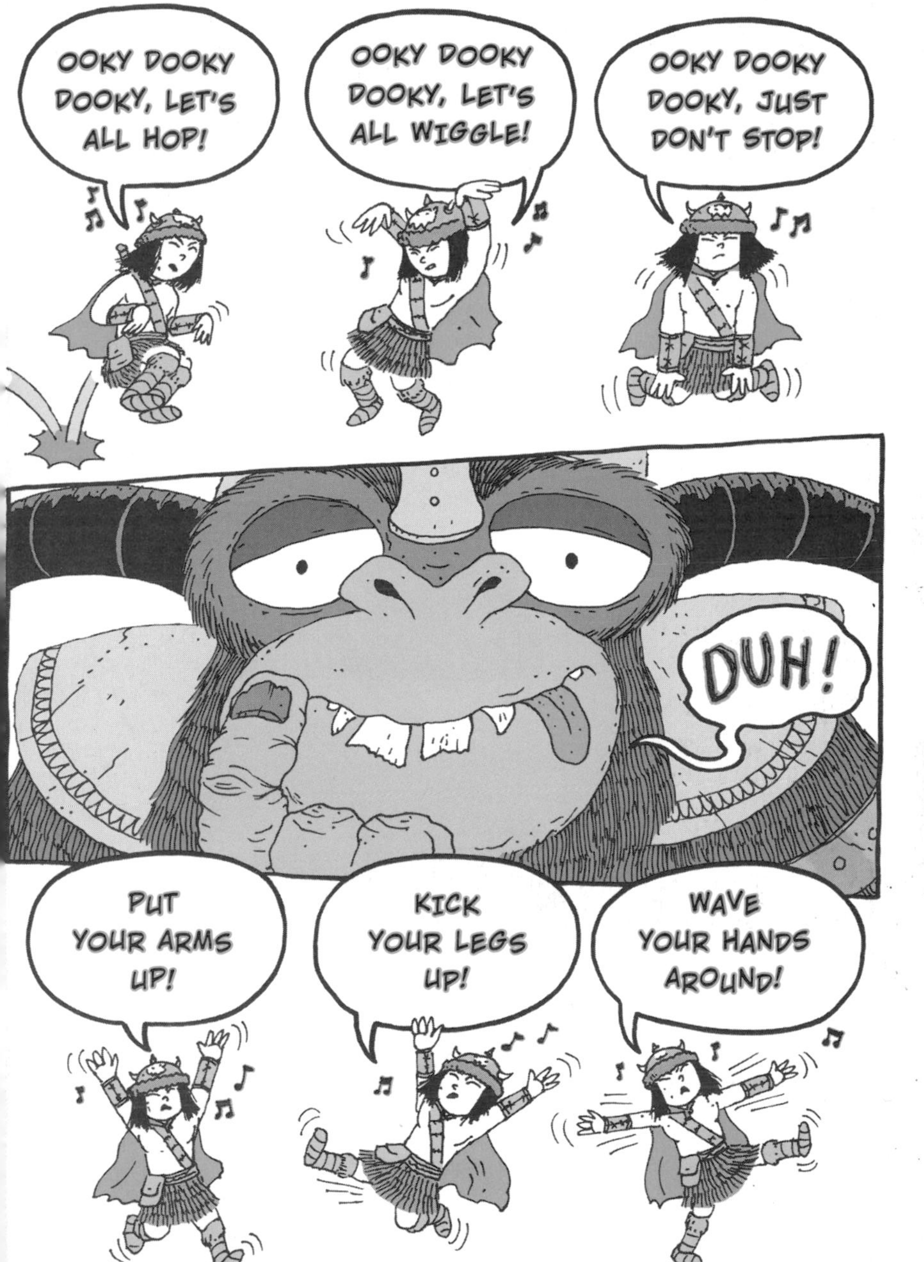
OOKY DOOKY DOOKY, LET'S ALL HOP!
OOKY DOOKY DOOKY, LET'S ALL WIGGLE!
OOKY DOOKY DOOKY, JUST DON'T STOP!
DUH!
PUT YOUR ARMS UP!
KICK YOUR LEGS UP!
WAVE YOUR HANDS AROUND!

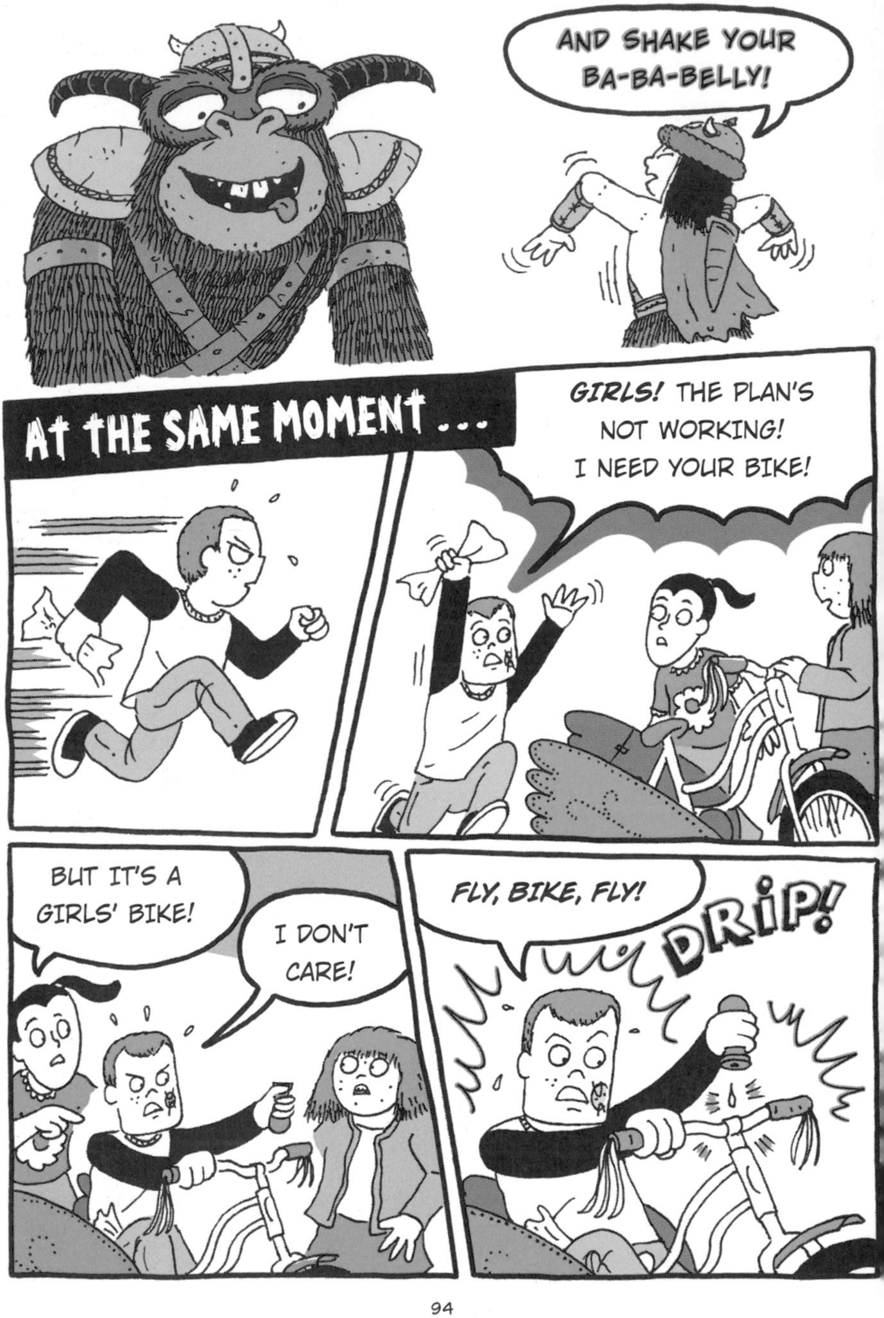
AND SHAKE YOUR BA-BA-BELLY!
AT THE SAME MOMENT . . .
GIRLS! THE PLAN'S NOT WORKING! I NEED YOUR BIKE!
BUT IT'S A GIRLS' BIKE!
I DON'T CARE!
FLY, BIKE, FLY!
DRIP!

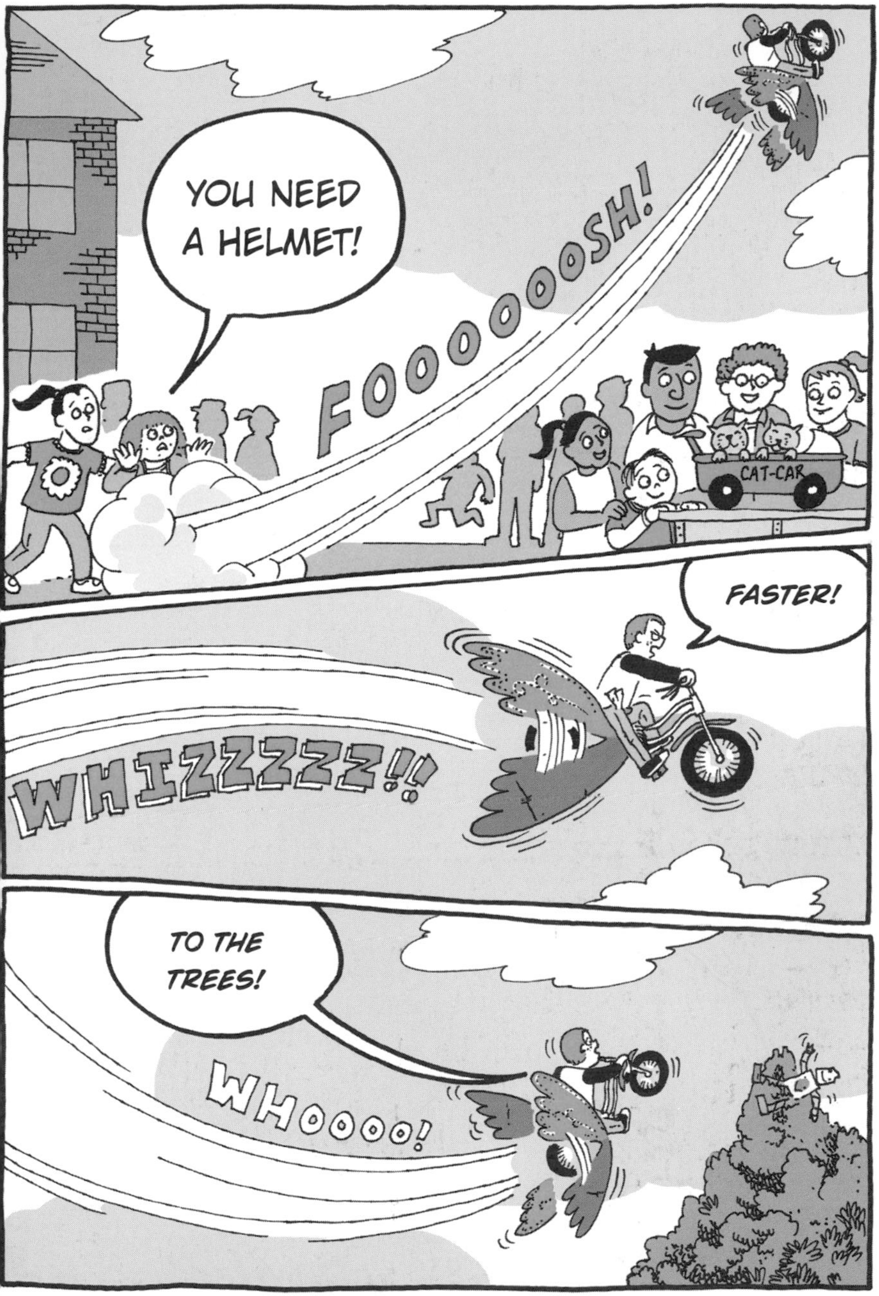
YOU NEED A HELMET!
FOOOOOOSH!
CAT-CAR
FASTER!
WHIZZZZZ!!
TO THE TREES!
WHOOOO!

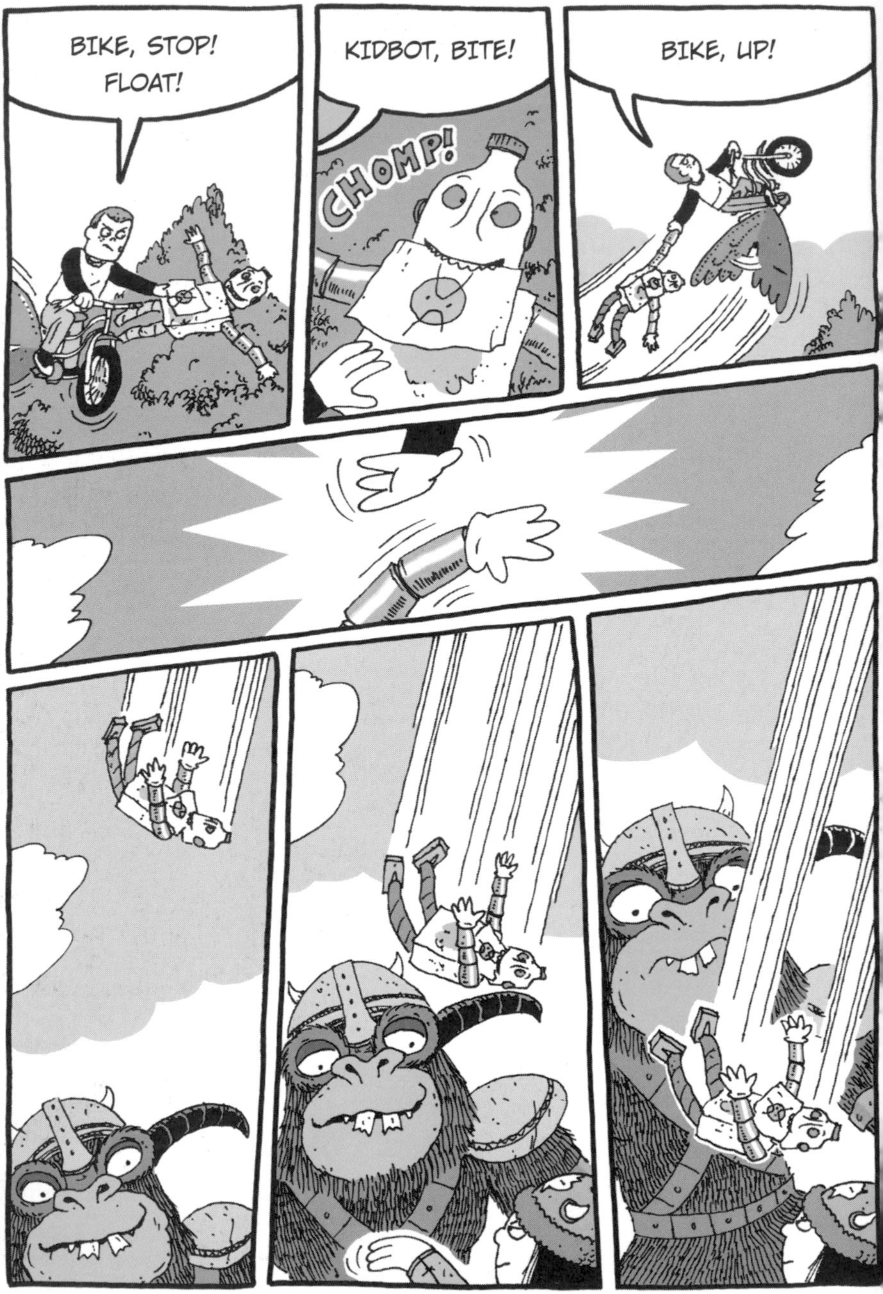
BIKE, STOP! FLOAT!
KIDBOT, BITE!
CHOMP!
BIKE, UP!

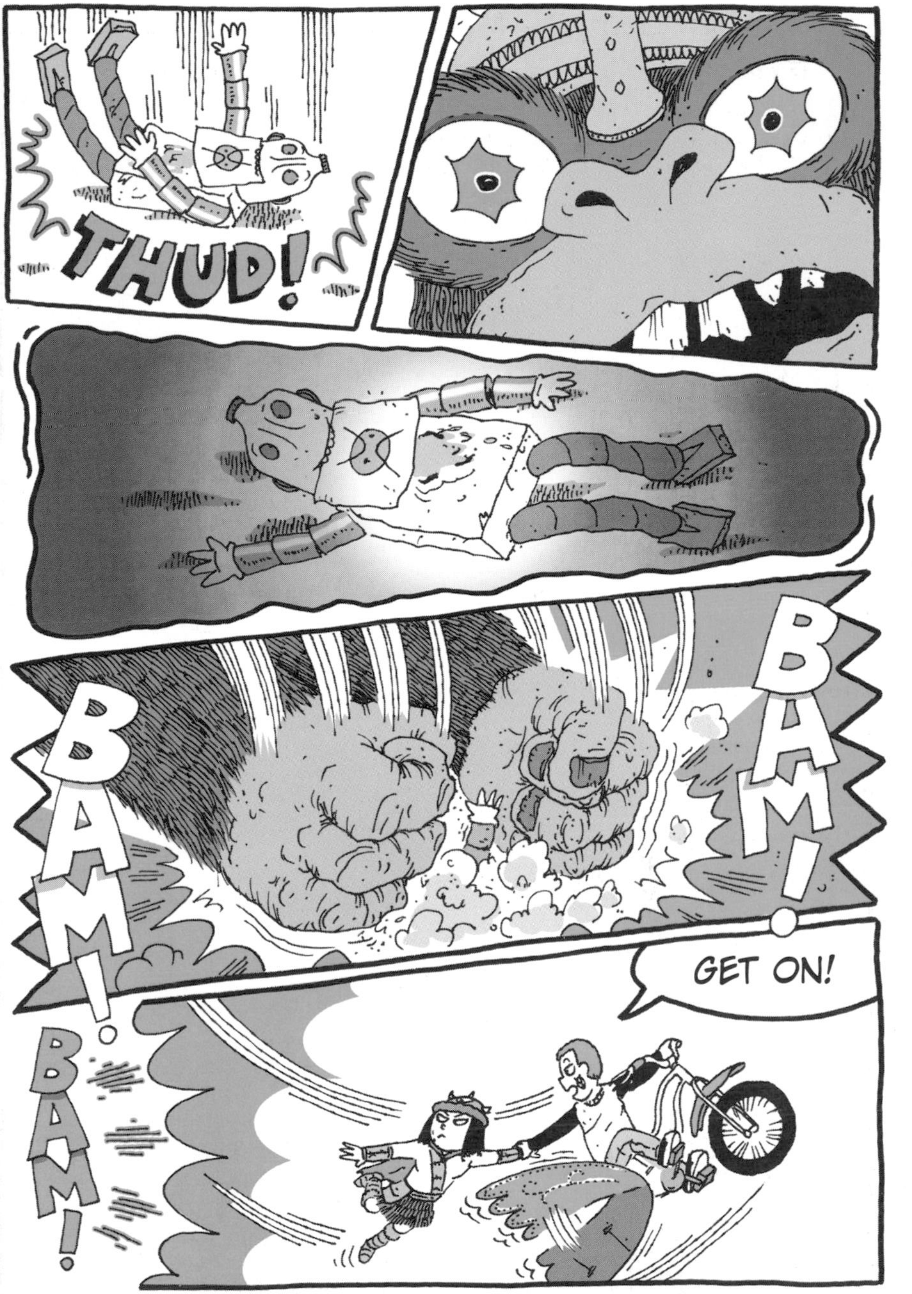
THUD!
BAM!
BAM!
BAM!
GET ON!

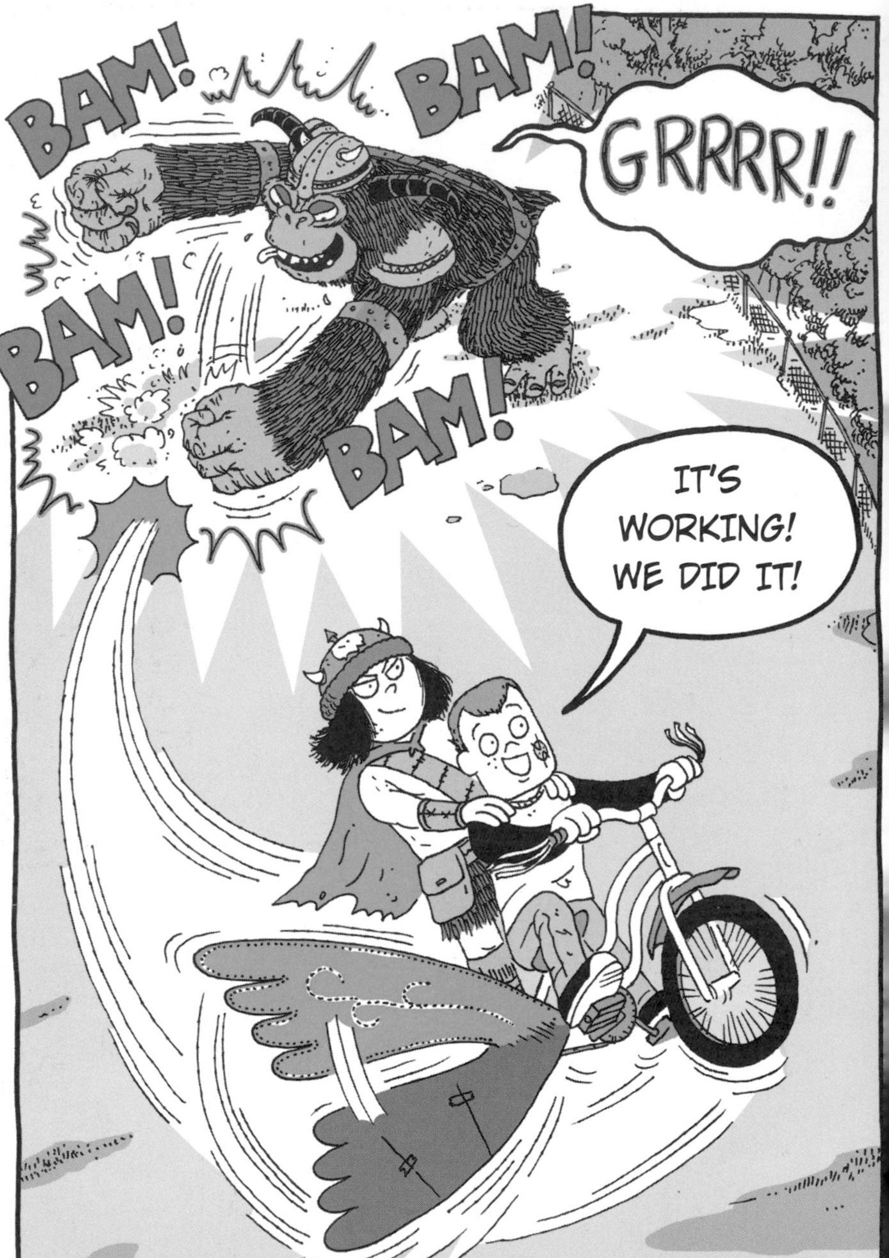
BAM!
BAM!
GRRRR!!
BAM!
BAM!
IT'S WORKING! WE DID IT!

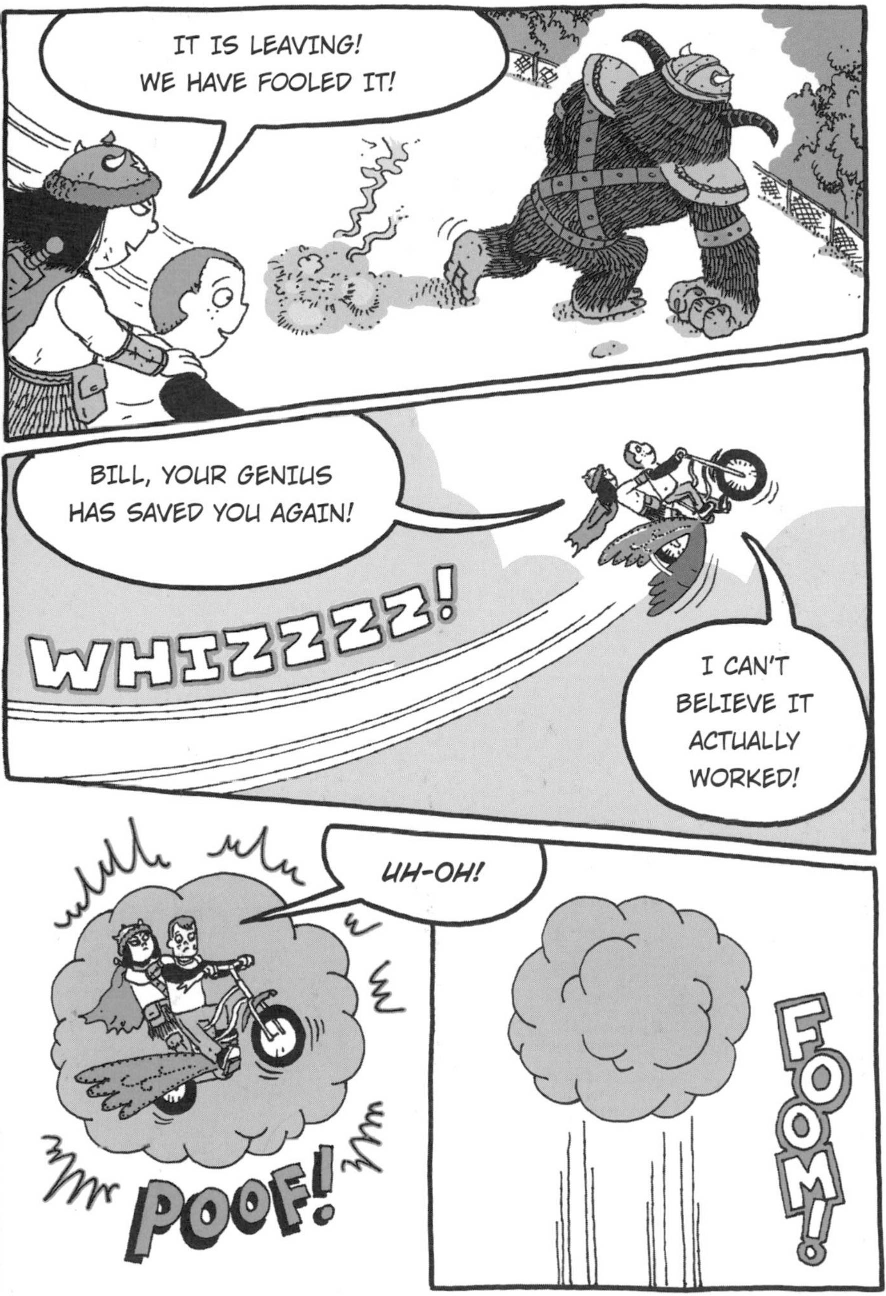
IT IS LEAVING! WE HAVE FOOLED IT!
BILL, YOUR GENIUS HAS SAVED YOU AGAIN!
WHIZZZZZ!
I CAN'T BELIEVE IT ACTUALLY WORKED!
UH-OH!
POOF!
FOOM!

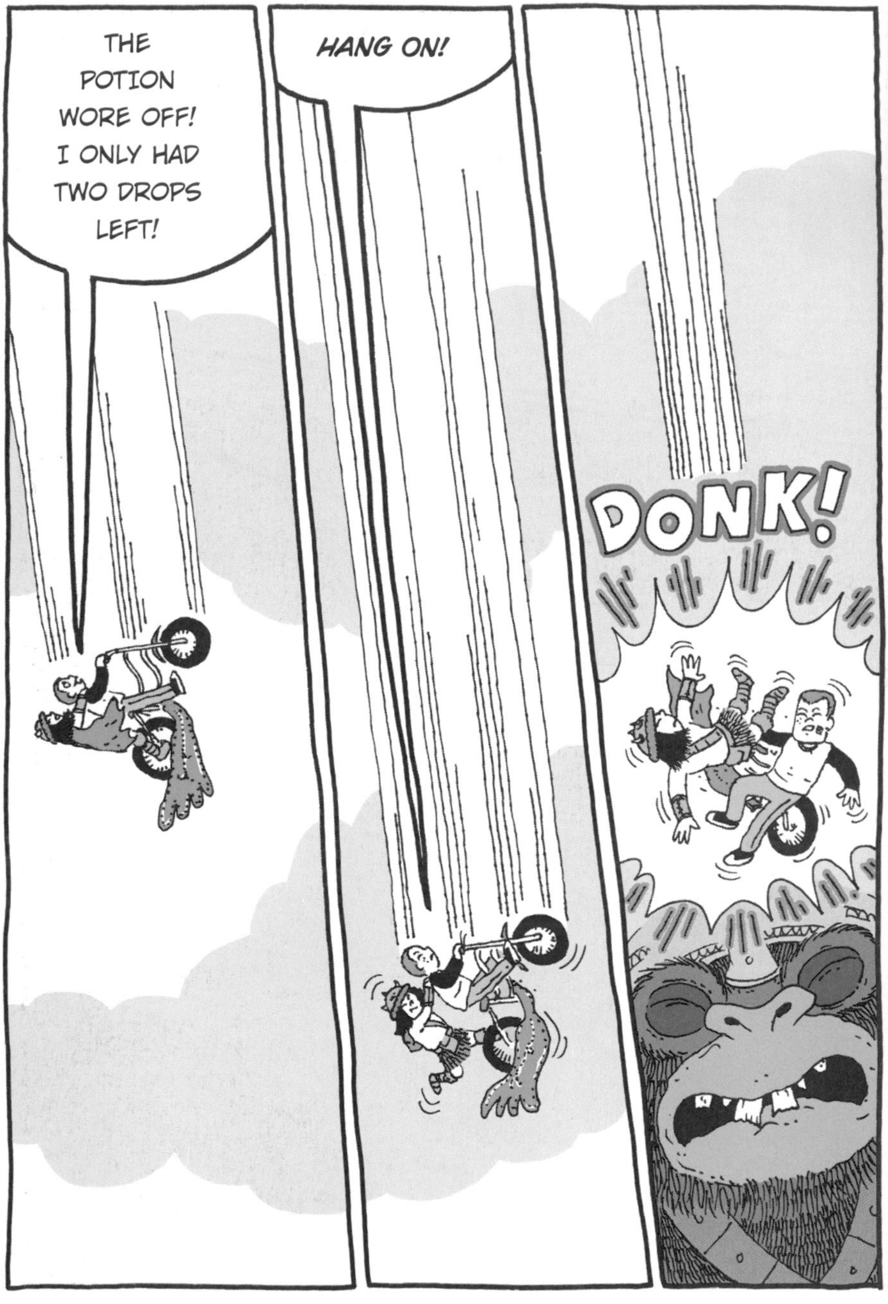
THE POTION WORE OFF! I ONLY HAD TWO DROPS LEFT!
HANG ON!
DONK!

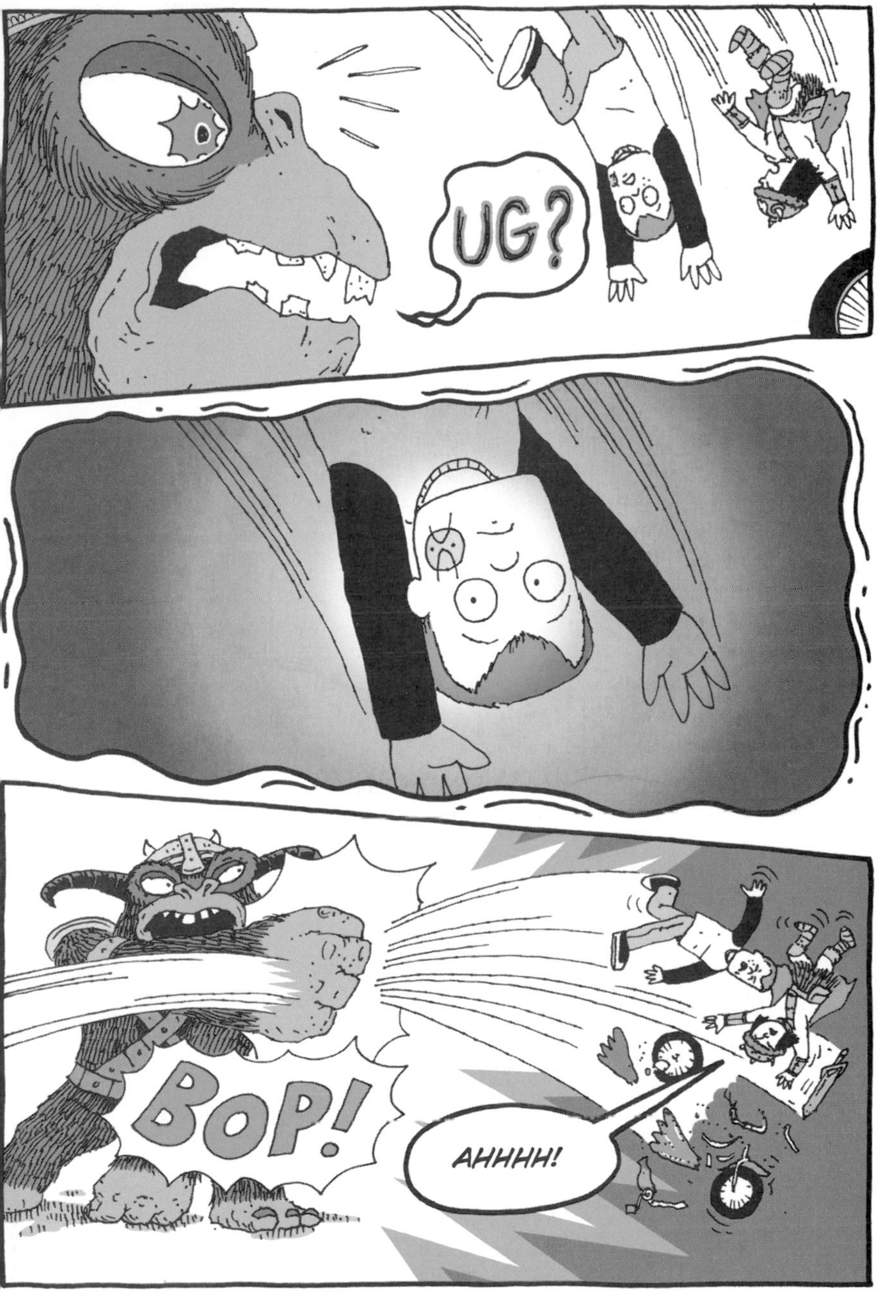
UG?
BOP!
AHHHH!

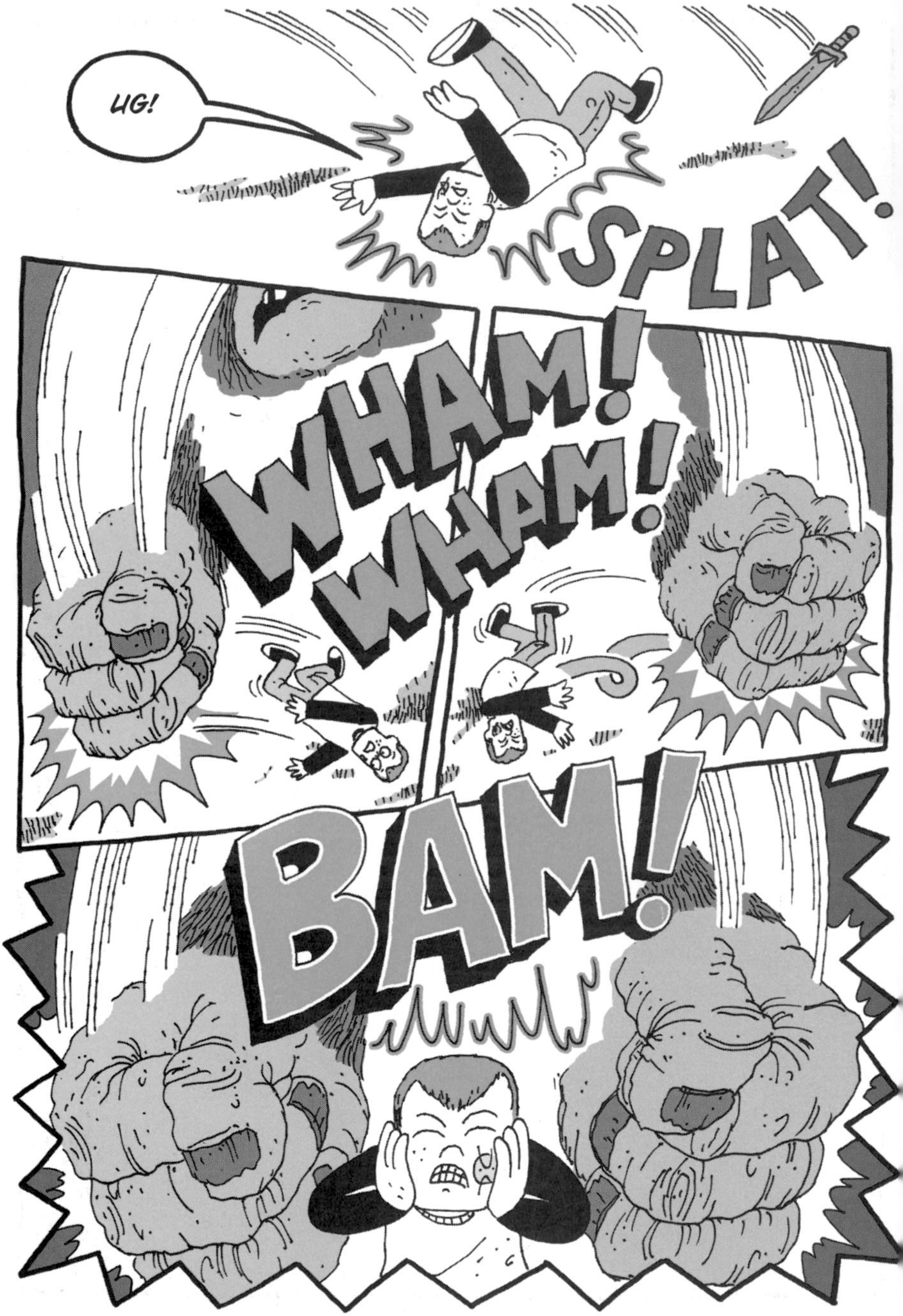
UG!
SPLAT!
WHAM!
WHAM!
BAM!

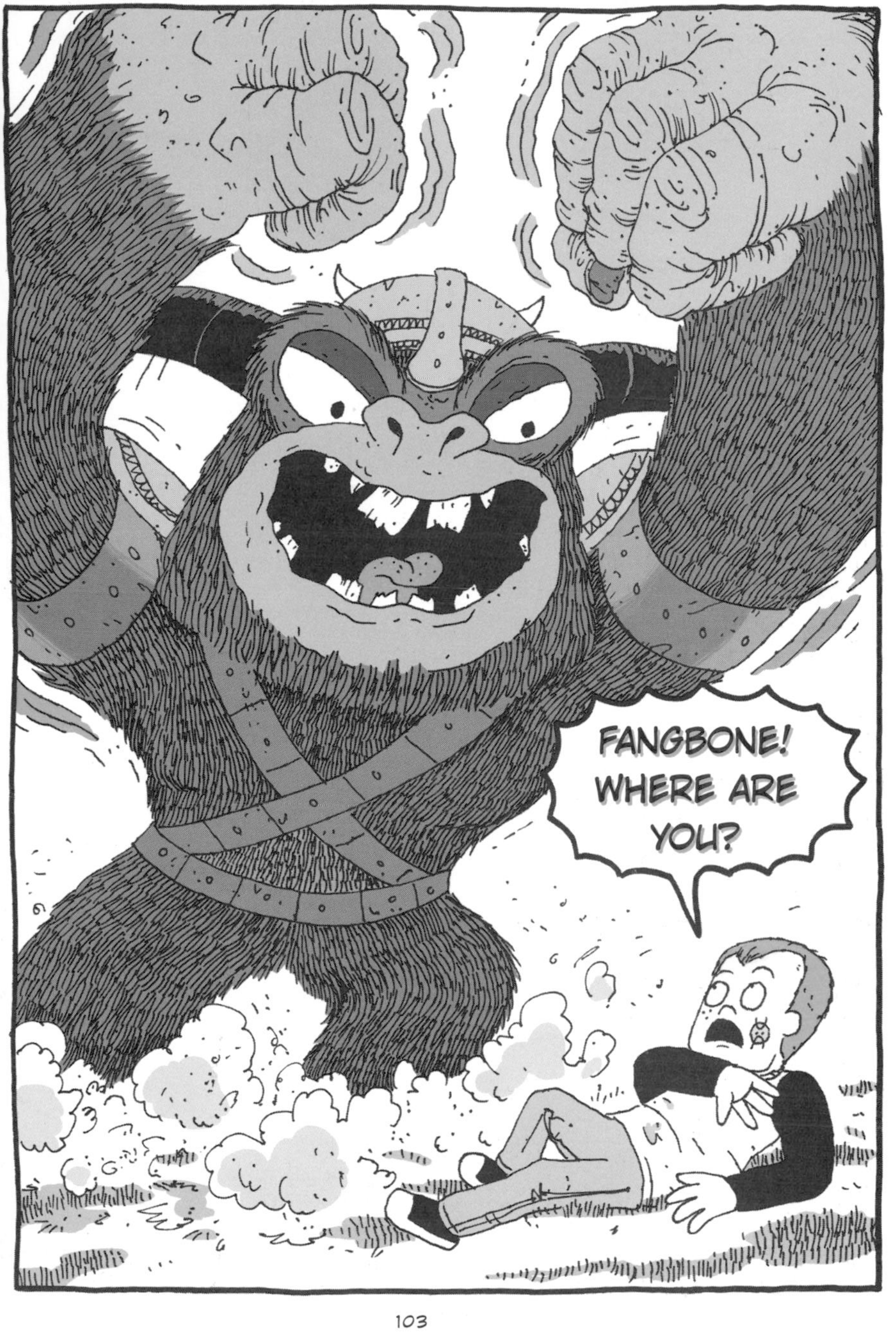
FANGBONE! WHERE ARE YOU?

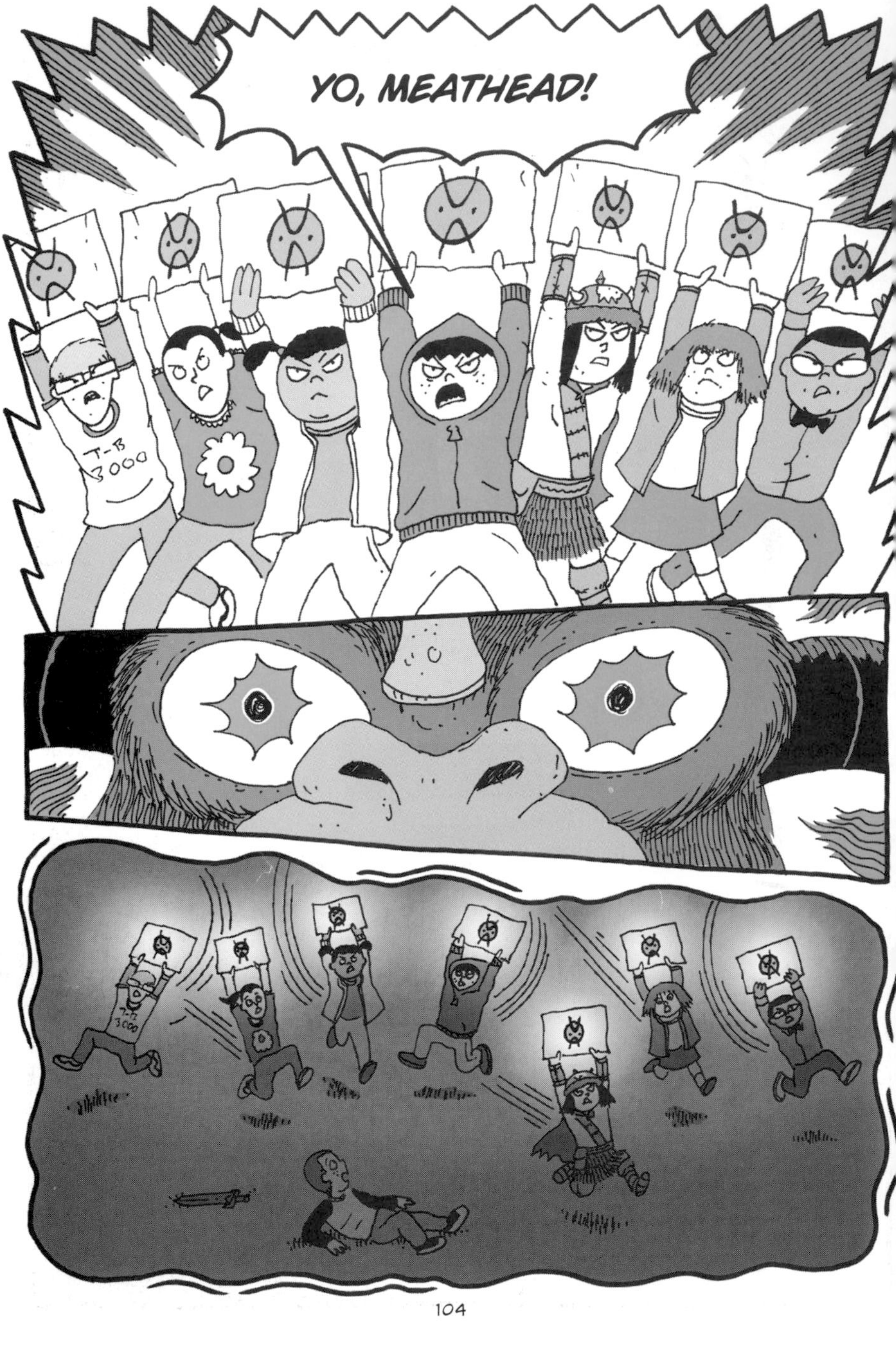
YO, MEATHEAD!
T-B 3000

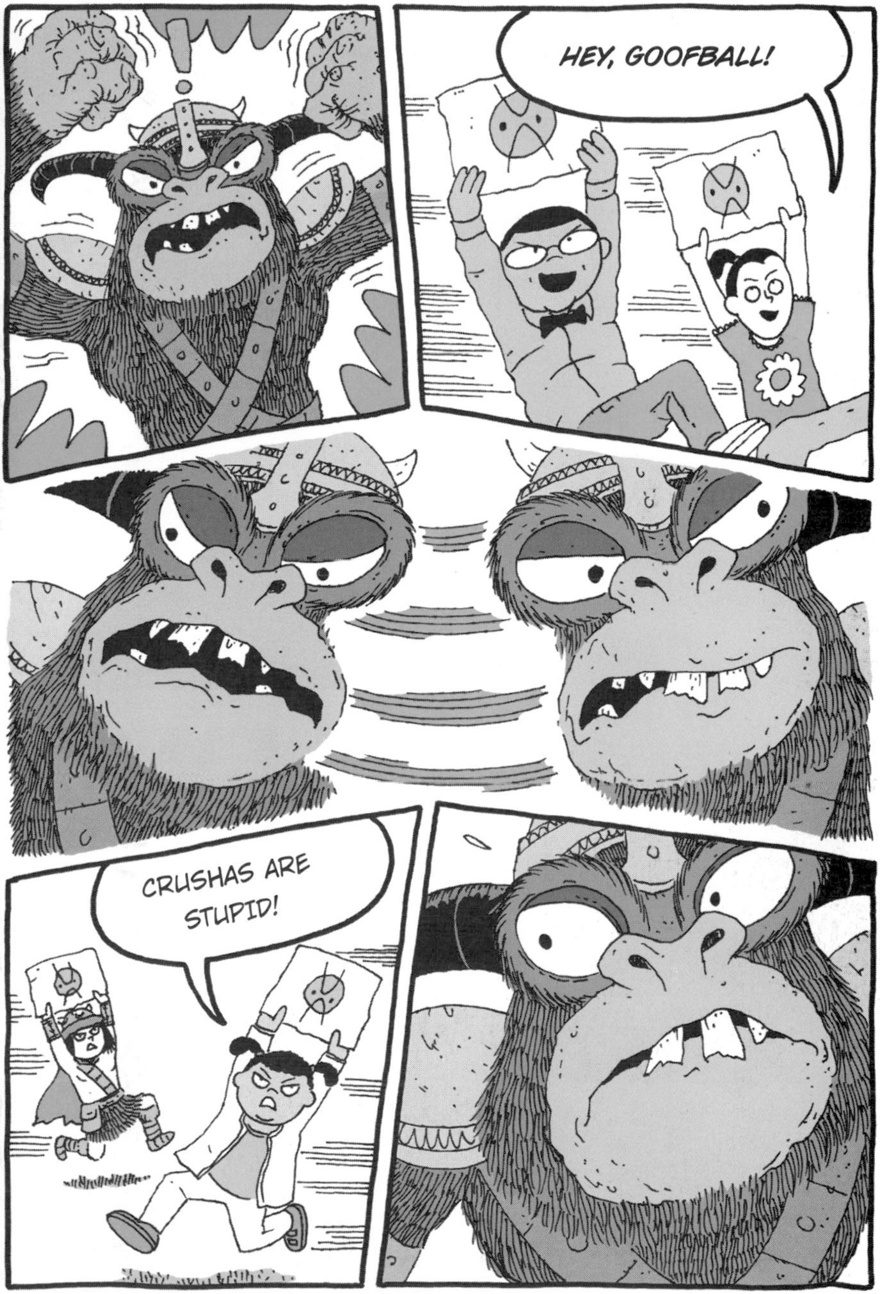
HEY, GOOFBALL!
CRUSHAS ARE STUPID!

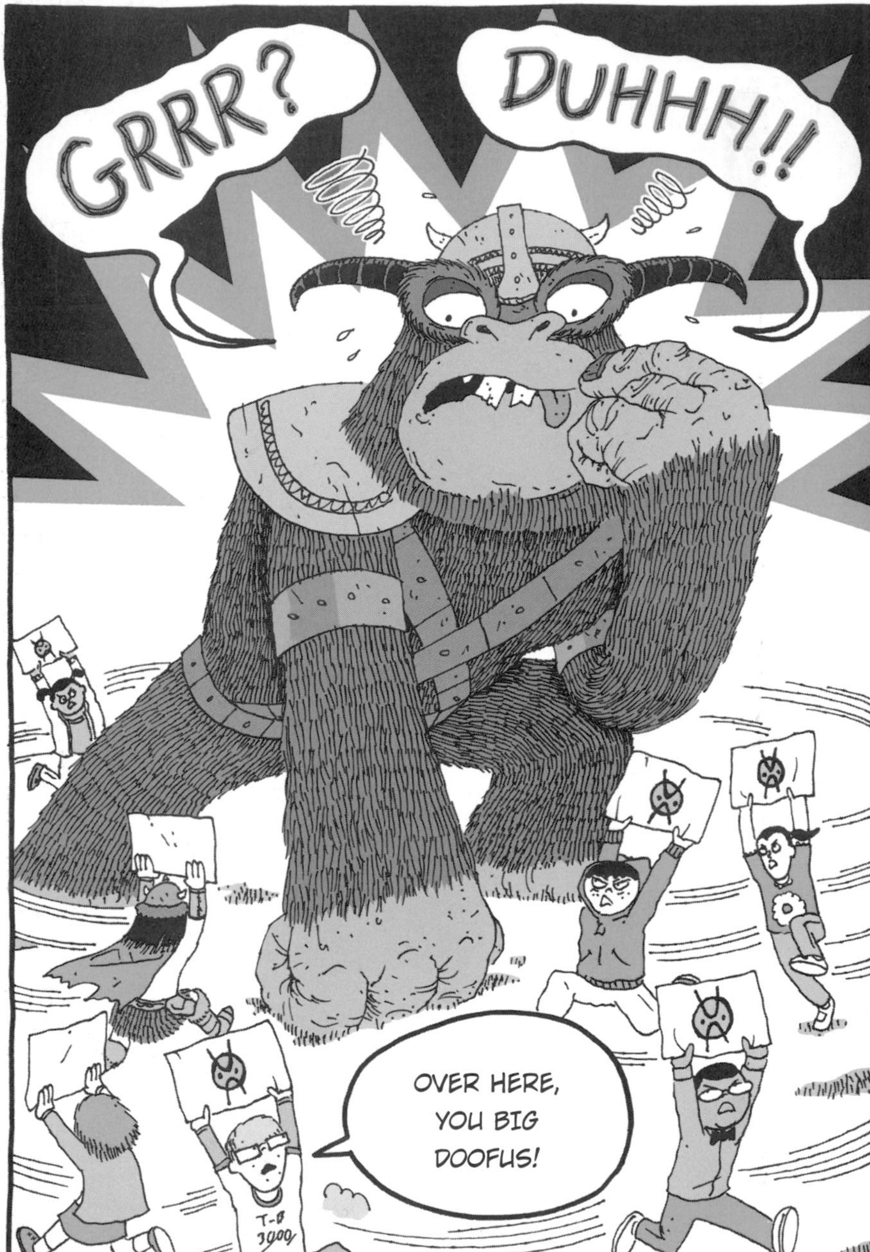
GRRR?
DUHHH!!
OVER HERE, YOU BIG DOOFUS!
T-B 3000

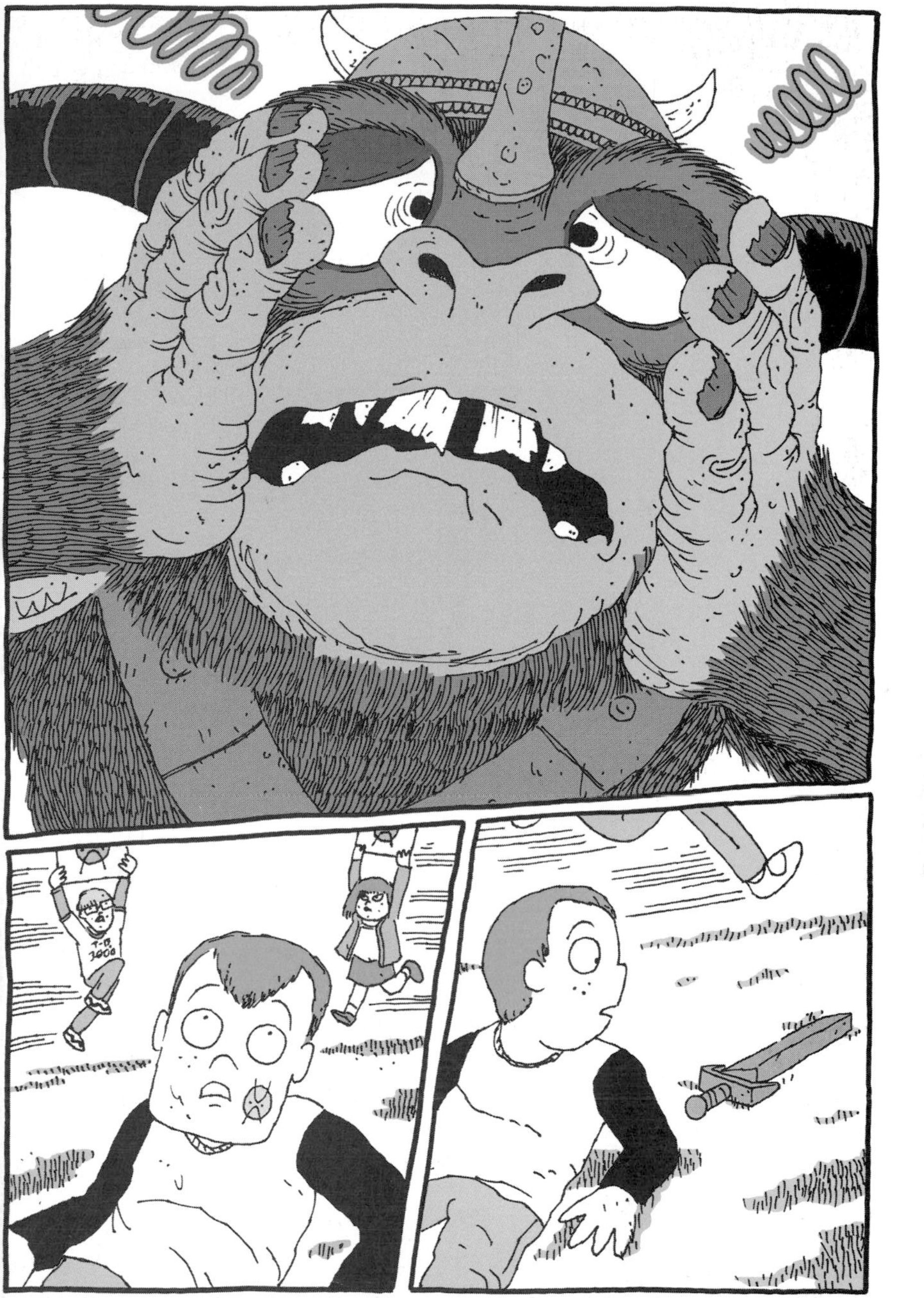

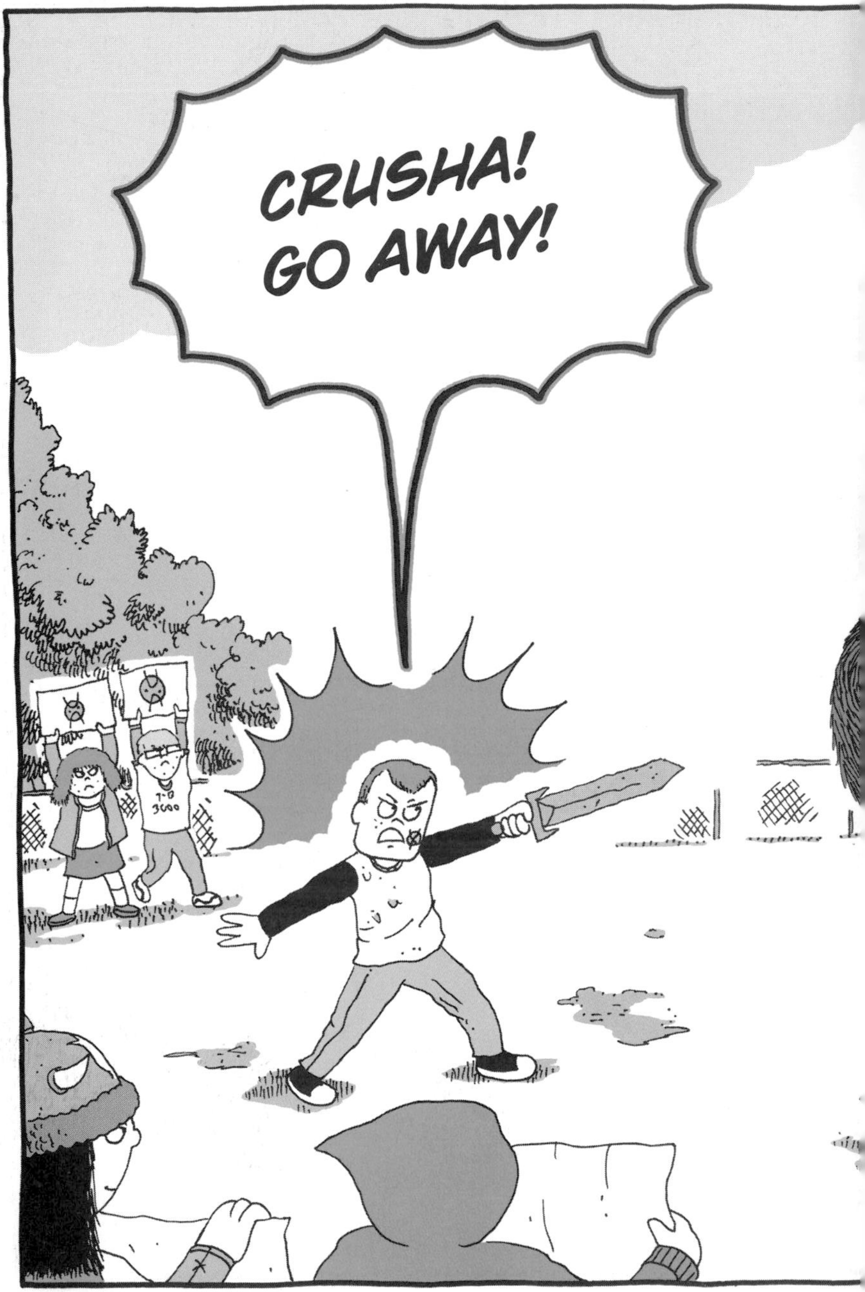
CRUSHA! GO AWAY!
T-B 3000

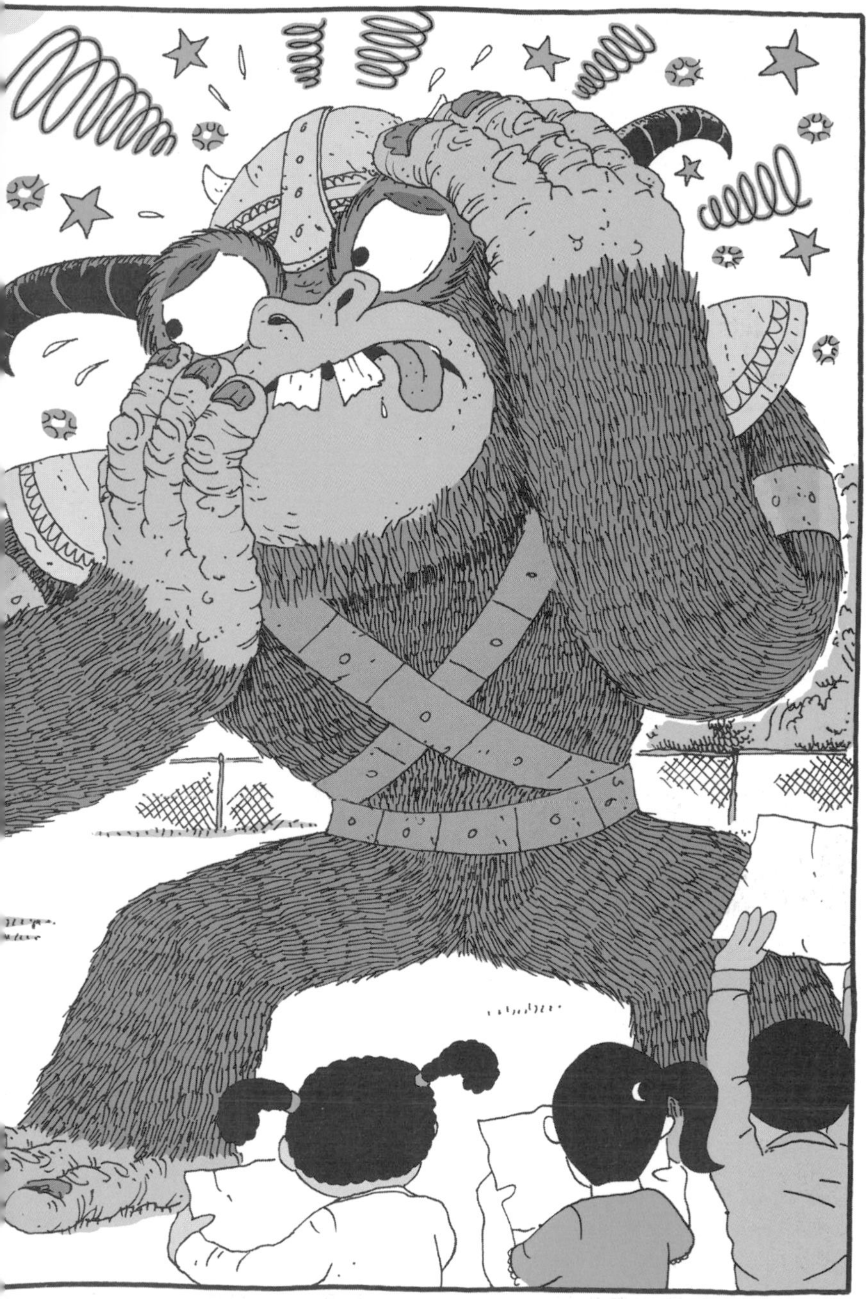

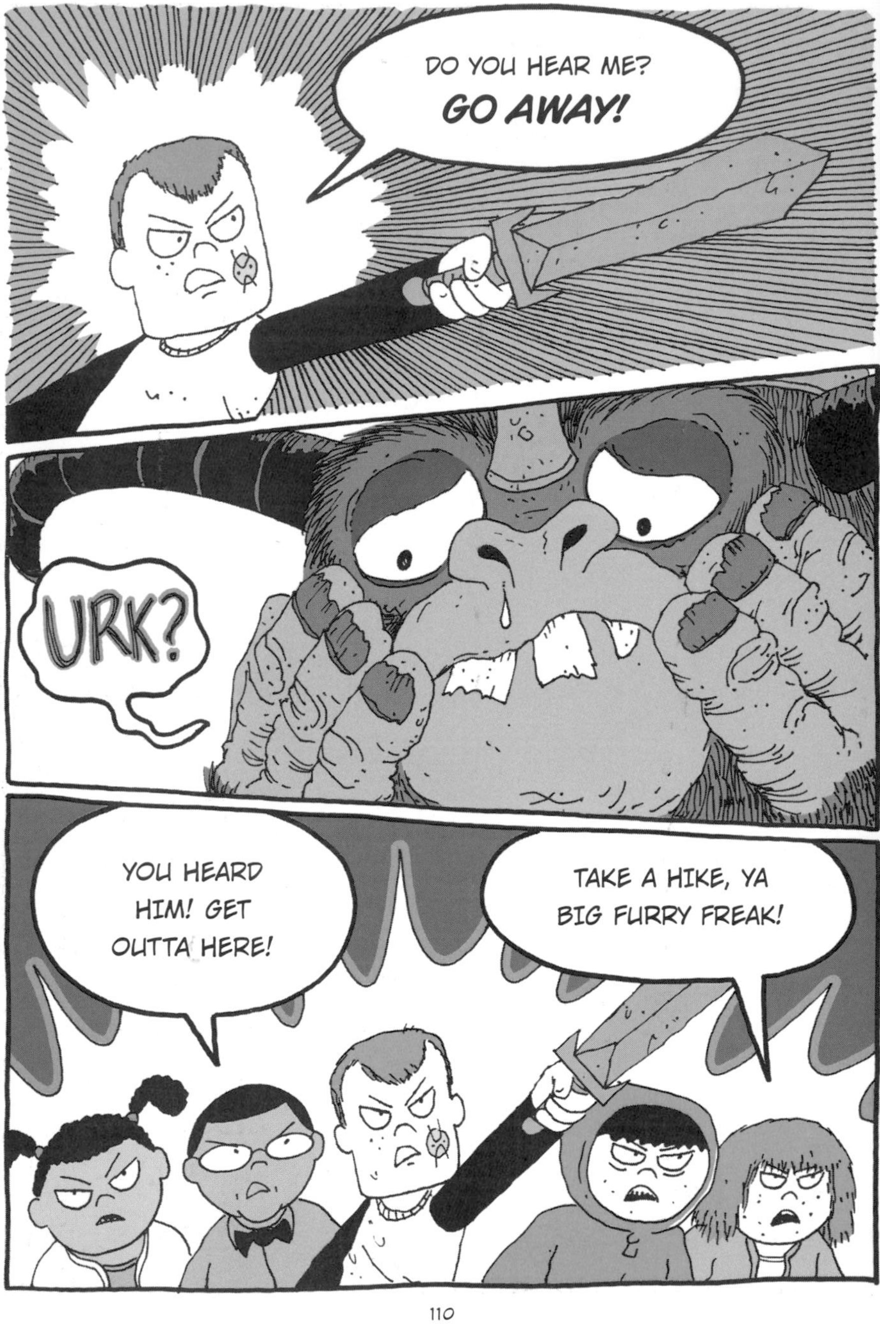
DO YOU HEAR ME?
GO AWAY!
URK?
YOU HEARD HIM! GET OUTTA HERE!
TAKE A HIKE, YA BIG FURRY FREAK!

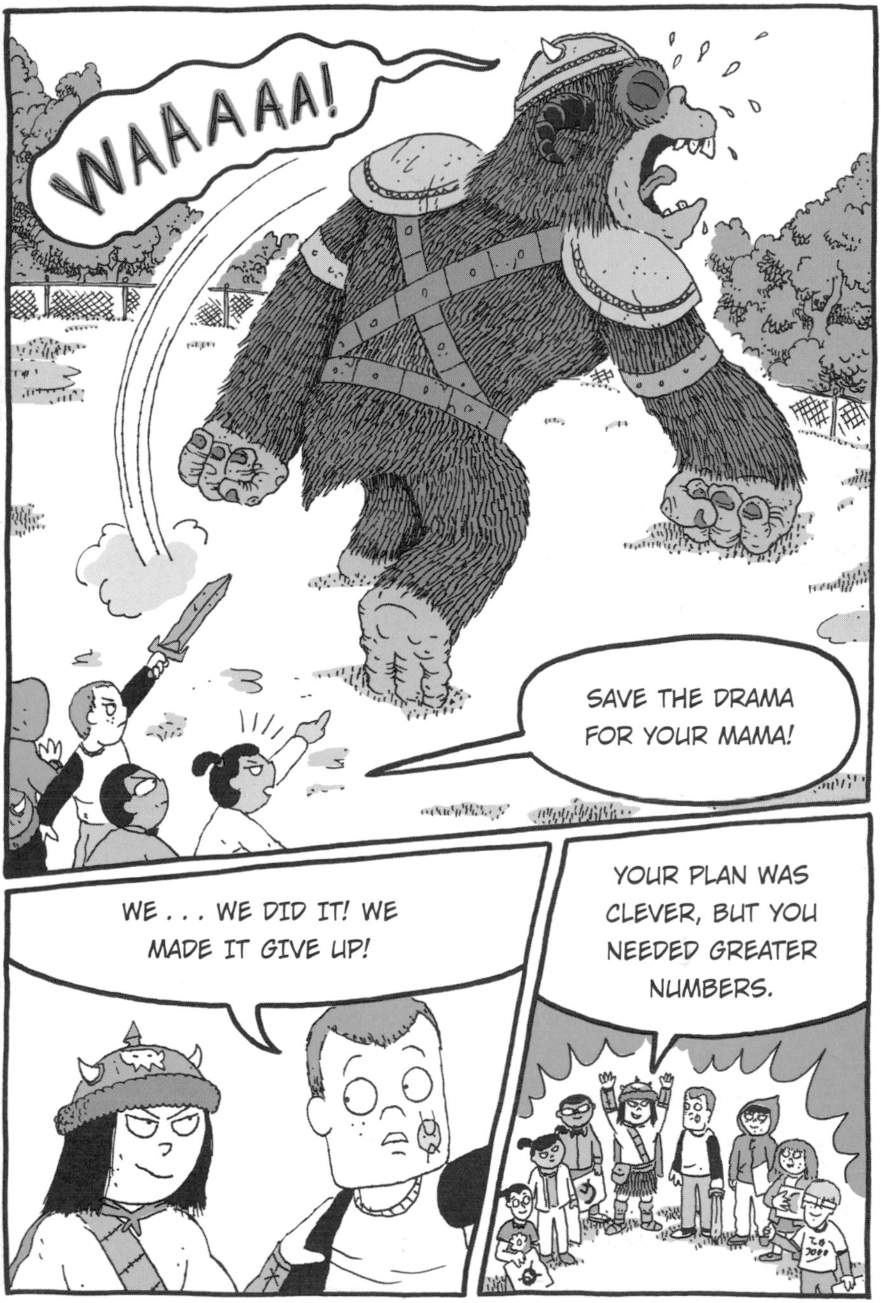
WAAAAAA!
SAVE THE DRAMA FOR YOUR MAMA!
WE . . . WE DID IT! WE MADE IT GIVE UP!
YOUR PLAN WAS CLEVER, BUT YOU NEEDED GREATER NUMBERS.

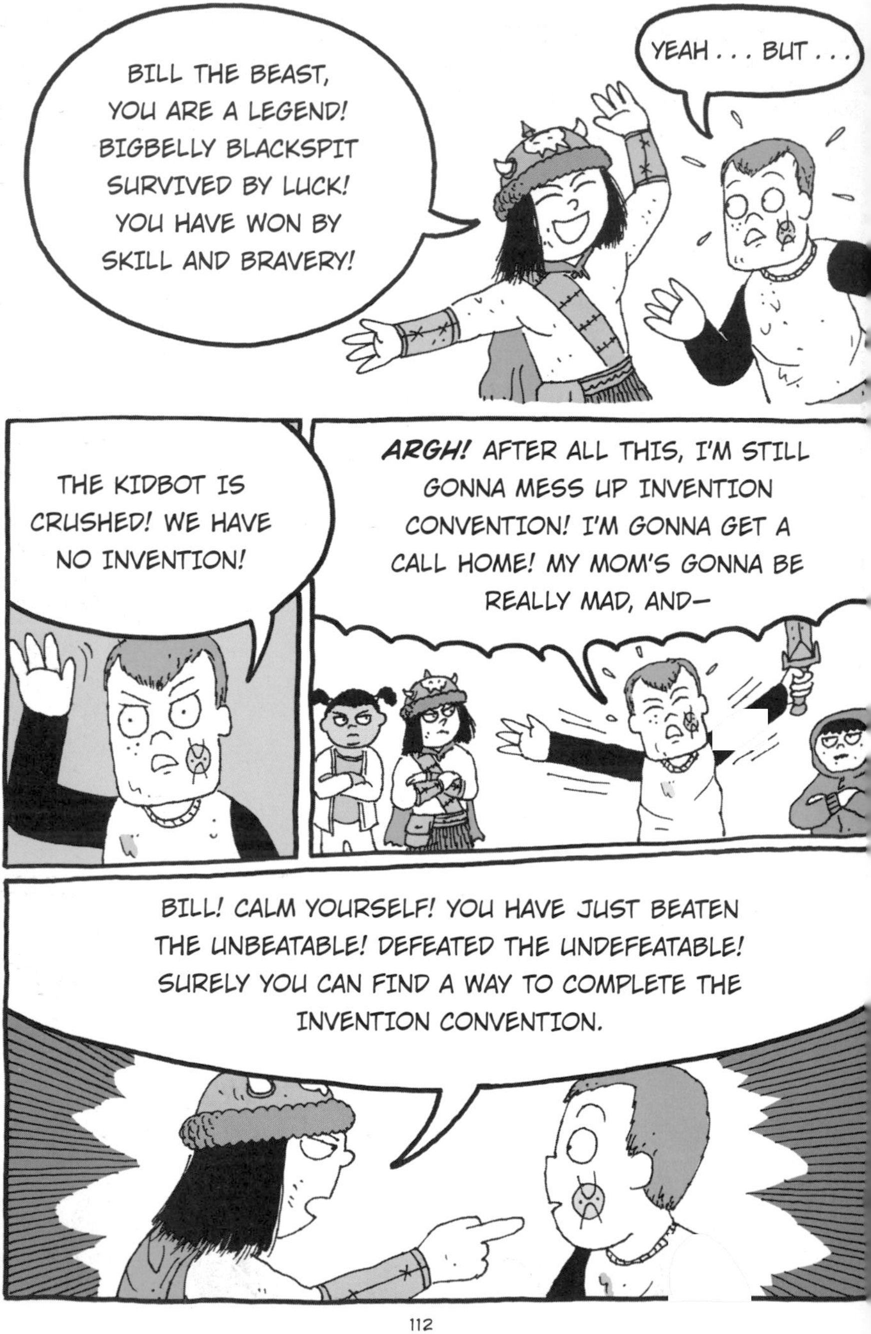
BILL THE BEAST, YOU ARE A LEGEND! BIGBELLY BLACKSPIT SURVIVED BY LUCK! YOU HAVE WON BY SKILL AND BRAVERY!
YEAH . . . BUT . . .
THE KIDBOT IS CRUSHED! WE HAVE NO INVENTION!
ARGH! AFTER ALL THIS, I'M STILL GONNA MESS UP INVENTION CONVENTION! I'M GONNA GET A CALL HOME! MY MOM'S GONNA BE REALLY MAD, AND—
BILL! CALM YOURSELF! YOU HAVE JUST BEATEN THE UNBEATABLE! DEFEATED THE UNDEFEATABLE! SURELY YOU CAN FIND A WAY TO COMPLETE THE INVENTION CONVENTION.

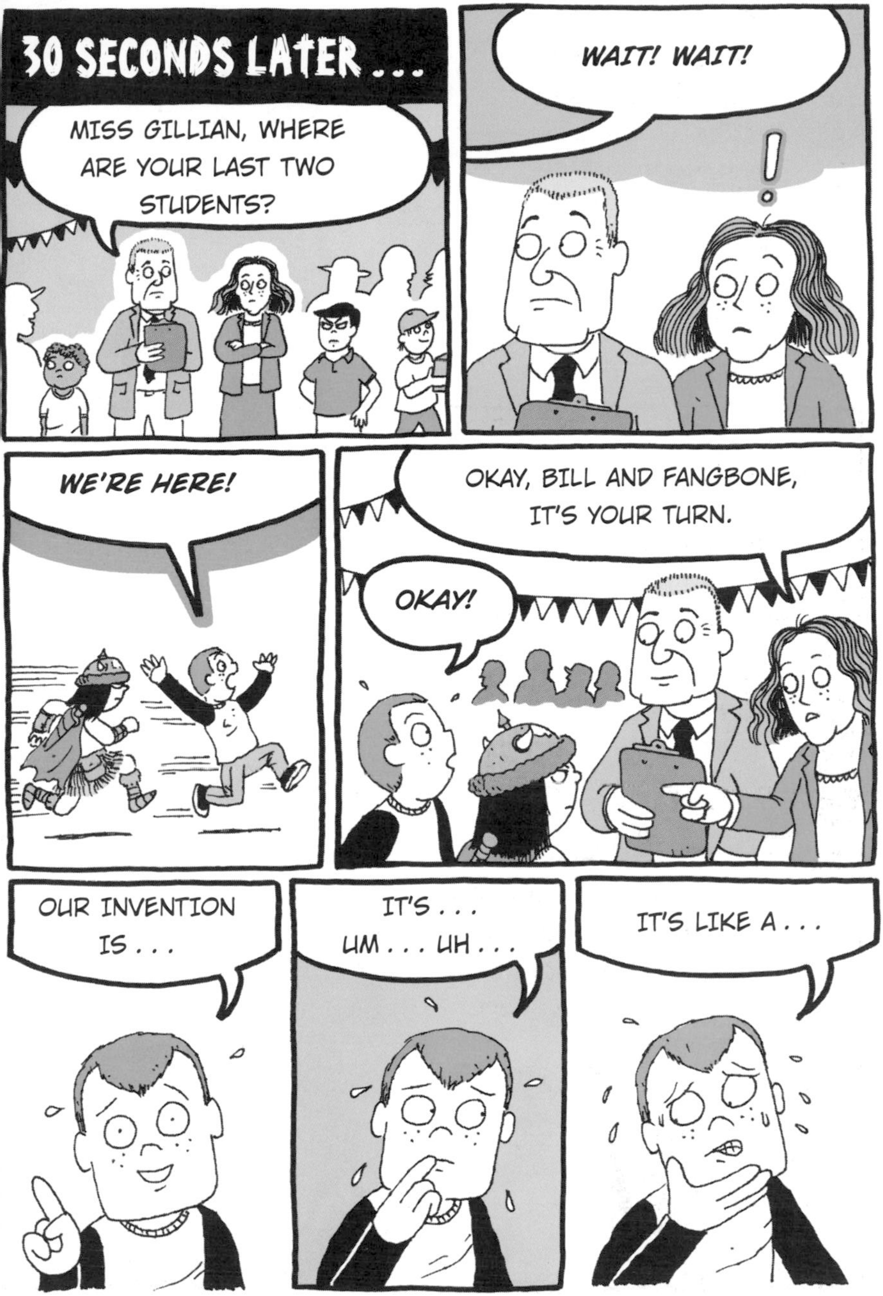
30 SECONDS LATER . . .
MISS GILLIAN, WHERE ARE YOUR LAST TWO STUDENTS?
WAIT! WAIT!
!
WE'RE HERE!
OKAY, BILL AND FANGBONE, IT'S YOUR TURN.
OKAY!
OUR INVENTION IS . . .
IT'S . . . UM . . . UH . . .
IT'S LIKE A . . .

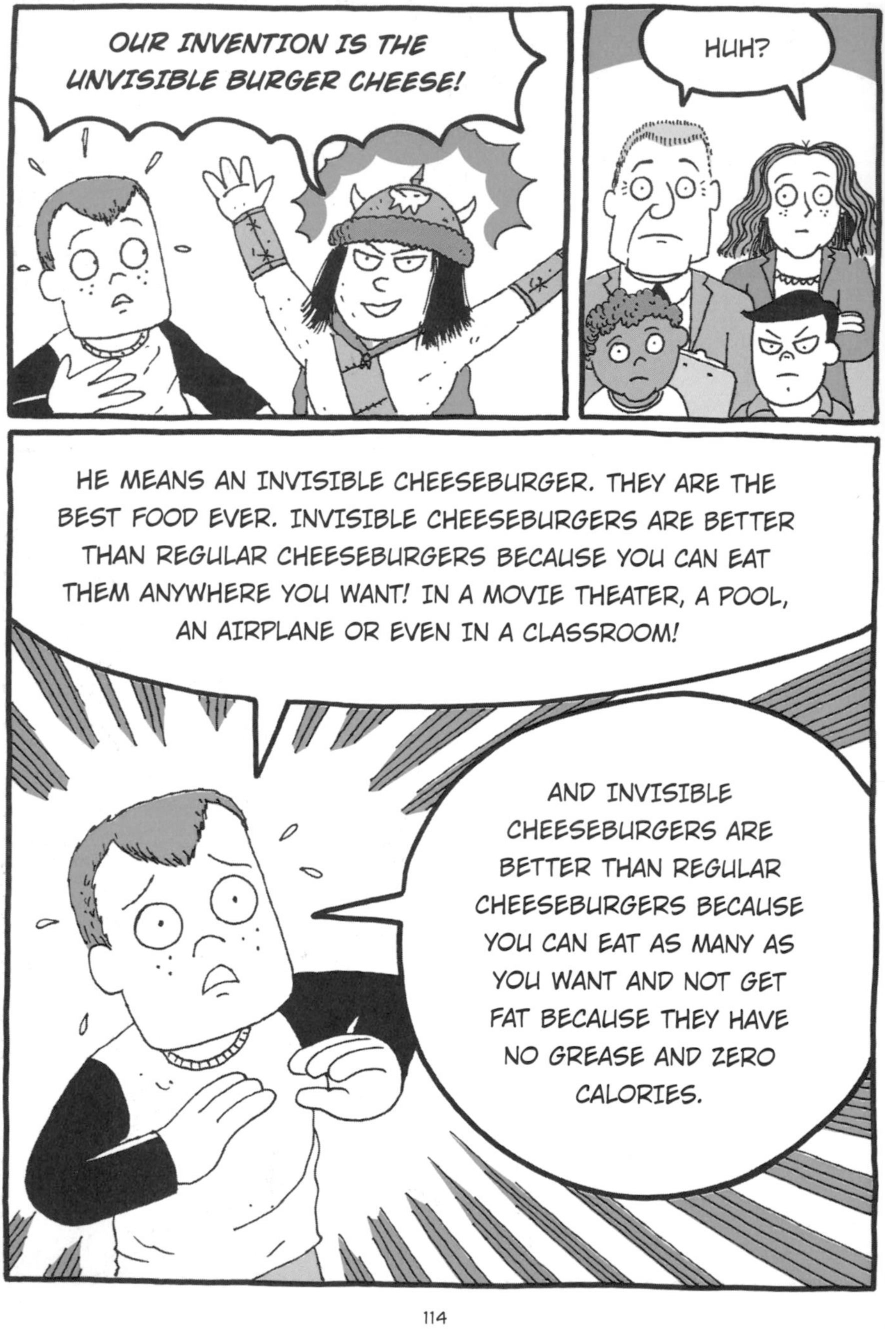
OUR INVENTION IS THE UNVISIBLE BURGER CHEESE!
HUH?
HE MEANS AN INVISIBLE CHEESEBURGER. THEY ARE THE BEST FOOD EVER. INVISIBLE CHEESEBURGERS ARE BETTER THAN REGULAR CHEESEBURGERS BECAUSE YOU CAN EAT THEM ANYWHERE YOU WANT! IN A MOVIE THEATER, A POOL, AN AIRPLANE OR EVEN IN A CLASSROOM!
AND INVISIBLE CHEESEBURGERS ARE BETTER THAN REGULAR CHEESEBURGERS BECAUSE YOU CAN EAT AS MANY AS YOU WANT AND NOT GET FAT BECAUSE THEY HAVE NO GREASE AND ZERO CALORIES.

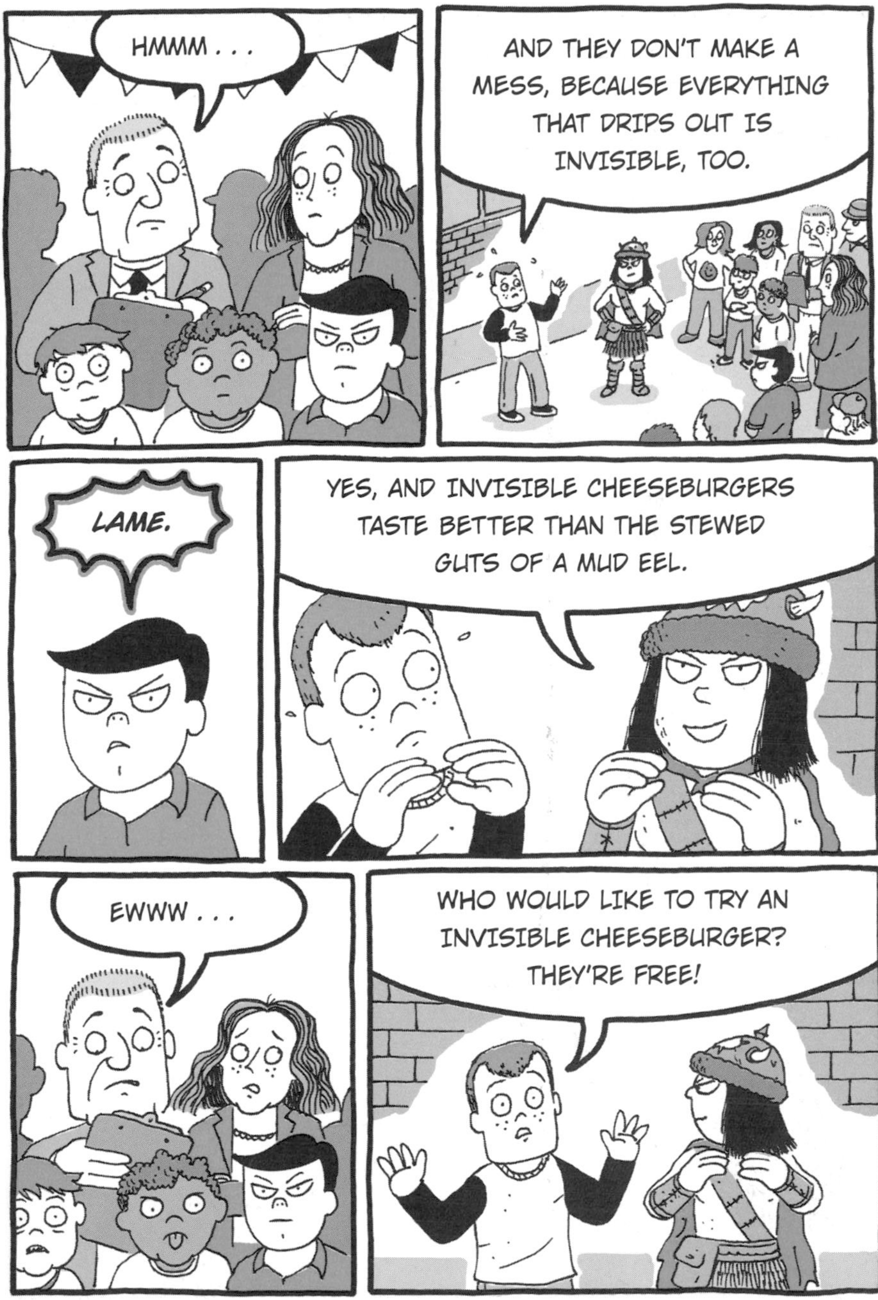
HMMM . . .
AND THEY DON'T MAKE A MESS, BECAUSE EVERYTHING THAT DRIPS OUT IS INVISIBLE, TOO.
LAME.
YES, AND INVISIBLE CHEESEBURGERS TASTE BETTER THAN THE STEWED GUTS OF A MUD EEL.
EWWW . . .
WHO WOULD LIKE TO TRY AN INVISIBLE CHEESEBURGER? THEY'RE FREE!

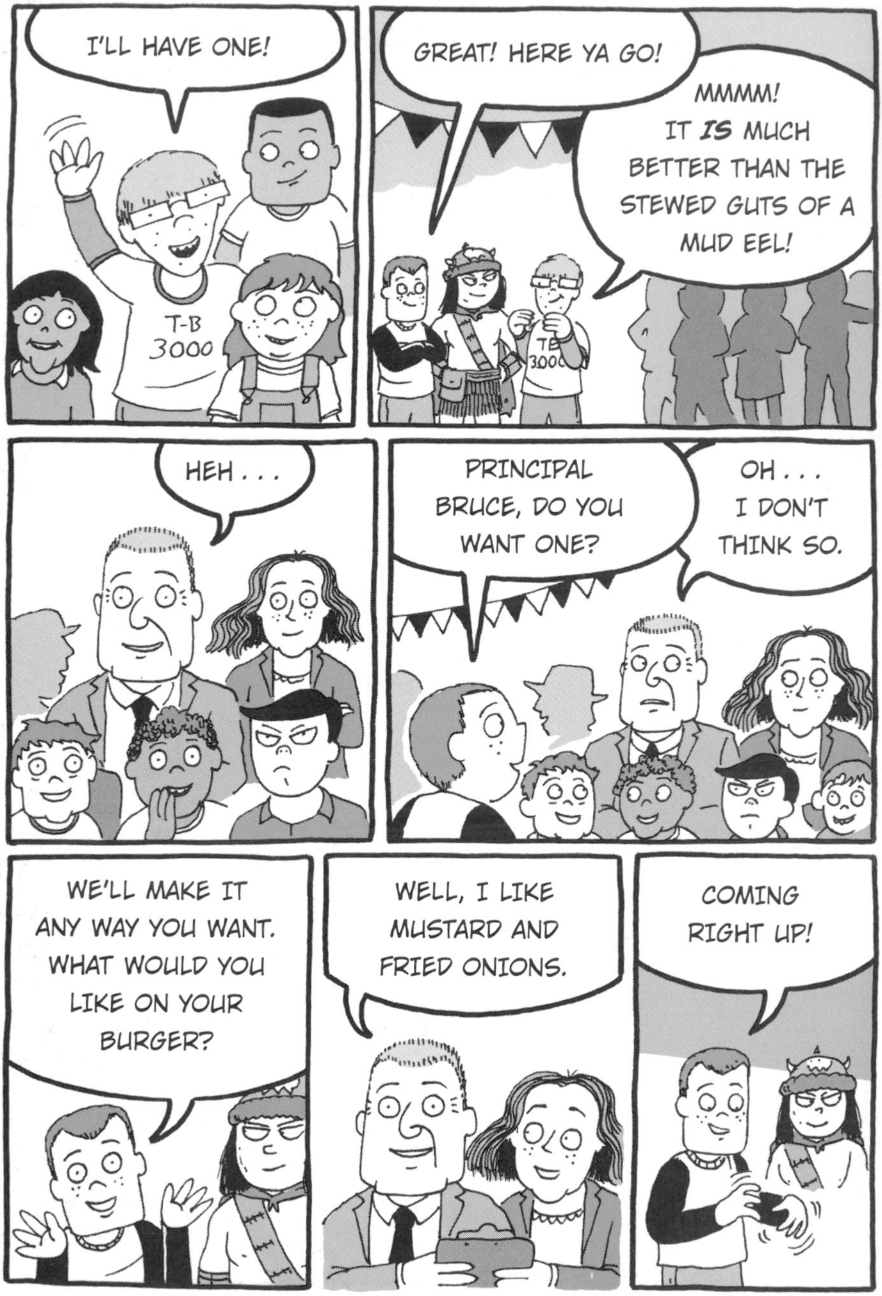
I'LL HAVE ONE!
T-B 3000
GREAT! HERE YA GO!
MMMM! IT IS MUCH BETTER THAN THE STEWED GUTS OF A MUD EEL!
HEH . . .
PRINCIPAL BRUCE, DO YOU WANT ONE?
OH . . . I DON'T THINK SO.
WE'LL MAKE IT ANY WAY YOU WANT. WHAT WOULD YOU LIKE ON YOUR BURGER?
WELL, I LIKE MUSTARD AND FRIED ONIONS.
COMING RIGHT UP!

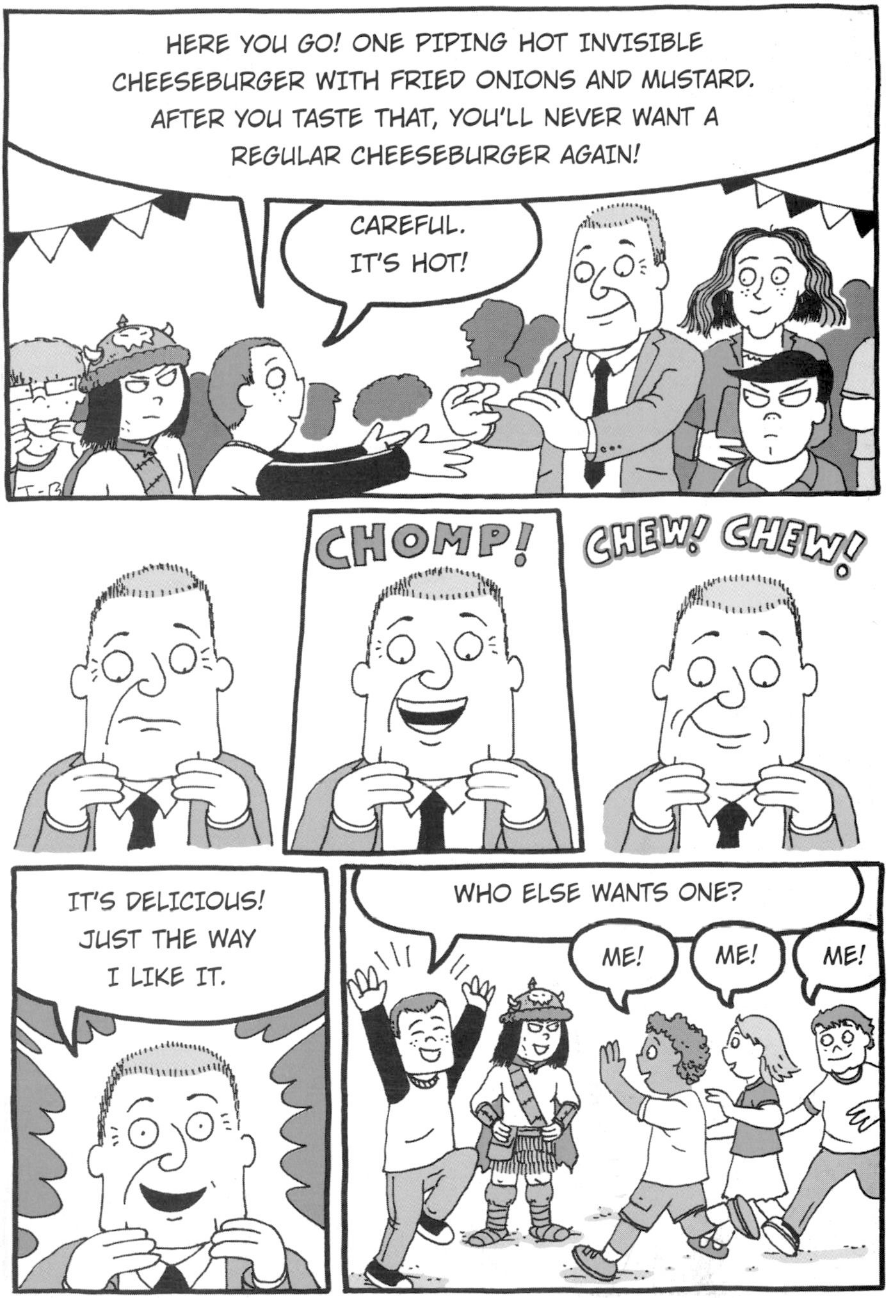
HERE YOU GO! ONE PIPING HOT INVISIBLE CHEESEBURGER WITH FRIED ONIONS AND MUSTARD. AFTER YOU TASTE THAT, YOU'LL NEVER WANT A REGULAR CHEESEBURGER AGAIN!
CAREFUL. IT'S HOT!
CHOMP!
CHEW! CHEW!
IT'S DELICIOUS! JUST THE WAY I LIKE IT.
WHO ELSE WANTS ONE?
ME!
ME!
ME!

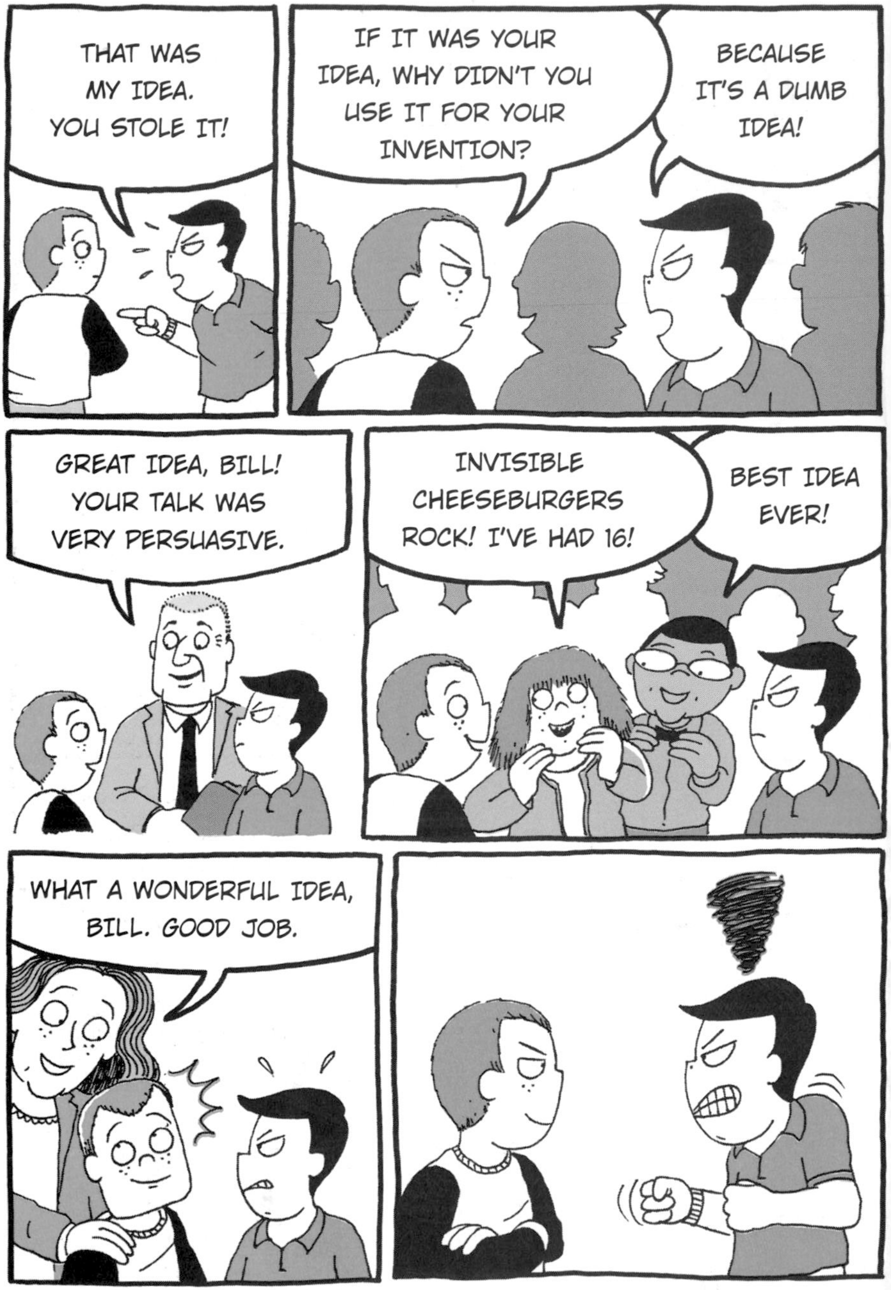
THAT WAS MY IDEA. YOU STOLE IT!
IF IT WAS YOUR IDEA, WHY DIDN'T YOU USE IT FOR YOUR INVENTION?
BECAUSE IT'S A DUMB IDEA!
GREAT IDEA, BILL! YOUR TALK WAS VERY PERSUASIVE.
INVISIBLE CHEESEBURGERS ROCK! I'VE HAD 16!
BEST IDEA EVER!
WHAT A WONDERFUL IDEA, BILL. GOOD JOB.

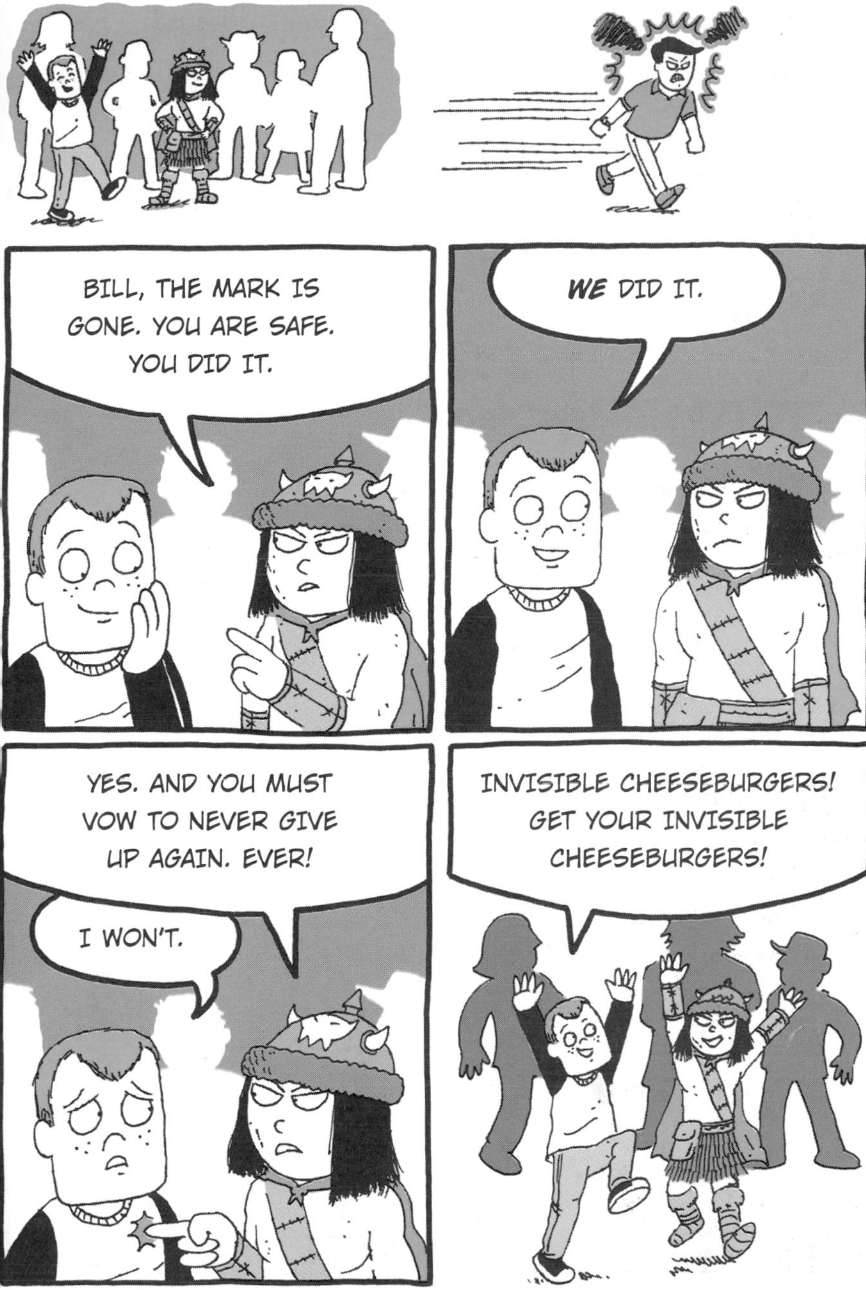
BILL, THE MARK IS GONE. YOU ARE SAFE. YOU DID IT.
WE DID IT.
YES. AND YOU MUST VOW TO NEVER GIVE UP AGAIN. EVER!
I WON'T.
INVISIBLE CHEESEBURGERS! GET YOUR INVISIBLE CHEESEBURGERS!

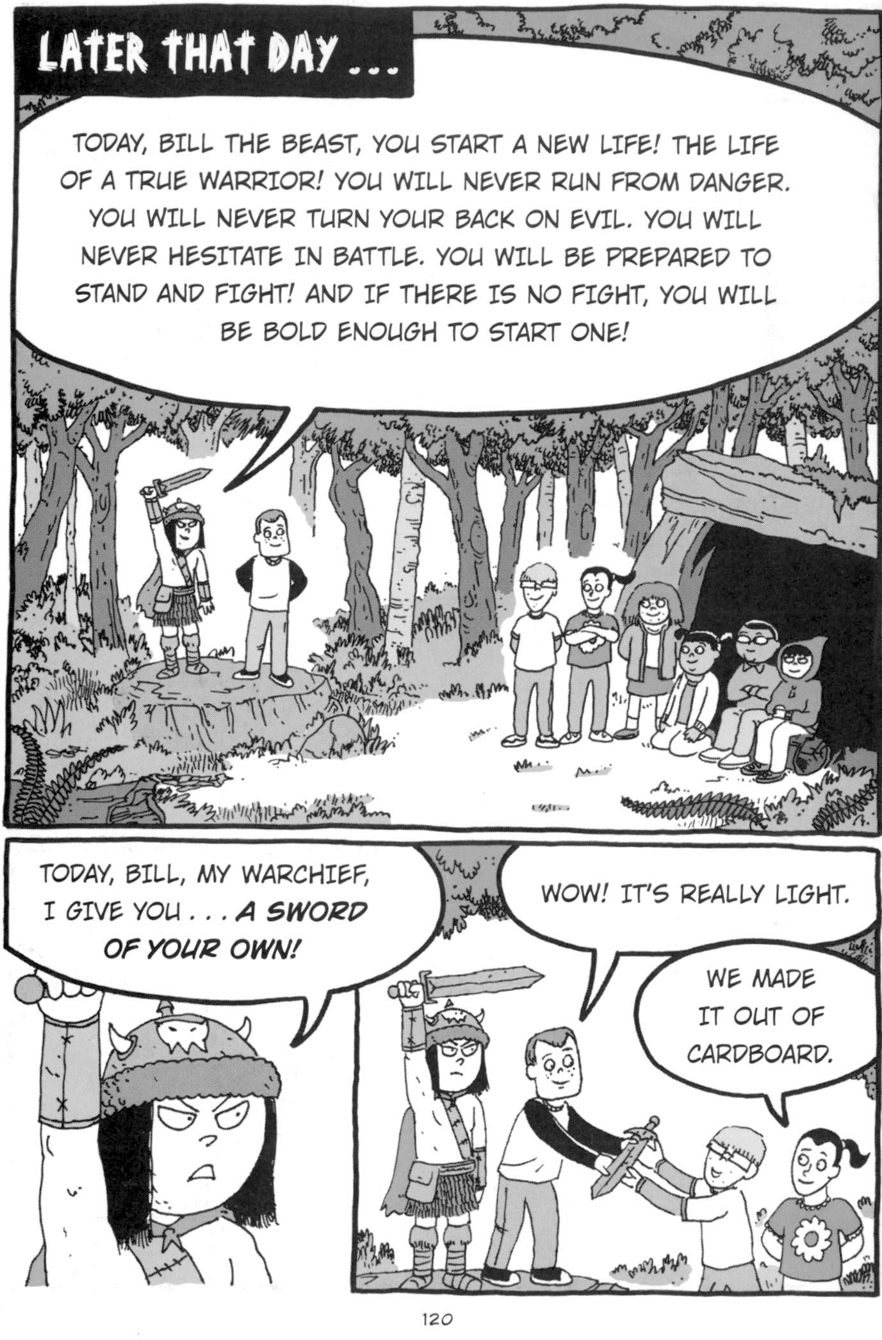
LATER THAT DAY . . .
TODAY, BILL THE BEAST, YOU START A NEW LIFE! THE LIFE OF A TRUE WARRIOR! YOU WILL NEVER RUN FROM DANGER. YOU WILL NEVER TURN YOUR BACK ON EVIL. YOU WILL NEVER HESITATE IN BATTLE. YOU WILL BE PREPARED TO STAND AND FIGHT! AND IF THERE IS NO FIGHT, YOU WILL BE BOLD ENOUGH TO START ONE!
TODAY, BILL, MY WARCHIEF, I GIVE YOU . . . ***A SWORD OF YOUR OWN!***
WOW! IT'S REALLY LIGHT.
WE MADE IT OUT OF CARDBOARD.

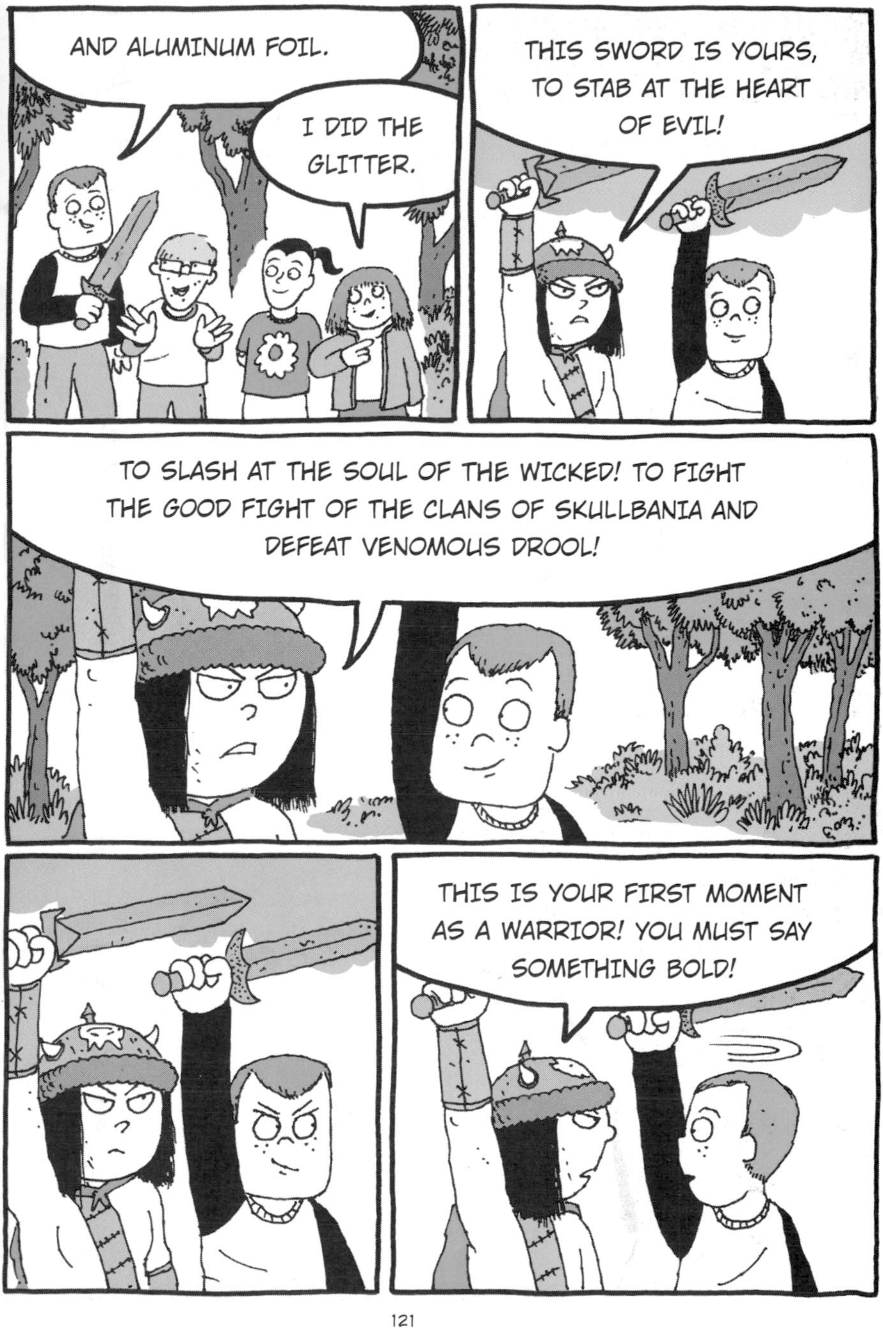
AND ALUMINUM FOIL.
I DID THE GLITTER.
THIS SWORD IS YOURS, TO STAB AT THE HEART OF EVIL!
TO SLASH AT THE SOUL OF THE WICKED! TO FIGHT THE GOOD FIGHT OF THE CLANS OF SKULLBANIA AND DEFEAT VENOMOUS DROOL!
THIS IS YOUR FIRST MOMENT AS A WARRIOR! YOU MUST SAY SOMETHING BOLD!

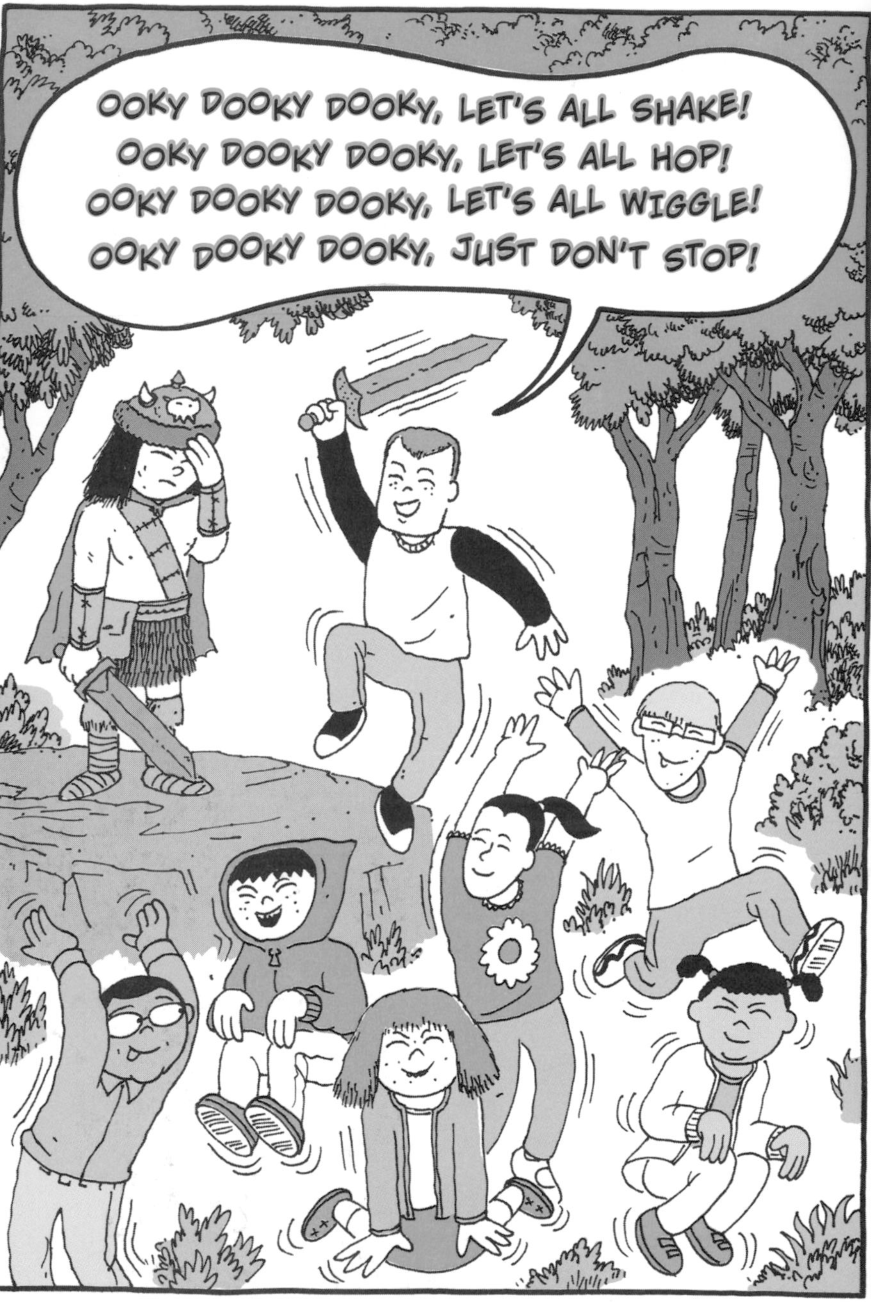
OOKY DOOKY DOOKY, LET'S ALL SHAKE!
OOKY DOOKY DOOKY, LET'S ALL HOP!
OOKY DOOKY DOOKY, LET'S ALL WIGGLE!
OOKY DOOKY DOOKY, JUST DON'T STOP!

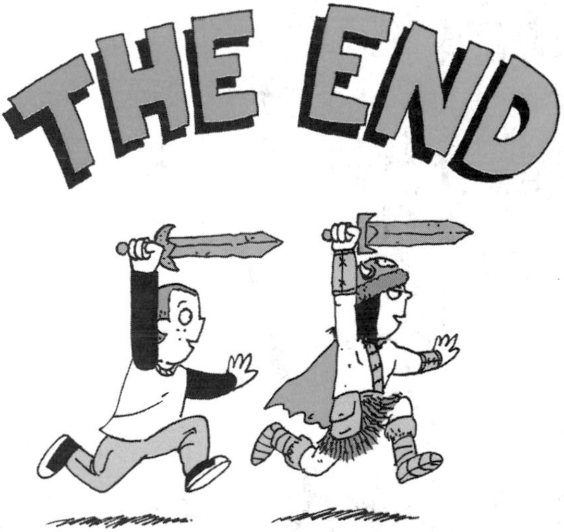
THE END

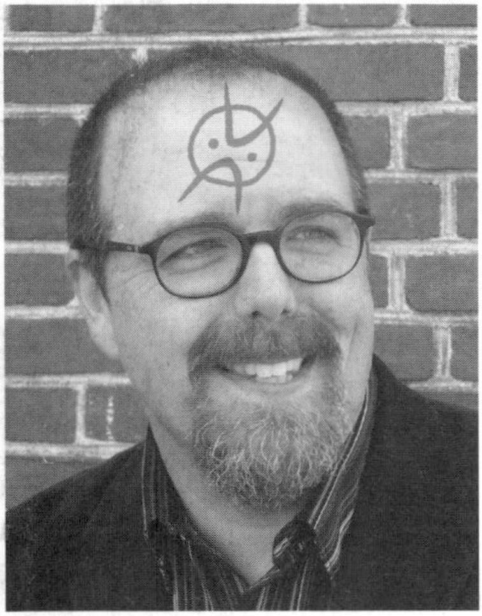

MICHAEL REX IS THE AUTHOR AND ILLUSTRATOR OF OVER TWENTY BOOKS FOR CHILDREN, INCLUDING THE ***NEW YORK TIMES*** #1 BESTSELLER ***GOODNIGHT GOON***. MICHAEL HAS A MASTER'S DEGREE IN VISUAL ARTS EDUCATION (K-12), AND WORKED AS A NEW YORK CITY ART TEACHER FOR FOUR YEARS. HE VISITS SCHOOLS ACROSS THE COUNTRY, AND HAS APPEARED ON ***THE CELEBRITY APPRENTICE*** AS A GUEST ILLUSTRATOR.

MIKE LIVES IN NEW JERSEY WITH HIS WIFE AND THEIR TWO BOYS.

FOLLOW FANGBONE AND FRIENDS IN HIS FIRST TWO EPIC ADVENTURES!

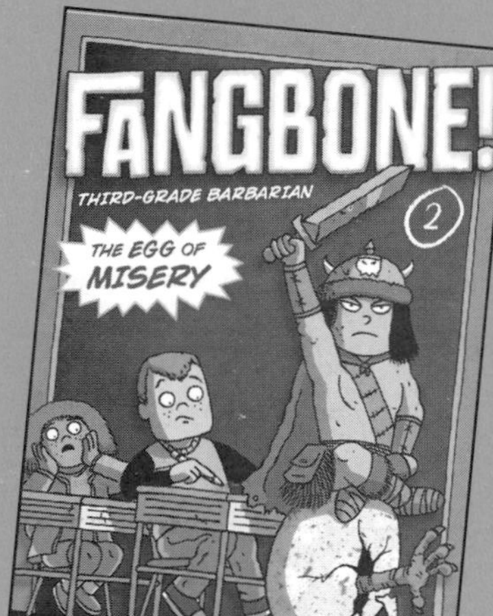
FANGBONE!
THIRD-GRADE BARBARIAN
THE EGG OF MISERY
2
MICHAEL REX
A NEW YORK TIMES #1 BESTSELLING AUTHOR

FANGBONE! THIRD-GRADE BARBARIAN: THE EGG OF MISERY
978-0-399-25522-9 / $5.99 ($6.99 CAN)

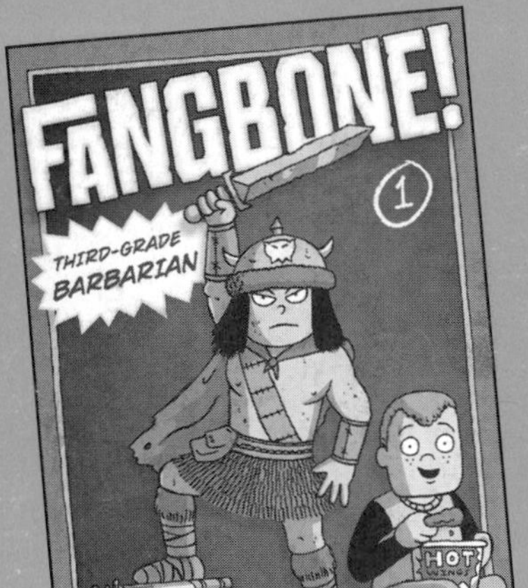
FANGBONE!
1
THIRD-GRADE BARBARIAN
HOT WINGS
MICHAEL REX
A NEW YORK TIMES #1 BESTSELLING AUTHOR

FANGBONE! THIRD-GRADE BARBARIAN
978-0-399-25521-2 / $5.99 ($6.99 CAN)